An extremely tall man with pale skin and blond hair ran toward them from the mansion. His uniform was as ornate as Daniel's and a great deal more colorful. He was dressed all in orange, but each garment was a different *shade* of orange.

"Didn't you hear me tell you to land at once?" the blond screamed. "By God, you'll know to do what I tell you the next time!"

He lifted his right hand for what was obviously intended to be a full-armed slap. He was rangy rather than bulky but he was also a good foot taller than Daniel.

"Pardon me, sir," Daniel said in a voice loud enough to be heard. "I'm a Cinnabar gentleman and an RCN officer. Don't presume—"

The blond swung. Daniel caught his wrist with his right hand and stopped the blow in the air.

The other rebels were watching, jabbering among themselves more in interest than anger. The blond was obviously a leader of some sort, but he was also a foreigner.

The fellow drew back a leg to kick. *Act harmless and a little stupid*, Adele had said. Daniel could see the logic of that, but he *was* a Leary.

He still held the blond's wrist. He let go of it. The fellow'd been straining to pull out of Daniel's grip, so he jerked himself off balance. Daniel grabbed the blond's raised boot with both hands and twisted hard. Because of the considerable leverage, the knee popped before the ankle did. He toppled backward, screaming.

"There, that's all right, then," Daniel said, straightening to smile brightly at the circle of watching rebels. *Bloody hell*, he thought, *he'd burst the left shoulder seam of his tunic . . .*

THE WAY TO
GLORY

DAVID DRAKE

THE WAY TO GLORY

A Baen Book

Baen Publishing Enterprises
P.O. Box 1403
Riverdale, NY 10471
www.baen.com

ISBN 10: 1-4165-2106-2
ISBN 13: 978-1-4165-2106-8

Cover art by Stephen Hickman

First Baen paperback printing, May 2007

Library of Congress Control Number: 2005000987

Distributed by Simon & Schuster
1230 Avenue of the Americas
New York, NY 10020

Pages by Joy Freeman (www.pagesbyjoy.com)
Printed in the United States of America

DEDICATION

For Gina Massel-Castater
With respect and affection

ACKNOWLEDGMENTS

Dan Breen continues as my first reader, I'm happy to say. He has particular merit on clerical issues, but he's very good on matters of size as well.

I'm occasionally asked how I keep details straight while writing complex novels in several subgenres in quick succession. The assumption tends to be that I have a cross-indexed file of names, etc, to which I refer frequently. That would indeed be a good way to do it.

What I actually have is a retentive memory and more recently a team of continuity checkers who do a much better job than I could if I were to concentrate on names instead of story. Dorothy Day and Evan Ladouceur carried out this duty splendidly on *The Way to Glory*. The mistakes remain my mistakes, however.

Incidentally, occasionally an error will lead to a bit of found art. When I realized that the I'd given the Alliance vessel *Moltke* fewer, larger guns than a Field Marshal Class heavy cruiser should mount, I didn't go back and change the equipment. Instead I renamed her *Scheer* and left her a pocket battleship, which opens possibilities for later books in the series.

My webmaster Karen Zimmerman both archived my daily files and provided (generally in a matter of minutes) information which I suddenly needed. Well, wanted: was it important that I have the real Haitian national anthem before me (in Creole and English versions) when I wrote a throw-away scene? I guess the answer is that it was important to me. There's a lot more story background in my head than ever gets onto the page . . . but if it *weren't* in my head, what was on the page would be thinner and paler. *I* think.

Andre Norton gets a specific note of thanks for noting how useful lizards could be as pets on a space-ship. I say "specific" because I probably wouldn't be writing adventure stories of this sort if I hadn't read Andre's when I met science fiction.

I had computer problems. My son Jonathan fixed them. An acknowledgments page reminds me of how very lucky I have been in life.

My wife Jo bore with me as I wrote another novel and my immediate neighborhood became a deepening morass of books, documents, and pictures. (I use a lot of references while I'm working.) I try to clean up my mess in the short intervals between novels, but I'm aware that it isn't a perfect existence for an ordinarily neat person.

My thanks generally to all those who've brightened my life by their presence in it.

AUTHOR'S NOTE

The general political background of the RCN series is that of Europe in the mid-eighteenth century, with admixtures of late-Republican Rome. (There's a surprising degree of congruence between British and Roman society in those periods.)

Major plot elements in *The Way to Glory*, however, come from the nineteenth century. Those of you who know some American history may note echoes of the *Somers* Mutiny, and if you're really well-versed you'll understand how greatly I simplified the details of political factions both in Washington (Whigs, Democrats, and the intimates of President Tyler whose own party had repudiated him) and in the U.S. Navy. Real history is a great deal more complex than anything I could make up.

The situation of the British North America and West Indies Squadron, based in Bermuda, would've been much as described during the eighteenth and even seventeenth centuries, with one important difference: Haiti didn't gain its independence till 1804. From that point through the 1880s (from which I've drawn several plot incidents) much of the squadron's work involved interceding in Haiti on behalf of British citizens (many of whom brought no credit upon their status) and refugees in general. One could scarcely ask for a better description of the term "thankless task." This one came with cockroaches.

In more recent times, the U.S. has taken over the former British role in Haiti. I suspect the roaches are still there; certainly nothing else has changed.

I'll note again that I don't invent systems of weights and measures for the background of the RCN series: the practice would neither advance my plot nor make the world a better place. I don't assume that people thousands of years in the future will still be using the systems in use today. Those who would quarrel with my choice here might usefully ask themselves, however, how long feet and inches have been in use thus far.

—Dave Drake
david-drake.com

Not once or twice in our rough island-story
The path of duty was the way to glory.

—Alfred, Lord Tennyson
"Ode on the Death of the Duke of Wellington"

CHAPTER 1

Xenos on Cinnabar

The pair of footmen at the head of the stairs bowed to Daniel; the older one said, "Senator Kearnes will be most pleased that you're able to attend, Lieutenant Leary."

"Pleased to be here," Daniel said. He smiled as he passed into the ballroom which took up most of the second floor of the Kearnes townhouse. Indeed, he *was* pleased.

The invitation to Lira Kearnes' fortieth birthday gala specified that officers were to wear full medals rather than ribbons. The request might well have been intended to display Lieutenant Daniel Leary at his most splendid; certainly it had that effect.

The Republic of Cinnabar Navy was the sword of the republic, not a weapon of party politics. High RCN officers couldn't attend this ball because Bruno Kearnes was the central figure in several political battles of the sort that the RCN kept out of. The unspoken ban on attendance didn't apply to a twenty-four-year-old lieutenant. The fruit salad on the breast of Daniel's Dress Whites would've been impressive even for an admiral, however.

Daniel, lately commanding the corvette *Princess Cecile*, had returned with dispatches from Admiral Keith's squadron just in time to give Senator Kearnes his show. Daniel in turn was getting the kind of adulation that came to those whom the citizens of Cinnabar decided were genuine heroes. It was Lira Kearnes' gala, but it was Daniel Leary's night.

Daniel scanned the crowd, checking for anyone he might know among those present. The invitation had been to all four officers from the *Princess Cecile*: Midshipmen Dorst and Vesey, and First Lieutenant Conn Medorn, who not coincidentally was the nephew of Admiral Keith.

The *Princess Cecile*'s signals officer, Adele Mundy, had been invited also—but not because she was an RCN warrant officer. Adele was Mundy of Chatsworth, head and sole survivor of one of the most noble families in the Republic. Her father—before his execution for treason—had been leader of the Popular Party. That was the territory if not precisely the title which Bruno Kearnes appeared to have marked for his own.

Daniel didn't see any of his fellows from the *Sissie*, but there was plenty of room in this swirling crowd to get lost. Besides, Daniel hadn't come here to find shipmates. . . .

The small orchestra in the loft above the balcony swung into a polacca. Couples who weren't up to the lively music left the dance floor in the center of the enormous hall, but others took their place.

A portly banker with investments in shipbuilding

remained with the younger couples, however; he danced with an enthusiasm that made up for his limited skills. His partner was probably closer to his granddaughter's age than that of his daughter. She complemented the banker's steps perfectly, just as the tiara of sapphires she wore complemented her blue eyes.

And those blue eyes caught Daniel's across the room as she dipped and spun.

Much of the Republic's wealth and beauty was here tonight. Daniel Leary could have any share of it he chose, *any* share, simply by stretching out his hand.

He grinned: which he'd likely do before long. He was a healthy young man, and the voyage back from the Galactic North with Admiral Keith's dispatches had been a long one.

"Leary!" called a saturnine man in a red velvet suit; his waistcoat flashed with metallic gold. *Mawhire of Rondolet*, recalled a rarely visited portion of Daniel's mind; an acquaintance of Daniel's father. Mawhire's clothing had made an impression on a child who even at seven was more comfortable hunting on the family estate than he was with the much crueler games that politicians got up to. "Daniel Leary! Come over here, boy, and let me introduce you to some friends of mine. My but you've grown since I last saw you!"

Which would've been about seventeen years ago, when Speaker Corder Leary broke the Three Circles Conspiracy and drowned it in blood. Daniel vaguely recalled that Mawhire had lost a cousin in the Proscriptions. . . .

"Daniel Leary, may I present Senator Russell—that's Russell of Walsingham, you know . . ." Mawhire said. Daniel bowed—nodded deeply—to a man with vacant eyes and more facets glittering on his fingers than there were in the crystal chandeliers above.

" . . . and Tomas Bayard of Bayard and Sons." Daniel bowed again, this time to an ancient man—he supposed Bayard was male—supporting himself in a walker. Stone-faced servants stood at either elbow just in case they were needed.

"Surprised to see you here, Leary," Bayard said in a cracked voice. "Given how your father and Bruno Kearnes get along. *Don't* get along."

He turned his head toward Mawhire, a quick motion that reminded Daniel of an ancient, poisonous, lizard casting for prey. "You know that story, Mawhire?" he demanded.

"I recall rumors," Senator Mawhire said, having the decency to look uncomfortable. "But it's not really a matter—"

"Speaker Leary and young Kearnes there don't get along because Leary and Lira Kearnes got along too well!" Bayard continued in glee. "Far too well!"

He broke into cackling laughter; it ended abruptly in a paroxysm of coughing. One of Bayard's attendants held his shoulders while the other slipped a large handkerchief over his mouth.

Daniel smiled pleasantly. *I hope you bring your lungs up, you nasty little bastard*, he thought. Aloud he said, "That would've been before my time, sir. And of course it's not the sort of thing a gentleman talks about."

"Gentlemen!" Bayard sneered. "All a gentleman's good for is feeding the worms!"

"That's the common lot of mankind, my dear Tomas," said a woman suddenly standing at Daniel's right elbow. Her voice was cultured and as smoothly cutting as a scalpel. "However the lieutenant here has already accomplished things that will keep *his* name alive after the worms have devoured what the doctors have left. Not so?"

"Faugh, glory!" Bayard said. "Women and fools set great store by it, I understand."

He started to turn away, but stiffness and the walker prevented him from doing so quickly enough. The woman added sweetly, "I suppose women you've had to learn about second hand, haven't you, you poor dear?"

Daniel allowed himself a satisfied smile toward the magnate's back. He wouldn't have responded to Bayard directly, out of courtesy toward a sick old man—however nasty—and from the sense of propriety ingrained by living within the rigid order of the RCN. He certainly wasn't displeased to watch somebody *else* kick the old bastard in the balls, though—and then put the boot in as he writhed on the floor.

He turned to the woman. She looked to be in her thirties, but that was probably as much a medical marvel as the fact Tomas Bayard was alive at all. She was undeniably handsome, but even "the thirties" was far too old for Daniel's taste.

"Mistress Jacopus," said Mawhire to the lady, "allow me to present the Lieutenant Daniel Leary of whom we've heard so much. I'd say Daniel was an old family friend, but in fact I can't claim to be any closer to Speaker Leary today than Kearnes is—or you are yourself, boy, from what I hear? Had quite a falling out with your father when you joined the navy, I heard?"

"I haven't spoken to my father in some years, that's true," Daniel said, letting his eyes rise as if to view the frescos of the high ceiling. Cherubs were teasing lions in various fashions in each panel, while between the paintings were stucco moldings of furious giants straining to burst through the frames they supported. He supposed the scenes were allegorical; another way of saying they were without interest to him. "I wonder if there's something to dr—"

"Do let me be your guide, Lieutenant," Mistress Jacopus said, taking his right arm in both hands; gently, but in a proprietary fashion nonetheless. "I have so many questions to ask you about your medals!"

The Jacopus family was famous for wealth and a determined neutrality in the Republic's rough-and-tumble—sometimes *very* rough—politics. Daniel had heard that one member of the family was the most famous hostess in Xenos; he didn't doubt that he'd just met her.

The orchestra was playing a hornpipe, but it was a restrained thing compared to what went by the same name in the spacers' bars around Harbor Three—or any other RCN liberty port. Daniel had spent his time in those bars when he was a midshipman, an officer by courtesy but not yet commissioned. Since fame had brought him invitations to dos like this one, he'd found little to regret about no longer being poor and obscure. The liquor was better and the women were much prettier. He'd never had much interest in dancing anyway.

Mistress Jacopus led him toward the refreshment table which was set in a corner, in front of double doors onto a parterre. Servants passed in and out, exchanging full trays and bottles to replace the those that had been browsed and drunk empty.

Jacopus was taking him by the long route, however, and at each step she nodded graciously and smiled to another guest. Occasionally she murmured a first name—"Dear Janni . . ."—or title—"Senator, how nice,"—as they passed, savoring the looks of respect and—from some of the women—fury.

"I hope you don't mind me showing off my trophy, Lieutenant," she said in his ear as though murmuring endearments. "Because you are quite a trophy, you know."

"Ah, mistress—" Daniel said.

"Christine, please," she said. "And you needn't worry that I'll embarrass you later. I know quite a lot about your tastes, including the sort of *young* friends you prefer for recreation. I'd offer to help you there, but I'm sure a handsome hero like yourself is capable of making his own arrangements."

"That's generally been the case in the past, ah, Christine," Daniel said. "And I do appreciate you, ah, helping me out of an awkwardness."

Daniel didn't like to talk about his father for a number of reasons, not least that he didn't have anything to say about Corder Leary. They'd had little contact even before the break—which was over Corder's remarriage, not Daniel's career. He'd joined the RCN in reaction to that blazing row, not as the cause of it.

Daniel had spent his childhood on the family estate of Bantry, learning a little about decorum from his mother—a saint, as everybody agreed—and a great deal about hunting, fishing and manhood from Hogg, a family retainer. There'd been Hoggs poaching on

Bantry from the days of the first human settlement, long before the Hiatus in star travel drew a thousand-year line through history.

In the eight years since the row, Daniel and Corder Leary'd had no contact whatever. Words had been said that would've meant pistols at dawn if those speaking hadn't been father and son, but even beyond that . . .

Corder Leary was a stiff-necked, stubborn man who'd never backed down in a fight. Daniel wasn't his father and wouldn't have wanted to be him; but much as Daniel revered his late mother, he knew very well that his temper and his backbone hadn't come from her side of the family.

There was a crush at the refreshments table. Daniel hadn't really been thirsty, just uncomfortable at the direction Mawhire had taken the conversation, and Christine Jacopus simply wanted to be seen with the lion of the evening. Instead of forcing his way through, he paused to look around again.

By the etiquette of upper-class Xenos, the only regular servants on the floor were those behind the refreshments table. The guests' personal attendants were in the balcony above. They could be summoned to meet their employer in a hallway if required or even escorted onto the floor by a member of the Kearnes household in event of an outside emergency.

Many of the guests—perhaps a quarter of the total, Daniel guessed, smiling faintly—were accompanied by silent men and women in simple dress. If you didn't know who they were, they could pass for poor relations of the glittering guests they stayed close to.

In fact they were . . . well, calling them guards would be harsh but not inaccurate. They were employed by various couturiers, jewelers, and pawn brokers. They accompanied not the guests but rather the clothing and accouterments which the guests wore and hadn't paid for; that they very probably *couldn't* pay for. By convention, nobody "noticed" them.

"What is this one, Daniel?" Christine said, touching the spray of gold feathers dusted with real rubies waving from the peak of his dress hat. She leaned against him a little more closely than she need to have done.

"Oh, the aigrette?" said Daniel, squinting sideways. "That's the Kostroma Star, a, ah, foreign decoration. From an allied foreign power, of course, or I wouldn't be permitted to wear it."

Though in truth the fourragere of gold and silver cords across his left breast was the Order of Strymon in Diamonds; the stones on the clasp at his epaulette were the size of a child's teeth. In theory it entitled the wearer to the freedom of Strymon, a planet Daniel didn't expect ever to visit again as an RCN officer.

It was stretching the point a good deal to describe President Delos Vaughn as an ally of Cinnabar, as the events that put him in power had been not only unauthorized by Cinnabar's Ministry of External Affairs but actively hindered by those well-meaning diplomats. Still, the award was too striking for Daniel not to wear it unless he were flatly forbidden.

Foreigners had vulgar taste, far inferior to that of Cinnabar, of course. But Daniel had learned that girls—the girls he found attractive—didn't object to a bit of vulgarity; and truth to tell, the taste of rural districts like Bantry wasn't nearly as muted as that here in Xenos, the capital.

Christine touched one medal after another, her

lips working silently. A circle of guests was forming about them like mother-of-pearl coating a sand grain in the mantle of a shellfish; not pressing, but rapt in anticipation of what they might hear. Powerful nobles and *very* beautiful women, wondering what the heroic Lieutenant Leary might say!

Daniel knew it didn't matter. These same people would howl and kick his naked body down the street tomorrow if he were disgraced and executed; they'd done that with many of those implicated in the Three Circles Conspiracy. The folk quickest to spurn the fallen were those who'd cheered the loudest in the days before their overthrow.

It didn't matter—but he was young and he was human. "That . . ." Daniel said as Christine ran the sash of red silk and cloth-of-gold between her fingers. He spoke to the older woman, but his eyes met those of the petite blonde beaming from just beyond her. " . . . makes me a Royal Companion of Novy Sverdlovsk as I understand it. I was fortunate enough to recover a valuable artifact for the throne and gained Sverdlovsk's support for a Cinnabar initiative in the Galactic North as a result."

The artifact was a diamond engraved with the continents of Old Earth before the wars in which asteroids had smashed the planet out of its former shape. Daniel had traded it for a warship, and with that ship he—and the finest crew that ever blessed an RCN captain—had smashed an Alliance squadron. The sash was showy. For the same incident Admiral Keith had awarded Daniel the Medal of the Republic in Red—a small bronze cross with a ruby point in the center.

Civilians marveled at the sash. RCN officers braced to attention and saluted when they saw the medal.

The orchestra played a few bars as a signal. Couples began forming for a sarabande.

"Now, Daniel," Christine said, holding his right hand with her left but turning to take the hand of the blonde beside her. "May I present Thora, the daughter of my great friend Senator Bencini?"

She brought their hands together. Thora simpered becomingly; her fingers gripped Daniel with more than formal enthusiasm.

"RCN forever," called a dry, carrying voice from across the circle of spectators. Daniel looked from Thora for a moment and caught the cool, amused eyes of Adele Mundy as she marched past them into the stately paces of the sarabande beside a fifties-ish man corseted into a Fencibles uniform.

"RCN forever," Daniel echoed gaily, raising the blonde's hand high in enthusiastic triumph.

It was good to be young and an RCN officer. It was good to be alive!

RCN forever!

If asked, Adele Mundy would've said she found dancing considerably less interesting than shelf-reading: going through the stacks of a library and placing misfiled volumes in their correct location. Still, dancing was an accomplishment expected in a noblewoman, so she'd learned it. Though Adele's parents were the leading lights of the Popular Party, they'd never permitted their children to forget that the Mundys of Chatsworth were among the first families of the Republic.

"Were" being the operative word there. Every Mundy save Adele herself, studying in the Academic Collections on Blythe—a member of the Alliance of Free Stars—had died in the Proscriptions by which Corder Leary had crushed the Three Circles Conspiracy. Adele's sister Agatha had been ten years old when her head was taken to decorate the Speaker's Rock in the ancient center of Xenos.

The music ended. Adele's partner was in the building construction trade. He turned to her and wheezed, "Mistress Mundy, it's been a pleasure to dance with you. A great pleasure!"

He bowed as deeply as his corset allowed him, which of course wasn't very deep. Even without the undergarment, his bright green Fencibles uniform had enough gold piping that it could stand up itself.

"Thank you, Colonel," Adele said, miming a curtsey by spreading her hands with a bare dip of her head. "The pleasure was mutual."

Which was more or less true: he hadn't trodden on her, always a possibility when Adele danced with out-of-condition men who were determined to show off. It was a worse problem off-planet, of course. Here in Xenos she was Mundy of Chatsworth, a person of rank but no particular importance. On the distant worlds where the *Princess Cecile* might land, Adele Mundy was a sophisticate from the capital, a personage of greater status than any other woman present . . . even in the minds of those women.

The latest style for the sarabande was to keep the toes of the forward foot straight down while executing the steps in slow motion. Adele filed the information as she filed all information. She'd be called on to demonstrate Xenos fashion soon enough, she was sure, in a ballroom of unpainted wood or on an open pavement under unfamiliar stars.

"Mistress Mundy?" said an attractive woman somewhat older than Adele's own thirty-two standard—that is, Earth—years. "I was told . . . well, *are* you Mundy of Chatsworth? I don't mean to intrude, but . . . ?"

The woman, a complete stranger to Adele, was dressed at the height of current style: her neck and wrist ruffs would make it impossible for her to feed herself. That was probably the point, of course, rather like the shoes you couldn't walk in that had been a fad among the nobility when Adele was a child.

"Yes," said Adele, knowing her voice held a hint of challenge. She didn't intend that—whoever this woman was, she clearly wasn't an enemy in the sense that Adele would need the small pistol in the side-pocket of her tunic.

But there *had* been enemies of that sort in Adele's life, even before she joined the RCN and became part of the Republic's most powerful instrument of policy. Reflexes you've gained on battlefields don't go away because you're standing in a ballroom now. "I'm Adele Mundy."

"I'm Lira Kearnes, Mistress Mundy," the woman said, obviously embarrassed. "I'd hoped to talk with you because you're a naval officer. Ah . . . I expected you to be in uniform, so though you were pointed out to me I wasn't sure. . . ."

"Oh!" said Adele in considerably greater embarrassment than Mistress Kearnes and for better reason. Here she was treating her hostess like a potential enemy, simply because the woman had wanted to talk with

her. Though why had she mentioned the RCN? "I'm
very sorry, I was thinking of other things."

And so she had been, thinking about things that
had no business in polite society. Even without the
hardships that resulted from her family's ruin, Adele
Mundy wouldn't have grown into a person whom
acquaintances would've described as cheerful and
outgoing. She regarded courtesy as the most important
social virtue, however, and she'd just been discourteous to her hostess.

Quickly she went on before Lira Kearnes could
resume speaking, "I received an invitation as Mundy
of Chatsworth, mistress. The invitation to the officers
of the *Princess Cecile* was limited to the commissioned officers. Or in the case of the midshipmen,
those who will *be* commissioned. I'm a technician; a
warrant officer, in RCN terms."

The orchestra was playing a rigadoon. It was more
sprightly than most of the guests cared to attempt,
but Midshipman Dorst of the *Princess Cecile* danced
with the athletic grace with which he'd carried out
any task requiring physical strength and dexterity. His
partner was a red-haired civilian, strikingly attractive
and just as good a dancer as Dorst was.

Midshipman Vesey, also of the *Sissie* and Dorst's
lover, watched from the edge of the dance floor with
a careful lack of expression. Daniel regarded Vesey as
a very respectable astrogator. That was high praise, as
it came from a man whom the RCN held the near
equal of the incomparable Stacey Bergen, Daniel's
uncle and the man who'd trained him in everything
to do with a starship. Vesey was even attractive . . .
but not the way the redhead was attractive.

As best Adele could tell, Dorst loved Vesey; certainly he'd willingly put his tall, muscular body between her and any danger. But tonight was likely to be a difficult time for Vesey, who seemed completely oblivious of the bevy of civilian nobles trying to catch her attention.

Adele sighed. She herself had no more interest in sex than the busts on either side of the marble mantelpiece did. There were others—Daniel Leary was a member of the class—who had an obvious animal enthusiasm for the business but then got on with the rest of their lives, utterly unscathed by those activities.

And then there were the Midshipman Veseys and apparently the majority of humanity, who were regularly turned inside out by what could've been a matter of simple biology. Adele's philosophy hadn't had room for a deity even before the slaughter of her family, but it sometimes seemed to her that the whole business was too illogical not to have been Something's cruel joke.

"Mistress Mundy . . . ?"

"I'm *very* sorry," Adele said, curtseying to Kearnes in honest contrition. "I'm afraid I'm distracted by the—"

She didn't know how to go on. Not with what she was really thinking, not to this woman who'd no more understand than if Adele began chattering in the language of a just-discovered planet which'd fallen into savagery at the Hiatus and never recovered.

"We don't have much occasion for events like this," Adele continued in a flash of inspiration. It wasn't exactly a lie. Not *exactly*. She made a gesture of cultured restraint to the glittering crowd. "I haven't seen anything to equal it since, that is, in a very long time."

Since my family was massacred; but that was another thing not to say here.

"Would you like to go . . ." Kearnes began. She caught herself and amended her words to, "Would you mind stepping into a drawing room with me, Mistress Mundy? I know it's my party and I shouldn't, but I really do want to talk with you. It's about my son, you see."

Adele went blank-faced. *Her son?*

"Yes, of course," she said aloud, meaning the private discussion rather than that she had any idea of what Lira Kearnes was talking about. It took conscious restraint to prevent Adele from pulling out her personal data unit and squatting on the floor to check the Kearnes family in a detail greater than what she'd thought necessary on receiving the invitation. It was always a mistake not to search deeply when you had the time!

Adele wore a double tunic and skirt. The translucent outer fabric was a misty gray which slightly blurred the geometric patterns embroidered in black on her inner garments. The data unit in a pocket on the inner skirt was hidden from view but instantly accessible. Through the unit's controlling wands—less bulky than a keypad—Adele had access to the wider universe in the only form she could really accept it: as tabulated information.

But it would be impolite to bring out the flat rectangle now, and Adele had already come uncomfortably close to being impolite to Lira Kearnes. Besides, there was a better—if not as natural to Adele—way to learn what the lady was talking about: she could ask.

"I'm not aware of having met your son, mistress," Adele said as footmen in violet frock coats swept open an unobtrusive door and closed it behind them. The drawing room beyond was tiled in patterns of circles, whorls, and multi-pointed stars. Instead of ordinary light fixtures, a screen brightened into the holographic image of an arched double window looking out onto a palm-fringed beach. Beyond, the sea combed over sand toward the window.

"Do sit, please," Kearnes said. There were chairs and a table, but she gestured instead to the ottoman beneath the "window."

Adele seated herself carefully, folding her hands in her lap. The tips of her fingers rested on the hard, hidden outlines of her data unit.

Kearnes sat on the other end of the ottoman and stared at the upholstery between them for a moment. When she looked up, she began, "It's my third son, Oller. He's joined the navy, you see. I didn't want him to go, but . . . Oller's a very high-spirited boy, extremely bright but, well, he has his own ideas. He'd signed on with a privateer, and it was only because my husband agreed to get him a special appointment as a midshipman that Oller gave up that plan."

"The RCN can be a fine career for a high-spirited youth, mistress," Adele said, choosing her words carefully. "It has been for my friend Lieutenant Leary, certainly."

But Daniel *was* high spirited. Reading between the lines of a mother's description, Oller Kearnes was a spoiled brat with romantic notions of what it meant to be one of scores or hundreds of people sealed in a metal box so full of equipment that even to turn around required caution.

Danger is another thing that's more romantic to read about than the reality of blood and burns and the screams transcending age and gender and even humanity. Pain can be a sound, pure sound, and pictures can't prepare you for the smell of a man trying to stuff his intestines back into his ripped abdomen.

"Yes, I know that," Lira Kearnes said. "That's why I wanted to talk with you, one of the reasons. I don't suppose you're a mother . . . ?"

And despite the wording, Kearnes obviously hoped Adele would say, "Yes."

"No," Adele said primly. "I am not."

"Ah," Kearnes said. "Well, I was sure you weren't. I couldn't talk to Lieutenant Leary directly. He, ah, his father was an associate of my husband's at one time, but they had a falling out. I thought you might be able to tell me what life's like for a midshipman on shipboard. And, well . . ."

She reached out impulsively and touched her fingertips to the back of Adele's right hand. "It helps that you're a woman," she blurted.

In biological terms you're no doubt correct, Adele thought. With some difficulty she controlled the instinctive curl of her lip. But that wasn't fair, because Kearnes was really saying it was easier for *her* to talk to a woman about her fears for her offspring. It didn't imply anything about the woman she confided in.

"I might better introduce you to Midshipman Dorst, whom you've invited tonight," Adele said. "But . . . midshipman is a responsible job. He'll be treated as an officer under most circumstances, but he's still in training and he'll be expected to pay attention to whoever may be instructing him. And of course RCN discipline is strict even for officers; perhaps especially for officers. Lives may depend on obedience to orders."

"Yes, that's what worries me," Kearnes admitted to her interlaced fingers. "Oller isn't a bad boy, please understand me, and he's *very* bright on so many subjects. But . . ."

Oller is a willful brat who's never stuck to anything long enough to learn if he has an aptitude for it, Adele translated silently. Aloud she said, "It's possible that discipline imposed by his superiors will teach your son the importance of self-discipline, mistress. That often happens."

Certainly being clouted across the deck by a bosun who took exception to your smart mouth would be a learning experience beyond anything a well-born youth was likely to have gotten at home. Woetjans, the *Princess Cecile*'s bosun, was also biologically female. She was six and a half feet tall and showed no hesitation whatever in using her immense strength to advance an argument with someone whom RCN regulations made her responsibility. As Chief of Rig, those responsibilities included teaching midshipmen the ropes as surely as they did teaching enlisted recruits.

"Yes, well . . ." Kearnes said. She forced a smile as she met Adele's eyes again. "Oller is on a cruise to Sexburga in the *Bainbridge* under Commander Slidell. They're taking dispatches for distribution there, but I gather it's really a training cruise. It should be a good experience."

The poor fool almost choked getting that last sentence out, Adele thought; half in pity, half in disgust. *Did the woman have any conception of what real hardship amounted to?*

But of course she didn't, because she hadn't allowed herself to think about uncomfortable things. Lira

Kearnes may well have walked past Agatha's head on Speaker's Rock, for example.

"A training cruise will give your son an idea of what service in the RCN really is," Adele said aloud, wondering if she should get up to put a stop to the conversation. Not *quite* yet. "I don't know what the regulations say formally, but I'm sure that if the boy feels he's really unsuited to a naval career, your husband will be able to arrange his separation easily enough."

"Yes, of course," Kearnes said, her smile real this time but wan. "I know that, but I still, well . . ."

In a change of subject that made Adele reach again for her data unit—and again catch herself—Kearnes continued, "The Captain Slidell commanding the *Bainbridge* is Aban Slidell. His elder brother Jan was Corder Leary's private secretary when he was Speaker of the Senate."

"Politics have never interested me, mistress," Adele said, tensing herself to rise.

"But you know that your friend Daniel's father is *that* Leary, don't you?" Kearnes said. Suddenly her voice was firmer. "I was wondering how you two came to be friends."

Adele looked at the holographic image. Waves rolled inshore. If you looked carefully, you could see the line at which the seeming water changed from gray-green to deep blue, following the sea's depth as sharply as anything a surveyor could draw on a map. The palm fronds moved in a pictured breeze as well.

"Mistress . . ." Adele said, choosing her words very carefully. If she hadn't been sure that there was *something* to this conversation that she hadn't grasped yet, she'd have left the room and this house instantly.

But Lira Kearnes wasn't simply being stupidly offensive. Good heavens, the woman had started crying!

"Mistress Kearnes," Adele said, turning toward the seascape again so that Kearnes could dab at her tears with a tiny handkerchief. "I'm not the sort of person who makes friends easily. This isn't anything to do with events in my life, it's just what I was born. I'm a librarian by instinct and training. Under normal circumstances I'd be running a major research institution now. I'd have the respect of my peers—and not to be unduly boastful, I'd *have* very few peers. But I'd have no friends at all."

"Please, I didn't mean to offend you," Kearnes said. "Please, I'm very sorry!"

She was reacting to the tone, Adele supposed, but not even Adele could control that now. People sometimes called her emotionless, but that wasn't the case: she was just very controlled, because the emotion Adele Mundy knew best was a cold, murderous rage that had no place in ordinary human society.

"I'm not offended," Adele said, rasping the words. Fighting to take the edge from her voice she repeated, "I'm not offended."

Taking a deep breath, Adele went on, "As you obviously know, my circumstances stopped being normal at the time of the Three Circles Conspiracy. I lost my family, but quite frankly I'd never been close to them either. I can be offended at what happened and I can quarrel intellectually with why it happened, but I don't imagine that I'd have any more contact with my parents and sister in the future I expected than I do in my present existence. I put a flower on the family cenotaph once a year."

Adele laughed. She was a proud woman, she knew that: proud of her intelligence and skills, proud of being a Mundy of Chatsworth; proud that she wore the uniform of the RCN.

But the greatest boast of Adele Mundy's heart was her honesty—and that she was proving tonight, in a fashion that surprised even her.

"But a very odd thing happened, Mistress Kearnes," Adele went on, wry humor suddenly bubbling in her voice. "Events have made me a member of the RCN. I have a family closer than ever my blood relatives could have become. And I have a friend, too. If he happens to be the son of Speaker Leary, then that's nothing to me—or to him either. Because we're *friends*."

"I . . ." Kearnes said. She smiled wanly and continued, "I think you're very fortunate, mistress."

"Yes, I am," Adele said, standing up at last. "And if what you really started to say is that you don't understand, then let me assure you that I don't understand either. But I'm very glad of the situation."

She turned the door latch but looked back over her shoulder before pulling the panel open. Lira Kearnes was still seated on the ottoman. Her expression was vaguely surprised when she met Adele's gaze.

"The RCN has been very good to me, mistress," Adele said. "I hope it'll prove equally good for your son."

"I hope so too," Kearnes said, rising to her feet with the composure to be expected of a noblewoman like herself. "Thank you very much for your time, Mistress Mundy. And your kindness."

The footmen had stepped to either side when they heard the latch click. After Adele passed between

them, they edged back to conceal as we~ ~
ing the doorway.

The tiny bead earphone in Adele's right ear b~
minusculely to get her attention. It was Adele's connection with her only servant, Tovera, who was paranoid
because at some level she believed that everyone else
was exactly like her. Adele suspected *nobody* was
exactly like Tovera, a murderous sociopath with no
more personality than a bowl of skimmed milk.

Tovera had knowledge which she'd gained as an
agent of the Alliances' Fifth Bureau—the spy agency
which reported directly to Guarantor Porra, whose
will was law everywhere the military forces of the
Alliance could carry it. She'd attached herself to
Adele in part because she'd seen that Adele through
art and instinct could gain information which Tovera's
practiced craftsmanship couldn't reach—

And also because she'd seen Adele kill as emotion-
lessly as Tovera carried out every aspect of life, killing
included. Tovera watched her mistress as an example of
how human beings behaved; Adele saw in her servant
an example of how easily she herself could become a
thing that was human only on the outside.

They both gained by the association. Mistress Bernis
Sand, the head of Cinnabar's civil intelligence service,
gained even more.

Adele had no way to answer, so she waited the few
heartbeats that Tovera always allowed after the attention signal. Three men had noticed her reappearing
from the drawing room and were walking toward her:
two fellows in their forties, both strangers to her, and
a one-time political associate of Adele's father whom
she'd thought was an old man even then.

messenger from the Navy Office came for Senator
_arnes," Tovera said. Radical signal compression and
Adele's tiny earphone would've stripped the emotion
from any voice, but in Tovera's case it didn't make
much difference. "*The* Bainbridge *has returned from
a training cruise under Commander Aban Slidell.*"

Mistress Kearnes will be pleased, Adele thought.

"*The Kearnes' youngest son had been aboard as
a midshipman,*" Tovera continued with the precision
that Adele expected and shared—making them a small
minority in that fashion as well as many others.

"Mundy of Chatsworth, is it not?" said the first of
the three men to reach Adele. The red rose in the lapel
of his sharply tailored one-piece suit marked him as a
Progressive, a political ally of Senator Kearnes. "I'm
glad to meet you at last, mistress. I knew your—"

There was an altercation on the dance floor. Daniel's
servant, Hogg, had appeared through a door that
must lead from the balcony. Two footmen had tried
to prevent him from going to his master without
approval and an escort.

Hogg had the face of a half-witted rustic and dressed
like an explosion in a trunk of theatrical costumes.
When he wanted to, he moved fast; which the footmen who'd grabbed his arms would remember that
after they regained consciousness. For now they lay
on the floor, bleeding from pressure cuts where Hogg
had slammed their foreheads together.

"*Slidell executed Midshipman Kearnes for attempted
mutiny along with two crewmen,*" Tovera said.

"What!" shouted a deep-voiced man. "What the
hell do you mean!"

Guests stepped aside. The Progressive who'd

addressed Adele turned and stared in the direction
of the noise. "Why, what's going on?" he said to no
one in particular. "Who's the navy man the Senator's
talking to?"

Adele hadn't met Senator Kearnes, but she recognized him from the images she'd viewed in researching
Kearnes when she received the invitation. She hadn't
had any active reason to study her would-be host, but
for Adele information was good in and of itself. *If
only she'd learned more about young Oller!*

"The Hell you say!" Senator Kearnes bellowed.
He was a big man with a bull neck and apparently
a bull's temper. The slim RCN lieutenant opened his
mouth to speak further. Kearnes knocked him down
with a clenched fist.

*"I think you'd better get out now before something
happens,"* Tovera said.

Daniel looked past Hogg to Adele; they exchanged
nods. Adele started for a side door. Daniel called
something to Vesey and Dorst, inaudible over the
rising babble of the crowd.

The orchestra was still playing. Dorst turned in
protest; Daniel grabbed one elbow and Hogg the other,
bringing the big midshipman with them regardless of
his opinion. The redhead who'd been dancing with
Dorst shouted something shrill and ran three steps
after them—then sprawled on her face when Vesey
stuck a leg between the civilian's ankles.

Tovera was paranoid, of course. She thought anything could be a threat. But when a man as powerful
as Senator Kearnes got angry, there was simply no
point in staying around to learn what he *might* be
capable of.

"Where's my wife!" Kearnes shouted. "Where's Lira!"

Adele stepped through the door. As worried footmen closed it behind her, she heard the Senator cry, "By God, someone's going to *die* for this!

No point at all.

CHAPTER 2

Xenos on Cinnabar

"The dashing Lieutenant Leary's buying," Lieutenant Pennyroyal said as she pushed open the door to The Lower Deck, a basement-level tavern three blocks from the Navy Office. There were closer bars, but The Lower Deck catered to lieutenants on half-pay when they adjourned yet again from the General Waiting Room without being summoned to an inner office and granted a place.

"Indeed I *will* buy," Daniel said cheerfully. "The first round, that is. Gaby?"

The only waitress on duty at this early hour looked up and beamed. She was a friendly brunette twenty years and forty pounds the wrong side of cute.

"A pitcher and four glasses for our booth, if you would," Daniel said, pointing to where Pennyroyal and Ames were already sliding toward the wall end of facing benches. That left Vondrian across from Daniel on the outside—and the natural choice to buy the second pitcher.

The four lieutenants knew one another well enough to be friends in the loose sense of the word. Pennyroyal had been Daniel's classmate at the Academy; Ames and Vondrian had been a couple classes ahead. They'd been thrown together in the General Waiting Room in years past, hoping to be called for a place. When they found themselves again sharing the same bench, it'd been natural to go off for a beer together when the levee ended with the usual lack of result.

Vondrian had family money and an uncle in the Senate. Like Daniel he'd been appointed Lieutenant Commanding—still a lieutenant in pay, but with greater status and a potentially greater share of prize money. The latter didn't apply in the case of Vondrian, captain of a stores ship assigned to the Glover Stars Squadron.

Pennyroyal and Ames had neither wealth nor influence. She'd been the Sixth Lieutenant of the battleship *Schelling*, returned for refit from the Glover Stars in company with Vondrian's vessel, while Ames had been Third Lieutenant of the heavy cruiser *Maspero*. Even in the midst of full-scale war with the Alliance, the Navy Board had condemned the cranky, leaky *Maspero* as uneconomic to repair. Ames and the cruiser's other officers were waiting for transfer to a new vessel fitting out.

Gaby bustled over with the beer immediately, though the fellow at a back table with six empty shot glasses lined up had called for another just as the four lieutenants arrived. "Throws his money around like a drunken spacer," was a cliche with a great deal of solid truth beneath it, but most of the patrons of The Lower Deck didn't have money to throw. Due to captured prizes, Daniel Leary was a striking exception.

Gaby did a half pirouette so that when she bent to set down the tray, her considerable bosom surged toward Daniel. She knew he tipped well any time he could, and she probably guessed that this afternoon he'd be showing off in front of his friends.

Daniel grinned as he slid out the coins. She was right, of course.

"So, what do you think about Slidell's court-martial?" Lieutenant Vondrian said, serving the others from the pitcher. "Are they going to hang him for murder to quiet the Progressives?"

"They can't do that," Ames scoffed. "Why, Slidell's wife is the daughter of Admiral Seens and the niece through her mother's side of Bokely, the Director of Construction. The RCN would never throw one of its own to the mob!"

Daniel sipped his beer, feeling a trifle uncomfortable about the subject. It was the obvious one, though. Everywhere RCN personnel gathered—in the dives fronting Harbor Three as surely as in the most exclusive clubs in Xenos where admirals played cards with members of the Navy Board—they were discussing the same thing.

The problem for Daniel was that he'd chanced to be present two weeks before when Senator and Lady Kearnes were informed of their son's execution. That made the victim to him a young boy with grieving parents instead of a problem in discipline which had been solved in a particular fashion. Death was a normal part of military operations; but execution for mutiny was a very different thing from the accidents, disease, and combat losses that filled the back columns of the *Naval Gazette*.

"It's time for somebody to take a hard line with the Progressives anyway," Vondrian said, lifting his own glass now that he'd filled the others. "What do you say, Leary? Your father's a politician."

"I wouldn't presume to speak for my father," Daniel said. "He and I have very little in common."

He forced a smile to hide the real weight of the words. Daniel never talked about Speaker Leary, but neither did he care to emphasize the degree to which he'd broken with his father. If they were going to talk about Daniel Leary—and they would; the RCN was like a girls' school with everybody gossiping about everybody else when they weren't present—then let it be for the things *he* was responsible for: his navigation, his reckless luck, or the swath he cut through women in whatever venue he found himself.

"And you shouldn't talk about him either, Vondrian," Pennyroyal said with a chuckle. "'Speak of the Devil and hear the rustle of leathery wings,' you know."

She glanced at Daniel. "Begging your pardon if I'm speaking out of turn, Leary," she added in embarrassment.

"Speaker Leary's been called worse things," Daniel said mildly. He looked around the tavern. Holograms of famous space battles formed a frieze under the tongue-and-groove ceiling. Several of the projectors were out, leaving patches like mildewed tapestry in the images. "I can't imagine him appearing in The Lower Deck, though."

Among the things Speaker Leary was called after the Three Circles Conspiracy were a conscienceless brute, a ruthless murderer; and the Savior of the Republic. The first two statements were certainly correct. Daniel was neither a politician nor a political historian, but he rather suspected the last was correct also.

"Mark my words," said Ames, raising a finger for emphasis. He had a baby-face, making a comedy routine of his attempt to look portentous. "They finished hearing the evidence yesterday. The court'll come back tomorrow or the next day, clearing Slidell of all charges. And they'll send him off-planet about as quick to quiet down any trouble the mob makes."

"They certainly convened the court without wasting time," Vondrian said, frowning into the last of his beer. He reached for the pitcher, but Pennyroyal already had it; they were all thirsty from their morning spent warming a bench. "Sending Slidell off-planet won't silence the Progressives, though. *Or* the mob."

"Give them their real name, Vondrian," Ames said. "Radicals. I ask you, what's a captain to do if it's the safety of his ship or the lives of a few mutineers? What would you do if it was you?"

"The thing is . . ." Daniel said, watching the foam on the last inch of his beer. The Lower Deck's draft lager was quite palatable. The house whiskey claimed to be rye but was probably processed from carbohydrate waste with a dash of coloring. It had a kick, though, and the price was moderate. Sometimes that was what you wanted. . . .

"The thing is," Daniel resumed, the eyes of his companions on him, "I've never heard of a mutiny that wasn't over when the ringleaders were in irons. Slidell had arrested young Kearnes and the two crewmen, so why did he decide he had to execute them the next day without a proper court-martial?"

"The *Bainbridge* is a training sloop, Leary," Ames

said. "Slidell didn't have any compartment where he could isolate the prisoners. What if the other mutineers made a rush and freed them?"

"I know how small the *Bainbridge* is," Daniel said sharply. "She's the same size as the *Princess Cecile* or next to it; and I'll tell you, spacers, that I can't imagine executing a man out of hand because I was afraid to bring him back to Cinnabar for trial!"

He gulped the rest of his beer. The pitcher was empty, but Vondrian was already signalling for Gaby.

Daniel had spoken more forcefully than he'd intended, but the whole business bothered him. To be sure, discipline was a more valuable asset to the RCN than another squadron of battleships without that discipline; and to be sure, mutiny was properly punishable by death.

If it *was* mutiny. And that was for a court-martial of five disinterested officers to determine, not for a captain to decide on whim.

"You've always had a picked crew, Leary," Vondrian said, taking a florin from his purse for Gaby. "You're a lucky captain, and so you have your choice. That isn't true of a lot of us, you know. It certainly isn't true for the tub *I* command."

"Look, I'm not judging Commander Slidell," Daniel said. "I'll leave that for a proper court-martial. All I'm saying is, I wish Slidell'd left it for a court-martial too."

Pennyroyal refilled the glasses. Daniel drank his down by two-thirds in a series of measured gulps, feeling uncomfortable.

He knew he'd been shading the truth when he said he wasn't judging Slidell, but the degree to which he felt the commander was in the wrong hadn't struck him till he heard the words come out of his mouth. A captain who executed spacers without authority was as surely in violation of RCN regulations as a spacer who refused a lawful order.

"I say Slidell did what he had to," Ames maintained, stubbornly but without heat. "We'd all of us done the same in his place."

Daniel looked at his fellow lieutenant. Ames grimaced and said, "Well, maybe we would. Anyway, it's for the court-martial to decide."

"This I'll say," Vondrian said, finishing the second pitcher. "And I don't hold with the Progressives, let alone the mob; you know that. But if Slidell *had* brought his prisoners home instead of spacing them through an airlock, the RCN and Cinnabar both'd be in a better place now. This is going to mean trouble and maybe bad trouble, depending on what the court decides."

Pennyroyal cleared her throat and very quietly said, "Should I order another round, then?"

Daniel tossed off the last of his beer. "No, no," he said. "I really need to be getting on. Maybe tomorrow will be the day for all of us, eh?"

He stood up. In fact the *Princess Cecile* would be another month in the yard, not so much from battle damage—though there'd been some—as the strain long voyages put on a small ship. That was fine with Daniel Leary, who had prize money to spend among civilians awed by a chestful of medals. Being on half-pay awaiting the convenience of the Navy Office wasn't a good thing for Pennyroyal, though. The relief in her face suggested she'd have had to walk back to her lodgings for want of tram fare if forced to buy a pitcher.

"Aye, I'll come to the tram stop with you, Leary," Ames said, sliding out of the booth after Daniel. Vondrian stood also, though his glass was still half full.

Lieutenant Aris Choravski came down the stairs from the street and paused, blinking in the tavern's dimmer light. He caught the RCN uniforms and called, "Say, you fellows. Did you hear? The court-martial's come out with a verdict on Slidell!"

Choravski had an appointment in the Personnel section of the Navy Office, so he should've been on duty now. Nobody who knew the man would be surprised that he'd ducked out of his office early to spread the juiciest piece of gossip to touch the RCN in many years.

"Well, what is it, then, man?" Daniel snapped. He was irritated with himself for blurting what he had to his fellow lieutenants—and irritated at the situation for being what it was. His frustration came out in his tone. Well, Choravski didn't deserve any better.

"They've acquitted him!" Choravski crowed, not in the least put off by Daniel's harshness. "Acquitted on all charges!"

"I told you so!" said Ames.

"Aye, so you did," Vondrian agreed. "And I told *you* that there'd be bad trouble if they did."

Daniel grimaced as he started for the stairs out of the tavern. By personal taste as well as revulsion against his father's life, he didn't think much about politics.

But he was pretty sure Vondrian was right.

The summons had been by means of a calling card, handed at noon to the doorman of Chatsworth Minor,

Adele's townhouse, by a seeming street urchin. He may have been a real urchin; regardless, the doorman said he'd run off immediately.

The printed front of the card read BERNIS SAND. On the back was written in pencil: *your westbound tram stop at 18:17*. There was no date or signature.

At 18:17 Adele stepped out of the townhouse with Tovera at her side. "I'll be going out for a few hours, Tiomka," she said to the doorman on duty.

"Sure you wouldn't like a few of us to come along, mistress?" Tiomka said. He and the other servants at Chatsworth Minor wore the blue-and-silver livery of the Mundys, but strictly speaking they weren't Adele's retainers. They were employed by The Shippers' and Merchants' Treasury, the bank which leased the townhouse from Adele but sublet the property on very favorable terms back to Adele and to Daniel Leary when their RCN duties found them on Cinnabar.

"No thank you," Adele said. "I'm not going anywhere I need to impress people."

The bank had acted through its managing partner, Deirdre Leary. Daniel knew his sister was involved, but he was too much an innocent in the realms of finance to understand how extremely generous the terms of his rental were.

Daniel *didn't* know that his father owned the controlling interest in The Shippers' and Merchants' Treasury. If he'd had an inkling of that, he'd have left the townhouse in a fury very different from Adele's cold rages but just as dangerous to anyone who tried to get in his way.

Adele had no affection for the man who'd had her family killed; but—possibly because she didn't have close blood relations herself—she was unwilling to prevent Corder Leary from doing what he could to secretly help his son. She wasn't hiding the fact from her friend: he'd never asked, because that sort of question didn't interest him.

And heaven knew, Daniel needed someone to look after his money. Daniel's idea of financial planning was to spend what he had—and a bit more. Annuities from The Shippers' and Merchants' Treasury paid comfortable returns on the prize money he'd earned at the risk of his life. The bank dribbled out enough money to weight Daniel's pockets nicely for as long as he lived; and not coincidentally, the form of the investment prevented him from touching his capital.

"You should take me, you know," Tovera said mildly. Her title was "private secretary." She dressed the part in a severely cut suit and attaché case. "There are people who know who you are. Everywhere you go, you're in danger."

Tovera's suit was fog gray; her complexion was so pale that if she'd worn charcoal, she'd have looked like a mime in white-face. The case held a variety of specialized tools, in particular a sub-machine gun.

"While I doubt that Mistress Sand would do me physical harm if I insulted her by bringing a bodyguard, Tovera," Adele said, "I believe I'd be risking things that are of more importance to me than my life is."

Tovera chuckled. "I understand, mistress," she said. "But your life is important to *me*. Who else would show me how to act human?"

Adele looked at her. She thought Tovera had just made a joke, but it was difficult to be sure. A servant like Tovera was rather like making a pet of a spider from the pale depths of a cave.

Chatsworth Minor was at the end of a close; the tram stop was on the cross street four doors up. A monorail car was leaving as Adele approached, but it was going east toward the center of the city. Two servants had gotten off, laden with large baskets of produce that they may well have brought from the family's country estate. They bowed politely as they passed Adele.

A westbound car was hissing toward the shunt, shifting the polarity of its magnetic levitators to trail rather than lead that of the support rail. From outside the car seemed to be full to capacity. The doors didn't open as they normally would when the vehicle stopped.

"Go back and wait for me, Tovera," Adele said. She reached for the latchplate, but the door accordianed open before she touched it. There were three figures inside, wearing cloaks over gray 2nd Class RCN uniforms. The rest of the crowd was an illusion caused by patterned film over the windows.

"As the mistress orders," Tovera said politely, but she didn't move until the door had closed and the tram began to whine away.

Personal transportation in Xenos was by foot or—most generally—by the monorail trams which covered all parts of the city and suburbs. The cars seated twelve and held twenty in reasonable comfort, though at rush hours they might carry double that number. They were individually programmed: a rider chose his destination on the touch pad at the stop where he waited. The system's central computer then directed to him the nearest car headed in the correct direction.

The wait for a car was rarely more than twenty

minutes except perhaps at the farthest reaches of the line. There was a great circular exchange at the Pentacrest, the physical and administrative center of Xenos, where riders might have to transfer; otherwise the cars took them to their destinations by the least circuitous route possible.

Many wealthy families had private cars which retainers set onto the tramline when the master or mistress had an appointment. Only governmental agencies had aircars, and wheeled transport was limited to delivery vehicles during the hours of darkness. Both prohibitions were enforced not by the police but by other nobles, who wouldn't hesitate to have their guards shoot a rival's aircar into a collander.

"Where's Mistress Sand?" Adele said with scant courtesy. The three officers—all men—in the car were strangers to her. She wasn't worried, but the situation wasn't what she'd expected and she didn't like it.

"She sent us to brief you," said the eldest of the three. "Because of the delicacy of this matter, you're not to contact her directly while the operation is running."

The fellow was in his fifties; he had sunken cheeks and a high forehead. The cloaks covered rank insignia and name tags, but if still on active duty he was at least a captain and possibly an admiral. His two companions were younger: a soft-featured blond in his twenties and a black-haired man of thirty-odd with the build of an athlete who'd let himself go to seed.

Adele glanced at a window; the film that counterfeited a carload of passengers also prevented her from seeing out. The tram was proceeding according to directions these men had programmed into it. There was no way that she could tell where they were going;

they might simply be riding in a circle back to where she'd gotten on.

She didn't like this at all. Well, she'd been involved in many things that she didn't like, especially during the fourteen years she'd lived as a penniless orphan.

"There isn't an operation till I've agreed to it," Adele said to the leader. "What are you proposing?"

"If you think—" the blond man began hotly. His superior silenced him with a raised finger, continuing to hold Adele's eyes.

The tram bounced hard at a junction. They were all standing. Adele and the blond man grabbed stanchions; the heavy-set man stumbled backward and had to stick out his hand to keep from falling on a seat. The leader rode the shock with the ease of a man who'd spent much of his life on maneuvering starships.

The jolt had broken the serious edge of tension filling the car. The leader smiled curtly and said without preamble, "The most serious danger to the Republic at the moment, mistress, isn't the Alliance of Free Stars but rather Radical agitation here on Cinnabar. Though of course the Alliance is funding it, you can be sure of that."

"*I'm* not sure of that," Adele said evenly. "But my duties have nothing to do with Cinnabar politics, so my ignorance is unimportant."

"Your duties are what the Republic says they are, mistress," the heavy-set man growled.

Adele looked at him; she didn't speak. The leader pursed his lips in irritation and said, "I'll handle this, More."

Smoothing his face, he resumed to Adele, "Mistress, you can be certain that the Republic wouldn't call you to this duty were it not important. You lived within the Alliance for many years. You know that the so-called Alliance of Free Stars is really the brutal dictatorship of Guarantor Porra, enforced by military power and a ruthless security apparatus."

"I agree," Adele said, smiling faintly. People tended to think "ruthless" meant "cruel." It didn't: it meant doing what was logically required without factoring in mercy.

She herself wasn't cruel; but she'd shot her way out of a trap on Kostroma, changing 20-round magazines several times. If any of the scores of people she'd shot that night weren't dead, it was simply because the light pellets from her pocket pistol hadn't penetrated their skulls as she'd intended.

She'd been aiming at their eyes because the bone behind the orbits is very thin, so almost all of the pellets would've penetrated.

In the hours before dawn Adele saw those faces and other dead faces more nights than she didn't. Nonetheless she'd do the same thing again if the situation logically required it. *She* knew what ruthless meant.

"The trouble is, most of the common people, especially in Xenos, don't have your experience," the leader continued. "They're easy marks for Porra's agitators and also for irresponsible Cinnabar politicians who think they'll gain votes by turning the common people against their natural leaders."

"A cancer," the blond man said, his head turned to the side as though he were addressing the images pasted onto the windows. "A cancer in the heart of the Republic!"

"Your late father is a hero to many of these people,

Mistress Mundy," the leader said earnestly. "Because you've been operating away from Cinnabar, they won't realize you've changed sides. You'll be able to infiltrate the traitors' inner circles very easily."

"I haven't changed sides," Adele said, reaching into her left side-pocket.

She wondered what Daniel would've said if some fool had made him a comparable proposition. He'd have been loud, she was certain; but that was Daniel, and she was Adele Mundy who rarely raised her voice.

"I don't have a side, gentlemen," Adele said. "I've never had politics. Politics were my parents' affair, and I fail to see the attraction of what their interest resulted in. Set me out of this car at once, if you please."

"Don't get above yourself, mistress!" the leader said sharply. "This isn't some academic game where you can choose whether or not to play. This is the safety of the Republic!"

Adele brought the little pistol out of her pocket. Lucius Mundy knew that his politics would lead to duels—unless his would-be challengers learned that calling out a Mundy was tantamount to suicide. He'd seen to it that every Mundy practiced long hours in the target ranges both at Chatsworth and the town-house, Chatsworth Minor. Young Adele had a natural skill with pistols that had stood her in good stead in recent years. . . .

"Say!" said the blond fellow. His voice rose abruptly in the course of that single syllable. "What do you think you're doing with that?"

"Are you willing to kill me, gentlemen?" Adele said mildly. "Because I'm certainly willing to kill you."

She fired into the tram's control panel. The pellet

from the little electromotive pistol snap/*crack*ed, the supersonic shock wave blurring into the impact that blew a divot from the plastic panel.

"Bloody Hell!" the heavy-set man squealed, throwing an arm over his eyes. Fragments of projectile or target must've splashed him.

"All right!" the leader said. Then, quieter but with real venom, "All right, we'll put you down. But don't think you've heard the last of this!"

He cuffed the blond man. "You have the key, don't you Dagenham? Well, use it!"

Adele lowered the pistol to her side, keeping the barrel well out from her trousers leg. The flux from even a single shot heated the muzzle enough to char cloth. Her face was as still as those on the film covering the car's windows.

The blond man took a key card from his breast pocket and inserted it into the control slot that allowed specified users to use the pad on the panel to direct the vehicle, overriding the central computer. He met his leader's eyes, got a snarled, "Yes, you bloody fool!" and shunted the tram car onto the next stop.

The doors didn't open. Adele slapped the latchplate with her right hand, then deliberately slipped the pistol into her pocket—it cooled quickly. She turned her back on the men as she stepped out of the car. She had no idea where she was.

The tram hummed off behind her. She'd expected one of the officers to shout some final threat, but they remained silent.

There were a dozen people on the platform, but they appeared to be sheltering here rather than waiting for a tram. The buildings nearby were four- and five-story apartments, probably tenements for the very poor. The spill-over, the poorer yet, was here at the tram stop. A pair of men hunched toward Adele, then stopped when they saw her face, cold as death, in the light over the call plate.

With her left hand in her pocket, Adele walked to the public phone on the other side of the kiosk from the call plate. A woman with an infant was huddled against the panel below it.

"Pardon," Adele said. "I need this."

"Hey, who do you think *you* are?" the woman said in a shrill whine.

"Shall I have you whipped out of the city?" shouted Mundy of Chatsworth, scion of one of the oldest houses in the Republic. "Get out of my way, you scum, or I'll do that and worse!"

The woman crabbed herself away. Her infant began to complain at increasing volume.

Adele punched a series of numbers into the keypad, hit the pause symbol, and then typed an almost identical sequence on top of the first. Almost instantly a woman's voice, cultured despite the tinny speaker, said, "Yes?"

"This is Mundy," Adele said. "I resign, effective immediately."

"Where are you now?" Mistress Sand said.

"I'm where your damned stooges left me!" Adele said, her voice rising despite herself. She knew she had an audience listening from the darkness around her, and she didn't care. "Somewhere near the outskirts of Xenos, I suppose. The number of the stop is—"

She paused to remember the number in stencilled in black letters above the call plate on the other side.

"Four four seven one, I believe," she added.

"I had nothing to do with whatever happened to you tonight, mistress," Bernis Sand said. "I'll be with you in fifteen minutes, less if I can manage it. Don't leave the spot."

The line went dead. Adele stepped back from the phone and looked around. A dozen pairs of eyes were on her. The platform smelled of spoiled food, human waste and other, sharper odors. So, she realized, did the people staring at her.

Adele began to laugh. *At least I'm in better company than I was a few minutes ago*, she thought.

CHAPTER 3

Xenos on Cinnabar

Adele, her back to the panel mounting the public phone, didn't hear the aircar approaching. While she worked with her personal data unit, the locals had circled her like animals watching a campfire. As they scattered they called, "The cops! The cops!" loudly enough to break her concentration.

She sighed, shutting down the air-projected holographic display and tucking the control wands away into the case. The unit didn't hold all knowledge, not even when it was linked—as it was now—to the enormous database in the Library of Thomas Celsus with all *its* attendant links, but it held enough to engulf any number of troubles and disappointments. In fact its ocean of knowledge was deep enough to swallow the cold, killing rage which a few minutes ago had filled Adele Mundy's mind.

She stood, sliding the data unit into its special thigh pocket and dusted the trousers with her palms. For the meeting Adele had worn unobtrusive civilian clothing,

45

in excellent condition but similar in type to the cast-off garments of the residents of the tram stop.

Adele had a thigh pocket in every outfit she owned, including her 1st Class RCN uniform where it was very much against regulations. She occasionally went out without her pistol because her destination banned weapons and enforced it with detectors; she was *never* willingly without the personal data unit.

A covered eight-place aircar set down beside the tram stop. The flanks of the vehicle were marked MILITIA in large letters; searchlights and loudspeaker cones were attached to short posts at the front and rear.

Mistress Bernis Sand got out. She was a short, heavy-set woman who looked bulkier for being in formal garb: white shirt and white cummerbund, with black trousers and frock coat. Adele wondered fleetingly what excuse the spymaster had made to leave some high-level gathering when Adele called.

"Do you mind walking with me?" Sand said. She loosened her cummerbund. "Stuffy doesn't begin to describe a Regents' Dinner—the atmosphere, mind, not the Temple Hall."

"As you like," Adele said, falling in to Sand's left. Up the street in the direction they were going was a construction site. She slanted them toward the middle of the pavement out of long-trained reflex.

"We're being watched discreetly," the older woman said. "You needn't worry."

"Mistress, I've lived most of my adult life in districts like this," Adele said in a thin voice. "I'm not worried. I'd just rather not have to shoot some fourteen-year-old sniffing solvent in a culvert, waiting to mug somebody for pocket change."

"Your pardon, mistress," Sand said, nodding toward Adele to make it more than a formal apology. "I'm upset about your other trouble tonight; for which I also apologize. I assure you I wasn't aware of it, but obviously it wouldn't have happened in the way it did were you not associated with me."

"The person involved . . ." Adele said. They were the only pedestrians out on the street, but scuttling from the darkness to either side hinted that scavengers of various kinds were active. "Is a retired admiral named Elric Kahn. He didn't use his own name, but he named his two flunkies. It was easy enough to find them on the Navy List and track their associations back to him."

"Was it indeed?" Sand said. She barked out a laugh. "For you I dare say it was, Mundy."

Sobering, she went on, "Being Kahn, he'll have been asking you to infiltrate the radical fringe of the Progressive Party, I suppose. A bloody fool thing to ask *you*, but I don't blame him for trying. God knows it's a real problem."

Sand jerked her thumb back toward the aircar, now nearly a block behind them. "There's riots tonight in three districts downtown. We were shot at on our way here, though it must've been a pistol and barely flecked the paint. Over the Slidell acquittal, you know."

"Is Senator Kearnes behind it?" Adele said, remembering her host's violent rage two weeks before.

"No, this is at a much lower level," Sand said, turning her hands palms-up as if weighing souls. "It's not about young Kearnes, it's the two common spacers murdered by uncaring aristocrats. But that's nothing to do with you, Mundy; as I would've told Kahn if he'd asked me."

Sand looked sharply at Adele. Without raising her voice, but in a tone that would've served for pronouncing a death sentence, she said, "Did they use my name?"

"Yes," Adele said. "They delivered your card with instructions on the back to my doorman."

She cleared her throat and added, "I destroyed the card immediately."

"Of course you did!" Sand snapped. "And of course that makes no difference. Mundy, I've been a fool in various fashions over the years, but never such a fool as to imagine that you'd lie to me."

She snorted another laugh. "You might shoot me; that I can imagine. But not lie."

"I'd regret shooting you, mistress," Adele said, smiling faintly. It wasn't really a joke, of course.

Sand sighed. "They shouldn't have used my name," she said. "For the rest, well, I'd say Kahn was a fool but I've always thought that."

Adele grimaced. "I was angry because I thought the approach *had* been made by you, mistress," she said. "Since it wasn't—Kahn and his flunkies are scarcely the only fools on Cinnabar. No doubt they meant well."

Shrugging, she added, "No harm done."

Sand turned to look at her as they sauntered along the empty street. The pavement was cracked and half the street lights were out, but they weren't in a hurry. "They used my name, Mundy," Sand said in the same flat tone as before. "*I* will deal with the matter."

A man shambled from between two buildings, holding out a bottle in his left hand. He kept his right hand close to his body. "Have a drinkie with me, girls!" he called. "Drinkie, drinkie!"

Adele stepped in front of Sand, pulling the pistol from her pocket. She fired into the pavement between the man's feet. The air at the muzzle fluoresced as the coil gun's magnetic flux ionized the light-metal driving band. The ceramic pellet sparkled like stardust, gouging a narrow trench in the street.

"God help me!" the man screamed, twitching both arms convulsively. The bottle flew in one direction, a knuckleduster in the other. He ran back toward the alley, moving much more purposefully than he'd approached.

Adele smiled coldly. Perhaps the fright had sobered him; and perhaps the rattle of trash in the alley was from stray dogs, not a pack of three of four other thugs waiting to rush onto their victims when their front man had grabbed them.

"The troubles mean we need to get you off Cinnabar, though," Sand said. If she had an opinion about what'd just happened, she kept it to herself. "If matters get much worse, one side or the other will decide you're working for their enemies and target you. Because of your father, you know."

Sand paused, grimaced, and added, "One side or *another*. These civil messes aren't limited to two parties."

Adele held the pistol out to the side to cool. She had eighteen rounds remaining; she hadn't brought extra magazines.

She laughed.

"Eh?" said Sand, taking a snuffbox of polished shell from somewhere on her person.

"I was thinking that Tovera was right today," Adele said.

Though the words wouldn't have been an explanation for many people, Sand chuckled in understanding. "The trouble with the Toveras of the world . . ." she replied. "Is that you always know what they're going to say before they open their mouths. And the Kahns too, I'm afraid. It limits the value of their analyses."

She looked sharply at Adele. "I'm not suggesting you can't take care of yourself, mistress," she said. "But there're a lot of them."

"It wouldn't be a comfortable way to live," Adele agreed, "even if it were possible."

For a moment bleak darkness filled her mind. *It isn't fair!* And then she laughed again, louder than she had in months if ever. Sand glanced at her but this time didn't speak.

"I'm human," Adele said simply. "I'm not an emotionless, logical machine. I know that because of the extremely foolish thoughts that come into my head."

"I never imagined you were emotionless, Mundy," Sand said. She cleared her throat. In a more businesslike tone she continued, "I don't have an operation that requires your particular skills at the moment, but you'd be a valuable asset to the Republic wherever you were. Do *you* have a particular desire?"

Adele thought through the offer—a quite remarkable offer, given who Mistress Sand was. But the truth was . . .

"The two greatest centers of knowledge are the Celsus Library here in Xenos and the Academic Collections on Blythe," she said, apologetic because what she was really saying was that Sand's generosity was of no value to her. "I'm being driven off Cinnabar, and because of the war I can't go back to Blythe.

In all likelihood, I'll never be able to go back to Blythe. I'll never be a civilian again in the mind of Guarantor Porra."

"Nor that of his Fifth Bureau," Sand agreed in a tone of regret. "Because of your association with me."

"Because of the choices *I* made," Adele said crisply. "You couldn't have forced me to do *anything*, mistress. No one could have."

"I'm aware of where my responsibility stops, Mundy," Sand said with slightly more of an edge. "I'm also aware of my responsibility."

"Yes," Adele said. She slid the pistol back into her pocket. She didn't notice its weight; rather, its absence was subtly uncomfortable. "Should we turn around now?"

"Not unless you want to," Sand said. "The car will pick us up when I call it, wherever we are."

They continued walking. The range of buildings to the right was an industrial concern of some sort, partially lighted now through grime-clouded windows. Adele heard heavy vehicles grunting and squealing from loading docks on the other side of the factory. She restrained her impulse to take out her data unit and determine what the business actually was.

Smiling at herself Adele said, "What I'd really like to do, since staying here isn't an option, would be to accompany a surveying expedition into regions that haven't been travelled since the Hiatus. There'd be a scientific head, of course, but the vessel itself would require a skilled captain. Lieutenant Leary would be the best choice for that post since his uncle retired twenty years ago."

"I intended to be a lecturer in Pre-Hiatus history,

Mundy," Mistress Sand said in a tone of wistful amusement. "As an avocation, of course—heaven forefend
that a member of the noble house of Caliwell actually
work for a living. I think I could still perform valuable
services in that fashion if circumstances allowed. I'm
rusty on the details, but I've learned how to collect
data and even more important, how to analyze it."

She looked at Adele with a wry smile. "Circumstances don't permit, of course. And in the midst of
a full-scale naval war, neither is the Republic going to
fit out an expedition for the sole purpose of expanding
human knowledge."

"Though that's a little more probable," Adele said,
"than that Daniel would go haring off into the back of
beyond when there's a war to fight on our doorstep."

She laughed. "He isn't a pugnacious man, I wouldn't
want you to think that," she said. "Let alone a blood-
thirsty one. But he's quite clear on the fact that the
RCN's primary duty is to fight the enemies of the
Republic."

Mistress Sand nodded, smiling faintly. "I think
we've done what we can here," she said, putting the
snuffbox away without having used it. She turned and
raised her hand.

Adele couldn't see the aircar far behind them, but
the idling purr of its lift fans built quickly to a whine.
The driver switched his red and green sidelights on
and started toward them, ten feet above the road's
broken surface.

"The driver and guard have been vetted, of course,"
Sand said. "But—"

"Yes, of course," said Adele, mildly irritated that the
older woman had said something so unnecessary. They'd

gotten out and walked, hadn't they, instead of having their discussion in front of Sand's underlings?

"We'll put you down at a tram stop east of your townhouse," Sand said, as though she hadn't heard the implicit rebuke. "That'll keep you clear of the trouble downtown."

"All right," said Adele, facing the oncoming vehicle as she mulled the distant past. Were these riots the beginning of what would end in another round of Proscriptions? Because if they were, she'd leave Cinnabar and never return. . . .

"Mundy?" Sand said, raising her voice to be heard over the approaching drive fans. "I need to make some inquiries, but I'll meet with you again tomorrow. I'm not forgetting you."

"I appreciate that," Adele said. Silently as the aircar landed, her mind added, *But sometimes I wish I could forget myself—the thing I am, and what made me such a thing.*

"My sister she works in a laundry . . ." sang Daniel Leary. He'd had a drink or two at home, but liquor was properly a matter for fellowship, not solitude. On a whim he'd decided to visit the Strip outside Harbor Three. *"My father, he fiddles for gin."*

The dozen civilians sharing the tram watched him and Hogg with nervous smiles. Their expressions seemed out of place to Daniel. He had money in his pocket and ahead of him the best sort of friends there were: the ones he hadn't met yet.

And he had a few drinks inside. Only a few, and a few nips from Hogg's flask as they clicked and rattled westward.

"My mother, she takes in washing . . ." Daniel warbled, winding up for the big finish.

He'd attended one gathering or another almost every night since the *Princess Cecile* landed. His host for dinner tonight, a wealthy ship chandler, had cancelled unexpectedly. Daniel didn't worry about being on his own. He'd always been able to find a party in the past.

The tram crunched to a shrieking halt: the emergency brakes had reversed polarity in the levitators, sucking them hard against the support railing. The civilians flew forward with no more control than if they'd been dropped from a cliff, but Hogg was holding a stanchion and Daniel stuck his right leg out straight to brace himself against the forward bulkhead.

He moved without thinking about it. Spacers who thought before acting disappeared into bubble universes in which they were the only life form after their ship moved on to the next bubble of the Matrix.

Daniel's reflexes didn't prevent an elderly woman and a much younger, much heavier man from slamming into his back. He grunted but didn't fall; that sort of thing happened on starships, too. Just about every sort of unpleasant surprise happened on a starship, one time or another.

Civilians shouted frightened curses. Daniel turned. The old woman moaned on the tram's floor as the heavy-set man knelt on her.

"Watch that, my man!" Daniel said. He grabbed the back of the man's collar and jerked some of the weight off the poor woman.

The fellow swung at Daniel. Hogg clocked him behind the ear with the liquor flask, stainless steel and sturdy enough for a countryman's use. It was certainly sturdy enough to roll the heavy man's eyes up as his body went limp. Daniel slung the burden to the floor beside the woman, then looked out of the car for the first time to see what was going on.

They were in a plaza, a junction for several monorail lines. They'd halted behind a private tramcar painted pink and violet. Daniel didn't recognize the livery nor the crest, some sort of four-winged bird.

The three-story buildings around the plaza housed laborers from Harbor Three. Their ground floors were given over to shops serving spacers: restaurants, clothing stores, and a better class of pawn brokers and bars than you'd find sharing the Strip with the brothels a few blocks to the east.

An angry mob filled the plaza. Men—with a few women, and not whores either—were swinging the private car to either side, trying to rock it off the support rail. In all likelihood they'd succeed very shortly.

The private car had opera windows, small ovals, to provide privacy for those within. Daniel saw the terrified face of a servant in pink and violet livery looking out the back; then the crowd shouted and flung the car almost sideways. A blond, wide-eyed woman peered from the thrashing chaos within.

"We'll be getting off here, Hogg," Daniel said, stepping toward the door. He had to push past civilians transfixed by what was going on outside.

"Right," muttered Hogg. "*Just* the sort of bloody fool thing I figured we'd be doing."

Daniel was wearing a 2nd Class uniform, gray with black piping. It satisfied the regulation requiring RCN officers to wear civilian clothes or a dress uniform whenever they were off-duty in public—but it was his third-best set of Grays, which made the word "best" something of a joke. The elbows and trouser seat were worn, the right sleeve had been sewn back when it started to part from the shirt-front, and you'd notice the oil stain on the tunic if you saw it in good light.

It was the sort of uniform you wore to go bar-hopping on the Strip. It would do equally well for Daniel's present purpose, though part of him regretted not also having stuck a length of high-pressure tubing through his belt. Still, if it came to a straight fight, matters weren't going to work out well anyway.

He reached for the door's manual latch. A middle-aged woman shrieked as she saw what he was doing. "Please," she said in a choking voice. "Please, please. Don't let them in."

Daniel looked around his fellow passengers. They were all ordinary folk, coming home from work or perhaps heading for dinner in a restaurant. They stared at him. Daniel thought of rabbits in the hutch at Bantry, about to be slaughtered for dinner.

"You'll be all right," he said, raising his voice so everyone in the car could hear over the growl of the mob. "They're not interested in the likes of you."

"And you *won't* be all right if you keep in our way," Hogg snarled. "I'm in a bloody poor mood already."

The woman half-stepped, half-staggered, to the side. She was weeping uncontrollably.

Daniel opened the door just as the mob managed to swing the private car off the support rail. It hit on its left side with a crash that buckled panels and popped out the rear window. The mob growled deafeningly, drowning the screams of those on whom the car had fallen.

The crowd'd surged back as the car dropped. Daniel used the disruption to push and elbow his way through the ruck to what had been the underside of the tramcar. He heard the door above him rattle open.

"Get me a little room, Hogg," Daniel said. He grabbed the car's dismounting step, now seven feet in the air—the width of the car. Hogg growled something lost in the crowd noise. Daniel swung himself onto tram's upturned right side with a hunch of his shoulders. The sleeves of his tunic ripped loose.

Daniel's rounded features would look soft to a stranger's first glance, but the captain of an RCN starship under way spends much of his time on deck with his riggers. The best way to judge energy gradients was to stand on a masthead and eye the rippling shimmers of Casimir radiation that surrounded the vessel. Daniel had the upper body strength of a professional gymnast.

He balanced on the quarter panel, looking into the vehicle. Inside were four footmen and the blond girl. She was quite pretty despite the blank, overwhelming fear that forced her eyes open and let her jaw drop. . . .

The servants were stripping off their tunics, hoping to be safer in their underwear than they would wearing livery. They looked up and saw Daniel's RCN uniform; their expressions changed from terror to unexpected hope.

"Help me!" a footman screamed, elbowing his mistress aside. He stepped onto an armrest and raised his hand. His three fellows trampled the girl in their haste to join him.

Daniel wondered if the servants would've been able to organize themselves well enough to lift and pull one another out if he hadn't been here. But he was. . . .

He bent, gripped the footman by the wrist instead of the hand, and jerked him up by flexing his knees. The motion wasn't very different from the way Daniel would've landed a heavy fish in the sea off Bantry.

Instead of helping the footman balance on the tram, Daniel deliberately flicked him off the side. The fellow pitched into the crowd with a despairing wail. Daniel bent, grasped the next footman, and repeated the process.

He didn't feel any particular anger against the servants. They weren't covering themselves with glory, but they'd have probably said they weren't paid to die for their mistress; Daniel more or less agreed with them.

On the other hand, an RCN officer quickly learned that no solution to a crisis was going to be perfect: you saved what you could. Daniel figured that a petite blond woman needed his help more than four able-bodied men did.

As Daniel half-pushed, half-threw, the third servant over the side, he noticed that two men from the crowd were trying to pull themselves up by the steps the way he'd done. They were getting in each other's way, so he ignored them.

The last footman was badly overweight and blind with tears. He waved his arms wildly, but not close enough to grab. Daniel knelt to bring himself a little farther down than he'd been while squatting, then took the chance of grabbing with both hands instead of keeping one braced on the door jamb; he got the fellow by wrist and elbow. He straightened at once, using the footman to counterbalance him. At the top of his lift, Daniel pivoted and dropped his burden after the others.

He glanced at what was happening in the street for the first time since he'd climbed onto the tram. Two of the servants were crawling away, stark naked and moaning. The crowd was still in the process of stripping off the third man's tights, jeering and punching him. Daniel figured that level of punishment was a cheap price for your life; and probably a lot cheaper than their mistress was going to pay if the mob had its way.

One of the men who'd been trying to climb had made a stirrup of his hands for the other. Daniel kicked the higher man in the face; he toppled backward with a squawk, falling on the lower man whom Hogg had just punched in the kidneys. Hogg hadn't gotten involved until he needed to. He knew as well as Daniel did that they couldn't fight the whole mob themselves.

Daniel leaned toward the girl. She was in a sitting position on the now-floor, staring up at him. He wasn't sure her eyes were focusing. The car began to rock. Daniel reached down with both arms and shouted, "Quick! They're going to roll it over again! We've got to get out first!"

His only chance was to act immediately. If the rioters tipped it onto its roof so that a dozen of them could reach the girl, it was all over.

She got up, closed her eyes, and jumped. Daniel grabbed her wrists. She weighed almost nothing compared to the footmen, and his system still blazed with adrenaline. He'd pay for this tomorrow; though he had to survive the next few minutes for that to matter.

Daniel wrapped his arms around the girl and lifted her, as if they were in a particularly passionate embrace. "Now, milady," he said. "I want you to hold on very tightly no matter what happens, and I apologize in advance for the inconvenience."

The tramcar Daniel had arrived on was hissing forward again, now that the private car was no longer blocking the support rail. The rioters shifted out of the way, uninterested as Daniel had expected in people more or less like them.

Daniel jumped down into the space cleared by the accelerating car, taking the shock on his flexed knees. The girl gave a despairing *eep!* but her arms tightened around Daniel's neck; she even wrapped her legs around his waist. So far, so good.

There hadn't been time to plan, but you could never plan for all the things that might happen. Daniel'd half thought of climbing onto the mounting step of the tram as it moved off, but there were too many rioters in the way already.

Across one of the streets entering the plaza near the overturned car was a bar; six spacers wearing the beribboned, heavily embroidered utility uniforms of RCN warrant officers on leave stood in front of the entrance. Daniel started toward them.

Five were men, the sixth a woman built like a fireplug. In all likelihood most of the bar's patrons had left as the mob gathered, but these senior warrant officers stuck around. They watched the mob with live and let-live expressions, but from the way they held themselves and the batons of one sort and another in their hands they were ready to defend what was probably a favorite drinking spot.

"Hey!" shouted a man close behind Daniel. "Here's the *uhh*—"

Hogg's rabbit punch was too late, and besides he wouldn't be able to silence everybody as Daniel bumped his way through the crowd. "There she goes!" a woman squealed. "There she goes!"

"RCN!" Daniel bellowed, breaking into a trot. He took the shocks with his shoulders when he could, but mostly he was using the girl as a battering ram. She grunted each time they knocked a civilian out of the way, but she didn't complain or lose her double grip. "RCN to me!"

"Bloody officers can find their own holes!" shouted a tall warrant officer with the butt end of a pool cue. A scar led up his forehead into a white streak across his scalp. "Calahan was a bosun, same as me!"

One of the mutineers Slidell'd put out the airlock of the Bainbridge *had been the bosun*, Daniel recalled. *The bloody fool!*

Somebody grabbed him from behind by the sleeve. He kicked back hard, but the section of the mob still between him and the building was turning to see what was coming their way. Slidell wasn't the only fool, that was clear, but Daniel hadn't argued with Hogg's assessment right at the start of this.

"I'm Lieutenant Daniel Leary!" he said. A man was braced squarely in front of him. Daniel kicked the fellow in the crotch. The man to the right of the one

doubling up grabbed the girl's shoulders and pulled;
the man to the left cocked back his fist with a brick
to ram into Daniel's face. "By God my *Sissie* never
shipped a spacer afraid of a fight! RCN!"

Hogg carried a pair of four-ounce sinkers joined by
a length of monocrystal sea-fishing line that could cut
unprotected flesh like a knifeblade. It was primarily
a throwing weapon, of small use in a ruck like this
Daniel would've said.

A sinker on six feet of line made a hissing arc past
Daniel's ear. The fellow with the brick fell screaming,
his arm dangling from a broken collarbone. He'd been
lucky not to have a dished-in forehead—and it *was* luck,
because Hogg didn't pull his punches in a brawl.

Daniel's right hand caught the man trying to take
the girl from him. He lowered his head and jerked
the civilian's face into the point of his skull, feeling
cartilage crunch. "RCN!" he called, but there were
too many of them and—

"RCN!" other voices shouted. Through the mob's
noise Daniel heard a series of cracking, slapping
sounds accompanied by high-pitched screams. "Clear
a path for the RCN!"

Two warrant officers stood in front of Daniel, the
bosun with the pool cue and the woman with a thick-
bottomed liqueur bottle in either hand. The green
glass was bloodstained. They parted to pass Daniel
and his burden between them; their four fellows were
holding the flanks.

"Hogg's with me!" Daniel called as he trotted/
stumbled toward the bar's entrance only a few feet
away. He didn't dare look behind. Suddenly he had
barely enough strength to stay on his feet.

"Here you go, sir," said the tense-looking barman standing just inside the doorway. He held out the open whiskey bottle in his left hand; in his right was a bung starter. "And will your good lady be having something tonight?"

"In a moment, perhaps," Daniel wheezed. He cleared his throat and went on, "Miss, we're all right for the moment. I believe you can let go now."

She unwrapped her legs but continued to hold onto Daniel's neck. Her body was trembling.

The warrant officers retreated to their previous position in front of the bar; Hogg was with them, Daniel was pleased to see. The mob backed away like surf curling off a beach. The girl was out of their sight, and the cost of coming in after her was obviously going to be high. There were other, less dangerous targets available.

"Hermy, phone the Shamrock and tell Woetjans her captain's here and could maybe use a hand," the bosun with the pool cue ordered the bartender. He caught Daniel's eye and added, "That's where your Sissies mostly drink, sir. Not that you're not welcome here with us Starchies, but I figured you'd as soon be with your own."

"I'm much obliged to you, bosun," Daniel said. The other warrant officers were watching sidelong while keeping one eye on the mob just in case something changed. "To all of you."

"We're sorry, Mister Leary," the woman said with a rueful grin. "We didn't see it was you, you know."

"I know," Daniel said. "And I understand."

Hogg still wore the mesh-armored right glove which permitted him to handle his weighted line without losing fingers. He'd emptied his flask and was prudently refilling it from the bottle the bartender had offered Daniel a moment before.

Daniel looked at the girl he'd saved; she eased back slightly. Well, saved from a bad time. A—he grinned to himself—worse time, anyway; she'd just about lost her tunic as it was.

"Mistress?" Daniel said. "My name's Daniel Leary, Lieutenant Leary, that is. Friends of mine should be arriving shortly. May we escort you to someplace you'll be safe?"

"I'm Marta Grimes," the girl said. She was no longer clinging to Daniel's neck, but she hadn't moved far away. She didn't seem inordinately concerned that she was wearing nothing but a gauzy bandeau above the waist. "My father's Grimes of Octagon though he's off-planet now. Our townhouse is only two blocks away, but it won't be safe. The servants couldn't . . ."

Her voice broke. She stared into Daniel's eyes, suddenly trembling again. "You saw what happened, Lieutenant Leary!"

"Indeed I did," Daniel said, putting his arm around the girl's shoulders. She squeezed herself to him as though she hoped he'd pick her up again. "May I ask if your father has liquor in the house? Quantity is more important than quality, for this purpose."

In the near distance he heard voices shouting, "Outa the way for the *Princess Cecile!*" The sound came from at least twenty throats, led by the rasping alto of Woetjans, the *Sissie*'s bosun.

"Purpose?" Marta repeated in puzzlement. "But yes, Lieutenant. Dad's cellar is famous."

"Then if you don't mind expending some of it in a

good cause," Daniel said, "I think we can keep you and your townhouse safe for the duration and make some of my shipmates very happy at the same time."

He looked at the warrant officers who'd rescued him. "You all are welcome too, I believe."

"Thanks, but Hermy's made us the same offer," the bosun of the battleship *Aristarchus* said. "I know Woetjans. You won't have no trouble."

"And what can I do to thank *you*, Lieutenant?" the girl said.

"For a start, you can call me—" Daniel began.

But that wasn't where the girl wanted to start, apparently, because her lips closed his before he finished the sentence.

CHAPTER 4

Xenos on Cinnabar

The line of officers signing in at the bar of the General Waiting Room was shorter than usual, even for the present wartime situation that placed a relatively high value on unassigned personnel. The riots had left Daniel in rather better shape than he'd have been otherwise, though. Instead of spending the night bar-hopping along the Strip as he'd intended, he'd wound up drinking very little after leaving his house.

Daniel still hadn't slept much, but he was used to that. Though as for his uniform, well, it was a good thing he wasn't going to be called to an interview in the personnel department. He hadn't been home to change, and the brawl hadn't helped what'd been marginal before the evening started.

The overage, overweight captain ahead of Daniel rose from the sign-in sheet with a wheeze. He took a numbered ivory chit from the supercilious civilian at the gate into the open bullpen beyond where the clerks sat. Daniel guessed the captain hadn't seen active service in a decade and must know he never would again. The General Waiting Room merely got him out of his house and into the society of other officers in the only fashion available to him.

And maybe that wasn't such a minor thing after all.

Daniel took the stylus and began to sign in. The attendant reading the sheet upside down suddenly stiffened and frowned. "Lieutenant Daniel Leary?" he said.

Daniel straightened with a flash of anger that he hoped didn't show on his face. Hogg had reattached the sleeves and mended the rip in the tunic, but a replacement saucer hat would have to wait for his return from Chatsworth Minor. Yes, Daniel was technically out of uniform, but it was no business of a *civilian* to tell him so.

"I am," Daniel said, his nostrils flaring.

"Don't bother taking a chit," the attendant said, reaching forward to lift the bar. "Go to desk four immediately."

"What?" Daniel said. "Why on earth?"

"Lieutenant," the attendant said with a touch of irritation, "I have absolutely no idea. The memo was waiting for me when I arrived this morning."

He glowered and added, "It's *very* unusual!"

"I see," said Daniel, stepping into the clerical enclosure.

He felt edgy. To a bureaucrat in the Navy Office, an unusual event meant his routine had been disrupted. That was a terrible thing—to a bureaucrat. To a spacer, however, "unusual" was likely to mean something lethally dangerous.

Clerk Four—a small plate on the desk's front corner with a stencilled number was the only identification—

was a thin, middle-aged woman who looked up with a disapproving expression from the data she was entering when Daniel reached her desk. He guessed disapproval was how she viewed most things; it didn't make him special.

"I'm Lieutenant Daniel Leary," he said. Without really meaning to—because she was a civilian too—he braced himself to Parade Rest, his feet regulation distance apart and his hands crossed behind his back. "I was told you have orders for me?"

The clerk sniffed. "Directions, rather," she said. "You're to go at once to the Bellerophon Club and ask for the gentleman in Room 247. One of the guards in the passage—"

She nodded minusculely toward the doorway at the back of the clerical enclosure. It led to the offices of the RCN's top bureaucrats.

"—will take you through the building to the back entrance of the Bellerophon and see to it that you're admitted."

She went back to her data entry.

"Ah," Daniel said brightly, hoping with the optimism of youth that if he paused for a moment the words would suddenly mean something.

They didn't.

The Bellerophon Club stood behind the Navy Office but faced the square on the other side. The chief figures of government, elected and appointed, were members but the club remained resolutely above party politics. Common report—which Daniel knew through his father was true in this case—said the Bellerophon gave enemies a place to bargain without the rhetoric and emotion of the Senate floor.

It wasn't anywhere a mere lieutenant was ever likely to enter. And if he were invited there, then he needed clothing more formal than Grays that looked like he'd worn them while performing maintenance in the *Sissie's* power room.

"Ah?" Daniel repeated, this time with a rising inflexion. "I'll just go back to my quarters and put on my Whites, eh?"

The clerk looked up again. This time her expression was positively frigid.

"I'm sure I wouldn't presume to tell a gentleman how to behave," she said with cutting dishonesty. "But my understanding has always been that an RCN officer's duty is to execute his orders, not to waste time in his quarters when he's been given clear direction."

"Ah," said Daniel. *That* he understood. Not why, but what; and "why" wasn't a proper question for a junior officer anyway. "Thank you, mistress. I'll see the guard in the passage immediately."

Daniel walked to the door in the back wall with his back straight, wishing very strongly that he'd worn a better uniform when he went out the night before. He felt that everybody on the benches was watching him.

They probably weren't. The only feeling *he'd* had about what happened in the General Waiting Room was occasional momentary envy that somebody else'd been called for an assignment interview and Daniel Leary hadn't.

The two guards in the hallway on the other side of the clerical enclosure were alert but unconcerned. They were RCN personnel wearing Shore Police armbands, not soldiers from the Land Forces of the Republic.

Daniel opened his mouth to say, "I was told that—" Before the words reached his tongue, he rephrased them to, "Clerk Four said one of you men would guide me to the back entrance of the Bellerophon Club. I'm Lieutenant Daniel Leary."

Passive voice was a sign of weakness and fear. Daniel felt weak, and he was afraid; but he'd be *damned* before he'd advertise the fact.

The younger guard squeezed a small data cube. An air-projected hologram—merely a blur of light from Daniel's perspective—formed above it briefly. "Yes sir," the guard said, sticking the cube away in its belt pouch. "If you'll come with me, please."

He opened a door in the opposite wall and preceded Daniel down a flight of stone steps cushioned with red plush. The stairs and the corridor beyond were dry and well-lighted, though they didn't appear to get much traffic. Daniel had passed through the door from the General Waiting Room a number of times in his RCN career but he'd never guessed the existence of this part of the building.

The guard with Daniel following made a short dog-leg to the right, then another to the left. Two more guards waited at an armored door. They brightened at the sight of company. "Hey, Binnings," one asked Daniel's guide. "This the package for the club?"

"Right," said the guide. "One of you want to take him over? Melies is supposed to be waiting for him."

"It ain't Melies at this hour," said the guard who hadn't spoken. "It's Roberto. And you bet I'll take him. It'll be the first sunshine I've seen in four hours."

Not unless the overcast unexpectedly burned away in the past few minutes, Daniel thought, but he didn't speak. He was being treated like an object—a package—not only by these flunkies but also the unguessed powers above them. He'd keep his mouth shut like a good package until he knew enough to comment intelligently.

Daniel grinned as the guards unlocked the heavy door. He wished he'd worn a better uniform when he went out last night, yes; but he didn't in the slightest regret not leaving the Grimes townhouse early enough to change clothes at home. The present mysterious business might work out very badly for him; and if so, the last hour and a half with Marta Grimes would be something to savor in bleak times.

With the guard, obviously disconcerted by Daniel's grin, leading, they stepped out into an alley. Though narrow, it was cleaner than many hotel corridors. Daniel glanced left and right as they crossed. As he by now expected, there were Shore Police at either end.

The door in the otherwise blank wall of the building opposite opened the instant the guard tapped on it. "Got your package, Roberto," he said to an elderly servant in livery of vertical black and white stripes.

"Ah," Daniel said. "I'm to see the man in Room two-four-seven."

"Of course, Lieutenant," the servant said, bowing slightly. "But he's asked that you join him instead in the roof garden. It's been reserved for your use this morning."

Daniel nodded. He didn't speak because his mouth was dry and anyway, he didn't know what he might've said. What in the name of *goodness* was going on?

They went up a circular staircase not unlike the companionways of a warship. You could armor a shaft against flying fragments and even decompression, but it was next to impossible to prevent the stresses of combat from twisting a tube enough to bind an elevator cage. Stairs were a better option.

Daniel had no difficulty following the servant up the four flights, but he was surprised at just how agile the old man appeared to be. Occasionally there were sounds through the doors they passed at each floor, but these were merely unidentifiable murmurs.

The servant opened one of three doors at the top of the stairs. Bowing he said, "You'll find refreshments already laid beyond, sir, so you won't be interrupted. I will wait here to escort you back when you're ready."

By a gentleman's reflex Daniel shook hands with the servant, slipping him the florin he'd palmed as he climbed. The old fellow smiled, the first human expression he'd displayed, and bowed as Daniel stepped past him. Another good memory to have if hard times followed. . . .

The roof garden was several hundred square feet in extent. Daniel had expected a view over the city—but that, he immediately realized, would've meant others might've observed those holding discussions in the garden. The walls were high, and the trees around the margin were evergreen spray-leaves from the planet of Peltin Major, a screen in any weather.

Natural history was one of Daniel's wide range of leisure delights. He wondered if the landscaper had placed pools for the climbing fish which pollinated the spray-leaves in their distant home . . . and smiled at the comforting pointlessness of the thought.

A heavy-set man in Whites sat reading from a

stack of hardcopy printouts at a table in one of the garden's trefoil groves. He turned and looked up: he was Admiral Anston.

"Sit down, Leary," said the most powerful man in the RCN, a highly successful admiral who'd retired rich to become possibly the best President of the Navy Board of all time. He waved to the serving table laid with a truly remarkable range of bottles, some of them new to Daniel. "Have a drink if you need one."

Without waiting for Daniel to respond, Anston lurched to his feet and lifted a tawny bottle. "Damned if I don't need one myself." He poured three inches, then pointed to the glass. "Rye good enough for you? There's likely mixers somewhere."

"Straight's fine with me," Daniel said, taking the glass and waiting while the admiral poured a similar slug for himself. Straight *was* fine under the circumstances; battery acid would've been fine if that's what Admiral Anston was offering. But normally, at least this early in the morning, Daniel would've added water.

Anston raised his glass, muttered, "Cheers," in the tone of a man responding to a funeral eulogy, and took a healthy gulp. "Sit down, boy. Dammit, sit down!"

Daniel obeyed, taking a careful drink lest he be snarled at for not doing *that* too. Anston was angry, and while Daniel couldn't imagine that the admiral was angry at him, he was the closest available target.

Anston sat down also, glowering at the papers before him. "This is ninety percent bullshit, you know, Leary?" he said, thumping the stack. "Ninety-nine percent! Most of what I do all day is bullshit."

"Sir," Daniel said, nodding. He didn't know what he was supposed to say or do. This was much worse than being reamed out for the condition of his uniform; *that* he could've understood.

"And this next part is bullshit also, but I'm going to do it regardless," Anston said, his voice suddenly firm. "The Republic owes you a good deal, boy. You know that and I know that. Every bloody soul in the RCN knows that."

"Sir," Daniel repeated. He was holding a full glass of whiskey and he had no desire whatever to take a drink. Bloody hell!

"But we don't always get what we're owed," Anston said. "You know that too?"

"Yes sir," said Daniel, his voice calm and his mind suddenly calmer as well. "I know that very well." He paused, considering, then finished his thought aloud: "And often enough, sir, we get more than we really deserve. I have, at any rate."

"Huh!" Anston said, smiling and tossing off half the remainder of his whiskey. "Well, you won't say that this time, I'm bound."

He eyed Daniel across the table's patterned marble surface. "You're a good officer, Leary," he said. "A good officer and a lucky one, which can be even better. Your uncle taught me things about astrogation that the Academy never dreamed of, and he taught you more—your record shows that."

Anston emptied his glass. Because there was a pause and a harmless response available, Daniel said, "Thank you, sir. Uncle Stacey was a good man and a great astrogator. Uniquely skilled."

The admiral still glowered, but he seemed to have relaxed somewhat. He set his glass down and didn't seem interested in refilling it.

"'Needs of the service' generally means some clerk isn't willing to do his job properly," Anston said. "That or somebody above you has the knife in for whatever reason. It shouldn't be that way, but it is. Only sometimes it means what it says: the needs of the service come before what any individual is owed."

"Yes sir," Daniel said. He cleared his throat and added, "Sir, I'm a Leary of Bantry and an officer of the RCN. I know that the RCN doesn't exist for my personal benefit."

"Aye," said Anston, "nor for mine either. But I've made a good thing out of it, I'll tell the world! And you will too, boy—if you keep the course you've charted this morning: doing your duty and keeping your head down."

He rose to his feet again, grinning. "And if you survive."

"Yessir," Daniel said, rising also. He drank, a mouthful and another mouthful and a third, emptying the glass. The interview was obviously over. It'd have been discourteous to leave a full glass on the table; and besides, it was very good whisky. "Rye" could mean a lot of things, particularly in a spaceport bar; but this was probably older than Daniel himself was.

"Pardon all this rigmarole, Leary," the admiral said with a scowl. "I'm not one to complain about politics—where would the RCN be without politics, I ask you? Sucking hind tit behind the generals and every other damned bureaucrat in Xenos, that's where! But sometimes there's hard choices. I wanted you to hear this from me personally."

He tapped the papers on the table and went on, "I'll tell you truthfully, it'll be my job if the wrong parties learn I've been talking out of school. Even me, boy."

"I appreciate your trust, sir," Daniel said as he set down the glass. He threw Anston a sharper salute than he—or any of his drill and ceremony instructors at the Academy—would've thought he had in him, then turned and walked back to the door at a measured pace.

Admiral Anston had just informed him that Lieutenant Leary wasn't going to be promoted as he perhaps deserved for his exploits in the *Princess Cecile*. Indeed, Daniel knew the betting gave him an outside chance of being jumped to full commander instead of lieutenant commander, the next step.

But he was smiling nonetheless. That meant he'd remain in command of the *Sissie*; and he was young enough that command of his handy, lucky corvette was still worth more than the increased pay and rank of a promotion that took him away from her.

"The *Princess Cecile*, the corvette you've been assigned to in the past . . ." said Mistress Sand, sitting across from Adele in the back room of O'Brian's Books and Manuscripts. She didn't look at the pre-Hiatus manuscript on the table between them; unlike Adele, Sand was neither a collector nor a compulsive cataloguer. "Is to be taken out of service as beyond economical repair. Your friend Leary will be assigned to a larger vessel to serve under the command of a senior officer."

Adele took the personal data unit out of her pocket and switched it on, silently considering what she'd just heard. Sand hadn't raised her voice or given the words any rhetorical flourishes, but the fact the spymaster'd opened the meeting with that bald statement proved she'd known exactly what she was saying.

The data unit's holographic display was its usual welcome pearliness, waiting for Adele to tell it where to start. She had no idea where to start; no idea at all. She shrank the starting display and met Sand's eyes directly.

"Why in the name of heaven are they doing that?" Adele said as calmly as if she were facing her opponent on a dueling ground . . . as she had done, and had killed him there. The first of uncountably many times she had killed. . . .

Sand must've understood where her words would send her agent's mind; it was Sand's job to understand, and she did her job very well. She didn't flinch.

She continued, "The court-martial upheld Commander Slidell's actions because the sitting officers—and those above them—felt that any other decision would seriously corrupt discipline in the middle of a war."

She shrugged and took out a polished black snuffbox different from the one she'd carried but hadn't used the night before. She must've noticed Adele's flicker of interest, because a wry grin flickered across Sand's stern face.

"Cannel coal," she explained, placing a pinch of snuff in the hollow between the back of her left hand and thumb. "And as for the court-martial's decision, perhaps it was correct. I don't choose to second-guess naval officers in their own bailiwick. The plan, as I understand it, was to send Commander Slidell on a deployment that would keep him away from Cinnabar for long enough that public feeling would die down."

Sand shrugged. "After last night," she said, "they've decided that simply hiding Slidell from sight isn't going to be enough to end the immediate problem. Eight square blocks were burned out, and there's reason to expect matters to get worse tonight."

"Are they planning to bring in the army?" Adele asked. Her tone was much the same as she'd have used if Sand were briefing her about the situation on a distant world. Dispassionate information-gathering followed by dispassionate analysis was the best choice for a person like Adele Mundy.

Not the only choice, though. A pair of sergeants in the Land Forces of the Republic had used their knives to cut off Agatha's head. If she ever met those men . . .

"No, not unless it's absolutely necessary," Sand said. "There's concern at the highest levels of government that this might lead to open warfare between soldiers and spacers from the warships in Harbor Three. They're believed to sympathize with the rioters, you see."

"Ah," said Adele as she brought up the display of her data unit again. "Yes, I do see."

Sand stopped her left nostril and snorted the snuff into her right. Her face screwed up as she fished a handkerchief from her breast pocket, then sneezed violently into it.

As she waited for the spymaster to continue, Adele viewed RCN personnel assignments. Slidell was listed as PENDING, scarcely a surprise. The next stage was to call up open slots for a commander in the RCN, then refining the sort further for off-Cinnabar deployments. . . .

"Your friend Leary's a hero," Sand resumed. "To the citizens of Cinnabar, and particularly to the enlisted ranks of the Navy."

"A captain who goes where it's hottest," Adele said with a mocking lilt in her voice to keep from choking on emotion—on pride and on love. Her mind had already arrived at where the spymaster's words were heading. "A captain who brings his spacers back with money in their pockets and with honor from every soul they meet, just for having served under Mister Leary."

"Yes," Sand said. She wasn't pleading—Adele didn't imagine that Sand would plead under any circumstances—but for all the spymaster's neutral words and flat delivery, she was asking for Adele's help. "If the Navy can show that Daniel Leary is willing to serve under Commander Slidell, then perhaps Slidell isn't such a villain after all. Then we don't have civil war between the army and navy, or alternatively have to stand by while Xenos burns down around our ears."

"The ship is to be the *Hermes*, an anti-pirate tender classed as a light cruiser?" Adele said, her eyes on her display. She held a wand not unlike a single chopstick in either hand. Their angles, both absolute and relative to one another, provided instantaneous control of the data unit without the space requirements of a keyboard, even a virtual one.

Mistress Sand said nothing for a moment. Her face remained expressionless, but now it had the stiffness of granite rather than flesh. "Yes, mistress," she said, "the *Hermes*."

Sand cleared her throat and continued, "Mistress, I wouldn't normally pry into your sources of information, but I had reason to believe that only two people in the human universe had that information until now. If my communications with Admiral Anston aren't secure, then I really *must* know that."

Adele didn't know what an anti-pirate tender was, so she cascaded into another data field. The *Hermes* was dumbbell-shaped, which didn't make sense till she brought up the image of a ship of the class in service. Smaller vessels, cutters, were docked against the central bar in two groups of three, slightly offset from one another.

Aloud Adele said, "I was simply searching data, mistress. You gave me the parameters when you told me the commanding officer's rank and stated that the purpose was to get him a distance from Cinnabar immediately. When I found that the prospective officers of a new-built ship meeting those parameters had been removed unexpectedly a few hours ago, I formed a hypothesis—"

Another person might have said, "took a guess." *That* person would never have gathered the necessary background information.

"—which I tested by asking you a direct question. It's what you pay me to do."

"I see," said Sand. For the first time in Adele's association with her, the spymaster looked distinctly uncomfortable.

Adele set her wands down. "I'm not sure you do, mistress," she said. "I'm extremely angry at what's happening to a friend of mine, probably the only friend I've ever had or ever will have. I embarrassed you deliberately because though it's not your fault, you're party to what's happening."

She grimaced. "And for that I apologize," she added. "If you want my resignation, you have it. Of course."

Mistress Sand's cheeks bulged and her sides began to

shake. She didn't speak. Adele watched in cold horror, wondering if their exchange had provoked a fit.

"For God's sake, Mundy!" Sand blurted at last. She staggered to her feet. "For *God's* sake!"

She's laughing. Adele's face became very still. She stood up also.

"Please, please, I wasn't laughing *at* you," Sand said, sobering instantly. "I was laughing at myself."

She got her breath, then continued, "Mundy, I've said a number of times that I'd league with demons if they'd aid the Republic against Guarantor Porra and the beasts who work for him. I just realized that I've apparently done that, leagued with a demon. But you're the Republic's demon, and I'm *bloody* well not going to let you go now that I've found you!"

That's flattering, in a way, Adele thought. A smile touched her lips. *Not least because it's more or less the way I view myself.*

The smile grew broader. *And how, I wonder, do Alliance spacers view Lieutenant Daniel Leary?*

Adele sat down again to make it easier to use her data unit. Whatever you learned brought up additional questions. To the extent there was a reason to continue living, that was the reason.

"What about a crew for the *Hermes*?" she asked, her eyes on the holographic display. "Will Daniel bring the Sissies with him?"

"Yes," Sand said, sitting down as well. Adele was barely aware of the movement. "The new crew combines spacers from the *Princess Cecile* with those from the *Bainbridge*."

"Saving the three whom Commander Slidell executed, one hopes," Adele said as her wands flickered.

Sand didn't respond, but a smile touched Adele's lips. It was the sort of joke that only Tovera was likely to think funny . . . but nonetheless it proved Adele Mundy wasn't the humorless machine she'd been called any number of times during her life.

And come to think, most RCN spacers would chuckle at the thought as well. Adele had been raised to judge "most people" by civilian standards. Spacers knew death too well to let it frighten them unduly.

"Mistress," Sand said, speaking very carefully again. "I don't ask you to spy on your friends, but I ask you for your opinion as an agent of the Republic: *will* Lieutenant Leary accept the new appointment, do you think? Because everything is predicated on that."

"Daniel will do his duty, yes," Adele said, keeping her tone perfectly flat. "Being his father's son, he'll understand the political imperatives behind the assignment."

She shrank her display to meet Sand's eyes again. "Now," she continued. "*I* have a request."

"Make it," Sand said. She didn't add, "Anything you ask will be granted," or the similar nonsense other people might've expected to hear. There were requests Sand wouldn't grant. They both knew that, and to suggest otherwise would mean one or the other party was a fool.

"Ganse, the First Lieutenant of the *Bainbridge*, is quite senior," Adele said. "Daniel won't ask this but I will: remove Ganse from the proposed crew for the *Hermes* and replace him with a lieutenant who's junior to Lieutenant Leary. The purposes of the Republic don't require that Daniel serve as *Second* Lieutenant under an officer of lesser distinction."

Sand smiled faintly. "I'll see what can be done," she said simply. She pursed her lips and slid the snuffbox along the edge of the table with her forefinger. Raising her eyes to Adele's she continued, "I operate on the assumption that you wish to accompany Lieutenant Leary wherever he may be assigned, Mundy. If that isn't correct, please inform me."

"It's quite correct," Adele said. "That's one of the few things that I don't expect to change."

In part that was true because she could no longer imagine living without the odd *dynamic* stability that Daniel Leary provided within the greater cocoon of the RCN. It was strange that you could live your life without something but then find it absolutely necessary from the moment of its arrival.

Sand nodded. "That's useful," she said, "because the *Hermes* will be posted to the Gold Dust Squadron based on Nikitin. There's information leaking from Nikitin. I'd very much like that leak to be plugged. I know that in the past you haven't been involved in *counter*intelligence work, but I don't believe there's anyone better suited to the task."

Adele shrugged; her wands moved with quick precision, as though each had a separate will. *Nikitin... Gold Dust Cluster, over three hundred stars many with inhabited planets; main export, naturally occurring anti-aging compounds... Piracy; volume, cost, suppression, Gold Dust Squadron...*

"It's all information," Adele said as she skimmed her data, mentally ear-marking sections for review at leisure. A quick side-trip brought her to Anti-Pirate Tenders, Under Construction, *Hermes* ... She smiled to have doubled back to familiar territory. "It doesn't really matter whether I'm looking for information about Alliance forces or information passing to the Alliance about our forces. It's all the same."

"You're the expert," Sand said with a smile of satisfaction. "Do you have anything further, mistress?"

"Perhaps," said Adele, hoping to keep the tremble out of her voice. She was about to meddle in matters which by no stretch of the imagination were the business of a private citizen. She shut down her data unit. "You said the *Princess Cecile* is being taken out of service. What will happen to her?"

"I can ask," Sand said. "What do you think should happen to her, mistress?"

Adele cleared her throat. "Let me preface this by saying that I'm not a naval architect," she said. "I've listened to Daniel and others discuss the construction of the *Princess Cecile*, but I may have badly misconstrued the actual situation."

"I accept you're not an expert on naval construction," Mistress Sand said, still smiling. "I'll further postulate that you've assessed other unfamiliar specialties accurately enough to turn the course of battles in favor of the Republic."

"Yes," said Adele. She allowed herself a smile. "Cinnabar builders favor one-piece construction for starships, creating very stiff, sturdy vessels. Many officers believe this to be the only proper way of building a ship."

"Go on, mistress," Sand said. She held the snuffbox between the tips of her index fingers, shifting it slightly so that the polished black casing glinted in the indirect light of the viewing room.

"The *Sissie* is Kostroman built and therefore has a

modular hull," Adele said. She deliberately used the corvette's nickname to emphasize to the spymaster that Adele Mundy was a part of a unique world: the community of those who sailed between the stars in flimsy metal boxes and who fought other, similar communities. "Long voyages loosen the structure in a fashion that wouldn't occur with a unit hull, but they don't actually affect the ship's basic integrity. She just needs to be tightened up."

"If it were that simple," Sand said, speaking with the care of someone who doesn't intend that a disagreement become a fight, "wouldn't the docks at Harbor Three have done the work instead of recommending the corvette be discarded?"

"So far as RCN personnel are concerned," Adele said, "a modular ship is by definition uneconomic to repair. They don't have the specialist expertise to do the work properly, and in their hearts they don't believe it ought to be done anyway. A small private dockyard, however, might be able to put the *Sissie* back in shape very easily."

"Simply thinking out loud . . ." Sand said. "If the *Princess Cecile* were sold as scrap to a private dockyard like Bergen and Associates, she might become an asset to the Republic in the form of a privateer or fast transport."

"Yes," said Adele. Bergen and Associates was a partnership between Daniel Leary, a legacy from his uncle Stacey Bergen, and Corder Leary. "I think she might. And it'd be a better end than rust for a ship which has rendered valuable services to the Republic in the past."

Sand laughed, but there was more wistfulness than

humor in the sound. "Do you think ships have souls, Mundy?" she asked.

"I don't think human beings have souls, Mistress Sand," Adele said harshly. "But if a ship *could* have a soul, the *Sissie* would."

"I take your point," Sand said. She slipped away her snuffbox and braced her hands on the table, preparatory to rising. "I appreciate your diligence toward the long-term best interests of the Republic, Mundy."

Adele also stood and put her personal data unit back in its pocket. Another person using the same words would've meant them ironically. Bernis Sand, though, could follow a chain of events through more layers of cause and effect than anyone else Adele had met.

"I'll drop a word in the right ear," Sand said. She gestured Adele to the door; they would leave the building by different exits and some minutes apart. "It seems to me that the Republic owes a proper reward to a ship which has always given more than duty required."

CHAPTER 5

Xenos on Cinnabar

The ground floor of Chatsworth Minor was given over to servants' quarters and the service infrastructure of the house. Adele lived on the third story, but with the door open she could hear Daniel coming up the broad staircase to get to his quarters on the floor below.

Adele stepped to the door of her study, casting her shadow in the fan of light across the gorgeously textured beewood boards of the landing. She felt her heart-rate rising. Though she was sure her face remained calm, her stomach was threatening to revolt in an embarrassing fashion.

"*Good* evening, Adele!" Daniel caroled as he looked up. He waved a bottle as long and slender as an Indian club of blue glass at her. "Good morning, in fact, and I do hope you've been celebrating too?"

Daniel was walking under his own power, though Hogg had backed up the stairs ahead of him and a pair of footmen were following to catch him if he tumbled backward. She'd never seen Daniel drunk when he was on shipboard or otherwise on duty, but neither was Adele sure she'd ever seen him cold sober when he thought the circumstances permitted a drink.

"I'm afraid I haven't been," Adele said austerely. "Daniel, please come up and listen to me for a moment."

There wasn't a good way to do this, so she'd do it in the fashion that best suited her and suited Daniel's temperament as well: by spitting out the bare facts without delay or adornment. To the degree that it's ever suitable to give or get crushingly bad news.

"Yes, of course," Daniel said quietly. He handed the bottle to his servant, saying, "Hogg, hold this for me, if you will."

Then, back straight and face composed, Daniel walked up the stairs and into the study at a measured thirty-inch pace. His left hand swung the door closed with a muffled thump.

In preparation for the discussion, Adele had cleared away the books and papers which normally covered the chair across from hers and the table of polished fluorspar. Without the pointless formality of waiting for an invitation, Daniel seated himself. "Proceed," he said.

"You're to be reassigned as First Lieutenant of the tender *Hermes*, under Commander Slidell," Adele said. "This is an attempt to damp down the protests, the riots, over Slidell's acquittal."

"Well I'll be damned," Daniel said. His face was completely blank. Adele had seen the same expression on a man eviscerated by a cable that'd snapped under tension. Then he repeated, "I'll be *damned*."

"Would you like a drink?" Adele said quietly.

Ordinarily she didn't keep liquor in the study—she had no use for it here—but she'd laid in a stock for this discussion. If Daniel took a notion for something beyond the half dozen choices immediately at hand, Tovera was waiting in the butler's pantry to bring up anything he suggested.

"What?" said Daniel, looking startled. He smiled wanly. "Ah. No thank you, Adele," he said. "I've had more than enough already tonight, I'd say."

He tensed to stand, then relaxed and smiled again. "The bottle I came home with," he said. "You saw it? Tears of Love, it's called. They make it on Lyrex."

He shook his head, smiling more broadly at the memory. "Make it from what, I wouldn't guess," he went on. "Public urinals, perhaps. But the bottle's quite lovely, don't you think?"

"Yes, I thought so too," said Adele, restraining the urge to bring out her data unit. She could learn in a heartbeat what the base of Tears of Love might be—and far more important, she'd escape from this room and this conversation.

The conversation was necessary. She kept her hands on the table.

Daniel pressed his fingertips together. Adele thought he might be restraining himself from rising to punch the door behind him.

"I see the logic of the plan," he said, forcing a smile. "I wouldn't have thought of it myself, but it's quite clever."

Even the false smile vanished. "*I* wouldn't have thought of it," Daniel repeated, "but my father very well might have. I wonder if he did?"

"The crews of the *Sissie* and Slidell's previous

command, the *Bainbridge*, are being combined," Adele said; adding useful information instead of simply changing the subject. Though she was changing the subject also.

"That's not a bad plan either, to tell the truth," Daniel said in a tone of professional appraisal. "Normally a sloop would be under a junior lieutenant, but the *Bainbridge* was a training vessel; thus a commander in charge. Mixing the trainees with a crack crew like my Sissies on a larger ship is an ideal way to polish them."

He chuckled. "To knock the edges off, at any rate, and maybe a head or two with them," he added. "Well, better lose a few in training than all of them in battle, you know."

Daniel's face hardened again. "I recall hearing Lieutenant Ganse was Slidell's First Lieutenant," he said. "I know Ganse's senior to me. He's quite senior, in fact."

"I understand that you will be the senior lieutenant in the *Hermes*' crew," Adele said with an austere lack of affect. "I can't swear to that, of course."

Daniel smiled faintly. "No," he said, "and you can't swear that the sun will rise tomorrow morning. Your understanding is good enough for me, though."

His smile suddenly became broad and warm. "Thank you, Adele," he said. "I understand now what Admiral Anston was trying to tell me this morning. He didn't dare use the real words, so I filled in the gaps with my own fantasies. I'm glad to have heard this from a friend instead of learning it at the Navy Office tomorrow."

He chuckled. "This morning, that is."

Daniel rose to his feet and turned. Adele brought out her data unit. As her friend's hand touched the door knob she said, "Daniel?"

He looked back over his shoulder. "Eh?" he said.

"Tears of Love is distilled from the pulp of the Terran sago palm, as grown in the soil of Lyrex," she said.

Daniel looked blank for a moment, then doubled over with laughter. When he had the outburst more or less under control he straightened and said, "Is it indeed? Well, Adele, I know where we could find an almost-full bottle. I propose that we finish it together and then get some sleep before sunrise. What do you think of that?"

"I think it's an excellent idea," Adele said, smiling coldly at him. "Since my data unit doesn't contain information about distilled latrine wastes, I'll apparently have to conduct a personal investigation."

Bellowing again with laughter, Daniel opened the door to retrieve the liquor from Hogg, who waited outside.

As Daniel sat in the General Waiting Room, he wondered how many hopeful officers had polished the bench with the seat of their trousers in the decades before him. Pennyroyal was to his right, with Ames, Vondrian, and Herondas—like Pennyroyal, a former Academy classmate—ranged further inward along the hard wood.

More than decades, in fact. The bench was made of steelgray which grew only on the east coast, not far from Bantry. It must've been a century since there were steelgrays large enough to provide single planks so wide.

The data printer beside the gatekeeper beeped and purred out a tape. She—a female clerk had the duty this morning—tore it off, frowned as she read it, and called in a cracked voice, "Two-nine-one!"

The eyes of every uniformed soul on the other side of the bar jerked down to the ivroid chit in his or her hands, even though all of them had instantly memorized the number they'd drawn this morning. Daniel smiled faintly. His was ninety-nine . . . though occasionally he held it upside down with his thumb across the bar beneath the numbers, pretending it was sixty-six. He had a vague feeling that six was his lucky number.

He already knew his luck had run out when Adele spoke to him last night. Still, he could kid himself.

A very stiff, military-looking captain wearing Whites walked down the aisle, holding her chit between thumb and forefinger. Her left foot dragged slightly, though whether that was the result of injury or simply circulation cut off by the wait on the hard bench was a matter for conjecture.

The other suppliants relaxed with a collective sigh.

Daniel wore a new set of Grays; his second-best saucer hat was on his lap. He'd embarrassed himself the day before with his sloppiness.

Spit and polish weren't the hallmarks of a fighting navy, but Daniel's previous disarray had been of a sort to bring the RCN into disrepute. Officially he'd escaped censure, but spacers were too close to the unfathomably powerful not to be superstitious. In Daniel's secret heart was a needle of fear that his slovenly appearance had something to do with the disaster overtaking him.

Because the appointment Adele had warned him to expect was a disaster beyond any question. Bloody *Hell*, to serve under an officer who was a butcher or a paranoid madman! Or both, of course.

"Four-four!" called the gatekeeper. "Forty-four."

A newly minted lieutenant, also in Whites and with full braid and epaulettes, leaped to his feet and trotted toward the clerical enclosure. He looked no more than fifteen years old, though he was probably the regulation minimum of eighteen. Regardless, he was somebody's nephew, headed for a plum appointment on the staff of a high officer.

Interest was a fact of life in the RCN, and it *should* be a fact so far as Daniel was concerned. He wasn't one to change a system that worked very well, thank you—as the series of RCN victories from time immemorial proved. Nonetheless Daniel sometimes wondered how his career would've been different if he weren't estranged from his politically powerful father.

He smiled broadly at his foolishness. If he hadn't had the fight with his father, he wouldn't be in the RCN at all. . . .

Ceiling ducts sighed as they blew air into the large hall through louvered vents. Daniel cocked his eyes upward, trying to isolate the additional sound he'd noticed.

Pennyroyal saw his interest. In a concerned whisper she asked, "What is it? Do you hear that squeal-*click* up there? Do you think one of the bloody fans is going to fall on us?"

"I hear it, yes," Daniel whispered back with a grin, proud that he could identify the sound. "But it's not the fan, Penny: it's a solitaire from Playa Grande.

They're mammaloids but tiny, small enough to fit on your thumbnail."

Pennyroyal stared at him, obviously wondering if he was joking. "What's it doing in the air system, then?" she demanded.

"Judging from the call, at the moment it's looking for a girlfriend," Daniel said. "Twice a Playa Grande year, that's about nine standard months, they're *not* solitary. Apart from that, they eat mostly spiders."

Which also weren't native to Cinnabar. Or Playa Grande, for that matter. If he were ever forced into retirement, he'd write a monograph on the fauna of the Navy Office, he swore he would!

"Ninety-nine!" rasped the gatekeeper.

For an instant, Daniel's mind went blank; then he jumped to his feet as though he'd been goosed with hot iron. He strode down the aisle, followed by Pennyroyal's whisper, "You lucky bastard, Leary!"

She won't say that when she hears what the assignment is, Daniel thought. Then he remembered the berth Pennyroyal expected, junior lieutenant on a battleship. That was a job with nothing to recommend it beyond the fact it was a job, providing full pay and perhaps some day a transfer to something better. Whereas the Gold Dust Squadron didn't offer much in the way of glory, but there was a very good chance of making a fortune by recapturing freighters from the pirates. Many an officer would trade his hopes of promotion for the benefit a posting to Nikitin brought to his bank account.

That was the trade Daniel *had* made. More accurately, the trade those in charge had made for him. So be it.

Daniel handed his chit to the gatekeeper without speaking; his mind was a thousand light-years away. The clerk said something, but Daniel heard the words only as a mumble. He glanced down at her.

"Don't look at me that way!" the gatekeeper said in a rising tone. She fumbled to lift the latch on the bar, letting it slip back with a clack the first time. "Desk One, the Chief Clerk. I don't have anything to do with it."

Daniel nodded and walked into the enclosure. He'd entered the enclosure before—a half dozen times all told, he supposed—but though the experience wasn't entirely unfamiliar, he still felt as though he were playing a part in a religious ceremony.

The chief clerk, a man of indeterminate age, sat at a desk on a dais knee-high above the remainder of the enclosure. Daniel didn't ever recall seeing a suppliant officer directed to him.

Beside the clerk's desk stood a thin, completely sexless figure in black with white appointments. He—she, it—looked familiar, but it nonetheless took Daniel a long moment to recognize the person as Klemsch, the Secretary to the Navy Board.

In theory Klemsch had a menial position. In practice, as the person who granted and more often refused access to the Board, he—Daniel *thought* Klemsch was male—had more real power than most Senators.

There were no steps up from this side of the dais, a symbol if not a barrier. Nor did the desk have a name plate like those of junior clerks. Daniel lifted his foot as he'd have done to mount a companionway two steps at a time. He restrained his instinct to salute, since even the chief clerk was a civilian, and said, "I'm Lieutenant Daniel Leary. I was directed here."

"That is correct, Mister Leary," the clerk said, handing Daniel a sheet of thick paper. There was a ribbon to tie it shut after it'd been rolled. "I must request that you review the document now and state whether you accept or reject it."

Daniel stiffened with the document in his hand. *Did they think he'd refuse a lawful order?* Aloud he said, "As you wish."

The orders were simple and in standard form, save that the details had been filled in by hand instead of being printed complete from a computer the way those of a junior lieutenant normally would be:

LIEUTENANT DANIEL OLIVER LEARY, UNASSIGNED

Lieutenant: So soon as you are able you will proceed to the RCS Hermes, *to which you are assigned, and take up the post of First Lieutenant. You will carry out the duties of this position as set forth in RCN regulations and such further duties as may be properly delegated to you by the officer commanding.*

Very respectfully

T. *Klemsch*
Secretary, at the direction
of the Navy Board

Daniel smiled ruefully. Right up to this moment a part of him had hoped that Adele's warning wouldn't actually come true. He'd never have let the hope reach even the surface of his conscious mind, but it'd been there . . . and its failure gnawed at the sinews holding his body erect.

"Very well, then," Daniel said, rolling the document so that he didn't have to carry it open in his hand. He'd give it to Hogg, waiting for him on the steps of the Navy Office which he as an officer's servant wasn't permitted to enter. "May I ask if the warrant officers assigned to the *Hermes* have received their orders yet?"

The clerk touched a keyboard built into the surface of his desk. It was otherwise blank save for a rack of pigeonholes at one end, each filled with a rolled document.

The rainbow blur of a holographic display bloomed before him, then vanished. "I believe they have, yes," he said in a tone of no more emotion than sand whispering through an hourglass.

Daniel nodded. "Then I'll proceed to Harbor Three as directed," he said.

"One moment, Mister Leary," the clerk said. He handed a tight scroll tied with blue ribbon. "You're to deliver this to Captain Slidell when you report to the *Hermes*."

"*Deliver?*" Daniel repeated in amazement. "What do you mean 'deliver'?"

He took the document by reflex but almost dropped it. On the outside of the scroll somebody'd written To: *Officer Commanding RCS Hermes* in a flowing copperplate hand. Then, below it: *To be read aloud immediately upon receipt.*

"I mean deliver, Lieutenant," the clerk said waspishly. "I know of only one definition for the word. And if you're wondering what the document is or why it's being transferred in this unusual—indeed, unique in my experience—fashion, then I have to say that I cannot even guess at an answer."

He glared like a basilisk at Klemsch. That worthy dipped his head in a minuscule nod. He said nothing and his expression, a thin smile, hadn't changed since Daniel first noticed him standing beside the chief clerk's desk.

"Very well," said Daniel. "Good day, gentlemen."

He turned on his heel and marched out of the enclosure. Pennyroyal and the other lieutenants who'd been sharing the bench with Daniel tried to catch his eye, but he continued down the aisle toward the exit from the building.

The *Hermes* was scheduled to lift in three days or as much longer as required to get a full crew aboard. Daniel wasn't looking forward to serving under Commander Slidell—

But he'd tell the *world* he'd be glad to get off Cinnabar and escape this cycle of events he neither understood nor wanted to understand!

CHAPTER 6

Harbor Three on Cinnabar

"When I looked at an image . . ." Adele said, saying the thing that was in her mind. She knew from long experience that this often disturbed those who heard her, but this was Daniel; and anyway, she was too old to change her ways now. "I thought the *Hermes* looked strange because it wasn't finished. It's finished now, though, isn't it? The outside, I mean."

Yard workmen in forklifts were hauling pallets of stores from the three-car monorail train halted on the siding beside the *Hermes*. All her hatches were open, and the sound of saws screaming on metal bubbled through them like particularly shrill bosun's whistles. Though the hull was complete, finish work on the vessel was continuing.

Adele judged the *Hermes* was about three hundred feet long. A third of the length was in the bullet-shaped bow section, followed by a small-dimension shaft some hundred and fifty feet long which connected the bow to the spherical stern element.

The tender floated on full-length outrigger pontoons in a construction slip. Her plasma thrusters were mounted on the sides of the bow and stern sections where they were clear of the water. The High Drive motors which combined matter and anti-matter were on the pontoons. The High Drive could only be used in vacuum, so it didn't matter that the motors were under water after the *Hermes* landed.

"Like a fish after it's been filleted," Hogg said somberly. "A real abortion, ain't it, young master?"

Harbor Three was an enormous artificial swamp laid out in groups of slips, each around a central lagoon from which starships could land and lift off in relative isolation. A vessel was running up its plasma thrusters in alternate pairs, burning in new nozzles. The thrusters echoed as they blasted ions into the water on which the ship floated. The roar could've come from almost anywhere in the reservation; the plume of steam charged with rainbow plasma lifted like a flag, however, not far from the tram platform where Adele with Daniel and their two servants viewed the *Hermes*.

"An anti-pirate tender's a very specialized tool, Hogg," Daniel said. Adele thought he sounded amused rather than upset, but she also realized that she and Hogg were being much more negative about the *Hermes* than would've been acceptable if Daniel were her commander. "Think of it as the equivalent of a gut-hook skinning knife, useful if not attractive. And of course with her cutters nested against the central spine, she'll look more like how one expects to see a ship."

Daniel grimaced, suggesting to Adele that perhaps

he agreed more with her and Hogg than he was willing to admit. "I see some officers on the slip," he said. "If Commander Slidell's among them, I'll present my orders."

He tapped the tied and wax-sealed scroll he'd retrieved from Hogg when they got off the tram at Slip 17Y. "And *this* bloody thing."

They started toward the slip, Daniel a half-step ahead of Adele. Both wore Grays, though the personnel on the slip were in utilities. Adele wondered how Daniel was sure they were officers, then noticed that he'd slipped his RCN goggles down over his eyes for a quick look.

The goggles had a range of viewing modes, including magnification as high as x128; with the internal stabilizer locked, that would be sufficient to read subdued collar insignia a hundred yards distant. It didn't surprise her to learn that Daniel had done so.

Hogg and Tovera followed obsequiously. Daniel as First Lieutenant rated a servant; a communications officer ordinarily would not, but Adele's orders gave her authority to appoint an unpaid civilian assistant for whom the RCN would provide rations.

When Daniel was commanding the *Princess Cecile*, the question of Tovera's position never arose. Under Commander Slidell it might very well—and Mistress Sand, as thorough in her way as Adele was in very different fashions, had taken care of the problem before it arose.

"The aft portion is almost entirely water tanks," Daniel explained, gesturing to the vessel as they approached. "Crew quarters are in the bow, and storage apart from the water—the reaction mass—is in the bow also. You could think of the bow as a ship by itself with the stern merely an appendage, if you liked."

"And the middle?" Adele asked, more from politeness than curiosity. If she'd simply wanted to know what the bar of the huge dumbbell held, she'd have brought out her personal data unit and squatted down on the pavement with it.

"The spine is just passages, airlocks, and the piping that feeds air and reaction mass to the cutters," Daniel said. "So long as the cutters're attached, they're completely supplied from the tender. That way when they separate, their tanks are topped off."

"She's got missiles though, right?" Hogg asked from behind them. "I mean, we're not going out on an unarmed ship, are we?"

"Well," said Daniel, "not unarmed, Hogg, but the tender's function is to support its cutters. They're the *Hermes'* real armament. And they don't carry missiles, no, because the pirate craft they're designed to fight aren't large enough to justify expending a missile. Instead they've got sheaves of chemically fueled rockets to destroy masts and rigging at short range. Much of their duty—our duty now—will be to retake merchantmen the pirates have captured. Often the original crew will be imprisoned on board."

"What if we run up against a real warship like we've done before in the *Sissie?*" said Hogg. "Then we saw 'em off because we had missiles . . . which this sway-backed pig don't. Do we get swallowed up whole?"

"Afraid to die, Hogg?" Tovera said. She sounded curious.

"I don't much fancy giving some Alliance bastards target practice without us shooting back, is all," Hogg muttered. Then he added in a tone of transparent dishonesty, "But I guess the RCN knows what it's doing."

An empty lowboy stood on the quay; the cab was tilted forward to expose the engine, but nobody was working on it at the moment. Adele made a slight gesture to catch Daniel's eye, then nodded toward the vehicle. He flashed a smile of agreement and strode toward the three officers conferring nearer the bow of the vessel. The youngest, a woman, was projecting holographic builder's drawings from a unit in one hand and touching them with the laser pointer in the other.

Adele set her data unit on the lowboy as an improvised desk. Hogg and Tovera halted with her, a polite distance from the commissioned officers. Adele noticed that Tovera wore an earphone and, though her eyes were ostensibly on the horizon, she kept one end of her attaché case pointed toward the officers. It seemed very probable that Tovera was eavesdropping on the conversation through a parabolic microphone—but that was Tovera's business.

For her own part, Adele viewed the plans of the tender. As First Lieutenant, Daniel's station would be in the Battle Direction Center—basically a duplicate bridge from which the ship could be sailed and fought in the event the captain and the remainder of the bridge crew became casualties.

The communications officer would normally be stationed on the bridge. Under the present circumstances, Adele believed the specialist equipment she brought as an agent of Mistress Sand would be better kept under Daniel's authority. She knew her espionage duties made

Daniel uncomfortable, but he could be trusted not to interfere or—what might actually be worse—show too much curiosity in what she was doing and how.

The question of where the *Hermes'* BDC *was* hadn't occurred to Adele until she actually saw the vessel. Having done so, a few twitches of her wands highlighted a chamber in the core of the spherical stern section. It was completely surrounded by tanks of reaction mass the way the pituitary gland is buried in brain tissue. That was probably as safe as any location on a starship could be, but seeing it gave Adele a feeling of disquiet.

"They're inspectors from the Bureau of Material, making a hand-over inspection of the vessel because it's newly built," Tovera said in an undertone. She flicked her eyes sidelong to indicate the three strangers with Daniel. "Slidell and Lieutenant Ganse aren't aboard, though they're expected momentarily."

Daniel was having an animated conversation, gesturing with the rolled document he carried. He had more technical competence and interest than most spacefaring officers because much of his upbringing had been in his uncle's shipyard—now his own shipyard.

"It seems hard on the master, to give up a pretty little thing like the *Sissie* and be put aboard a wallowing pig like this one—and not as captain, neither," Hogg said in an undertone. "Though I hear there's money to be made in the Gold Dust Cluster. Prize money, and good money besides on private cargoes—and not *just* the smuggled ones."

But smuggled cargoes too, Adele amended, since it was Hogg speaking. Well, nobody'd appointed Adele Mundy a Commissioner of Revenue.

"Lest you be concerned that the *Hermes* is clumsy compared to the *Princess Cecile*, Hogg . . ." Adele said, reading operational histories of anti-pirate vessels from her data unit as she waited for Daniel to take them aboard. "It appears that the cutters operate individually and are crewed by personnel from the tender. It appears to be quite normal for a tender's First Lieutenant to take charge of a cutter, and they're said to be quite handy little vessels."

"Handy little ships that fight at knife range," Tovera said. She giggled, a sound with as little humor as a crocodile's smile.

A tram clinked to a stop on the platform. Two officers in Dress Whites stepped off and started toward the *Hermes*.

"Guess that's Slidell," said Hogg. "Can't say I like the look of him any better'n I do the pig of a ship he captains."

Adele eyed the oncoming officers. The older man wearing the open circle insignia of a commander had an ascetic face, but it was now distorted by a scowl as he glared at Daniel Leary.

I tend to agree with Hogg, Adele thought. The way her mind had turned made her suddenly aware of the pistol in her jacket pocket.

The notion was completely inappropriate, but it was oddly comforting. Adele smiled, and she was aware that Hogg and Tovera were smiling also.

"There's Slidell and Ganse coming now," said Lieutenant Commander Avars, head of the yard's inspection team. "It's been a pleasure talking with you, Leary."

"And do keep an eye on the High Drive motors,

won't you?" Lieutenant Episcopo added as she stowed her projection unit back in its belt pouch. "I'm not saying anything against Apogee Engineering, but any time a start-up company underbids the established firms, well . . . there's testing and believe me we tested; but you're likely to be twenty days out from Cinnabar if anything goes wrong."

Daniel nodded to his new acquaintances as he turned and composed his mind for meeting Commander Slidell. They were all good fellows. Once they realized the new first officer wasn't a swashbuckler quick to damn all yard personnel as grafting incompetents, they'd pointed out the care they'd taken to make sure the inevitable trade-offs didn't seriously degrade the tender's safety and performance.

Which Daniel understood. A private yard, even a scrupulously honest one, had to compromise also if it was to stay in business. Bergen and Associates, now with Daniel as managing partner, expected increased profits as it entered its third decade.

"We need to go over the Power Room still," Avars said to his colleagues. They were making an in-house check before the final inspection in company with the *Hermes'* officers for formal hand-over. "Though I don't think anything remains there other than the missing louvers."

The three inspectors started toward the boarding bridge thirty feet down the quay, their boots scrunching. Daniel transferred the rolled documents—his orders and the mysterious scroll he was delivering to Slidell—to his left hand so that he could salute properly. Or at any rate, as properly as he ever managed.

"Leary?" Episcopo called to his back. "I know the

Hermes's not the sort of ship you're used to, but she's a solid craft if you give her a chance."

Daniel smiled. The comment had broken his concentration—which was exactly what he needed, because his mind had been focusing on the series of unpleasant reactions he might have to face when he met his new captain.

The situation was uncomfortable for Lieutenant Leary. It was bound to be hugely irritating to the far senior Commander Slidell, who was being rushed off-planet with a First Lieutenant whom he'd almost certainly see as a minder.

Slidell and Ganse took in the fact that Daniel wasn't from the dockyard staff as they must've thought at first. Ganse stumbled and muttered something to Slidell in a low voice; the commander snapped a curt reply without taking his eyes off Daniel.

Daniel stood at Parade Rest. His eyes were on a tram pylon just inside the distant perimeter of the port reservation; he could still follow the approaching officers with his peripheral vision. When they'd approached within eight feet—three formal paces, call it—Daniel thudded his heels together and saluted, bellowing, "Sir! Lieutenant Daniel Leary reporting as ordered!"

Slidell replied with an effortless, perfectly formed salute. When the commander's arm dropped, Daniel slid his right foot to Parade Rest. He held out the open document between his thumb and index finger, offering it to Slidell. "Sir!" he said. "My orders!"

He kept the remaining scroll in his left hand for the moment. One thing at a time.

Slidell took the orders and read them sourly. He

was a slender man of a little more than average height. He looked forty standard years old, but Adele said he was only thirty-seven; his high forehead and expression of cold disgust increased his apparent age.

"Look at this, Ganse!" he said, offering the thick parchment to his companion. "I couldn't believe they'd really make such a grotesque mistake, but here it is. First Lieutenant indeed!"

Slidell returned his attention to Daniel, looking even more disapproving than before. "I'm sorry to disappoint you, Leary," he said, a lie if Daniel had ever heard one, "but when I heard the rumor of your posting to the *Hermes*, I checked dates of commission. Mr. Ganse is of course your senior in grade, by almost three years, in fact. You'll become the Second Lieutenant—unless perhaps you'll refuse the appointment now that you see an error was made?"

"Sir," Daniel said truthfully, "I don't understand the situation. I trust the Navy Office will provide us with clarification shortly."

What Daniel suspected, based on his discussion with Adele, was that the hasty orders transferring Lieutenant Ganse off the *Hermes* hadn't caught up with him yet. The lieutenant was a good-looking fellow with curly red hair that suggested a heartiness which his reserved demeanor and his quietly-blameless record belied. He looked puzzled and concerned by the situation—but not hostile, unlike Commander Slidell.

"I really don't see what there is to clarify," Slidell said forcefully, rattling the orders forgotten in his hand. "Do you, Ganse? It's simply a mistake and that's already clear."

Daniel cleared his throat; this was probably as

good a time as there was going to be to deliver the remaining document, though it wasn't a good time at all. "Sir?" he said, holding out the scroll. "I was directed to deliver this to you when I presented my orders."

"What?" said Slidell, staring at the rolled parchment. He didn't extend a hand to take it. He looked like a man who's opened a door and met a snarling animal. "What in the name of the Great God is this, Leary?"

"Sir," Daniel said, "I don't know. Secretary Klemsch told me—"

A slight liberty with the literal truth, but completely accurate in implication.

"—to deliver this to you with the direction that you were to open it immediately and read it aloud."

Daniel continued to stand at Parade Rest rather than relaxing, and he kept his eyes focused on the horizon. Animals—and human beings at a visceral level, particularly men, *were* animals—tended to react to a direct gaze as a challenge. The last thing Daniel needed now was to raise the emotional temperature still higher.

He knew from discussions with other RCN officers that Slidell—before this latest business—had the reputation of being an able officer and a cultured gentleman. Either the stress of recent events or whatever underlying problem had caused him to put three men out an airlock without a formal court-martial had Slidell close to the edge of his temper now; that would be obvious to anybody. Daniel couldn't imagine any good result for himself if his new captain snapped and, for example, threw a punch.

"I've never heard of anything so absurd," Slidell said, snatching the scroll from Daniel's hand. "I swear, Leary, if this is some jape of yours . . ."

His voice trailed off as he broke the seal and unrolled the document. Slidell might think based on the stories going around that Daniel Leary was a childish, grandstanding fool whose luck would run out shortly, but he couldn't really believe that Daniel would forge a document and take the name of the Secretary to the Navy Board in vain.

Slidell focused on the writing within. His face went blank, then thunderous.

"I don't believe this," he said on a rising note. "This is impossible!"

"What is that, sir?" asked Ganse, looking over the commander's shoulder. "Does it explain . . . ?"

Daniel held a rigidly formal silence. To have reminded Slidell that the direction was to read the document aloud wouldn't have been . . . well, it would've left "impolitic" behind on a fast ship.

"It's infamous!" Slidell shouted. "I've never heard of anything like this! Completely infamous! You!"

He pointed the document in Daniel's face in a trembling hand.

"What do you know about this?"

"Sir," Daniel said; quietly, truthfully, his eyes following a tram entering the reservation. "I don't know anything about it. I was directed to deliver the document. It was made clear to me that I wasn't to question—that an RCN officer *didn't* question—orders."

He was shading truth again, though again without being misleading. *Good Lord, what* was *in the second scroll?*

Slidell drew himself up stiffly and offered the document to Daniel. In a tone of icy anger far different from the honest fury he'd displayed to this point, he said, "Do please read it, then, Lieutenant. Since it concerns you so closely, I'm sure Admiral Anston won't mind. In fact, won't you read it aloud for us? Perhaps I'll find it more intelligible if I listen to it."

Daniel took the opened scroll. Both scrolls, in fact: his own appointment, crumpled now, came with it.

He cleared his throat. The second document was inscribed in a bold holograph, perfectly legible. Daniel read, "*My dear Slidell. I'm writing to save possible embarrassment. Early tomorrow morning the Senate will decree Special Honors to the late Commander Stacey Bergen for his services to the Republic in the fields of exploration and navigation. As the Commander is deceased, these honors will take the form of the extraordinary elevation of his closest living relative, Lt. Daniel Leary, on the Lieutenant's List. Leary's appointment will be put back to the date of his uncle's retirement from the RCN twenty-one years ago.*"

Daniel cleared his throat again. "And it's signed 'Anston,'" he added quietly, meeting Slidell's eyes for the first time.

"Well, I suppose we have no choice then, have we, Ganse?" Slidell said to his companion. "Justice, tradition, and propriety have no chance of prevailing against the Senate and Navy Board, do they?"

Ganse still wore a puzzled expression. He was looking from Daniel's face to Admiral Anston's note, then back again. "Well," he said, "I've never heard of such a proceeding, but Commander Bergen was a great explorer. A truly great . . ."

He met Daniel's eyes and gave him an honest smile. "I envy you knowing Commander Bergen, Leary," he said. "And I've heard of your exploits, of course. It'll be a pleasure to serve with you."

Ganse's arm twitched as he started to extend his hand to shake Daniel's. Commander Slidell stared at him in glacial rage. Ganse looked startled and stiffened to Parade Rest.

"You'll need to remove your duffel from the First Lieutenant's cabin, Ganse," Slidell said, his eyes on Daniel again. "I'll follow you aboard after I have a few words with Mr. Leary."

"I'm perfectly willing to take the starboard cabin, Ganse," Daniel said. The billets of the First and Second Lieutenants were ordinarily identical except for their location, across a corridor from one another and adjacent to the wardroom. "No need to move for me."

"On ships under my command, Leary," Slidell said in a poisonous voice, "matters are conducted properly. I hope you can learn to adapt to this change from your own practice. Mr. Ganse, carry out my orders if you will!"

The red-haired lieutenant trotted toward the boarding bridge without looking around. Daniel felt suddenly calm. The situation wasn't going to fly out of control as he'd initially feared it might. It was unpleasant, certainly, and the voyage to come was likely to be extremely unpleasant; but Daniel had done many unpleasant things in the past. That was simply a part of life.

"I know why you've taken this appointment, Leary," Slidell said. He sounded calmer than he'd been. "And it's not going to work."

"Sir," Daniel said quietly. "I accepted this appointment because I'm an RCN officer and this is where the Navy Office in its wisdom determined that I could best serve the needs of the Republic. I didn't seek this place—"

And *that* was an understatement if ever there was one!

"—but I'll carry out my duties aboard the *Hermes* to the best of my ability."

"So you say," Slidell said without particular emphasis. "Well, let me tell you something, Leary: there was a conspiracy against me on my last voyage. The record shows I knew how to deal with it, and I haven't forgotten how. Be very clear on that point!"

"Sir!" said Daniel, clicking his heels to Attention again and preparing to salute. Slidell had already turned and was striding toward the boarding bridge.

Daniel let his body relax, though his mind was still in the state required by battle or a tricky maneuver. Adele and the servants were coming toward him. They'd have to get their gear aboard quickly, because he was quite sure Slidell would lift ship whether or not that part of the preparations was complete.

Daniel smiled. Treating the situation as a command problem rather than a personal one made the salient points stand out more clearly than they would in a sea of emotion.

On one aspect, he simply didn't have enough information to make a prediction. Daniel knew *he* wasn't going to lead a conspiracy against Commander Slidell. The difficulty was that he wasn't sure Midshipman Kearnes had been doing anything of the sort either . . . and Slidell had put Kearnes out an airlock.

CHAPTER 7

Harbor Three on Cinnabar

The *Hermes'* Battle Direction Center was a utilitarian chamber with six central consoles spaced in an inward-facing circle. On most warships, even a small corvette like the *Princess Cecile*, one of those consoles would be an attack board. There a junior officer would plot missile launches in case the gunnery officer on the bridge became a casualty. The *Hermes* had no missiles, so Adele could take that console without disrupting the tender's normal assignments.

Three technicians had installed a special communication and decryption module within the console; they and Adele were the only people within the Battle Center. Though the techs wore RCN utilities without name tapes or rank tabs, they'd come from Mistress Sand; it was very unlikely that their names appeared anywhere within the Navy Office.

The young female positioned the access plate over the opening in the console base, then locked the clips home by tapping the corners of the plate with the heel of her hand. She rose to her feet.

"That should serve," said the senior tech, a middle-aged man. He turned to Adele and said, "Do you want us to wait while you test it?"

"I think not," said Adele. "I'll want to go over it thoroughly. I'll let you know if I find any problems."

Adele much preferred not to have anyone else present when she was working. Once she got started it didn't matter: she sank into a world of her own in which the data cascading at the direction of her wands walled her off from intrusion.

When she started, though, she was likely to cast around for a time. She couldn't avoid feeling that an observer was judging and condemning her waste effort.

Harbor Three was an ideal location to put the gear through its paces. Eavesdropping on the business of the largest military port on Cinnabar would let Adele know very quickly how much she'd be able to learn in a comparable Alliance base. A number of independent powers had considerable military strength, but none was in the same communications-security league with the two principal adversaries.

The technicians exited, leaving the armored door open behind them. A fourth member of Mistress Sand's organization joined them. He'd been lounging in the corridor outside, not as a guard but to explain to anybody who wanted to enter that the BDC was closed while delicate calibrations of the commo equipment were being carried out.

There was no need for a guard: Adele had set the mechanical interlocks from the inside after she closed the door behind the technicians. Nothing short of a missile could enter the chamber until Adele reopened it.

Adele switched on the console and started to sit, but as the newly installed equipment hummed to life she heard Woetjans bellow, "Hargood, if you don't take three seconds off your time, I'll derate you to Landsman. Bloody *hell*! I'll transfer you to the Power Room, see if I don't!"

Smiling, Adele left the console as it was and walked into the passage connecting the tender's bow and stern sections. Hatches to the outer hull were open. The hacksaw voice of Woetjans, the *Sissie*'s bosun, was unmistakable as she whipped her riggers into shape after the drink and dissipation of a long leave.

She was now the bosun—the Chief of Rig; the warrant officer responsible for a starship's antennas and sails—of the *Hermes*. It struck Adele that there might've been debate as to who took the chief's slot on the tender when the crews were combined, were it not for the fact that Commander Slidell had executed the bosun of the *Bainbridge*.

"All right!" Woetjans said. "That's enough for the port watch, and a piss poor lot you look, too! Starboard watch to the mastheads and back, *now*!"

Adele looked through the hatch above her. She could see Woetjans' hand when the bosun gestured broadly, but the opening was above Adele's reach even if she'd had enough upper body strength to haul herself up.

"May the darkness eat my bones, Wesso!" Woetjans said. "I've seen *babies* crawl up the rigging faster than you're climbing!"

"Woetjans?" Adele called.

The bosun's face suddenly appeared in the hatchway, glowering from habit and the present process of getting the riggers back in shape. Her expression suddenly spread into a smile. That didn't make the bosun beautiful—nothing could—but it gave her face the gnarled attraction of a mighty tree.

"Mistress Mundy!" she cried. "By *God* mistress, I'm glad to see you! Now I know we'll be all right, with you and Mister Leary both! You want to hop up here?"

Without waiting for an answer, she reached down. Woetjans had the long, powerful arms of a tree-climbing ape. They made her remarkably nimble in a starship's rigging, and they were just as useful when she waded into a brawl swinging her weapon of choice, a length of high-pressure tubing.

Adele gripped the bosun's hand in both of hers. She'd thought Woetjans might lower a ladder to her; which meant she hadn't been thinking at all. . . .

"I can't—" she said, meaning to finish the sentence with, "pull myself up," or "do much to help," something like that. She didn't bother, because the bosun straightened in a single easy motion and snatched Adele onto the deck.

Well, deck of a sort. The bar connecting the tender's bow and stern had flat catwalks top and bottom, port and starboard. Adele stood with Woetjans on the uppermost of these.

Woetjans noticed Adele glancing at the surface and explained, "The connecting hull curves a bit too tight to be safe in the Matrix. I mean, nobody experienced is going to have a problem, but a newbie could lose the grip of both his boots and go floating off into nowhere."

Adele heard a hint of apology in the bosun's voice. She wasn't apologizing for what she'd said, but Adele could guess what the bosun had been thinking. With a smile of self-awareness, Adele said, "A newbie or someone as notably clumsy as I am, you mean. Though I generally have sense enough to wear a safety line."

"That you do, mistress," Woetjans agreed in relief. "And that's always a good plan for those who don't, you know, have much call to be out on deck."

The bosun transferred her attention to the riggers. The *Hermes* had four rings of antennas, three around the bow section and one at the cardinal points of the stern. The *Sissie*, a much smaller vessel, had six, and a battleship of 80 thousand tons might have twenty or more.

At present the dorsal masts were extended. The other sets were telescoped and folded against the hull.

The antennas and yards spread electrically charged sails to shift a vessel among the bubble universes of the Matrix. The sails didn't drive the ship—that was accomplished by the inertia imparted by the High Drive in the sidereal universe. Rather they blocked calculated amounts of the Casimir Radiation which streamed through *every* universe in unvarying degree, pushing the vessel from bubble to bubble to take advantage of differing constants of time and velocity.

The more sails, the greater subtleties of action within the Matrix; and therefore greater speed and maneuverability in relation to the sidereal universe. Anti-pirate tenders were tubs.

Adele smiled coldly. Tenders were tubs with a purpose, however. In this instance the *Hermes* would also serve the purposes of Mistress Bernis Sand.

"All right, port watch up and down!" Woetjans said. "Up and down, you scuts, and try and look like you're Sissies and not gutter scrapings!"

"Aw, Chief, we been at this two bloody hours!" a rigger cried. "Give us a break, hey?"

"That's right, Patco!" Woetjans replied. "Two bloody hours, and two more if I have to. Remember, they're delivering the Bridgies yet today. I'm damned if I'm going to have my people showed up by a load of kids and retreads off a training ship! Up and down, Sissies!"

The riggers swarmed up the lines. They reminded Adele of the way liquid spreads through fabric: some spacers a little ahead, some a little behind, but all moving as a single entity toward a common purpose.

"Can't say I'm looking forward to this voyage the way I have some in the past, mistress," Woetjans said quietly. "Oh, I know you and Mister Leary'll make it right if anybody can, but it's God's truth that I'd sooner not be shipping under Commander Slidell. I think that and all the Sissies think that. And I'll stake my left arm that mosta the lot from the *Bainbridge* think that too."

The bosun shook her head. "I knew Calahan," she said, "that's the bosun who went out the lock. He was a hard man and no mistake. He'd run guns and I shouldn't wonder if he knew about piracy from the other side, if you take my drift. But I don't believe he was planning to mutiny on an RCN warship. That's just crazy."

Adele shrugged. "I don't have any knowledge about that, Woetjans," she said.

A line of seven tram cars, their blue-gray paint chipped from hard service, rattled to a halt on the quay. The doors of the first and last car opened, disgorging two squads of Shore Police with sub-machine guns and an officer.

The latter checked to make sure his platoon was ready, then touched a control box on his belt. Only then did the other five cars open. Spacers with downcast eyes filed out and shambled toward the *Hermes*.

"There's the Bridgies," Woetjans said glumly. "The rest of our crew."

"Why, they're being treated like prisoners!" Adele said in amazement. She'd often seen liberty parties stagger back to the ship in the morning, every soul hung over if they weren't still drunk. Never had she encountered so crestfallen a group as this draft from the *Bainbridge*.

"That's just what they are, mistress," Woetjans said. "Locked up as soon as Slidell reported what he'd done. 'As witnesses' they said, but everybody knew it was so they wouldn't talk before they could be shipped off Cinnabar again. And now we're *all* locked up till lift-off—saving you and the other officers, I mean."

Formally, the bosun and Chief Engineer were the most senior warrant officers aboard a ship; in practice Woetjans and the rest of the Sissies always treated Adele as a noble rather than a junior technical specialist. She was both, of course; and while she didn't ask to be treated with deference, the practice had done nothing to impair the efficiency of the *Princess Cecile*.

"This is a very regrettable situation," Adele said, her eyes narrowed.

"Aye, so it is," the bosun said grimly as she pulled on the heavy gauntlets hanging from her belt. They were part of the rigging suit she'd wear while working in the Matrix. "Well, I got my work cut out for me, that's the bloody truth."

In a bellow she continued, "All you Bridgies with riggers ratings, you hold right where you are! I'm Woetjans, I'm Chief of Rig, and after I hear your names we're going to see what you can do!"

Instead of going in through the hatch and walking to the quay via the boarding bridge, Woetjans gripped the line snubbed at her feet. She released the shackle, then swung down. She'd obviously prepared this maneuver to impress the crewmembers who didn't already know her.

She impressed Adele as well. Anyone glancing at Woetjans would expect physical prowess, but this had taken careful planning. She'd had to rig a line to the yard of a forward antenna and belay it to the stern in order to come down precisely in front of the boarding bridge. Not at all a stupid person, Woetjans, for all that she could barely read her own name.

Adele had known the bosun would take her comment as agreement; that was her intent. In truth, while she knew the ruthlessness of the Navy Office—and of the Senate; who should know *that* better than the last surviving Mundy of Chatsworth?—she was by no means sure the situation was as cut and dried as Woetjans supposed.

Slidell was not only well-connected, he had a very good record. That was why he'd been given command of a training vessel, after all.

But with the ship's captain deeply suspicious of Lieutenant Leary and everyone connected with him, well . . . there were othes besides Woetjans who had their work cut out for them.

The tram pulled into the siding, halting with a click as it settled onto the rail. Besides Hogg and Daniel there were six people in the car, going home and at this hour anxious to be there, but likewise too tired to protest when the doors opened to a gust of rain.

"Hogg, you really can go back to the house, you know," Daniel said. The storm had gotten worse since they left Chatsworth Minor, and it'd been bad enough then.

"Aye," said Hogg, snugging his collar close as he stepped from the car to the leeward side of the kiosk. "And I could join the priesthood, too, which I guess is about as likely. I been out in worse'n this, young master. We both of us have."

Hogg wore high, soft-soled boots, a hat whose broad, floppy brim directed runnels out beyond his body, and a full-length cloak of raw wool, tightly woven with the natural oils still in the fabric. The cloak repelled rain without the glints and rustling a hard synthetic fabric might have caused. Those were important attributes for a hunter, and even more important for a poacher who risked more than the loss of a trophy.

Daniel got out, waiting beside his servant for a moment while the tram hissed down the street. He'd probably never see the other passengers again nor they him, but it was a matter of courtesy not to come hammering on the door of Mistress Maeve Astola with a crowd of strangers looking on.

The *Hermes* would lift tomorrow in what was actually a shake-down cruise though classed as a fully operational deployment. Quite a lot could go wrong with the ship, and her crew was even more problematical.

A First Lieutenant in such circumstances could choose to spend his last night on Cinnabar in various fashions. Most would decide to go over matters they'd checked three times already. Commander Slidell was doing that now, prowling the tender's antennas with a handlight, examining joints that might stick and hinges that might shear.

And some of them *would* stick and shear, to an overwhelming statistical probability. A starship in operation was too powerful and too complex not to stress portions of its fabric beyond the breaking point. But by now, only testing in actual service could determine *which* pieces were going to break. Daniel believed he'd be better able to deal with the inevitable failures if he spent the night in relaxing activity.

"You know she was laying for you, don't you?" Hogg said sourly. "Bints like her don't hang out in spacers' bars."

"Well, The Lower Deck isn't the Shamrock, after all," Daniel said, thinking about his brief contact with the lady.

"It is to the likes of her," Hogg said, quite truthfully. As another blast of rain lashed the street. "All I'm saying is, don't figure you know for sure what she's got in mind, young master. There's people who want more from you than what you carry between your legs."

"Well, Hogg," Daniel said as he ducked out of the kiosk in what he hoped was a lull. "That's quite true, but I'm afraid the only way to learn is to test it in practice."

Mistress Astola was a black-haired beauty whose slender waist set off her hips and bosom perfectly. She'd walked up to the table where Daniel was saying goodbye to friends, whispered an invitation, and left the bar as suddenly as she'd appeared. The offer couldn't have been better timed. Daniel'd intended to look for company at the party the Richelets were giving, but he'd been working hard enough to prefer a simpler alternative tonight.

The address was fifty feet from the tram stop: a four-story townhouse of similar age and quality to Chatsworth Minor. Daniel stepped into the triple-arched door recess and tapped on the panel. The remainder of the lady's directions were quite simple: "*A servant will open the door, then leave. Go down the hall to the right to the lighted drawing room.*"

He glanced back at the tram kiosk. A small light in the ceiling had been on; it no longer was, leaving Hogg completely concealed on this rain-swept night.

Daniel didn't know what Hogg was worried about. Perhaps he wasn't worried at all and was just doing his duty as he saw it. Men like Hogg didn't ask *why* a gentleman's servant should wait in a downpour while his master met a lady in complete privacy; they just did it, because it was their job.

While Daniel grew up on Bantry, Speaker Leary had generally been in Xenos on political business. Corder Leary had neither time nor the inclination to be a father to a boy who shared none of his interests. Hogg had filled the place, raising Daniel in his own conception of duty. It'd served Daniel well as an RCN officer, and as a man.

The door opened inward with a gentle *hoosh*; a

slim figure, probably female, stood half-concealed in the anteroom. "Please go on through, sir," she whispered.

The inner panel was ajar; light glowed around the open edge. As Daniel pulled it toward him, he heard the street door thump shut.

The ornate staircase to the upper floors was offset to the left. There was a light somewhere upstairs, casting a diffuse glow through the banisters, but none of the wall sconces in the frescoed entryway were lit.

More light wavered softly from the hallway to the right. Daniel walked toward it, his careful footsteps soundless on the thick carpet. He entered a room covered with age-darkened wooden panels. A shaded candle on the table cast the only illumination; the figure seated on the other side was clearly male.

"Don't bother posturing, boy," the figure said. "There's only the two of us here, and bluster isn't going to impress me. Sit down and listen."

Daniel stared at him. It'd been eight years since he last saw his father; he hadn't expected ever to see him again.

"Sir, you have nothing to say to me," Daniel said. He was dizzy with surprise. If he'd met a squad of gunmen he'd have known how to react, but this . . .

"And I have nothing to say to you!" Daniel said. He'd gone white; now his face flushed and he felt as though his skin was burning. His fists were clenched.

Daniel gripped the back of the chair before him, not to sit in but from a momentary urge to hurl it into the wall. He needed to *act* to burn off the adrenaline that had set his muscles trembling violently.

"I said, don't bluster!" Corder snapped. "I'm not

here because I want to be, boy. This is family, and *don't* tell me you're not a Leary. I've watched you, and there's never a Bergen born who'd go into a fight the way you do. Now, sit down and listen."

Daniel opened his hands but left them resting on the chair back. He took a deep, shuddering breath. He didn't think it helped, but he managed to say without stammering, "There's other things than fighting, sir."

"Sure there are," Corder said. "And there's other people to do them, too, while we Learys do the things the others can't or won't. You've got a chestful of medals, I suppose; but the real reward is knowing there's places that Cinnabar traders can go now that they couldn't if it hadn't been for a Leary making it safe for them."

Which was true. Daniel hadn't thought anybody else, not even Adele, understood that.

Corder'd been hunching forward slightly; now he straightened in his chair. He was four inches taller than his son; his face was still craggy though his waist had expanded considerably since Daniel last saw him. The Speaker had joint problems, Daniel had heard; you *do* hear things, even if you're not trying to.

"And the fact that Cinnabar's a republic and not an Alliance protectorate like Porra tried to buy with the Three Circles Conspiracy," Corder continued in the same hard, certain voice. "*That's* a Leary's doing too, boy."

Daniel looked across the table, wondering if he should turn and walk out. The humor of a thought struck him; he barked a laugh.

"Eh?" said Corder; his tone a question, not a challenge.

"I'm not in the habit of running away from a fight, sir," Daniel said, grinning beneath the words. "Say what you have to say, and then I'll leave."

"Aye," Corder said grimly. "We'll both leave, and this meeting won't have happened."

He spread his big hands flat on the table; the knuckles seemed enlarged. He resumed in the same tone, "Oller Kearnes is my son. Was my son, before Slidell killed him. And Oller being my son is *why* Slidell killed him—revenge for his brother, you see."

Daniel let the words dance in his mind as he tried to fit them into a pattern that made sense. He wished Adele was here, for advice and especially for companionship. The idea was so ludicrous that it broke his mood.

"I don't see at all," Daniel said, with a lilt though not quite open laughter. "Who was Commander Slidell's brother?"

Corder grimaced. "Jan Slidell was my legislative aide," he said. "I thought I could get him into the Senate in a few years; he might've been useful. But instead he stuck a knife in my back for the Cullert faction."

Daniel opened his mouth, then closed it again. He didn't even know how to frame a question that would bring him closer to his father's meaning.

Corder saw and perhaps understood what was going on in Daniel's mind. "All right, you need background," he said harshly. "Bruno Kearnes and I were in partnership to get control of the dyeweed trade from Hise; the Cullert brothers were heading another syndicate. There was a lot of money at stake."

He looked up sharply. "A *lot* of money."

Daniel nodded. He understood that when Corder Leary used the phrase, it meant something very different from the pot of a florin-ante poker game.

"And . . ." Corder said, knotting his fingers and staring at them. "And I was seeing Lira Kearnes on the side."

He looked up, glaring at Daniel. "And I don't need a lecture!"

That's the first anger he's shown tonight. Because he acted like a fool and knows it. . . .

Daniel said calmly, "You weren't going to get one from me. Go on."

His father shook his head. "No, I don't suppose I was," he said. "All I can say, boy, is I hope you get it out of your system sooner than I did, because my pecker's got me in more trouble than the Alliance ever thought of doing. Including this time."

Corder turned his hands palms-up and went on, "It should've been safe enough. I never met Lira except in public or just the two of us together; Slidell made all the arrangements for our meetings, not me. So when it *did* come out and the Hise arrangements went into the dumper, I knew who'd done it; and I knew how to make sure Jan's pay-off didn't do him any good."

In a tone of savage gusto he said, "I *broke* him, boy. I broke him good. He shot himself a few years later, which saved me the trouble of keeping my thumb on him any longer."

"And you believe Lira Kearnes' son—" third son, wasn't it? "—is your offspring?" Daniel said carefully. It was a bloody strange conversation to be having, not least for the fact he and his father were talking, not screaming, at one another.

"I *know* Oller's my son," Corder said. "The timing's right, and Bruno Kearnes had his prostate out a year before the boy was born."

The older man started to get up but winced and settled back on the chair. "I never had anything to do with the boy growing up," he said to his hands again. "I haven't exchanged a word with Bruno since then, not even on the Senate floor. It was a bloody fool thing to have done, but I can't take it back. And now the Slidells have got back at me by killing the boy. Raw murder, and aimed against *me*."

And how much did you have to do with me *when I was growing up, you arrogant bastard?* thought Daniel, his face expressionless. Aloud he said, "I don't believe a respected officer like Commander Slidell would use the RCN as a tool of private vengeance, sir. I know I wouldn't do so myself."

Corder Leary straightened with a look of fury. This time he managed to lurch to his feet. He'd understood what Daniel was saying—all of what he was saying.

"Are you saying you're going to let Slidell get away with murdering your own brother, boy?" Corder demanded. "You know you could take care of him quietly when you're in the back of beyond!"

"I know that I'll not murder a man, sir," Daniel said. He wasn't angry, but he was horrified and suddenly drained. "Not for you, not for the Leary family. Not even for the RCN."

He'd moved the chair while he was gripping it. Now he set it back in alignment with the table.

"Good night, sir," Daniel said, turning on his heel. He closed the door behind him as he walked out.

That was a mistake—the candle within would've

lighted the hall to some degree—but he managed not to trip over the occasional table he remembered against the corridor wall. When he reached the entryway, he opened the inner door to the anteroom. The servant was waiting there.

"Please," she said. "Please, Lieutenant, let me apologize to you."

She'd thrown back the hood of her cloak. Because Daniel's eyes had adapted, he recognized her even in the dim glow as Maeve Astola herself . . . or at least the woman who'd used that name in The Lower Deck.

Daniel recoiled. The woman gripped his right hand with hers and said, "He forced me, please believe me. The only choice I had was to go through with the deception or take poison. And as soon as I'd let you in, I knew I'd made the wrong choice. I should've killed myself!"

Daniel analyzed her words with the things she hadn't said. What hold did Speaker Leary have over her? Any of a hundred things, depending on what the woman was in her heart. And this one seemed to be a decent person. . . .

"I doubt anything you did would've changed tonight's events, mistress," Daniel said. "He'd have seen to it that I met him at a different address, that's all; no harm done. But if you don't mind I'll take my leave now."

He didn't add that his father would've carried out whatever threat he'd made. Corder Leary didn't bluff, and he didn't do things halfway.

"He'll have gone out the back," the woman said, holding him with both hands now. "Please, come upstairs with me. I'm so sorry, so very sorry."

Daniel stiffened. *Do you think I need charity?*

But the words didn't reach his tongue. He laughed and said, "Mistress—Maeve, if I may call you? Maeve, if it hadn't been for your invitation I've have been attending a party at the Jonas Richelets' tonight. Would you care to come as my guest? And we'll see how the evening develops from there."

She threw her arms around Daniel, blubbering with relief. Quite a pretty little thing; and seemingly a decent person. . . .

CHAPTER 8

Harbor Three on Cinnabar

The steam had dissipated, but Slip 17Y was still muggy from the blast that tested the *Hermes'* twenty plasma thrusters, and their iridium throats radiated heat. Daniel was crawling beneath the vessel with Chief Engineer Pasternak—who'd come with him from the *Sissie*—and the five midshipmen assigned to the tender as they viewed the thrusters through their goggles.

Because Harbor Three was a major port, the slips had gratings that extended to cover the water on which vessels floated. That way work on and inspection of a vessel's underside didn't require use of a boat. The lower curve of the *Hermes'* hull floated only four feet above the surface, however, and nobody'd call the conditions comfortable. They were more comfortable than many of the things an RCN officer was expected to do, however.

"Sir?" said Midshipman Bragg, a slender, blond youth who thus far had impressed Daniel as being earnest but slow. He was the most senior of the three midshipmen who'd come from the *Bainbridge*, but—fortunately, to Daniel's way of thinking—he was nonetheless junior to Dorst and Vesey. They'd passed their exams and were waiting for appointments as lieutenants if all went well.

"Yes, Bragg?" Daniel said, looking over his shoulder. Bragg was staring at the stern section.

"The hull plating's discolored here, sir," the midshipman said, pointing. "Is that the way it's supposed to be?"

"The eight stern thrusters have to be placed closer together than the twelve in the bow, Bragg," Daniel said patiently. "There's more discoloration as a result—or rather, it occurs more quickly; after six months' service you won't be able to tell the difference. But if you'd switched your goggles to infrared as you were directed to do, you wouldn't be seeing that anyway."

"Oh!" said Bragg. "Sorry, sir!"

"Bloody farmer!" muttered Midshipman Blantyre, a stocky woman who seemed competent but a little too sure of herself. Daniel turned and looked at her. He didn't speak, but she felt the implied criticism and said, "Sorry," under her breath with a quick nod.

Daniel smiled slightly. Blantyre and Cory had been with Bragg for at least the past six months aboard the *Bainbridge*. Given how wearing Daniel found the fellow after less than a week, he had a degree of sympathy for Blantyre.

"Mister Leary!" Commander Slidell called from the quay. "Come out from under there and join me, if you will. And bring the midshipmen with you."

Slidell was the sort of man who probably sounded severe when he was making love, but he certainly wasn't making love now. "After me, Hermies," Daniel said, scrambling on all fours toward the narrow part of the hull where he'd have room to stand up. "And hop it!"

The six cutters were in their davits, clamped firmly to the spine so that they wouldn't swing about during the violence of liftoff. Unlike the *Hermes* herself, the cutters were well-used vessels. There was probably twenty years difference between the oldest and newest, but Daniel suspected all of them had been built before he was born.

The saving grace was that the cutters had been given new spars and rigging before they were assigned to the *Hermes*. Leaks in an older hull weren't especially serious: at worst the crew could wear atmosphere suits, uncomfortable but not dangerous. A cutter had only eight antennas, though. Losing one or more made it very difficult to maneuver in the Matrix.

A ladder up from the grating to the port outrigger and a catwalk from there would bring Daniel and his covey of midshipmen to the quay. Pasternak followed at the end of the line. They'd completed their work and, though it was still several hours to scheduled liftoff, tugs were already maneuvering to draw the *Hermes* from her slip to the center of the pool.

The inspection had been real, but Daniel was more interested in training the midshipmen than he'd been concerned about the newly installed thrusters failing. On infrared pits and cracks in heated nozzles would show up brighter than the surrounding iridium because they radiated over a greater surface area. Eroded nozzles could be replaced—if spares were available—or favored if that was the only option. The habit of checking after every landing could save ships and lives.

Slidell waited at the end of the catwalk, his hands crossed behind his back. He wore a utility uniform like everyone else as the *Hermes* prepared to lift off, but his was apparently brand new. Daniel had dressed to crawl under the ship on a grate that was certain to be wet and probably oily besides; he'd have looked grubby even if he hadn't been right to expect oil.

"Sir!" said Daniel, saluting. He couldn't step onto the quay while Slidell stood where he did. "I've been showing the middies how to examine hot thrusters."

"Very commendable, Leary," Slidell said, "but the present danger is that one of the cutters will come adrift in the atmosphere. I've decided I want them manned on liftoff so that they can separate safely if that happens. The crews can come back aboard when we're in orbit. You and the midshipmen will captain them. I've assigned Mister Ganse to your post in the BDC."

"Aye aye, sir," Daniel said. He'd never heard of such a proceeding, but it wasn't flatly foolish. Paired davits held each cutter. If one fractured on liftoff, the smaller vessel would flail itself and probably the tender as well to junk unless it were cast away instantly. Dropping a two-hundred ton cutter onto an inhabited area wasn't a good practice either.

Daniel turned to the midshipmen stopped along the catwalk behind him. "Bragg, you'll take six-one-oh," he said. "Blantyre, one-one; Cory, one-two. Vesey and Dorst take one-four and one-five, and I'll be in one-three."

That put the three former Bridgies in the cutters on the dorsal side of the *Hermes*. It would be much easier to successfully eject from there during liftoff than it would from the tender's underside while the thrusters were at full output. Cutter 613 in the bow ventral position would be a bitch and no mistake, so Daniel took it for himself.

He faced Slidell again and said, "Sir, we'll take our assigned stations now if you like."

And if you'll get out of our bloody way.

"Yes, all right," the commander said, stepping back and away. His grace and erect, military posture were impressive even in so small a thing. "And Leary? We're on an operational deployment now. Salutes are improper, even if you didn't look like a clown when you attempt it."

"Yessir," Daniel said, striding toward the boarding bridge with an apologetic nod. He'd been told by people who liked him a good deal more than Slidell did that military courtesy would never be his strong suit. That barred Daniel from a place on an admiral's staff—which made his inept saluting rather a benefit, he felt.

The midshipmen had sprinted ahead, eager to get to their stations. Daniel knew it'd be an hour before Slidell even closed up the ship, so he walked only as briskly as he thought the captain's eyes boring into his back required. Pasternak caught up with him at the entry hatch on E Deck.

"Sir, I know what regulations say," Pasternak said in a low-voiced growl, "two power techs and wipers to each cutter's crew. But please, that's for cruising at 1g and nothing for the Power Room crew to do but try not to fall asleep in front of the gauges. Can you get along with short crews on the cutters while we lift this girl the first time for real?"

Bloody Hell, why is he asking me instead of the Captain? Daniel thought. Though the answer was obvious enough: Daniel Leary *was* the Captain in the Chief Engineer's mind.

Pasternak had been a very senior man for a corvette like the *Princess Cecile*; the larger *Hermes* was a more proper berth for him. He'd shipped with Daniel before because he'd needed money and Mister Leary had the reputation of being a lucky officer who made his crews rich from prize money. That was very well, but for Pasternak to act behind the back of a man like Captain Slidell could have no good results for any of the parties involved.

Daniel raised a finger to halt the engineer in the tender's main entry compartment. Armored companionways to left and right led to the four higher decks and to the bulk storage holds on F Deck below. There were four airlocks in the bow section and two in the stern for the riggers who adjusted the sails in the void, but this large chamber—not an airlock, though any compartment of a warship could be sealed off from the remainder of the vessel—was the normal means of access while on a habitable planet.

Keying his commo helmet, Daniel said, "Captain? May I request that we reduce the cutter crews to a single power technician each? If something goes badly wrong, I'd prefer to lose a cutter than have the whole ship go down because there weren't enough eyes on the gauges of a new vessel. Even if I'm on that cutter. Over."

There was a brief pause. *"Yes, all right, Leary,"* Slidell said. *"Captain out."*

"The Captain approves, Chief," Daniel said. Grudgingly from the sound of his voice, but the words were all that mattered. "Make it so."

"Thank *you*, sir!" Pasternak said as he bolted down the right-hand corridor toward the Power Room. He was calling names over the ship-side intercom channel, reassigning personnel who were already going to cutters according to their previous orders.

Daniel entered the right-hand—upward—companionway. The helical stairs were broader than the *Sissie*'s, capable of serving two spacers abreast even if they wore bulky rigging suits. The hatches were open for the time being—they'd be dogged shut at liftoff. They echoed with the racket of boots on the steel treads and last-minute preparations on all the *Hermes'* decks.

He stepped out on D Deck, reflexively sticking his head around the hatch coaming first to make sure nobody was coming the other way. Yermakova was trotting down the corridor through the central portion of the tender.

"Sir!" she called to Daniel as she swung herself into the downward companionway. Behind her were five Power Room techs from the *Bainbridge*—one named Schmidt, but Daniel with a jolt of shame realized he couldn't identify the others except to group them by rating.

The six were the cutter personnel whom Pasternak had recalled to the Power Room. Normally a single tech kept track of four or more drive units—plasma thrusters on liftoff and landing, or High Drive motors when the vessel was out of the atmosphere and could use the much more efficient matter/anti-matter conversion process. With a vessel whose thrusters had never been run simultaneously at full output, the Chief Engineer was right to have as many trained eyes as possible looking for anomalies before they ballooned into catastrophic failure.

The six hatches at intervals off the corridor were open. The midshipmen had boarded their commands, but the last of the riggers were still entering the cutters when Daniel arrived.

Normally both rigging watches would've been waiting in the airlock foyers to exit onto the hull to raise the antennas as soon as the *Hermes* reached orbit. Shifting from there to the cutters meant going up or down three decks and then along the passageway. They'd done just that in the time it'd taken for Daniel to saunter aboard even though they were wearing rigging suits which put ruggedness over flexibility.

The riggers' helmets were hinged down against their backplates; they'd swing up and latch them to seal the suits, but there was no need of that yet. Dasi, a senior rigger from the *Sissie*, was the last to enter *Cutter 613*. He looked over his shoulder as Daniel boarded behind him and cycled the airlock closed.

"Hey Barnes!" he called in delight to the friend just ahead of him. "It's Mister Leary what's our captain!"

"Hey, three cheers for Mister Leary!" called Sentino, seated in front of the Power Board. She was a small blonde, a Sissie whom Daniel knew was the most senior tech on the *Hermes*. Pasternak had withdrawn Bridgies whom he didn't know well and Yermakova who'd just gotten her rating, leaving the cutters with experienced people in case they were needed to nurse the thrusters.

"Belay that, Sentino!" Daniel said sharply. "Anyway, there's nothing to cheer about. We're just passengers while the folks aboard the *Hermes* do all the work of getting us to orbit."

He squeezed to the command console forward but didn't sit down yet. On larger vessels the console swivelled, but in the cutter's tight interior everything had to be fixed in place. No starship had much room, but a cutter with a full crew was significantly more crowded than even a sloop or corvette.

613's interior was a single chamber without internal barriers. The fusion bottle and anti-matter converter were in the far bow, disconcertingly obvious to riggers—and to Daniel as well—who were used to having an armored bulkhead between their living quarters and the Power Room. The single airlock was in the stern, on the long axis because the cutter was too narrow to build it into the side of the hull.

Sentino was to Daniel's left; the muscular youth beside her must be her wiper, useful for carrying out physical repairs on the power plant once somebody else had diagnosed them but unable to read the gauges himself. At the attack console on the right was Rocker. He'd been striker to Sun, the gunner's mate on the *Princess Cecile* and now the *Hermes*.

Cutters were armed with a cluster of twelve chemically-fueled rockets with explosive warheads. The rockets followed ballistic courses, so they were aimed by gunnery specialists rather than the missileers who programmed the main armament of larger warships. A missile was a multi-ton starship with a High Drive and anti-matter converter, capable of accelerating to a significant fraction of light speed. Missiles weren't fitted with warheads because at their velocities even a nuclear blast couldn't add to the effect of their kinetic energy.

"Mr. Leary?" Rocker said, turning around at his

console. "Hogg says not to worry, he'll be watching things for you."

Daniel frowned. Speaker Leary and now Hogg were determined to make a normal RCN appointment into a feud between noble families . . . and very possibly Captain Slidell viewed matters in the same light.

Of course it *wasn't* really a normal RCN appointment.

Aloud—loudly enough for everyone aboard to hear— Daniel said, "I don't think there's any reason to be concerned, Rocker. And if Hogg is determined to behave otherwise, he'll find himself back on Bantry mending fishing weirs."

Chimes rang through the hull connection; an electronic equivalent beeped from Daniel's helmet and the command console: thirty minutes to liftoff, close up ship. Quicker than Daniel would've expected, though the sooner the better.

"Begin cycling your systems, Sentino," Daniel said. He glanced at the motorman. As he expected, she was already throwing switches on her board.

Daniel turned to his display and put a command lockout on thruster ignition. Pumping reaction mass through the feed pipes at once ensured that there wouldn't be air bubbles in the lines if it became necessary to light the thrusters. A blast of plasma from the nozzles while 613 was still coupled to the tender would be a disaster, however.

Disastrous at least to Daniel's hopes of advancement in the RCN. He didn't imagine Sentino would make such a boneheaded mistake, but officers who operated on the assumption that people didn't screw up had short, unhappy careers.

Dasi'd apparently been waiting for Daniel to look back into the compartment. "Sir?" he said. "Some a' the Bridgies, they think you got sent here to report on Cap'n Slidell. Is that so, sir?"

Daniel grinned at the blunt effrontery of the question. Riggers tended to be a free-spoken lot, in part because their normal job was more dangerous and unpleasant than any punishment short of execution. Small ships didn't allow real separation of commissioned and enlisted personnel, and Daniel wouldn't have been one to insist on punctilio anyway. Even so . . .

Aloud he said, "No, Dasi, that isn't the case. In fact I believe my assignment had more to do with impressing people with the fact that the Navy Office fully supports Captain Slidell. As it should, from what I've seen of the way the Captain has prepared the *Hermes* for deployment."

A cutter normally carried eighteen to twenty personnel. Because cutters were little more than platforms to carry sails, their crews were biased heavily toward the rig. *613*'s present ship-side crew was Daniel, Sentino and her wiper, and Rocker; but she carried fourteen riggers. The latter, Daniel noted on a quick survey, were drawn equally from former Sissies and Bridgies. On full complement she'd have over thirty crew but in the same general proportions.

A Bridgie caught Dasi's eye. "Go on, Terrel," Dasi said. "It's Mister Leary. You can talk to him."

Daniel didn't know what Captain Slidell would want him to do at this point, nor was he sure what a court-martial might say on the subject. His first thought was to tell the rigger to hold his tongue; but the truth was, Daniel himself couldn't help but be curious about what had really happened during the *Bainbridge*'s most recent cruise.

"If you have something to say, Terrel," Daniel said calmly, "say it. I won't take your words beyond the confines of this hull."

"The Kearnes kid was talking all sorts of crazy schemes, sir," Terrel said, his face scrunched into a look of unhappiness. "Mutiny and turning pirate, sure; but sweeping down on Pleasaunce and blowing up the Guarantor's Palace too, *all* sorts of crazy stuff. He'd listen to Calahan blowing wind, making the kid feel good, you see; and the kid'd slip Calahan liquor from the officers' storeroom, you see."

"Princhett's the other one Captain Slidell spaced," muttered a rigger far back in the stern. "He was a simple lad, but there wasn't no harm in him. He'd believe it if you said you could teach him to fly."

Daniel looked at the double line of expectant faces, knowing that whatever he said now would be through the whole crew within an hour of the time the *Hermes* reached orbit. He could refuse to speak, but that'd get around also. If anything, Daniel's silence would be taken as a more damning indictment of Captain Slidell than any words he could say.

Daniel smiled faintly. He'd made his reputation by acting in situations where none of the choices were good; this was just one more of them.

"Well, fellow spacers," he said. "I don't have an opinion about the legality of any action Captain Slidell took aboard the *Bainbridge*. A court-martial sat on those matters, and its findings are final."

A rigger—Haughtry, a former Sissie—murmured an angry protest. Daniel locked the man with his eyes.

"Sorry, sir," Haughtry mumbled, leaning sideways to put his face behind the bulk of the man ahead of him.

"I'll say this about the life of a spacer, though," Daniel continued. "And a hard life it is, that we all know. You can make a little mistake, and you've lost a finger or lost your life; or the ship itself breaks up with you and all your fellows lost. Not so?"

"Bloody well told it's so!" said Barnes forcefully. There was a chorus of grunted agreement.

"Now the best thing you can say about these three fellows that went out the lock for mutiny," Daniel said, "is that they talked bloody foolishness; which is a mistake anywhere and assuredly a mistake in the RCN. If it cost them their lives, well, that's what mistakes *do* cost, spacers."

He looked up and down the double row of enlisted spacers, meeting every pair of eyes that were willing to meet his. After a long moment he repeated, "Not so?"

"Ach, it's done with," said Dasi, shrugging in his armored suit. "We just wanted to hear what you felt about it, sir."

Daniel dropped into his seat, putting his back to the crew. They could all look at his image in their electronic goggles, but it wasn't the same as real face-to-face.

"What I feel," said Daniel through the intercom circuit. "Is that we're about to lift off. Any of you lot who aren't strapped in tight are likely to bounce tail over teacup—which isn't half what Woetjans'll do to you when she hears about it. Prepare for liftoff, spacers!"

Amid general laughter aboard *Cutter 613*, Lieutenant Ganse said over the general channel from the tender, *"One minute to liftoff!"*

Daniel checked his display and waited, his left hand poised to remove the ignition lockout the instant something went wrong with the *Hermes'* thrusters or the davits. He smiled with satisfaction. Things had gone pretty well, considering how badly they might've gone.

Or anyway, he thought they had.

Adele's face didn't change when she heard Captain Slidell reassign Daniel; she simply opened video channels from all six cutters to her console. Bleak, violent possibilities seethed through her mind, but—she smiled wryly—that was a common enough experience for her.

Tovera sat at a console that would otherwise have been empty; Hogg was in a jump seat folded down from the bulkhead. An engineer's mate from the *Bainbridge*, Peeker, was at one console; another was reserved for Lieutenant Ganse in place of Daniel.

Sun, the gunner's mate from the *Princess Cecile*, was on the bridge controlling the *Hermes'* defensive armament: a single turret with a pair of 4-inch plasma cannon. Ordinarily Sun's striker would back him up in the Battle Direction Center, but every other crewman with gunnery training, let alone a rating, was aboard a cutter.

As of course were the midshipmen who'd otherwise fill the remaining places. Their presence in the BDC was as much for training as for the real help they'd be if something happened to the tender's commissioned officers, though.

Adele wondered whether the ship's computer could plot a course home by itself if all the *Hermes'* human astrogators were lost. She smiled again. *That begs the question of where home is*, she thought. If she had to answer the question, she'd say it was wherever the crew of the *Princess Cecile*, her RCN family, happened to be.

Lieutenant Ganse entered the chamber hurriedly and set the armored hatch to cycle shut. Adele glanced at him past her holographic display on which her console cascaded message traffic from across Harbor Three.

"Sorry," he muttered as he seated himself at a console. "I was in my rigging suit when the Captain reassigned me. I, ah . . ."

His voice trailed off in a frown. Ganse glanced at the engineer's mate, murmured, "Good to see you, Peeker," and paused at Tovera, who met his eyes with her usual lack of expression.

"Tovera is my assistant," Adele said primly. Tovera had a great deal of technical training, but it was entirely hardware oriented; she could do little with a command console beyond using it for basic communications. "My striker, I suppose you'd say."

Adele turned slightly and indicated Hogg with a nod. "And Hogg is Mister Leary's servant," she continued. "He has no action station, so this is a good place for him to keep out of the way."

"Ah," said Ganse. "Yes, of course, Mundy. Hogg, you'll want to strap in for liftoff. That handgrip to your right pulls—"

"I know what it does, master," Hogg said firmly. "I'll hang on to the seat bottom when we lift, like I done plenty times afore."

Hogg wore his usual shapeless, ugly garments. They were bulkier than those of ordinary spacers and thus dangerous in the tight passages and whirling machinery of a starship. On the other hand, you could conceal a great deal beneath them without it showing: a covey of game birds, Daniel had said once; or enough weapons to outfit an infantry squad. Adele didn't suppose Hogg was hiding poached game this afternoon. . . .

"Ah," Ganse repeated, obviously more uncomfortable than either of the servants. "Well, you know what you're doing, then."

He brought his console live, focusing on the engineering readouts. One quadrant of his display echoed the information from Captain Slidell's command console. Adele knew that because she checked Ganse's display just as she'd done with Slidell's earlier. A communications officer shouldn't have done, and shouldn't have been able to do, that.

Adele's smile flickered again. Most communications officers *wouldn't* have be able to.

Satisfied with what he saw, Ganse looked up and gave Adele an awkward smile. "Ah," he said, "we haven't had much contact, Mundy, though I'm sure we'll get to know one another better during the cruise. I've, ah . . . I've heard of you. You've shipped with Mister Leary before, I believe?"

He ended the question on a bright note. He was honestly trying to be friendly, Adele decided, though he was nervous and possibly afraid. *What has he heard about me?*

"Yes," she said, "I suppose you could say that Lieutenant Leary drafted me into the RCN during the business on Kostroma several years ago. I'm a librarian by training. There proved to be a great deal of overlap with the things a communications officer needs to know."

Forcing a smile as a friendly response to Ganse's friendliness, she added, "Though I'm very weak on procedures and naval ceremony, I'm afraid."

"Well, there won't be much call for that in the Gold Dust Cluster, I expect," Ganse said. He pursed his lips and added, "I shouldn't have thought a librarian would, well, be able to . . . well, you have a very high reputation, you know?"

And what do you think a librarian does? Adele thought behind a tight, false smile. *Do you think that data—enormous volumes of data—magically form themselves into the answers that the Captain wants?*

Or Mistress Sand wanted, of course; but that was no business for Lieutenant Ganse or Captain Slidell either one. Aloud Adele said, "Think of me as an information specialist, Lieutenant. Routing simple communications is one of the easier tasks that a librarian performs."

Another chime rang through the ship. "*Ship, ten minutes to liftoff,*" Slidell said on the intercom channel. "*Mister Pasternak, light your thrusters but keep them at minimum. Out.*"

The information went to the cutters also, because Adele relayed it over an input-only link. The cutters' internal communications weren't copied to the *Hermes*—except to Adele's own console.

"*Roger, Captain,*" Pasternak's voice replied. The ship gave a series of thumps as though heavy rubber balls had bounced from its underside.

"Captain Slidell likes to preheat the thrusters thoroughly before putting power to them," Ganse said to Adele. "That's especially important with new nozzles like these, but he's a very careful officer."

"I understand that care is a very necessary trait in captains who hope to survive," Adele said in a neutral voice and with a neutral smile. "Though of course I'm not qualified to judge the matter myself."

The *Hermes* trembled softly. The thrusters buzzed, ejecting ions which vibrated at high frequency, but there was also the quiver of exhaust-hammered water rebounding from the walls of lagoon in which the vessel floated.

Adele flashed a view from the sensors on the dorsal spine. She found, as she expected, only a wall of steam glowing with traces of plasma. She could import a signal from one of the half dozen other vessels sharing the lagoon with the *Hermes*, but she didn't need to. She'd seen vessels lifting off many times in the past.

"Yes, that's quite right," Ganse said, though his tone wasn't so much one of agreement as of desperate pleading. It wasn't the way a commissioned officer should've been talking to a warrant officer, a mere technical specialist. He'd definitely heard rumors about Adele Mundy. "He's plotted the entire course to Nikitin even before we lift from Cinnabar. All seventeen days in the Matrix, with the interim returns to normal space to take star sightings."

Daniel had said he thought the *Hermes* could make the run in twelve days; that the tender mightn't be as clumsy as folk thought, not if the captain stayed out on the hull and watched the ghostly shimmering of universes beyond the bubble that enclosed his own ship. It was possible that Slidell could reach the Gold Dust Cluster as quickly or nearly so: from his record, Slidell was a highly skilled astrogator himself.

Adele smiled as she completed her analysis: the

difference was that Slidell saw no present need to press the ship and its crew to the limit, whereas Daniel would see no reason *not* to. No doubt the RCN needed both types of officer, but there was a reason Lieutenant Leary wearing full medals could be mistaken for an admiral.

Ganse looked as though he were about to say more, but the five-minute signal rang. The *Hermes* used an electronic chime quite different from the *Sissie's* solid brass bell. Though this was a perfectly good signal in its own right, Adele's face froze with irritation every time she heard it.

She smiled in reaction. On the other hand, she'd gotten used to greater changes in the past.

"Mister Pasternak, bring the thrusters to sixty-percent flow but keep them open," Slidell ordered. *"Ship, this is the Captain. Close all hatches, repeat, close all hatches. Captain out."*

Ganse stared at his display, his left hand dancing across the number pad by practiced reflex. *"Ship, all hatches are closed,"* he announced. Adele heard the words in her helmet earphones a heartbeat before they reached her through the air. *"Battle Center out."*

The thrusters roared into the pool, buoying the tender on a pillow of steam. Because the nozzles were flared, the plasma dissipated instead of trying to lift the ship into the air as the present flow might do if concentrated.

By now Adele knew that it was better to close the nozzles with the thrusters already at high output than to lift on rising output, since the nozzle petals were more uniform than the feed pipes might be. She knew quite a lot about how an RCN warship should operate, because she'd spent years aboard one of the best. . . .

Ganse looked toward her again. "Ah . . ." he said. "I suppose you've heard about the mutiny on the *Bainbridge*? Well, of course you have. Everybody has."

"Yes, but gossip doesn't interest me, Lieutenant," Adele said with a frown. She returned her eyes to her own display. *Unless my duties require me to be interested, of course.*

Adele monitored traffic throughout Harbor Three. Since the ionized exhaust washed across the radio frequency bands, that meant tapping the harbor's modulated laser transponders and decoding the downloads . . . which she and her equipment did very handily. The results were of no significance, but the practice would stand her in good stead at future, more dangerous, times.

"It isn't what people are saying!" Ganse blurted. "The Captain was being careful and he had a right to be careful. The *Bainbridge* is a very small ship. There was no way to be sure other plotters wouldn't have freed the three we had in irons and taken over the ship still."

"*Cutter crews, prepare for liftoff,*" Captain Slidell said. The cutters *were* fully prepared, of course, because Adele had chosen to pipe the tender's general communications to them from the first. Insets across the top of her display gave her miniature panoramas of the interior of the six small vessels.

"You understand that, don't you?" Ganse begged.

Adele looked at him. That was a direct question, so she couldn't ignore it. She'd give a good deal to know who Ganse thought he was talking to, though. Lieutenant Leary's friend? Mistress Sand's agent? Or some third thing his mind and his despair had invented? He certainly wouldn't have been talking this way to the warrant officer in charge of the *Hermes'* communications.

"Lieutenant Ganse," she said, "I understand that you believe . . ."

Her voice trailed off. Because she was Adele Mundy, she wouldn't speak a near truth that was a lie. She looked Ganse in the eye and said, rephrasing the statement, "I understand that you believed the executions were necessary at the time they occurred. I don't know what you believe now, nor do I care."

"Ship, this is the Captain," Slidell said. *"We are lifting off. Out!"*

The roar of the thrusters redoubled; Adele felt acceleration begin to weigh her body.

"Next stop, Nikitin!" Hogg called cheerfully.

Adele wasn't quite sure, but she thought that despite the thunder she heard Tovera's cool voice reply, "For some of us, anyway."

CHAPTER 9

Above Nikitin

The environmental system moaned as it ventilated the
Battle Direction Center, and the consoles themselves
whirred and squeaked. Even so, the *Hermes* was as
quiet as an operational starship ever got.

Adele paid no attention to Nikitin, the planet they
were orbiting, beyond noting that it was a glowing
blue ball of ocean dotted with islands. That was true
of many of the worlds where the RCN based its outlying fleets.

Sea worlds made it easy to refill tanks with reaction mass—any liquid would do, though water was
ideal—but that was a relatively minor consideration.
Broad seas gave a ship with mechanical problems a
wide variety of places to land safely: thrust reflect-
ing from hard ground created dangerous turbulence
in the instant before touchdown, the last thing the
captain of a vessel with a clogged feedline or cracked
nozzles wanted.

And if things went wrong anyway, a ship crashing

into the ocean was less likely to fling dangerous debris into the port facilities than one hitting the land. Naval planners had to include that possibility in their considerations also.

"*Very* satisfactory for a shakedown cruise," Daniel said. He lifted his helmet and rubbed his fingers through his fine blond hair with a pleased expression. "Aside from those three seventy-foot spars fracturing at the central weld, that is, and that just meant we had to fish the others from that batch."

Adele suspected that he would've been disappointed if nothing had gone wrong during the voyage. Daniel wasn't the sort to stir up trouble where there wasn't any, but he always seemed just a touch more alive when there was a serious problem to solve.

Her mouth quirked into her familiar wry grin. Daniel had certainly chosen a profession to suit his temperament, because an RCN officer was rarely faced with a shortage of life-threatening situations. Nor, she'd noticed, was a librarian who chose to accompany Lieutenant Daniel Leary.

As a vessel newly arrived over Nikitin, the *Hermes* remained in unpowered orbit until Planetary Control in Sinmary Port cleared them to land. Because Nikitin was a major naval base, an orbital minefield of X-ray lasers pumped by fusion bombs protected it. They'd automatically destroy any vessel that did anything but float in orbit till Planetary Control vetted it and gave permission.

Adele disliked weightlessness a great deal. The *Hermes* would probably be cleared to land in a half hour or so, but to fill the gap she threw herself into the mass of information which a new planet offered her. So long as Adele's mind was occupied, she didn't care—didn't *know*—what her body was doing.

Several data strands combined into something extraordinary. "Daniel," she said, ignoring his cheerful prattle. "The *Cornelwood*'s been damaged. That's the—"

"Good God!" said Daniel. *"That's the flagship of the Gold Dust Squadron! Was she attacked?"*

Although she and Daniel were at adjacent consoles, Adele had spoken over the intercom connection she'd set up for the two of them alone. She was using her console's sound-cancelling feature to prevent anyone nearby from hearing her words directly.

Peeker, the engineer's mate, a gunner's mate named Enescue, and two midshipmen were at the other consoles. The remaining three midshipmen sat on jumpseats along with Hogg and Tovera. Adele didn't mind the others knowing the information she was providing to Daniel, but she didn't want to advertise to them that *she* had learned it. Based on the way Lieutenant Ganse had talked, there were already too many rumors regarding Mistress Adele Mundy going around.

"No, it seems to have been an accident," Adele said, sorting as she spoke. "On landing after returning from Haislip Prime . . ."

Her control wands flickered through reams of extraneous data as if she were a miner clearing overburden. Recent communications—and there was an enormous volume of them; most of the base traffic for the past three days was devoted to the subject—dealt with salvage and repair. Getting back to the cause of the trouble was unexpectedly difficult.

"Yes, I see!" Daniel said. Sinmary Port was directly below the *Hermes* at this stage of her orbit. Daniel

had switched his display—echoed in miniature on Adele's—to a real-time image of the harbor, then magnified it till a single large vessel completely filled the field. "*She's sunk on her port side. The outrigger must've ruptured, but there should've been at least six separate compartments. . . .*"

His fingers hammered commands into his console's virtual keyboard. *You could've asked me to find the information*, Adele thought in momentary annoyance—and caught herself with a grin of self-awareness.

And so he could have, but on this particular point Daniel was faster than she'd have been searching for data which to her was unfamiliar. He'd simply highlighted the vessel half-sunk in the natural harbor and called up design particulars with a keystroke.

"*Right, ten sealed compartments in each float,*" Daniel said with satisfaction. "*It should've been that many for a heavy cruiser, but the Tree Class has enough other design problems that I wouldn't have sworn they hadn't skimped on safety measures. How in hell did they manage to lose integrity on the port side almost completely?*"

"There!" Adele said. She'd finally gotten to the correct file in the archives of Squadron HQ. It was classified, which didn't keep her out, but it'd kept the location from appearing during her initial data search. "A thruster nozzle burst as they were coming down."

There was even imagery of the accident, taken by automatic cameras in the harbor and on the cruiser's underside to aid investigation of situations just like this one. At one moment the vessel's thrusters were all spewing rainbow jets of plasma. In the next, a nozzle midway along the vessel's port side blew into glowing tungsten shards.

"*Ah!*" Daniel said as he watched the archival feed. "*What bad luck . . . though I* would *say they were coming in rather hot.*"

Plasma-streaked steam enveloped the image of the *Cornelwood*, smothering the ship's own cameras and those of the port facilities as well. The present file was optical only, which was probably sufficient; but being who she was, Adele reminded herself to look for microwave or sonic imagery as soon as she had a moment.

The *Cornelwood* splashed into the harbor and reappeared, bobbing violently as the curtain of steam cleared. To the distant cameras she was obviously listing to port; the ship's own imagery showed rips in the port pontoon until they sank beneath the surface. The nozzle had burst like a bomb, riddling the whole length of the float.

The other portside thrusters were still glowing from what'd probably been overload to counteract the cruiser's too-swift descent. They cracked one after another in gushes of steam as they dipped into the water. Their failure wasn't violent enough to damage the float further, but it was already a total loss.

The images from the *Cornelwood*'s cameras went black. Their mechanisms were sealed against worse environments than this, but they couldn't see through harbor scum.

"*What* very *bad luck,*" Daniel repeated, this time in a tone of wondering amazement. "*Raising and refitting her's going to take the whole port establishment, so we'll have to do all our own repairs.*"

"Should we report this to the Captain?" Adele

said. If Daniel had been in command, the answer would've been, "Yes, of course!" but Daniel *wasn't* in command.

"*We should, but I'm afraid he'd think we were boasting,*" Daniel said, voicing Adele's own thought. "*He'll be informed by the port authorities as soon as we're on the ground, so—*"

"*Sir?*" said Midshipman Vesey on a BDC-only channel. "*There's something wrong with the flagship. She's too deep on the port side, and there's barges around her in the water, over.*"

Though Vesey was in a jump seat, gathering data through her helmet display, she'd seen what Bragg and Cory at the consoles had missed. Her partner Dorst was viewing a signal imported from her helmet—Adele checked by reflex—but Blantyre beside them was searching for the image with her mouth set in a grim line.

"*Roger, Vesey,*" Daniel said, winking at Adele. "*Break, Captain this is Leary. Midshipman Vesey has noticed that the flagship is half-submerged. Salvage appears to be in progress. Over.*"

After a moment, Slidell's voice replied, "*Roger, Mister Leary. It looks like we'll have to handle our own refit, and I wouldn't wonder if they drafted some of our crew for their project as well. My regards to Mistress Vesey; that's the sort of observation that the RCN needs. Out.*"

Without asking permission, Adele clipped Captain Slidell's comment and relayed it to Vesey. The midshipman straightened in her seat, beaming like an angel.

"*Sir?*" Vesey said. "*You've got experience lifting a ship with another ship, and they're certainly not going to get the cruiser up any other way. Over.*"

"*We'll see what my superior officers wish, Vesey,*" Daniel said. He grinned at Adele and added over their private channel, "*Though from my viewpoint, it'd be rather a vacation not to be directly under Commander Slidell's eye the way I've been during the past seventeen days!*"

Daniel, wearing his best 2nd Class uniform with a saucer hat instead of a commo helmet, stood in the entry hold. To his left was Captain Slidell, to his right the five midshipmen in declining order of seniority. Lieutenant Ganse remained on the bridge as duty officer—the traditional place of the junior lieutenant at a new landfall.

Neither Pasternak nor Woetjans, the Chiefs of Ship and Rig respectively, were present. A crew of six techs under Brouwer, a Senior Mechanic from the *Bainbridge*, were in the hold with a large toolchest, but they weren't members of the party waiting to greet the delegation from the port establishment and the staff of Admiral Milne, who'd come aboard as soon as the slip cooled enough.

"*It seems quite idyllic,*" Adele said through the miniature phone in the canal of Daniel's left ear. He couldn't respond, of course, but it was nice to have her coolly chatty presence as he wasted time in an uncomfortable fashion. "*There're trees up to eighty feet over all the islands that I've checked, except where colonists have cleared them. The flowers are striking, so I suppose you'll have plenty of new animals to observe too.*"

Daniel smiled; so long as his First Lieutenant held himself at Parade Rest, Captain Slidell couldn't complain that his mouth had quirked. Adele wasn't any more interested in flowers than she was in manufacturers of plasma thrusters. They and most of the rest of the world about her were bits of data to be stored and classified, generally at the whim of someone else.

Hydraulic pumps whined, forcing the main hatch open for the first time since the *Hermes* closed up on Cinnabar. It squealed loudly: metal surfaces have a tendency to migrate in vacuum, so the hatch and its coaming had grown minusculely together during the voyage. Steam and a hint of strange spices curled in as the ramp lowered.

"Another bloody hellhole," a tech muttered. "It seems it's always a jungle or a bloody glacier. How's about a nice city some time?"

The senior mechanic caught Captain Slidell's glare. He muttered, "Belt up, Murtagh."

It wasn't that Adele didn't have personal interests—she could discuss books and manuscripts with as much enthusiasm as anyone in the human universe. But so far as Daniel could tell, most of his friend's attention went into what she could do for others.

He smiled again, then let the expression fade. That made Adele Mundy sound like a saint . . . which in an odd fashion she might be. A fashion that included the pistol in her pocket, and the cold certainty with which she used it at need.

The ramp squawled, then stuck halfway. "Coop and Filippa, get the number three jack, and you get the heavy hammer, Murtagh!" Brouwer snapped. He and his team rushed to the jammed lower hinge. Captain Slidell scowled, then seemed to relax.

"The islands are made by coraline algae," Adele continued. *"Plants that form limestone."*

She paused, then continued, *"Hmm. The algae grows from the top, but the mats reach down as the lower portions die. If they touch the bottom, they form islands. I'd never heard of anything like that."*

Nor had Daniel, and it gave him something interesting to ponder while he waited silently. He understood the need for drill and ceremony. He'd never be much good at it, but he wouldn't be a good engineering officer either; that wasn't the problem. It simply didn't seem to him that the landing of a tender at a distant station was a proper venue for formality.

"I got it, chief!" Murtagh said. "Gimme room, just gimme some bloody—"

The rest of Brouwer's team leaned or stepped backward, depending on where they stood. Murtagh brought the sledge around in a three-quarter's circle that ended in a bell-like *whang-g-g*. The ramp jumped, then settled into smooth downward movement till it squelched into the ground at the edge of the slip. The maintenance crew moved out of the way with murmurs of satisfaction.

Murtagh and the rest of the team Brouwer had chosen for the present duty were former Bridgies. From what Daniel had seen during the voyage—and now—they knew their business. He'd have been happier if Brouwer had integrated his crew, though, the way Woetjans had done with her rigging watches.

The last of the eddying steam cleared, leaving a familiar stench of baked loam that would linger for days. The slips of Sinmary Port were of natural earth rather than being concrete lined, so volumes of organic compounds burned when plasma vaporized the water they were suspended in.

The two lieutenants waiting on the quay sauntered up the ramp. One wore utilities, while the other was in Grays but with no decorations except the scarlet collar flash of a staff officer. There was no sign of the formal greeting party Captain Slidell had obviously expected.

"Commander Slidell?" the man in Grays said cheerfully. "I'm Sloan Pontefract, Admiral Milne's Flag Lieutenant. The Admiral sent me to invite you to tea this afternoon, say seventeen hundred local. She served with your wife's father and brother, perhaps you know."

Pontefract took in the spectacle of the *Hermes'* officers standing in line at Parade Rest. He halted at the head of the ramp and threw Slidell a salute which was razor sharp despite being clearly off-hand.

"I'm sorry, sir," he said. "We don't stand on ceremony much here in the back of beyond. No offense intended, I assure you."

Slidell returned the salute. "None taken, of course," he said grudgingly. He turned to Daniel and snapped, "All right, Leary. You and the midshipmen are dismissed."

"Commander?" said the other lieutenant. "I'm Farschenning from the port office. I'm afraid the facilities here are rather stretched at the moment as we've had a bit of an emergency. If you need repairs, I'm afraid they'll have to wait—unless your own complement can carry them out, of course?"

"We noticed the flagship's situation," Slidell said. "How in the name of heaven did something like that happen?"

Farschenning and Pontefract exchanged glances. Farschenning pursed his lips and said, "Bit of a disputed question, Commander. Some think the thrusters were overstressed, while others believe that yard maintenance here at Sinmary Port may have been to blame. And of course some times you have bad luck. That's perhaps the most likely explanation, though of course there'll have to be a Navy Office inquiry to get to the bottom of the matter."

Daniel kept a neutral expression as he considered Farschenning's careful statement. Squadron command and the base establishment—which reported to the Bureau of Material on Xenos, not to Admiral Milne—had started out by blaming one another for an event which'd been just short of disastrous. The likely result of such a public brawl would be half a dozen people forced into retirement for negligence or worse.

Cooler heads seemed to have prevailed, though. The parties were uniting to claim an Act of God that'd save everybody's career.

"The major problem now is to lift the *Cornelwood* so we can repair her," Farschenning continued. "The, ah, repercussions from the accident will be easier to deal with if the damage is repaired."

Lieutenant Pontefract nodded grimly. "The *Cornelwood*'s the only real *combat* unit in the squadron, you see," he said, admitting what Daniel had noticed when he first he looked at the ship-list for the Gold Dust Squadron. "Oh, I don't mean the others aren't warships, but they're a frigate and patrol cruisers configured for station-keeping and landing operations. Or your tender, Commander. All very well for chasing pirates or pulling civilians off Yang when they're having another of their bloody revolutions—"

"Bloody is right," muttered Farschenning. "The poor

devils in the *Garnet* got the job of dealing with the savages this time. I don't envy them."

"—but not for slugging it out with other warships," Pontefract went on. He'd paused, nodding agreement while Farschenning spoke. "Of course that's not likely to happen since the Alliance doesn't have any bases within thirty days of here, but not having the capacity would . . ."

He rolled his palms upward with an apologetic smile rather than put the rest of his thought into words. Daniel could finish the sentence easily: a squadron commander whose error degraded his force below the level required to face a putative enemy could expect to be recalled if not cashiered when Xenos heard about it.

"Yes, a very difficult situation," Slidell said, pursing his lips and nodding. "We've got a variety of problems to deal with—the *Hermes* is directly out of the builders' hands, you see—but I understand your priorities."

He gave the two station officers a wintry smile and went on with the closest thing to a joke that Daniel had heard from the Commander: "I even agree with them, though I doubt Admiral Milne was concerned about whether I did or not."

"You'll have to lift the *Cornelwood* on the thrust of another ship attached by cables, won't you, sir?" Vesey said to Lieutenant Farschenning. "The only alternative's to drain the slip, and the mud bottom makes that problematic."

Daniel looked at Vesey in surprise. The midshipmen had remained to listen to the station officers, standing with polite informality. That was perfectly proper—their primary duty was to learn the business of a commissioned officer before they themselves received commissions—but they weren't expected to take part in discussions unasked.

"We'd come to that conclusion, yes," Farschenning said, his eyes slightly narrowed but his tone polite. Vesey's observation had been both insightful and accurate, after all. "You're welcome to observe—"

He nodded to Slidell.

"—if your commanding officer approves, of course."

"You see, sir . . ." said Midshipman Dorst. He was a big, extremely fit young man. Vesey could spot him quite a few IQ points and still come out ahead, but Dorst never hesitated to put himself between others and trouble. The RCN needed officers like that as well as clever ones, and there were few better than Dorst. "Lieutenant Leary has personal experience with using one ship to lift another. He did it on Morzanga."

The station officers stared at Daniel. Captain Slidell turned, his eyes flicking from Dorst to Daniel and his lips forming a tight line.

"Good God!" Pontefract blurted. "You're *that* Leary? Leary of the *Princess Cicily*?"

Daniel nodded curtly. "The *Princess Cecile*," he said, "but yes. I don't think the business on Morzanga makes me an expert, though. That was very much a matter of 'needs must when the devil drives,' I assure you."

"Well, you're certainly the closest thing to an expert on Nikitin right now!" Lieutenant Farschenning said. "This is very good luck indeed. But what are you doing on . . ."

He caught himself with a guilty look at Commander Slidell. The rest of his sentence was just as clear as

Pontefract's unspoken discussion of how the *Cornelwood* was damaged: what's a dashing officer like you doing as First Lieutenant of a tub?

"I can't speak for the Navy Office's reasons," Daniel said to cover the embarrassment. *Can't speak in public, at any rate*. "But my service has been primarily on a single vessel, and I'm learning a great deal on the *Hermes*. If I'm assigned to cutter operations—"

He gave Slidell a deferential nod. The Captain preserved a stony silence.

"—then I'll have a chance to hone my ship-handling skills in still another fashion."

"Well, it's certainly good luck for the Gold Dust Squadron," Pontefract said. "Leary, I'm sure you'll be receiving orders assigning you to the project as soon as I get back to Squadron House."

He glanced at Slidell and flashed a wry grin. "I'm sorry about snatching your First Lieutenant away when you've got refitting of your own to do, sir," he said, "but you understand the priorities."

"Indeed I do, Lieutenant," Slidell said with heavy sarcasm. "I trust the *Hermes* will somehow manage without the remarkable Lieutenant Leary."

The station lieutenants exchanged puzzled glances. Daniel kept his face expressionless. He was glad to see the midshipmen did also.

"Well . . ." said Farschenning. "We'll take our leave, sir. Send in your supply requests and we'll fill them as quickly as we can."

"And don't forget the Admiral's invitation, Commander," said Pontefract. "She's looking forward to seeing you again."

He threw Slidell another sharp salute. It looked easy

when he did it; Daniel always felt that he'd grown an extra elbow when he tried.

"Indeed," said Captain Slidell as he returned the salute. "Perhaps the Admiral and I can discuss priorities."

Daniel returned to Parade Rest, waiting for what Slidell would say when the station officers were out of earshot. In fact the Captain said nothing, only turned on his heel and stalked up the companionway toward the bridge on A Deck.

Daniel looked at the midshipmen. Both Vesey and Dorst wore broad smiles. And after a moment, Daniel smiled back.

CHAPTER 10

Sinmary Port on Nikitin

"Stop here, Hogg," Daniel said when he realized that otherwise they'd drive straight through the swamp to the group overseeing salvage operations on the *Cornelwood*. The utility vehicle from the *Hermes* had six broad wheels. It'd likely get to the other side, but that'd mean chewing up the narrow pedestrian way and drenching the officers with muddy water.

One of those present was Captain Molliman, the Port Commander. At the very best irritating him wouldn't speed the supply of food and spares to the *Hermes* . . . which in turn wouldn't improve Captain Slidell's opinion of his First Lieutenant.

Hogg pulled around in a tight circle so that the vehicle's blunt cab faced the road back to the *Hermes'* slip. "All around the barn to get here, and we could *see* the sucker before we started," he grumbled to Daniel beside him. "Why'd they design the port like this?"

"Well, they didn't, Hogg," Daniel said mildly. From the air all the islands dotting Nikitin's equatorial ocean—not just Sinmary—looked like games of dominoes. Straight lines branched at ninety degrees and sometimes formed tee intersections with one another, creating messy sprawls in the shallow seas. "This is how the algae grows, and the site planners simply used what they found."

He glanced over the dozens of other vehicles already at the site. Most were cargo-carrying hovercraft, pulled up on the quays framing the slip, but there were a number of aircars also.

A pair of barges were anchored beside the listing *Cornelwood* to receive heavy stores through its hatches. The cruiser's 13,000-ton bulk dwarfed the low-lying surface craft.

"Besides, it looks as though the locals use water transport," Daniel added. "Be thankful the *Hermes* had a truck and we didn't have to walk."

"Aye, the pig," Hogg agreed, if it was really agreement.

Woetjans and the squad of riggers in the bed of the truck were out before Hogg had shut down the multi-fuel turbine. "Now keep civil, you lot," she thundered. "You're Mister Leary's Sissies and so the best in the RCN, but this is somebody else's turf. We're to help as we're asked to, not to take the job over ourself."

Daniel sighed. The bosun had just given good advice to her crew, senior people who'd worked on Morzanga. It was a pity she'd bellowed it in a voice that everyone in the slip must've heard.

"I'll lead, if you please, Woetjans," Daniel said, stepping to the truck's running board. He hesitated before dropping the remaining thirty inches to the ground.

He could've jumped to the ground, of course, but from the look of the soil he'd probably have sunk in to his ankles. Chances were he'd get muddy enough in the course of things—quite a number of people were working in the water, and Daniel wasn't one to stay comfortable while his subordinates did dirty, dangerous jobs. Still, it was better to introduce yourself to senior officers in a clean uniform.

Sinmary looked extremely flat from orbit . . . and so it was, no more than a twenty-foot drop from the spine of the jagged island to the shore of the almost-tideless sea. Because of the vegetation, though, sight distances were short except over water. The trees had trunks like inverted bells to catch rainwater, circled by diadems of foliage. They covered the equatorial islands. On Sinmary there'd been no effort to clear them except to build base facilities and the residences of the planters.

According to the *Sailing Directions*, Nikitin did a considerable business in fresh fruits and vegetables grown for nearby stars which in turn produced anti-aging drugs. Hundreds of nearby islands were under cultivation, but most of the wealthy landlords had a colony on the North Coast of Sinmary and commuted by aircar instead of living in scattered isolation on their estates.

The island-forming algae itself provided the ground cover. It trapped rain like the trees, in its case by creating rectangles whose edges threw up membranous sheets on calcite stiffeners. The organic portion decayed nightly to slush and was replaced the next morning. Where the island's surface wasn't tree roots or artificial, it was generally a bog.

Daniel started toward the officers. Beryllium mono-crystal woven into a coarse mesh formed a walkway with a natural non-skid surface. The same material was used for catwalks connecting starships to quays beyond reach of their boarding ramps, but here it was supported on pilings rather than pontoons. Though immensely strong, the yard-wide ribbon bobbed and swayed under Daniel's weight as if it'd been floating.

Lieutenant Farschenning looked over his shoulder as Daniel approached. He called cheerfully, "Here's Leary now, Captain. And it looks like Slidell was able to spare some of his riggers after all."

Daniel managed not to grin. He'd been on the bridge when the two messages came in, so he knew exactly what'd happened. When Slidell opened the message from the Port Commander's office, he'd snapped, "No, of course I can't spare riggers if I'm to make the *Hermes* ready without any help from the dockyard staff! And if Molliman thinks he can order me, I'll remind him that I'm not in his chain of command."

The second message was from Admiral Milne. Slidell stared at it expressionlessly, then said, "Mister Leary, direct the bosun to pick a squad of riggers who were with her on Morzanga and accompany you to the salvage site. Dismissed!"

The officers were standing on the concrete top of the quay. Through cracks in it rose ankle-high membranes of shimmering algae, some of them recently trampled down. Earth, compressed with a plasticizer, made a better surface for any purpose that didn't involve high heat because it was more resilient. The construction engineers hadn't used it on Nikitin because lime for concrete was readily available, while the closest thing to dirt was the gooey organic sludge from decayed algae.

Daniel halted a pace from Captain Molliman and saluted, saying, "Sir! Lieutenant Leary and twelve riggers reporting as ordered."

"Yes, yes, Leary, and we're glad to have you," said Molliman. He looked at the enlisted personnel, squinting to read the bosun's name tape. "Glad to have you too, Woetjans," he went on. "Report to Senior Chief Takami on Barge 73—if he isn't in the *Corny*, I mean. We're lightening ship at the moment, mostly lift and carry."

"Aye aye, sir!" Woetjans said. "We'll take one of the little skimmers if we may?"

"What?" said Molliman. He waved the Sissies toward the surface-effect vehicles pulled up at a slant nearby. "Oh, right, you're on foot."

He returned his attention to Daniel. Molliman was an overweight man of fifty with a limp and a built-up sole on his right boot. He couldn't have gotten through the Academy with that physical impairment, so it must be a service-incurred disability—and the reason he was now in a desk job.

"Be a good chap, Leary," he said. "Don't keep making people salute, eh? This isn't Xenos."

Daniel flashed an apologetic smile in reply.

"We're all glad to see you, Lieutenant," said a man in his early thirties, one of the two lieutenant commanders in the group. Nodding to the other LTC, a woman a few years older, he went on, "Tooney and I have been talking about how we'd manage the lift.

She's got the *Cutlass*, I'm Peggs of the *Chrysoberyl*. And I'll tell you frankly, Leary, I'm glad you know how to do it. Because neither of *us* think it's possible."

The challenge in Peggs' tone was mild and so far as Daniel was concerned perfectly justified. Nobody enjoys being told an outsider—and a junior besides—says he can do what you can't. Nonetheless, Peggs wasn't flatly hostile to the notion.

"You're related to Commander Bergen, Leary?" Tooney asked.

"My uncle, sir," Daniel said, nodding.

Tooney shrugged to Peggs. "I served with the Commander," she said. "There's nothing God could do with a ship that he couldn't, in the Matrix or in a gravity well, either one."

She fixed Daniel with her eyes again. Tooney's face was thin and ascetic; it reminded Daniel not a little of Adele Mundy. "I'm willing to learn anything you can teach me about the business, Leary," she said. "And if you want to take the controls yourself, I won't fight you for the honor."

"With respect, Commander," Daniel said, "I don't believe it *is* possible to lift the *Cornelwood* that way. Certainly not with me at the controls of an unfamiliar ship. I pride myself on my ship-handling, to be sure—"

He quirked a grin at the local officers. He wasn't going to pretend false humility, because the truth would make his point much better.

"—but I'd had years with the *Sissie* and knew her quirks. More important, though, the freighter I righted was on dry land and didn't weigh half what a heavy cruiser does, even if you manage to gut her down to the hull. I don't believe any practical net of cables can survive sufficient thrust to bring the sunken outrigger to the surface."

The local officers looked at one another. Farschenning and the other two lieutenants kept blank faces, but the lieutenant commanders began to smile. Molliman wore a look of grim satisfaction.

"Well, I shouldn't say it, Leary," Peggs said, obviously speaking for all of them, "because I'd like to see the *Corny* back in service ASAP . . . but I was a little concerned that somebody else thought he could succeed at what I expected t' be a disaster if I tried it."

"Somebody who didn't talk through his hat, you understand," Tooney added. "We know the Gold Dust Cluster is out in the sticks, but even here we've heard about you, Leary."

"That leaves us the problem of righting the cruiser, though," Captain Molliman said glumly. "And don't say build a coffer dam, drain the slip, and jack up the hull—because the bottom of the slip won't bear the weight. It's porous limestone and less than ten feet thick. And under that is three hundred feet of sea-water, which isn't much of a help."

"A reputation's like a snowball, sir," Daniel said, nodding to Tooney. "It gets bigger the farther it gets from where it started. But Captain? I think there *is* a trick that might work."

"Well, I'd like to hear it," Molliman said, his eyes narrowing. "And I hope it doesn't require sacrificing a black goat or something. Mind, I don't say I wouldn't do it."

He flashed Daniel a wry smile. It struck Daniel that Molliman knew perfectly well that his career was seriously at risk, but he'd managed to remain professional when many officers would either be ranting or drinking themselves into oblivion.

"I've compared site imagery with as-built drawings of the other ships available," Daniel said. "The *Cutlass* has too wide a footprint by several yards, but there's room for either of the Jewel Class cruisers to fit in the slip alongside the *Cornelwood* as she lies. That's the *Chrysoberyl*, or the *Garnet*, which I gather's due back from Yang momentarily?"

"Mister Leary," Peggs said, his tone quiet but full of amazement, "I couldn't possibly land *Chrissie* beside the *Corny* there without winding up on top of her in the surface eddies. I couldn't, God couldn't, and I very much doubt you could either."

"And even if you could," Molliman said, frowning but not angry, "the exhaust'd hammer the cruiser to a wreck. We've got enough problems already with water damage."

"We'd planned to have the lifting vessel in the next slip," Tooney said. "That way the quay protects the *Corny* from the blast."

"I believe the *Chrysoberyl*—" Daniel bobbed his head toward Peggs "—can be towed into the slip by liftoff tugs if you have them here—"

"We don't," said Molliman, "but—"

"—or winches, maybe anchored on other ships," Daniel continued. In the enthusiasm of the success he saw looming, he'd just cut off an officer three pay grades higher than his. Right now they were talking as peers, and the Port Commander was at least equally excited. "And *then* tie her to the *Cornelwood* and float her up gently instead of jerking her with the thrusters—"

"Wait, wait!" Tooney said. "It won't work, a patrol cruiser doesn't have enough excess buoyancy to lift a heavy cruiser. But—"

"We can get the top of the outrigger above the surface," Molliman said, drawing his engineering calculator from its belt holster. Daniel had already done the calculations. It'd be close, but still on the right side. "Patch the holes there, blow in air and lift to the next holes, then do the same. If we can return two more compartments to integrity, we've got it. We've got the bitch!"

A thrumming in the high sky made them all look up, slipping their goggles or—those who were wearing helmets—visors down to protect their eyes from the actinics in plasma exhaust. It was a moderate-sized vessel; Daniel reached up to boost his goggles' magnification, then caught himself with a grin and said, "A freighter? Or is this the *Garnet*?"

Molliman was talking over the radio, his voice blanked by his helmet's noise-cancelling feature. He raised his visor again and said, "It's the *Garnet*. I was just making sure they'd been assigned a slip at the east end of the harbor. They left for Yang three days before this happened—"

He nodded grimly to the *Cornelwood*.

"—and might just drop into their usual berth, Slip 12, right the other side of the cruiser."

"My *Chrissie*'s up for the next run to Yang," Tooney said to Peggs with a grin, "but if we're going to be lashed to the *Corny*, I guess you'd better start plotting a course, Peggs."

"As if I don't have it memorized," Peggs muttered, shaking his head. "Well, your turn in the barrel'll come up soon enough, Tooney. Yang's not going to settle down any time soon. We ought to station a ship there permanently. Of course she'd have to stay in orbit the whole time, because otherwise the whole crew'd desert and hop freighters off-planet."

"I'd resign my commission if I got that assignment," said one of the lieutenants, speaking for the first time. "A week at a time's bad enough."

"What's so awful about Yang?" Daniel asked. "And besides, it's not a Cinnabar dependency, is it? What're we doing there?"

"Wasting our time, mostly," Tooney said. "Cinnabar citizens *will* go there—mostly citizens from client worlds here in the Cluster, but according to the Ministry of External Affairs they're owed the same protection as a Senator from Xenos. Only Senators have better sense 'n to go to Yang."

"And as for what's wrong," said another of the lieutenants, "you can take your pick. The women, the water, the food, the liquor—they'll all kill you, sometimes faster, sometimes slower."

His name-tape read Teiro, the name Daniel vaguely recalled for the First Lieutenant of the *Cutlass*. The *Cornelwood*'s own officers must be aboard their vessel directing the sensitive internal aspects of the salvage while external matters were under the control of the Port Commander.

"I'd say they were all pigs on Yang," said Farschenning, "but my family kept pigs back on Cinnabar. The people on Yang don't measure up to pig standards. They got their independence from the Alliance eighty years ago and it's been downhill ever since."

"Independence?" Daniel repeated incredulously. "The

Alliance doesn't let anybody go. Guarantor Porra's bad, but he's not much worse than any of his predecessors. The only way a planet leaves the Alliance of Free Stars is for Cinnabar to pry it loose."

He chuckled. "And we're not in the habit of letting our valued allies change their minds either, I'll admit," he added.

Captain Molliman grunted. "Yang was an exception," he said. "There's anywhere between twelve and twenty clans on Yang. They each think they ought to be running the planet, and the only thing they agree on is killing whoever says he's in charge. Usually that's whichever clan says it's on top, but so long as there was Alliance troops on the planet *everybody* shot at 'em. It didn't pay, not a tenth the cost. Things hadn't changed in a century and they weren't going to change in another century."

He shrugged. "Nor has it," he added. "Not in eighty years, anyhow."

Peggs nodded agreement. "There's money to be made on Yang," he said forcefully. "Not so much anti-aging compounds but other drugs. Which means you can always hire enough guns and shooters to say you're a popular revolution."

"The local hash'll lift the brain outa your skull and put it in orbit," Lieutenant Teiro said. Everybody looked at him. He wetted his suddenly-dry lips with his tongue and added, "That is, you hear that."

The *Garnet* settled into a slip at the far end of the harbor. The snarl of the thrusters merged with and smothered the thunder of steam lifting as an incandescent plume from the water. Talk paused while the low-frequency roar echoed over the harbor's surface.

"And of course nobody on Xenos has the faintest

idea what the place is really like," Tooney said bitterly when it stilled. "As far as that goes, the Navy Office is as bad as External Affairs."

"Watch it!" said Peggs, looking past Tooney's shoulder toward the northeast. A large aircar had curved out over the open sea to avoid the *Garnet*; now it arrowed toward the *Cornelwood*'s slip.

Catching Daniel's eye Peggs continued in a murmur, "That'll be Admiral Milne bringing some of her local friends to see how the job's coming. She spends a lot of time with the planters when the squadron's in Sinmary Port."

Peggs' tone was neutral, and the words weren't criticism on their face. Given that they came from an RCN officer talking about another RCN officer, the statement was implicitly damning. The rest of those present were nodding agreement.

The aircar landed twenty feet down the quay from the group of salvage officers; a gust of wind plastered Daniel's utilities against his body before the driver, an RCN enlisted man in Grays, feathered his fans. He was the only person aboard in uniform.

Daniel hadn't met Admiral Milne, a beefy, frog-faced woman in her sixties, but she was easy to identify from imagery even though she now wore a trousered suit with broad vertical stripes. Verticals were a good idea for the Admiral's build, but the lemon and fuchsia stripes were not.

The car's six passengers formed three couples, though the striking thirty-ish man in the middle seat with the Admiral certainly wasn't her husband. As the newcomers got out of the vehicle, Daniel whispered to the local officers, "Should I salute?"

According to regulations, the answer was simple: you didn't salute unless both you and the other party were in uniform. Admirals were likely to think their whims were the word of God, and in outlying stations like Nikitin there was nobody to tell them they were wrong. Daniel couldn't guess how Milne would react.

"I'll take care of it," Molliman muttered. He stepped forward, putting himself between the others and Milne's contingent. Raising his voice he said, "Admiral, good to see you. I think we have an answer to the problem of raising the *Cornelwood* safely. Lieutenant Leary from the *Hermes*, here—"

He gestured.

"—has been quite helpful."

"I've heard of Leary," Milne growled, eyeing Daniel but pointedly not speaking to him. "I'd advise you to be careful, Molliman. The trouble with these lucky ones is that when their luck finally goes sour—and it always does!—you have to look sharp not to be caught in the same bloody smash."

Daniel kept his lips in a mild, slightly vacuous, smile. He had enemies in the service; anybody did if his career wasn't as bland and colorless as tapioca pudding. Daniel had never had contact with Admiral Milne, but she'd obviously met some of those enemies. There was nothing for it but keep his mouth shut and his face pleasant.

It was possible that the particular enemy Milne had talked to was Commander Slidell. Well, worse things happen in wartime. . . .

"The Tylers," Milne said, gesturing to the couple from the back of the aircar in a grudging effort at introductions on her part. The wife was half the age of her husband and dressed in what'd been Xenos fashion in the recent past.

The other couple wore matching jumpsuits of shiny aquamarine fabric. Milne nodded to them. Daniel couldn't imagine where the outfits came from, though the effect rather pleased him. "And the Vallevas. And this is Master Mondreaux, of course."

The young man at her side gave Daniel, presumably the only stranger, a nod that was almost a bow. Mondreaux dressed like a fop, with ruffs at throat and wrists; but he moved gracefully, and the muscles under his even tan were firm.

He looked to the side and said, "Ah, I see that Lady Raynham has decided to come after all. She and her daughter Geneva both hoped to meet you, Lieutenant Leary—"

Mondreaux bobbed slightly to Daniel. The surface of his expression was a bland smile.

"—but the lady's companion Master Buscaigne thought they had more pressing business than to greet the great hero from Xenos."

Another aircar was approaching from the north, smaller than the first but very well appointed. A slick-looking man was driving. The woman beside him was middle-aged and too big to fit comfortably into the garments she was wearing, but the girl alone in the back seat was very nice indeed.

The car settled next to Admiral Milne's. During the moment it hovered, Lieutenant Farschenning leaned close to Daniel and said through the thrum of the fans, "I won't say anything against Lars Buscaigne, but I don't recommend you play cards with him."

Daniel nodded. He knew the type. Master Mondreaux was another of them. . . .

Violent activity alongside the heavy cruiser drew everybody's eyes. A pair of spacers using atmosphere suits as makeshift diving apparatus shot to the surface, sloshing violently.

"What is *that*?" Mistress Tyler shrieked on an ascending note. Staring at the commotion, she grabbed her husband with one hand and Mondreaux with the other.

A man in the stern of the nearer barge hurled a gallon bucket into the water beside the risen spacers. The container started sinking, then burst in a gout of steam shot through with white fire. A ripple that looked like water out of a sluice peeled from one of the divers and merged with the churning slip.

Mister Tyler had been detaching his wife's hand from Mondreaux. The younger man stood impassively, unaffected by the nearby violence and seemingly unaware of the lady's grip.

"Bloody hell!" Tyler said, shocked in turn. He looked at Admiral Milne and said, "Quicklime, I suppose? Is that safe with the men right there?"

"Safe enough," Captain Molliman replied instead. "Caustic won't harm the suits, and usually the lime doesn't splash the fabric directly."

He looked at Daniel and explained, "There's big one-celled animals here. Blobs, we call 'em. In the harbor where they've got garbage and sewage to eat, they get to the size of bed quilts. If there's not a crack in your suit, they're not dangerous—but nobody likes to have one crawling on him, either."

"The water around the islands's very acid from

decaying algae," added Lieutenant Farschenning. "It's not the heat so much as for making the water basic that we drive them away with quicklime when they show up."

"I once saw a ship being raised from a swamp," Mondreaux said, looking out toward the *Cornelwood*. "A tank of reaction mass was empty though the gauge read full, and a bank of thrusters failed on liftoff."

The water of the slip still stirred, but for the most part the lime had slaked itself to quiescence. For the time being the divers continued to cling to a net over the side of the barge.

"The swamp was full of great carnivores," Mondreaux continued, turning again to his companions. Everyone but the trio coming from the second aircar was looking at him. "They were cold blooded, I gather, but they certainly weren't sluggish. There were more people defending the salvage crew than there were raising the ship. It was a constant battle, and the stench of the corpses rotting was beyond belief."

He chuckled. "Maybe they should've tried chasing them away with quicklime instead of killing them with impellers and plasma cannon," he added in a light tone. "I think after the first day or two, it was the smell of meat that drew the creatures more than the workmen around the ship."

The older of the women from the second aircar stepped out in front of her companions. The man with her, Lars Buscaigne, laid a hand on her arm to rein her in; she jerked herself free.

"Hello!" she said, holding both her hands out to Daniel, palms down. "I'm Celia Raynham, *Lady* Celia, but that's only because my dear late husband had a

title of sorts on Lindesfarne before he came here and
made so very much money. You must be the Daniel
Leary we've heard so much about!"

"Madame," Daniel said, bowing low to forestall
the hug with which he was pretty sure Raynham was
about to enfold him. She'd gotten an amazing amount
of information out in the form of a simple greeting.
An interesting woman, but not in the least interesting
to him *as* a woman.

"Yes," said the younger woman with a bright, cruel
smile. "Poor Mommy would be quite alone now in her
later years if it weren't for darling Lars here. He's in
constant attendance on her, aren't you, Lars?"

She held out her hand to Daniel, drawing demurely
back but managing to place herself in the direct line
between him and her mother. "I'm Geneva Raynham," she said sweetly, "but please call me Ginny. It's
enthralling to read of such heroic exploits by a man
not much older than I am myself."

Geneva turned to her mother, keeping the same
smile. "I'll bet it reminds you of back when you were
young too, doesn't it, Mommy?" she added.

Daniel didn't expect Geneva Raynham would age
any better than her mother had, but that wasn't a
present concern. She couldn't be much over twenty
standard years old, though she was obviously quite
sure of what she wanted.

Which seemed to be the same as what Daniel wanted.
The future wasn't going to be an issue. Repairs to the
Hermes would be complete in five days probably, eight
at the outside. The tender'd go off to her assigned station among the Burwood Stars. With luck Daniel would
never see the lady again. That'd probably suit Geneva

as well, but that wasn't a question he need ask himself once he'd lifted off in the *Hermes*.

"Very good to meet you both, ladies," Daniel said, bowing again. He didn't have to look at Admiral Milne to know how their fawning would affect her. "We of course have work to do here, but perhaps at a later time we can pursue the acquaintance."

"I wonder, Zita?" Mondreaux said unexpectedly. It was only by checking the direction of his glance that Daniel realized that he was speaking to Admiral Milne. "Of course I'm only a civilian, but it doesn't seem to me that one recently arrived lieutenant is really necessary for this business. Perhaps Lady Raynham and her daughter could show Leary the sights of our charming planet? I notice that there's a seat open in their aircar."

"That would be quite impossible!" said Lars Buscaigne, his face flushing dangerously. He was a good ten years older than Mondreaux, though he'd been to considerable pains to disguise the fact. "The extra weight—"

"*Really*, Lars," Celia Raynham said. "I'm sure the car will carry four. And if it can't—"

She threw Daniel a broad smile.

"—perhaps the Lieutenant can replace you as driver. You can drive an aircar, can't you, Lieutenant?"

In fact Daniel couldn't, but there was no danger of the situation arising. "No, no, I will drive, of course!" Buscaigne said. "It was only your safety that I was worried about, Celia. My skill is equal to the challenge, I am sure."

Mondreaux was whispering in the Admiral's ear. Milne snorted and said, "Well, why not? Do you need Leary here, Molliman?"

"No sir," said the Port Commander, "but I do want to emphasize that it was Leary who showed us the way to get this business done fast and safely."

"Yes, yes, I heard you before," Milne said peevishly. "Get along with you, Leary. I'll square it with Commander Slidell. And try to stay out of trouble, if you can manage that!"

Celia Raynham seized Daniel's right hand. "Come, Lieutenant," she said. "We'll show you the Grand Gallery. And I'll ride with you in the back of the car to point out sights."

Her daughter gripped Daniel's other hand. "I wouldn't think of tearing you away from dear Lars, Mother," she said. "I'll ride with the Lieutenant. Daniel—may I call you Daniel?"

Buscaigne didn't speak as he stomped toward the aircar on Celia's other side. Daniel had been eight years in the RCN and a regular visitor to his uncle's dockyard for a decade before that. A glimpse at Buscaigne's expression suggested that if the fellow *had* spoken, Daniel might still have heard some new curses.

There were various ways for Adele to have gotten from the *Hermes* to Squadron House. She was on Navy Office business, so she could even have summoned an RCN aircar from the base establishment.

Instead she chose to walk. Tovera followed a pace behind her mistress, like a modest and dutiful servant.

Adele smiled faintly. She supposed Tovera *was* modest, at least in the sense that she'd never brag or claim more than her due, and she was dutiful to a fault. One had to be very careful what one told a sociopath who'd been trained to kill: a word to Tovera was very like pulling the trigger of a pistol. In neither case would another's conscience override your expressed will.

Fortunately, Adele was *very* careful.

A starship was landing at the east end of the harbor, the hammer of its thrusters redoubling as their shockwaves began to echo from the water. The walkway trembled. It wasn't a serious problem, but the way the beryllium mesh shivered at the best of times made Adele feel as unsteady as if she'd been walking on black ice.

She chuckled. "Mistress?" Tovera asked quietly.

"I don't like aircars," Adele said. She nodded to the vehicular track alongside the raised mesh pedestrian-way. It was two parallel ruts filled with black muck except where an unusually deep cavity gaped in the limestone substrate. "And the roads here are bad enough that ground traffic must bounce instead of rolling if it's at any speed. I wonder if the Navy Office would approve a request for a Xenos-style tramway to carry me between the ship and Squadron House?"

"It wouldn't be necessary to ask Cinnabar," Tovera said. "Commanders of detached squadrons have large discretionary funds at their disposal. Admiral Milne could approve the project herself. As, of course, could anyone else who had the Admiral's authentication codes."

Adele wasn't sure whether Tovera actually had a sense of humor or if she made jokes in the same way that she acted as though she had morals: by analyzing jokes that normal people told and reproducing their elements in workmanlike fashion. Either possibility amused Adele, albeit in a gray fashion. It brought her a smile nonetheless.

The walkway zigzagged between two-story barracks blocks and small duplexes, housing for the port's permanent staff. The yards were raised with dredged material confined by retaining walls. Children played among the buildings, watched by women and a few men. Often they waved as Adele and Tovera walked by.

Many of the duplexes were surrounded by impressive displays of off-planet species, and even the barracks had planting boxes. Gardening seemed to be a favorite pastime here, presumably aided by the same climate that made Nikitin a planetary truck farm for neighboring worlds.

"It'd be a quiet place to live," Adele said. "I noticed when I went over the staff lists that forty percent of the personnel have been here five years or more."

Squadron House, a rambling three-story structure on what constituted the high ground inland of Sinmary Port, was easily visible. The building's walls were blocks of coarse brown limestone. Lesser structures were roofed with sheets of dull blue or green extruded plastic, but on the headquarters building sunlight gleamed from glazed ceramic tiles like the white heart of a lime kiln.

"Do you want a quiet place to live, mistress?" asked Tovera. She didn't sound concerned; she never sounded concerned. She just seemed curious about how human beings felt.

"Not without a library," Adele said. And in truth, probably not even with a library. She wouldn't say she'd become addicted to . . . excitement, danger, adventure.

However you chose to describe it, the words meant the same thing while you were undergoing them: chaos and generally misery.

But that was the only life Adele had known since the Three Circles Conspiracy left her an orphan and exile at age sixteen. Many spacers preferred home brewed slash when they could get better liquor, just because they were used to it. She supposed that was a definition of home: the environment you were used to.

A spacer in Grays was on guard at the entrance to Squadron House. He sat in a chair. His sub-machine gun lay beside him on the edge of a planting box filled with hyacinths and a red spiral flower. Adele didn't know the red flower's name, but she'd seen them frequently on her way here. She'd look them up when she had a moment, not because she needed the information but because it *was* information. . . .

"Signals Officer Mundy with my assistant," she said, offering the guard her ID. The embedded chip provided complete identification, including her retina scan and DNA patterns. "I have an appointment with Commander Rittenhouse."

"Yes, ma'am," the fellow said, waving her through without checking the ID in his reader. "Ground floor, take the corridor to the right and it's all the way to the back. The door says Communications, but it'll probably be open."

"Thus far I'm not impressed by their security," Adele murmured to Tovera as they walked in. The entrance hall was the full height of the building, and the three corridors leading from it were broad and airy.

"Would you be able to enter their data banks if you'd been barred from the building?" Tovera asked.

Adele frowned. "Yes, of course," she said. She'd already done so. She *always* sucked the information out of the local control center when her ship arrived in port, whether it was friendly or hostile.

"Then perhaps the guard had the right attitude," Tovera said blandly.

Adele looked at her servant. Tovera smiled at her. *That had to have been a conscious joke.*

The guard inside the open door marked COMMUNICATIONS was leaning on the desk of the very feminine-looking male receptionist and chatting. When he saw Adele coming down the hallway, he retrieved his weapon, a stocked impeller tilted against the wall, and said, "This is a restricted area, ma'am."

Adele held up her ID. "I have an appointment with Commander Rittenhouse," she said. "My name is Mundy. This is my assistant."

The guard handed the chip to the receptionist to check. "You just in from the *Garnet*?" he asked. "Any change in things on Yang?"

"I'm from the tender *Hermes*, not the *Garnet*," Adele said. "Are you expecting a change on Yang?"

The guard laughed bitterly. "Not in *my* lifetime," he said. "Or in my bastard grandchildren's neither. I was just making conversation, I guess."

"Well, it's correct," said the receptionist, eyeing Adele doubtfully as he handed back her ID. "But . . ."

"Then announce me to the Commander, if you will," Adele said sharply. If a thing was correct—and of course her identification was—then there were no buts: you carried out your duty promptly instead of delaying your betters by hemming and hawing.

The Communications Center was a large room. Ten

workstations faced inward in the middle, but only one was occupied. There were three private offices on the right side; the doors of the two nearer were closed. Dissonant music drifted out of the open third door.

The receptionist keyed his intercom and said, "Commander? The survey officer from Xenos is here."

The receptionist paused; the music from inside the office shut off. In the silence, Adele heard Tovera ask the guard about local liquors. While Adele was closeted with the Commander Rittenhouse, the Cluster Communications Officer, Tovera would be learning the routines of the office personnel and scouting places to put bugging devices in the unlikely event that Adele decided such were necessary. Tovera did that sort of thing as naturally as Adele herself dug into the heart of whichever information source was handy.

"Yessir," said the receptionist. He wasn't using sound cancellation, though his desk communicator had the capability. "But she's a *warrant* officer, sir. Yes sir."

The receptionist pursed his lips and looked at Adele. "He says you're to go on back," he said. "He figures there's a mistake, but he'll clear it up himself."

Adele looked at the handsome young fellow. *It wouldn't take a great deal to convince me to clear you up*, she thought. She'd intended to keep her face expressionless, but the receptionist squealed and drew back. Adele strode past the fellow, knowing that he wasn't worth the price of a pellet from the gun in her pocket.

But then, neither was she. She and the receptionist were both human and both flawed. There was no point in getting angry at one more twit in a universe which seemed to be largely populated with twits.

Adele entered the private office. The back wall—west-facing and on the exterior of the building—had been replaced by an expanse of frosted glass. Rittenhouse sat behind a desk pushed so far forward that there wasn't room to sit between it and the door, though there were comfortable chairs to the sides. The rear half of the room was a burgeoning confusion of flowering plants.

"Mistress Mundy," Rittenhouse said in a frowning tone that echoed his expression. "When I was told the Navy Office was sending an officer to review our information and communication systems here at Cluster Headquarters, I expected someone of commissioned rank. And properly of very high commissioned rank, I must say."

Rittenhouse was a military-looking fellow whose moustache flowed into his closely trimmed beard. He'd donned his 1st Class uniform to meet the officer from Xenos, but he obviously hadn't worn it for some while in the past. The tunic closed so tightly around his neck that his face was turning red.

That excused the Commander's testiness to some degree, though in her heart Adele believed that one didn't allow mere physical discomfort to affect one's behavior. Especially if you were uncomfortable because you'd gotten fat, an unacceptable weakness. . . .

Adele smiled. There were other weaknesses, of course—like Adele Mundy's tendency to feel everybody should behave the way she did. Apart from anything else, that would be a polite but exceedingly dangerous world in which to live.

Her smile had taken Rittenhouse aback: his expression wavered between amazement and outright fury. To calm him and because the situation suddenly amused her, Adele said, "Well, Commander, I'm quite sure I wasn't chosen because I'm the Mundy of Chatsworth. Admiral Hagbard—"

The Director of the RCN's Bureau of Communications and the person whose signature was on the orders under which Adele was operating, though Mistress Sand had dictated their content.

"—is far too professional to allow mere social concerns to influence his duties to the RCN."

The statement was completely true, at least to the extent that Adele's birth had nothing to do with her appointment. Hagbard was rather a snob, but his only connection with her presence is that he'd signed the orders *pro forma*.

Commander Rittenhouse assumed Adele was lying, of course. Occasionally Adele found herself trying to correct lies useful to her which somebody else had invented, but intellectually she knew that was an absurd thing for her to do.

"Oh!" Rittenhouse said, straightening in his seat. "Oh. Well, I trust the Admiral's judgment completely, Mundy. Have a chair, won't you?"

He gestured to the one on his right. "Are you a gardener yourself by chance?"

"No sir," Adele said, sitting in the chair opposite the one Rittenhouse had indicated. That one was under the curve of a fleshy plant whose blossoms dangled at or a little below the height of Adele's short-cropped hair. "Most of my experience with the natural world comes through written descriptions, though my shipmate Lieutenant Leary is a gifted amateur."

"Indeed," Rittenhouse said in evident disappointment.

"Well, regardless, what is it that you and the Admiral want from me, Mundy?"

"All I require is access for me and my assistant," Adele said. "How many coupled consoles does Squadron House have in all?"

"Well, there's the group here," Rittenhouse said, waving vaguely toward the main room. "I think seven of them are working. We've had some problems, you see. But we don't really have enough trained personnel here in the Cluster for that to make any difference. We're rather forgotten here, I'm sorry to say."

Adele noticed that a line of what she'd thought were little blue flowers on the stem above the Commander's head followed his motion. They were animals of some sort. Daniel would be interested. . . .

"And there's four more in the major departments in the building," Rittenhouse continued. "Plus the one in the Admiral's mansion. Admiral Milne had a console moved there so that she could access the system without coming to Squadron House. She's got a full office in one wing."

Adele frowned despite her intention of remaining expressionless. "I'd think that would raise security concerns," she said carefully.

"Oh, my goodness," Rittenhouse said with a chuckle. "You mustn't think this is like Xenos, Mundy. The only intelligence we in the Cluster deal with is piracy, and that's entirely a small-scale business—mostly a village clubbing together to buy a clapped-out starship and man it, hoping to steal a load of anti-aging drugs before their ship falls apart on them. They aren't going to break into the Admiral's mansion. And as for the wretched situation on Yang—"

He threw up his hands.

"I think you could mix up the past ten years of intelligence reports on Yang and not be able to tell the difference. Nothing changes on Yang."

"I see," said Adele mildly. What she saw was that Rittenhouse was even stupider than she'd thought, which was saying a good deal. Intelligence about the Cluster was of no great concern, but Squadron HQ received the general RCN distribution by courier vessels. That included information of potential value to Alliance operations in every zone of conflict.

She cleared her throat and added, "So there's no security whatever on Admiral Milne's personal console?"

"Oh, heavens, Mundy!" Rittenhouse said. "We may be a little relaxed by your Xenos standards, but we're not a pack of fools here on Nikitin. The Admiral's office is sealed off from the rest of the mansion. There's a guard at the door. Entry's limited to the same authorized personnel as this department, with the additional requirement that Admiral Milne herself has to be present. Why, not even her husband is allowed into the office!"

You're wrong about not being a pack of fools, Adele thought, but the precautions as Rittenhouse described them seemed reasonable by the standards of the Gold Dust Cluster. She wouldn't prejudge the source of the leak.

"I'll get to work, then," she said, rising carefully to avoid brushing a plant which she'd swear had stretched its violet-streaked flowers closer to her while she'd been sitting there. "I expect my assessment to take three days, but it might be a day or two longer. And I'll need access to Admiral Milne's console."

"Umm . . ." said Rittenhouse, getting up also. "I'm

not sure that'll be possible, Mundy. The Admiral's quite picky about who she allows into her office."

Adele noticed that he shifted sideways to stand upright; a shrub whose stem and branches were double spirals arched over his chair. Service on Nikitin was idyllic in many respects, but it seemed to have driven the Commander insane by the standards of Cinnabar society.

"I regret that it'll be necessary nonetheless," Adele said. Most of what she'd be doing was checking each console's internal history: what information had been accessed through it, when, and what passwords had been used. Because these were purpose-built RCN consoles, the internal histories couldn't be wiped without physically destroying the machine.

A team of experts might be able to create a false log, but that would require time and effort well beyond what was required to steal the information in the first place. If Adele didn't discover the source of the leak by checking the access histories, she'd have to consider the possibility of false logs along with others even less probable, but for the time being she was confident that the logs'd tell her how if not necessarily by whom the information was abstracted.

"Well, that's between you and the Admiral," Rittenhouse said, following Adele to the door. "I can't help you there at all."

A young lieutenant in utilities was standing at the front desk. The receptionist turned and said, "Commander? This is Mister Zileri, the First Lieutenant from the *Garnet*, you remember? They're still having trouble with their commo."

"Right, Commander," the lieutenant said. He had dark, curly hair and a round face whose normal expression was probably more cheerful than the one it wore at the moment. "It's the same thing as before, half the time we think we're sending but no signal's getting out. The only thing that helps is switching the unit on and off a couple times when we notice the problem, and that doesn't always work either. Can you get your techs on it again and this time solve it? Because my commo officer sure can't."

"Look, Lieutenant," Rittenhouse said, "I'm sorry about your problem but I'm not a miracle worker. This isn't Xenos, you know. If my technicians couldn't cure it before, they can't cure it now. And besides, how do you know that it wasn't fixed and you people broke it again after it was out of our hands?"

Adele wondered how often on average the phrase "this isn't Xenos" occurred in one of the Commander's work-related discussions. She herself had found no lack of lazy incompetents on Xenos, but the greater pool there allowed for a certain number of people who actually *could* do their jobs.

"Excuse me?" she said, inserting herself in a conversation that obviously wasn't going anywhere useful. It was none of her business, of course, but it was a problem and very possibly one she could solve.

"Yes?" said the lieutenant, raising his eyebrows in friendly inquiry. Commander Rittenhouse remained calmly aloof, rather like one of his plants standing silently while two birds twittered to one another.

"Is your communications system part of the main navigation computer or do you have a dedicated unit for commo alone?" Adele asked.

"I don't have any idea," the lieutenant said, frowning in concentration. "I don't *think* there's a separate computer. But say—neither unit's been changed in the past three years, but the problem only cropped up five or six months ago."

"Has your navigational software been updated recently?" Adele said. She didn't bother to argue about the definition of "changed," just pursued the problem as it took shape before her. "Say in the last five or six months?"

"Well, yes, that's a regular thing," the lieutenant said. "Every time the courier arrives from Xenos, actually—every month or so. But that's been going on too."

Adele nodded. "One of the updates may have changed a default, however," she explained. "It may give absolute priority to astrogational computations."

She shrugged. "There's no need for that under normal circumstances," she added. "Commo takes almost no computing power compared to astrogation, but a software engineer with no practical experience may very well have ignored that reality. You just have to reconfigure your defaults to the original settings. If that's the problem, of course."

"Bloody *fucking* hell!" the lieutenant said. "I—"

His eyes narrowed as he peered at Adele's name tape. Then his face brightened and he said, "Mundy? Is that the Mundy who's done so much with Danny Leary? Because I hear he's on the *Hermes* now and she's in port."

"Yes, that's right," Adele said with a degree of reserve that almost certainly wasn't justified, given the lieutenant's friendly enthusiasm. She *was* a cautious, reserved person. She saw no point in trying to change the personality that was natural to her and which had kept her alive in circumstances which had been fatal to others.

"Well by heaven!" the lieutenant said, reaching out

to clasp Adele's hand in greeting. "I'm Paolo Zileri. Danny and I were great friends at the Academy. I've been looking forward to seeing him once I got this commo mess cleaned up. By heaven!"

"If you're satisfied now, Lieutenant," said Commander Rittenhouse, "then I'll return to my duties."

He disappeared into his office without waiting for an answer. The door closed and the dissonant music resumed.

Zileri snorted. Adele merely let an almost-grin lift a corner of her mouth. If Rittenhouse hadn't spoken, nobody would've noticed he was leaving. . . .

"Look, Mundy," Zileri said. "I know this is an imposition, but is there any chance *you* can fix this for us? It's not your duty, but it'll be me and Hernandez otherwise. Even with you telling us where the problem is, I'm not . . . well, I don't think Hernandez is up to the job and I *know* I'm not."

Adele thought for a moment. She had nothing to do aboard the *Hermes* at the moment, and her duties to Mistress Sand weren't pressing in the sense that the delay of an hour would make a difference.

"Yes, all right," she said. "We'll take care of that immediately."

She started out of the Communications Center beside Zileri. "Mind," she added. "I'm not guaranteeing that I've diagnosed the real problem."

"But knowing Mistress Mundy . . ." said Tovera unexpectedly from behind them. "I'm sure that she *will* have solved the problem before we leave. I'm as sure as I am of death."

That was, Adele thought, another joke. In its way. In a way she shared with Tovera.

CHAPTER 11

Sinmary Port on Nikitin

An enlisted spacer flew Lieutenant Zileri with Adele and Tovera back to the *Garnet* in the vessel's small aircar. The patrol cruiser was good-sized, nominally of three thousand tons displacement—the same as the *Hermes*, though arranged in a cigar shape rather than the tender's uncommon dumbbell. Even to eyes as inexpert as Adele's, the *Garnet* looked worn.

The ship had eight rings of antennas. Each should've had four masts—dorsal and ventral, port and starboard. Starboard Three and Four were missing, and it seemed likely there were other gaps in the Port and Ventral rows which Adele couldn't see from her present angle.

She thought it was an illusion that the cruiser was riding lower on the starboard side than on the port, but when the aircar settled to the quay she saw it was actually true. Spacers and others who wore the dull blue of ground staff—or at any rate, wore scraps of blue uniforms, mostly cut-off and grease-stained—were at work on the starboard outrigger. A large pump powered by its own fusion bottle waited alongside on a flatbed, though it hadn't been hooked up to the outrigger as yet.

The aircar landed gently on the quay. Mud which ground vehicles had tracked onto the concrete had dried, so a doughnut of dust lifted from beneath the car and straggled away on the gentle breeze.

One of the men on the outrigger waved to Zileri, then started toward them across one of several catwalks laid for the purpose. He wore a commo helmet and utilities with the sleeves buttoned short.

"Say, Captain!" Zileri called over the descending whine as the fans slowed. "We're in luck. This is Signals Officer Mundy who's serving with my friend Danny Leary. She's going to fix the commo suite for us!"

That's getting a little ahead of yourself, Adele thought. But it was certainly what she intended to do . . . and judging from past experience, she'd probably succeed.

Adele found it difficult to be objective about herself, and her tendency not to trust the future was a learned reflex. You could arrive on Bryce, preparing to begin a lifetime of study, and learn in a few days that you were a penniless orphan. . . .

"Mistress Mundy," Zileri said, turning to make introductions. "This is Captain Andy Toron, as good an officer as you could hope to serve under. Andy, this is the Sparks who figured out what Cluster HQ wouldn't have in another million years."

"You're just trying to butter me up in hopes I'll leave you on the ground when we head back to Yang in a few days," Toron said. He was a short man—barely taller than Adele's five-feet five-inches—but in extremely good physical condition. It was obviously something he worked at. "No such luck."

"Aw, don't even joke about that," Zileri said, walking with Adele and the Captain to the boarding ramp just down the quay. Tovera followed behind. "We ought to be able to go two, maybe three months before we're up for that duty again, right?"

"I wish it was joke," Toron grumbled. "No, it's not. Kwo, the consular agent on Yang, sent a dispatch by freighter just after we left. Seems the government captured a couple hundred mercenaries from Burwood fighting with the rebels. They're Cinnabar citizens, so he wants a naval vessel to free and repatriate them. And you heard they managed to half-sink the *Corny* landing her?"

"Yeah, how'd they do that?" Zileri said. They strode up the ramp, Adele between the two officers and Tovera a pace behind. The internal hatches were all open, so the entrance hold echoed with the sound of tools and the calls of those using them.

"Hell if I know," Toron said. "What matters is that the crews of the *Cutlass* and *Chrissie* are fully committed to raising the *Corny*, so guess who that leaves to take care of the situation on Yang? Again!"

They entered a companionway and started up. A rainbow-colored animal the length of Adele's hand swooped through the air past her. She started instinctively.

"Aw, don't let the lizards bother you, mistress," Zileri said. "They keep the cockroaches down, as much as anything can anyhow."

He muttered a curse and added, "I wish somebody'd downed that bastard Kwo on Yang before he sent that stupid report, though. Who the hell cares if a few wogs from Burwood get whacked on Yang? They took their chances, right?"

"Look, if you wanted to make citizenship policy for the Republic, you shouldn't have joined the RCN," Toron said wearily. The two officers were letting off steam, not really arguing. "And don't blame Kwo. He did us a favor, tried to anyhow. He probably had that report before we lifted, but he held it a day figuring somebody else would get a turn in the barrel instead of keeping us on Yang."

They came out on A Deck. The main corridor and the bridge just forward of the companionway were much better lighted than the companionways. For an instant, the bulkheads seemed to shiver; then Adele realized she was seeing a wave of large cockroaches scurrying away.

Another lizard, this one bright yellow, ran a few steps along the bulkhead before launching itself on flaps of translucent membrane stretched by its three pairs of legs. It snapped up a roach on the fly and sailed back to perch on a ventilator grating. The roach's wing covers fluttered to the deck.

"They make good pets," Zileri said, following Adele's eyes. "Once you get used to them, anyhow."

"And there's nothing else for the roaches," Toron said. "Venting to vacuum doesn't kill the egg cases, and you can't use poisons when you've got to recycle your air for God knows how long."

The entered the bridge. The bosun seated at the command console turned and said, "Sir?"

"Stay where you are, Gorney," the Captain said. "I'm just bringing Sparks from the *Hermes* to take a look at our commo."

The only other crew member was a young, intense-looking man with Signals Branch lightning bolts on his lapels. He had a wiring schematic on his display, but from his scowl it wasn't helping him a great deal. At Toron's words, he turned with a look of relief and said, "You think you can fix it? Because I been tearing my hair out since we got back from Jacobean way last year. I can't find a bloody thing wrong!"

"I'll try," said Adele. "If I can—"

She hadn't gotten the request out before the signaller, Hernandez she remembered—the name tape on his utilities was too faded to read—jumped from his console. "Please!" he said. "Any bloody thing you want. You want me to dance on the maintop, I'll do it if that'll get the commo suite fixed."

"I don't think it'll require that," Adele said with a faint smile as she seated herself at the console. She brought out her personal data unit. For most tasks she found it quicker to use the little unit with her wands as a controller coupled to the primary system, rather than to adjust herself to a console set up in an unfamiliar way.

The display blurred; another yellow lizard—this one with a bright red tail—had sailed through the air-formed hologram, distorting it. Adele was by no means sure that *she'd* get used to the creatures, though it seemed that she might have to if the *Hermes* remained here on station for the year or more she expected.

"Say, you heard we're going back to Yang, didn't you, Lieutenant?" the signaller said to Zileri as Adele completed linking her unit to the console. "D'ye suppose we'll have to fight this rebel cruiser?"

"Any fighting we do's going to be trading shots on

the ground, Hernandez," Captain Toron said. "And our problem's with President Shin's government, anyway. Not that there's much difference *I* can see."

"This batch of rebels have an old Baltoon post ship, Mundy," Lieutenant Zileri explained as Adele cascaded the data across her holographic display. The trick was finding the correct directory since you couldn't trust the descriptions which other people had given the information. "They armed her and call her the *Beacon of Yang*, but long odds she couldn't lift into orbit. It's just bragging."

"Everything on Yang's just bragging," Toron said in a resigned voice. "Bragging and dirt. Every kind of dirt there is."

Adele had the navigation directory. The headers were alphanumerical, nonsense groupings so far as she was concerned, but by checking for times of entry she quickly set out the inputs occurring at just over six standard months and just over five. She opened the first.

"We'd be saving ourselves time if we slagged this *Beacon* while it's on the ground," Zileri said with a touch of enthusiasm. "If we make a pass over the area, you know they'll shoot at us. Bloody hell, they shoot at refugee ships! We've got a right to shoot back, right?"

"The trouble is, they've got anti-ship missiles in place around the *Beacon*," Toron said. "That was in Kwo's report, too. Mind, I wouldn't be surprised if he'd brokered the missiles to the rebels himself. The cruiser, so called, that's no threat to us, but a sheaf of hittiles through our Power Room and it's all over."

The astrogational data in the file proper meant nothing to Adele, but the format sidebar was clear—and was clearly the problem. She made a series of quick changes then shifted to the next similar input.

"Maybe we could come in at low level?" Zileri said, not so much hopefully as in the tone of a man toying with a puzzle. "Of course, if we've got to trick them into shooting at us, it doesn't help to take them by surprise so they can't."

The navigational update five-plus months back appeared to be the only one that had changed defaults. Perhaps it'd been compiled at a different location? Though it might be as simple as someone going on vacation and his standard task being handled by a different person.

"They're on Big Florida Island," Toron said. "We'll just route around them into and out of Heavenly Peace. If they ever do get the *Beacon* into space, she'll be easy enough to deal with then."

"All right," said Adele, sliding her wands into their carrying case, then getting up from the console. "I've corrected the problem, I believe. Mister Hernandez, if you and Lieutenant Zileri will take a look at the file, I'll show you where to make the correction if the problem recurs after a later astrogational update."

Hernandez slipped into the seat Adele had just vacated. "All right," he muttered. He highlighted the change in the file history without needing Adele to point it out. "All *right*, yes! Mundy, this is brilliant!"

"You can test it by setting the computer to run an astrogational problem, anything at all so long as it's running," Adele said to the two commissioned officers. "And use your commo for normal traffic. But I don't think you'll have a problem."

Captain Toron beamed. "Say, Mundy," he said. "You

wouldn't like a transfer to the *Garnet*, would you? She doesn't look like much, but she's a regular little money-spinner for her crew. We took, retook from pirates I mean, a freighter a couple months ago with a million and a half florins of anti-aging drugs aboard."

"Thank you," Adele said as she returned her data unit to its pocket. "But I think I'll stay with the *Hermes*."

"Anything we can do for you another time, then, mistress," said Toron. "It's hard enough duty here in the Cluster even when we help each other, and you've sure helped us."

"Yeah," Zileri said. "And I don't want to explain to Danny how we snatched away the magician he's got for a Sparks. Well, that Captain Slidell has, I guess."

"You were right the first time," Tovera said in a dry voice as she followed Adele toward the companionways.

A lizard with blue legs and a bright green body sprinted along the corridor ahead of them squeaking, then launched itself and curved through the hatch airborne. The squeaks echoed faintly after the creature itself had disappeared.

Adele smiled faintly. *Yes, Zileri had been right the first time.*

The only thing the Raynham mother and daughter had agreed on was that the other wasn't going to sit beside Lieutenant Leary, so Daniel rode in the front of the aircar with Buscaigne. The sea breeze was fitful with occasional gusts over the steep edge of the island that made flying tricky, but Buscaigne set the vehicle down with an expert fluff of the fans.

"Admiral Daudell built this parking area when he opened out the Grand Gallery," Celia said brightly. "It'd become quite overgrown, though, till dear Zita had it and the Gallery too cleaned up for the ball she gave last Republic Day. Zita really takes an interest in our little community, not like some earlier Admirals."

Admiral Milne was personally wealthy from her eighth of all prizes taken by the Gold Dust Squadron, so she might very well have hired farm laborers or civilian personnel from the port when they were off duty to clean and renovate the gallery and its attendant facilities. If that's what she'd done, Daniel would cheerfully add his praise to Lady Raynham's.

The chances were, though, that Milne had simply detailed spacers from the ships under her command to do the work. That was what admirals did, after all; and so did other powerful people, including politicians like Speaker Leary. It was the way of the world, and Daniel didn't lose sleep protesting it . . . but the fact that spacers were prettying up the landscape for a party instead of pulling maintenance on their vessels might have something to do with the failure that left the *Cornelwood* half-sunk in the harbor.

Celia Raynham sat directly behind Daniel. Buscaigne hopped out of the car while the fans were still spinning and trotted around the front to get to her before Daniel could.

"Allow me to hand you out, my dear!" he said firmly. Given that Daniel had no more desire to touch the lady than he wanted to be embraced by one of the giant amoebas from the harbor, he heartily approved of Buscaigne's procedure.

"And will you be *my* gallant, Danny?" Ginny Raynham said, holding her arm out over the side of the aircar in invitation.

"Yes," said her mother. "Dear Geneva really does need someone to take care of her. She has scarcely a bean of her own, poor thing, just the tiny trust fund Lord Raynham settled on her before he passed. All the rest came to me."

Daniel set his arm for Ginny to take as she stepped lightly from the vehicle. He didn't imagine Celia thought money was of any real significance to him—certainly not in anything having to do with women. She was just making a point of being nasty, rather as Ginny did about Celia's age. Like mother, like daughter, he supposed; though probably Adele would say something harsher about humanity in general.

He smiled. And that harsh judgment might be right; but that was Adele, not him. What *he* felt about the present situation was that Ginny Raynham was a very attractive girl who was determined to get to know him better—for a time.

Daniel looked about. The island's margin stood ten or twelve feet above the sea here; take two steps southward from the parking area and you'd drop straight into the water. The ground across a gully on the north side of the area sloped upward, though by no means steeply by the standards of most planets. Daniel saw the mouth of a cave not far up the hillside.

The roof of the rambling Admiral's Mansion was in sight a quarter mile to the east, but the intervening terrain was native forest. A path led along the seafront from the port housing to the parking area. There was probably a spur up to the mansion, but Daniel hadn't noticed it as they flew here from the harbor.

A metal footpath, this one a full five feet wide, dropped into the gully before rising into the woods.

It'd been freshly repaired. Daniel started down it with Ginny clinging to his arm. Behind them he heard Buscaigne and Lady Raynham speaking in low voices; the words were unintelligible but both sounded peevish.

To Daniel's surprise, the path kinked to the left instead of continuing toward the opening he'd spotted from the parking area. "Isn't it this way?" he said doubtfully, pointing into the woods with his free hand. From this angle he couldn't see the cave, but he thought he could find it easily enough.

"No, no, follow the path, Leary," Buscaigne called in a tone barely within the bounds of politeness. The mesh flexed with his weight and that of Lady Raynham as they followed the younger couple. "Do you think we're such bumpkins here on Sinmary that we'd build a track off to nowhere?"

Daniel grinned instead of bristling. The gibe had called to his mind the only circumstances in which he could visualize Buscaigne doing physical work: as part of a prison labor gang, preferably chained to other convicts.

Ginny leaned her left breast against Daniel's arm as she pointed up the slope. "Those are the Wormholes up there, Danny," she said. "There's ever so many of them, but they don't really go anywhere. They're like a ball of knotted string."

"The Grand Gallery wasn't open to the surface until Admiral Daudell opened it," explained her mother as she and Buscaigne joined them. "Such a shame that I couldn't have brought you here for the ball last month, Danny. With fairy lights glued to the ceiling it was just enchanting!"

"Come along, Celia," Buscaigne said. His lips smiled,

but he was guiding her clear of Daniel with more determination than affection. "I think we'll find the natural light even more romantic than we did that glitter."

Ginny had been clinging to Daniel's right arm. Now that her mother was in front of them, she tugged his arm around her waist instead. Daniel let his hand rest lightly on her hip, allowing just enough pressure to feel the muscles shift beneath the layer of smooth padding.

The path made another angled turn—beryllium sheeting had to be laid in straight lines—and ended in an arch cut through the limestone with power saws. Steps led downward into relative darkness. The workmen had made a half-hearted effort to sculpt framing pilasters with the same tools. Decades of weathering had softened the crude outlines into something mildly charming.

Celia hesitated at the entrance, but Buscaigne applied pressure till she trotted down to keep from overbalancing. Daniel raised an eyebrow to Ginny, but she grinned in response and led him through by the hand.

There was considerably more light in the Grand Gallery than there'd seemed from the outside. Besides the limited amount that trickled through the shaded entrance, seven tall keyholes were cut in the south-facing wall of the cliff. Daniel's first impulse had been to draw his light-amplifying goggles down, but after a moment he found that the sort of gray half-light the openings cast through the cavern was enough to see by.

There wasn't a great deal *to* see, though the vault's very size—it stretched for several hundred yards—was impressive. The arched ceiling was generally more than twenty feet above the cave floor, but icy-looking stalactites reached down to half that distance in some places. A zigzag of lacy stone curtained the back wall midway into the cavern.

Besides litter on the floor—paper trash, discarded garments, and the frequent wink of broken glassware—there were few signs of human intrusion into this world. Thirty feet from the entrance, movable stands held a plush rope circling a hole in the floor. Two other sinkholes were roped off at roughly equal intervals.

"Come here, Danny," called Celia, gesturing to Daniel as she strode toward the nearby sinkhole. Now that she was inside, the hesitation she'd shown before entering the cavern had vanished. She stepped briskly, kicking aside a fist-sized chunk of rock that'd fallen from the roof. "You're interested in animals, aren't you?"

Indeed Daniel was, though the fact Lady Raynham knew that was more than a little surprising. He walked over to her, smiling deliberately instead of frowning as he'd otherwise have done. Ginny didn't try to hold him back, though she kept a firm grip on his arm as she matched him stride for stride. Buscaigne followed Celia, his eyes on the ground save for a single quick glare of hostility toward Daniel.

Celia tipped over two of the supports, then squatted on her haunches at the edge of the sinkhole. "Look," she said to Daniel, pointing downward.

He knelt with his knees on the plush rope instead of squatting. The hole was filled with water to a few feet below the edge; Daniel couldn't quite have touched the surface without bending over at the waist. Micro-organisms gave the sea a milky luminescence, making the cavity brighter than the main cavern above it.

Tiny shapes slithered in schools; then, with shocking abruptness, a broad ribbon longer than Daniel was tall shimmered through the lesser fish. Teeth flashed. The predator vanished again, leaving behind rags of blood and fragments of the prey it'd savaged.

Buscaigne had placed himself between Daniel and Lady Raynham; he jumped back when the large fish struck. Celia didn't move and her daughter, standing with a hand on Daniel's shoulder, asked, "Were you frightened, Lars dear?" in mock concern.

"Is the sinkhole open to the sea?" Daniel asked. From the wildlife survey he'd read during the voyage from Cinnabar, he recognized the predator as a glass shark. They got even larger than this one, but he'd understood they were open-ocean creatures as adults.

"It connects to the sea on the north side of the island, not this side," Ginny said, pointing toward the openings in the cliff face. "All three of them do. But Admiral Daudell put a mesh over the openings so that only little fish could get in or out. Those that grow can't leave."

"Umm," Daniel said, rising to his feet. The pool continued to swirl from the strike of the glass shark, but the fingerlings had resumed their dance. *How deep was the sinkhole, anyway, and did it . . . ?*

"Are all the pools connected?" he said, pointing to the other roped-off openings. He started toward the next in line, carefully skirting this one. A six-foot glass shark could give a human being a dangerous or even fatal bite, but it probably wouldn't because its normal prey was much smaller.

Still, mistakes happen. The water was a glowing fog in which a man's flailing arm might look like a separate entity of just the size for dinner.

"No, they're separate," said Ginny, taking his arm

again as she walked alongside. "Do we have a light along? In the last pool there's a rock squid that's just *beautiful*."

Daniel checked his equipment belt by reflex, though he already knew the answer. "Yes, I do," he said. "I have my service light, anyway."

He took out his light, a squat tube the size of four fingers extended together. It threw a bright spot onto the lace curtain when he switched it on briefly. Reflection spread the output into a soft glow across the twenty feet ahead of him. "Will this do?"

Celia hugged him closer in agreement.

"Admiral Daudell used convicts to open the Gallery," Celia said, following behind them. As best Daniel could tell, she was speaking simply to be noticed. "Convicts from Cinnabar, I mean."

Daniel nodded. He hadn't heard that but it was certainly possible. A generation or two ago, the Republic had transported criminals to outlying planets to serve a term of hard labor, then remain as colonists. The practice got criminals off Cinnabar, but it'd led to a serious security problem on worlds which the Alliance attacked. The prison gangs provided Alliance troops with a ready-made Fifth Column.

Daniel glanced into the second pool. To his surprise the water was dark except for rainbow twinkles like the sun lifting fire from the facets of diamonds. Though both were open to the sea, this habitat was completely different from the one a hundred yards closer to the Gallery's entrance.

He shone his light down. Hand-sized invertebrates cruised in slow circles, their gill rings expanding and contracting as they filtered anything that could provide food from the water. When Daniel's beam struck them directly, they collapsed into themselves and sank. A fingernail-sized organ at the end of a long filament flashed nervously behind them.

"Come and see the last one," Celia said, putting her hand over Daniel's like a child leading her little brother. "It's lovely!"

"I don't think we need to go so far, Geneva darling," her mother said. Her tone was outwardly warm, but the words had a peevish color when they echoed from the cavern walls. "Perhaps Danny would like to come back to my house for tea?"

"He has his duties, Celia," Buscaigne said.

"You don't have to come, Mother," Ginny called, resting her cheek on Daniel's shoulder briefly as they walked along. "In fact, why don't you fly back to the house? Danny and I can walk to the port. I'll find a ride there when I'm ready to come home."

Lady Raynham didn't respond, but Daniel heard her footsteps—and those of Buscaigne—pattering determinedly along behind. He turned his lamp off, making do with the indirect light through the windows. The cave had been cleaned recently enough that only a few rocks littered the floor.

"The convicts didn't only open the Gallery, you know," Lady Raynham continued. "Admiral Daudell used them to bury his treasure—and the rumor is that he had them all murdered then so that no one would know where it was hidden!"

"Oh, Mother," Ginny said. "That's a fairy tale! Things like that don't really happen."

Daniel blanked his face without speaking. It wasn't completely beyond imagination that an RCN admiral would've murdered prisoners, but it was unlikely. More important, if it *had* happened, word would've gotten out. That was the sort of story that Uncle Stacey and his former shipmates talked about over a bottle in the office of Bergen and Associates while little Danny Leary listened entranced in the corner. Besides, what treasure would Daudell, an ineffectual though well-connected man, have amassed?

"I'm not surprised you say that, Geneva," Celia said in a cool voice, "because family has never meant anything to you. My father, the grandfather you never knew, was Superintendent of Works at Sinmary Port. He was responsible for feeding the convicts while they worked under Admiral Daudell. He said that Daudell continued drawing rations for the gang three full days after work on the Grand Gallery was complete. So there!"

Daniel cleared his throat. "Is it possible that the Admiral was selling the rations?" he asked. "To landowners to feed their laborers, perhaps?"

"It is not," Celia said firmly. Then, probably because she knew the statement was nonsense—of *course* there was a market for RCN rations, and if Daudell was too great a paragon of virtue to line his pockets at the Republic's expense then he was more unusual than an admiral who massacred prisoners—she added, "Not without my father knowing about it, I mean. He said he and his staff themselves distributed the rations to the convicts, not to navy personnel."

Daniel pursed his lips again. That sounded believable—because it implied that Lady Raynham's father had been concerned to get his share of any graft. He'd probably been as surprised as Daniel was that the delay in releasing the convicts to other projects hadn't been a profitable dodge on Daudell's part.

"Geneva has no sense of family," Lady Raynham continued in her martyred tone. "I think that might be why my dear Lord Raynham left her only a pittance."

"It had a great deal more to do with favors which I wasn't willing to provide *dear* Lord Raynham, mother," Ginnie replied in a tone like glass breaking. "Fortunately I'm not forced to buy companionship. It may be decades before I have to do that."

"Now what is it I'm to see here, Ginnie?" Daniel said in a louder voice than he'd have used if he weren't trying to break up a cat-fight.

The last sinkhole was larger than the other two, a perfect circle nearly twenty feet in diameter. It filled the back of the cavern—or almost filled it; when the cave floor collapsed to form the pool, it'd left a narrow rind of stone along the right edge.

Daniel shone his lamp across, sending shimmers from the wet rock. The cavern's tail kinked off around a corner where the beam couldn't follow.

"Point your light down," Ginnie said, lowering the line of plush rope as her mother had done the previous ones. "Straight down, all the way to the bottom."

Daniel leaned forward, sighting along his beam of light. The water here was dark, but the lamp flashed from the sides of fish fluttering like pennants in a breeze. He didn't recognize the species, though he hoped he'd be able to identify them when he got to a natural history database.

"Just wait a moment," Ginnie said, her hand caressing his shoulder. "Keep the light—"

The flash came from all around the pool, diamonds

winking in a closing net. The water surged, then cleared. The swimming fish vanished out the seaward channel.

Daniel recognized the rock squid. It was one of the major coastal predators on Nikitin, but the database hadn't suggested they got *this* big. Normally the creatures lay on the bottom with their hundreds of tentacles spread in living mats. When suitable prey swam overhead, they swept the tentacles inward with hooked claws extending from the inner surface of each one.

Here in the sinkhole the beast's technique was similar, but instead of stretching its tentacles on the bottom it'd covered the walls with them. They'd slashed inward and down together, ripping the entire school of fish. The squid's maw gaped momentarily, displaying a circuit of crystalline teeth which blazed in the lamplight like a sectioned geode.

"Beautiful . . ." Ginnie repeated softly. Daniel continued to look into the pool; he had a feeling he didn't want to see the girl's expression at just this moment.

The squid slowly spread its arms again like a flower opening to the sun. The tentacles were corpse white while they were extending, but when they reached the sinkhole's walls they shaded into the pitted yellow-grayness of the rock they lay against. The claws had drawn back within the concealing flesh.

"There's no treasure," Lars Buscaigne said unexpectedly. "Daudell was building a secret entrance to his mansion through one of the Wormholes."

Daniel switched off his lamp and turned. "How do you know that?" he asked. Buscaigne and Lady Raynham were blurs against the shadows until his eyes readapted, but shining the powerful beam on them would be too aggressive—at least for the moment.

"How do I know the sky's blue?" Buscaigne snapped. "Because it's obvious. And because I've watched that tramp Mondreaux come this way a dozen times and disappear. There's no place he could be going except into one of the caves, and he wouldn't do that unless it took him to his lover."

"His *lover?*" Daniel repeated. He wondered whether he looked as much like a beached fish as he felt. Presumably the bad light covered his gaping stupidity.

"Yes, Pontefract," Buscaigne said. "Admiral Milne's husband makes sure all her aides-de-camp are gay. Pontefract's having an affair with Mondreaux, slipping him into the Admiral's office where they can be sure nobody will barge in on them. Daudell probably had the tunnel built for a similar reason, to keep his private business away from a nosy wife."

Ginny Raynham turned. "Do you suppose Lieutenant Pontefract is a spy?" she said. "My, do you suppose Master Mondreaux is?"

"I wouldn't put it past that one," Buscaigne agreed. "There's more to him than he shows, that I'm sure of."

Daniel got to his feet, his face carefully blank again. Ginny didn't sound as though she believed that they'd just uncovered an Alliance spy ring, but this latest unexpected information fitted very neatly with what Daniel already suspected.

"Danny," Ginnie said with bright certainty. "You and I will go search the Wormholes right now. *We'll* find the entrance."

That wasn't the best way to locate a secret entrance to the mansion, but of course the girl didn't really believe there was any such thing. It was a perfectly satisfactory way to get her and Daniel out of Lady Raynham's sight, however.

"Really, Geneva," her mother said. "I don't think you should be tramping through the muddy forest. Why—"

"We owe it to the Republic, Mother!" Ginnie said. "Danny, are you coming? We'll take the tarpaulin from the car in case we need to rest."

"Yes, let them go, Celia darling," Buscaigne said in a soothing voice. "This is a romantic setting, do you not think, my dear?"

That was rather stretching it, Daniel thought as he let the girl hustle him toward the Gallery's entrance. Still, he appreciated what Buscaigne was trying to do—obviously on his own account, but nonetheless helpful to Daniel's short-term interests.

He very much wanted to discuss his suspicions with Adele, but that could wait an hour or two. And after all, maybe he and Ginnie *would* find a back entrance to the Admiral's Mansion.

That wasn't the first thing on his agenda, though. Nor on Ginnie's, he hoped and believed.

CHAPTER 12

Sinmary Port on Nikitin

Daniel, whistling "What Do You Do With a Drunken Spacer," walked into the Battle Direction Center. The hatch was open. The tech on guard nodded when she saw who was coming down the corridor and went back to her conversation with the trainee who had the signals watch.

Those two and Adele were the only people in the BDC at the moment. Adele was off duty, but Daniel hadn't been surprised when she'd told him by radio where she was. She didn't look up when he entered, but at least she didn't jump when he said, "It's a pleasant evening, Officer Mundy. Come watch the sunset with me from the outer hull, if you will."

When Adele turned, Daniel held up a pair of magnetic boots—the light variety for use with an air suit, not rigger's boots which weighed five pounds apiece. "I brought these in case you'd like to slip them on."

"More than I'd like to slide off the hull into the sea," Adele said dryly as she drew the boots on over her deck shoes. "I'm able to swim, but it'd make conversation difficult."

The starboard hatch in the corridor just outside the BDC was wide open. If Daniel had been on his own, he'd have pulled gloves on and swarmed up the line that'd been fixed to a bollard below the hatch, but the ladder welded to the spherical hull was a perfectly good alternative.

Well, maybe it was. "Ah, Adele?" Daniel said, gesturing through the hatch. "Will you be able to, ah, use the ladder?"

"Yes," Adele said. She stepped onto the hatch coaming, gripped a stringer with one hand, then lurched onto the ladder. "And very shortly we'll know whether I was able to use it successfully."

Daniel smiled faintly as he followed his friend up the ladder. Adele was in good shape and as physically adept as the next person—so long as there was gravity. By this point he doubted she'd ever learn to move like a spacer in freefall.

Except if she had to shoot something. *That* she'd been able to do any time she'd needed to.

Because the ladder curved from vertical to horizontal, Daniel'd normally have walked upright on the rungs without using his hands. That might've looked like he was mocking Adele, plodding along with all four limbs, though he was sure it wouldn't have bothered her. Even so, it hurt him to follow her as though he hadn't been trained to run the yards in the Matrix the way the riggers did—fast rather than safely, because when all Hell was breaking loose there was no safety *except* through speed.

He hoped Woetjans and the other senior riggers

weren't watching. He'd be a joke from here to Cinnabar if they were.

Adele reached the platform at the base of the dorsal mast and stood up. "Here?" she said to Daniel.

He looked around. A party of riggers was working on Antenna Port C, one of those which'd repeatedly failed to extend properly during the voyage from Cinnabar. They were well out of earshot, and nobody else was on the tender's hull.

"Yes," Daniel said, smiling. "This will do very well."

After he and Ginnie Raynham had played Find the Entrance to the point of mutual exhaustion, Daniel'd used his commo helmet to call Hogg in the utility vehicle. Hogg had driven to them, dropped Daniel back at the *Cornelwood's* slip, and carried Ginnie home to what was apparently called Raynham Tower.

Daniel had worked the remainder of the watch, calculating buoyancy and reviewing possible cable attachments, then returned with the draft from the *Hermes* when Hogg came to pick them up. Only when he'd showered and changed into clean utilities did he come aft to see Adele.

Now she looked westward over the seaweed-covered slip and the forest beyond, frowning slightly. "Surely the sun isn't setting already, is it?" she asked.

Daniel glanced at the flat chronometer on his wrist. "It won't set for another thirty-one standard minutes," he agreed, "and in these latitudes the sky stays bright enough to read by for another half hour. But it seemed a reasonable thing to say, Adele."

Adele blinked. She'd already taken out her personal data unit. "Oh," she said. "Yes, I see. For privacy."

"Yes," Daniel said, sitting on the platform with his back to the antenna. He motioned Adele to settle beside him as he regathered his thoughts. "Adele, what can you learn about Master Mondreaux? He's supposedly a local planter."

Adele went to work with the data unit resting on her thighs. Daniel watched her for a moment, then looked at avians—they were four-winged, warm-blooded, and feathered—circling low over the harbor to snap up insectoids.

He wondered if he'd ever know his friend well enough that she couldn't surprise him. She wasn't in the least innocent, but the degree of literalness she applied to the minute details of life was quite amazing. Words weren't *just words* to Adele Mundy, and she found "polite fiction" an oxymoron. You had to say exactly what you meant if you expected her to understand you.

And you could be quite sure that Adele would say exactly what *she* meant, with no intention of being insulting. Being insulting was just a side-effect.

"Daedalo Mondreaux, a dealer in art from recently rediscovered worlds," Adele said, squinting as her wands flickered. Her personal unit was coupled to the tender's database, but knowing Adele she also had immediate access to every networked data storage on Nikitin. "Primitive art, you'd probably say."

She grinned. "Actually, you'd probably say 'crap,' and from the imagery I'm able to call up I don't know that I'd disagree with you. Though I'm sure my mother would. Would have. Mother was very clear that it was our duty to appreciate the pure merits of the children of savagery while working to return them to the light of civilization and social justice."

Her wands paused. She glanced sidelong at Daniel with an expression he couldn't read and added, "I don't think Mother knew a great deal about savagery. At least until they nailed her head to Speaker's Rock."

"Mondreaux said he'd watched the salvaging of the *Golden Argosy* at Port Hagener," Daniel said as his friend resumed her search. He didn't know how to react when Adele talked—joked?—about the massacre of her family, so he didn't react at all. "He didn't use the name. He's not a naval person himself, so I doubt he realized that he was describing a unique event that somebody might be able to identify."

"That Daniel Leary might be able to identify," Adele said, smiling again as her wands flashed. "Did anyone else catch the reference?"

Daniel acknowledged the smile. "I'm not sure they did," he admitted or boasted; even he couldn't be sure of the right word.

"The thing is," Daniel went on, "Port Hagener is a major Alliance naval base. The *Golden Argosy* was chartered by Fleet Command as a supply ship. And the crash was just over five years ago, while we and the Alliance were at war."

From the forest west of the harbor an animal called, "*Room room room!*" It sounded enormous, bigger than any animal in the archipelago was supposed to get, but the trumpet-shaped tree boles would make perfect amplifiers.

"Mondreaux seems to have spent most of his adult life in the Alliance," Adele said. "I'm going by sales records attributed to him. I don't have census data, but fortunately one of the planters is an art collector and has a very complete auction database."

She shrugged and continued, "A year and a half ago a relative died, leaving Mondreaux a legacy including a villa on Sinmary. He retired here."

"Ah," said Daniel. He felt disappointed, though he supposed he should've been glad that there wasn't a spy in Cluster Headquarters after all. "Then it's perfectly reasonable that he'd have seen the *Golden Argosy* being raised. Well, I'm glad I checked with you before I made a fool of myself by accusing, ah, somebody."

"I'm glad you checked with me too," Adele said, turning to meet Daniel's eyes directly. "Because it's not at all reasonable that he'd have seen the event if he was an art dealer as he claimed. Certainly there's civilian travel between the Republic and the Alliance even when we're in a state of war, but all Hagener was a closed military reservation at the time. There shouldn't 've been any civilians on the planet, let alone a Cinnabar national."

"Ah!" said Daniel. "Ah."

He smiled broadly. "Then let me tell you the other thing I learned," he said, "and we'll see what else you can tell me."

Adele preferred working in a cubicle to the open air—it was what she was most used to, whether at a library console or the cramped quarters of a starship. On the other hand, her surroundings didn't really matter: when she really got into a task, it involved her totally. She suspected she wouldn't notice she was falling into the harbor until the splashing water interfered with her display.

She glanced up and saw Daniel grinning at her.

Does he know what I'm thinking? And just possibly he did, or at least he'd come to the same thought on his own. You learned to know your friends, and you had to accept that they knew you. It was oddly *comforting* to have friends.

"So you see . . ." Daniel was saying. "While I wouldn't trust Buscaigne's word on many things, his judgment that Mondreaux's a professional rival of his has a ring of truth. I don't know whether Lieutenant Pontefract has family money—"

"Yes, he does," Adele said. That was one of the first things she'd checked. "He's a second son, though. If money were the only criterion, Lady Raynham would be a much better target. Though of course if Mondreaux himself is gay, then he wouldn't be interested in the widow."

"I very much doubt Mondreaux has a sexual orientation toward anything except money," Daniel said. "That's certainly what Buscaigne believes, because he's been keeping a much closer watch on Mondreaux than anything but fear for his meal ticket explains. Though watching hasn't gotten him very far."

"Yes," said Adele. "Well, he didn't have the proper tools. Which we do."

She'd found what she was sure was the correct directory and now started opening files. Text in that one, she'd go back to it if necessary, but . . . Text there too, a mere letter of transmittal from the private contractor who'd carried out the survey ninety years before. And the third file—

"There," she said. "There! Daniel, take a look at this. It's the sonogram of Sinmary Island, made before the base was constructed."

She adjusted her display. Ordinarily the air-formed hologram was an image only to her eyes: anyone looking toward the display from a different angle would see a blur of colored light, as meaningless as the heart of an opal.

The personal data unit had a briefing mode which let anybody see the display, but Adele felt a twinge of discomfort as she switched it on. Somebody on the far shore with magnifying apparatus—even simple binoculars—could see what she was doing.

And if they did, what would it matter? Even in the unlikely event that the putative watcher understood what the image was? You *could* live your life viewing everything as a threat until it was proven otherwise; Tovera was proof of that. But Tovera wasn't fully human, and Adele didn't have to look very far down the path paranoia led to see herself as Tovera was. She wouldn't let that happen, or at least she'd fight against it happening.

"Now here . . ." she said, highlighting a straggle of narrow caves. "These are the Wormholes. And here's the Admiral's Mansion in white, and Squadron House to give you the scale."

She raised the magnification, focusing down on the block containing the highlighted elements. "You'll note that none of the Wormholes come anywhere near the mansion."

"Right," said Daniel, his voice calm with concentration. "There's a crack in the island. It's channeling rainwater to eat away the rock around seams lower down."

"All right," Adele said. She knew nothing about geology; if the explanation satisfied Daniel, that was good enough. "But here—you said you were in the Grand Gallery? Look here."

Metal belled loudly, breaking even Adele's concentration. There was a loud splash and the hull quivered beneath her. She looked toward the bow section. Something had happened—something had gone wrong, obviously, given the way people were shouting curses—among the party working on a starboard antenna.

"They were trying to cure the antenna from binding when it extends and retracts," Daniel said, watching the events. He'd apparently guessed that she didn't have any notion of what'd been going on. Well, he *did* know her. "They managed to drop the upper two telescoping sections into the harbor."

His lips pursed, Daniel's usual alternative to a frown. "Marbury's in charge, a bosun's mate from the *Bainbridge*," he went on. "He seems to be a bit on the hasty side. No real harm done this time since the slip's less than twenty feet deep, but I think I'll suggest that Woetjans have a talk with him. If it were my ship, I'd . . ."

He smiled cheerfully. "But of course it's not," he said. "And I'm not going to suggest to Captain Slidell to disrate the man till he gets some more seasoning, because it'd be a waste of breath. And probably unfair besides. I suppose I'm prejudiced in favor of my Sissies."

Adele thought about the statement. "I haven't noticed any prejudice on your part," she said, "except in favor of people who do their jobs well. To some degree I suppose that does benefit the people who served under you on the *Princess Cecile*, yes."

She cleared her throat and continued, "I was showing you a sonogram of the Grand Gallery. You mentioned the sinkholes. Here they are—"

This time she used yellow to highlight the cavities. The initial hue was unpleasantly insistent, so she muted it with a mixture of gray. She rotated the image ninety degrees to demonstrate that the channels into which the floor of the Grand Gallery had fallen ran northward out of the focal block.

"—but you see the last one isn't the end of the gallery. It continues here for another considerable distance."

A pigtail void twisted northward from the western end of the Grand Gallery. Daniel leaned forward, his face expressionless. "How high is it?" he asked. "I can't tell at this scale. Is it large enough that a man could get through?"

"It's no less than five feet high and thirty inches wide at the narrowest point," Adele said. "That's the throat just beyond the sinkhole. It changes direction there too. At the far end, it reaches to within fifty feet of where the foundations of the Admiral's Mansion are now. At the time, of course, nothing had been built."

"Three days would be plenty of time to cut a fifty-foot tunnel through coarse limestone," Daniel said to her, grinning triumphantly. "With stone-cutting saws and experienced workmen, which they'd have been by that point. I think you've found the way Mondreaux is getting into the mansion, Adele."

He paused. "Though that doesn't prove anything is going on except sex," he admitted. "Which I'm glad to say isn't a crime. And I can't believe Lieutenant

Pontefract is an Alliance spy. I don't know him well, but he was a senior when I entered the Academy, and I just don't believe . . ."

"Lieutenant Pontefract could be innocent of everything except bad judgment in picking bed partners," Adele said, searching in a sidebar while the sonogram filled the main field. "Which, as you say, isn't a crime."

Did that sound waspish? And of course it wasn't *quite* what Daniel had said. Adele couldn't understand—or at any rate couldn't allow herself to understand—why the women who interested him had to be not only young and pretty but also complete bubbleheads. She shrugged, as much a comment on what she hadn't verbalized as on what she had.

"But if Mondreaux is a trained intelligence agent, a spy," she continued, "he'd be able to plant discreet devices in the office portion of the mansion without Pontefract's knowledge. The only practical way to find them would be through their transmissions to the outside. If the spy were able to reenter the office regularly, he could collect the data manually and avoid that risk."

She cleared her throat, wondering whether to say more. *This is my friend Daniel. Perhaps the only friend I've ever had.*

"I think you can take it as a given that information is leaking from the console in Admiral Milne's private office," she said. "Based on console histories."

"Ah," said Daniel. "Ah."

He cleared his throat. "I don't suppose it'd do any good to tell Admiral Milne that her Flag Lieutenant might be involved with an Alliance spy," he said. "Not

without evidence. But you think Master Mondreaux
would be carrying spying equipment when he returned
from a meeting with Lieutenant Pontefract?"

"I think so, yes," Adele said, meeting Daniel's calm
eyes. "It would be the safest way to get information
out of the sealed office."

"Then I think Hogg and I will go hunting tonight,"
Daniel said. He grinned broadly. "Would you care to
come along to identify our bag, Adele?"

"I'd be very pleased to," Adele said. "Very pleased
indeed."

It was such a strange and wonderful thing, to have
a friend. . . .

CHAPTER 13

Sinmary on Nikitin

Adele settled herself, feeling the log beneath her gurgle a little against the soggy soil. Her utilities were waterproof within limits, but she suspected she'd be exceeding those limits tonight.

Not that it mattered, of course. Her data unit was sealed against dampness and the weather was warm enough that her fingers wouldn't stiffen on the control wands. Mere personal discomfort was too ordinary a part of her life to be worth considering.

Adele, Daniel and Hogg were in the gully that led to the Grand Gallery, simply because it provided concealment. They were well to the east of the parking area and a full five hundred yards from the entrance. Tovera had placed herself to watch for Mondreaux's approach without alerting him.

Adele hadn't asked where Tovera'd be. The pale sociopath had training in that sort of thing, and Adele herself did not.

"I wish we had a camera in the cave," Daniel said softly. "If we can't be inside ourselves."

"He's on the way," Tovera said. *"He's walking from the housing estate instead of flying here. He'll reach the parking area in two minutes or less."*

Adele and Daniel wore RCN commo helmets; Hogg did not, but Daniel made a quick hand-signal to him and got a nod in return. They were, Adele recalled, old hunting companions.

"We can't be inside," Adele said, "for the same reason we can't have a camera there. Tovera says if he's a member of the Fifth Bureau—"

Which Tovera herself had been, the intelligence agency reporting directly to Guarantor Porra.

"—he'll have been taught to sweep the area for watchers and electronic devices before he enters it. We have nothing to gain by assuming Mondreaux is badly trained or incompetent."

The first of Adele's five surveillance cameras showed movement. She expanded the image on the right half of her display. A man in a brown, shapeless cloak and a broad-brimmed hat came down the pathway, showing neither haste nor obvious caution. Only Tovera's identification made Adele sure he was Mondreaux.

Hair-fine optical cables linked the miniature cameras to Adele's personal data unit. The lines had no thermal or electro-optical signature, and to infra-red sensors the cameras themselves looked like the local equivalent of cicadas calling from tree branches. Even so Tovera'd been unwilling to risk placing one in the Grand Gallery itself.

Mondreaux walked past the first camera and into the field of the second; Adele expanded that image in turn. Though he was abreast of her and her companions, fifty yards of earth and vegetation hid them from one another's direct sight. The mesh walkway squealed against the posts that supported it, but the pedestrian's feet made no sound at all.

Mondreaux reached the parking area and the field of the third camera. He kept to the edge framed by knee-high bushes, not concealing himself exactly but positioning himself so that his outlines were blurred. He stepped into the gully, crossed it, and followed the broader path into the woods on the other side.

Tovera had placed the fourth camera to cover as much of the route as possible, but Mondreaux was occasionally out of sight among the trees. Adele found she tensed each time she lost the image, but Daniel and Hogg scarcely seemed to notice.

Hogg slipped a set of brass knuckles onto his right hand and clenched his fist. Adele said nothing, but she winced internally. She couldn't interrogate Mondreaux if his jaw was broken.

On the other hand, the knuckle-duster wasn't the worst option Hogg might've picked. She smiled slightly. Hogg's tool of choice for close-in work was a large folding knife, which would make interrogation even more difficult. . . .

The last camera was pinned to a tree fifty yards from the cavern's entrance. Because of its height, it had a narrow but uninterrupted line of sight through the Gallery. By increasing its magnification and light-amplification, Adele could get as good an image of the third sinkhole as she could've from the end of the cavern proper.

Mondreaux paused at the entrance to the Grand Gallery, then walked down the steps slowly with his left arm slightly raised. He might've been looking at a wristwatch. Adele presumed he was checking a multi-function sensor disguised as a watch.

Within the cavern he sauntered along the left-hand—seaward—side. He looked mostly ahead and to his right but occasionally turned suddenly to glance back at the entrance. His behavior dispelled any doubt that Adele might've had that Mondreaux was more than a gigolo . . . though in fact, she hadn't had many doubts.

She'd set her display on briefing mode again; Daniel watched it intently, but Hogg gave most of his attention to their present surroundings, the gully and the vegetation to either side. Adele assumed—and Hogg probably did also—that Tovera would warn them of any threat from outside, but Hogg watched anyway. He regarded it as his task to keep the young master safe. It wasn't one he delegated, ever.

Mondreaux reached the end of the Grand Gallery and pulled the rope supports out of the way. "Do you have a sound pickup in the cavern?" Daniel whispered urgently.

"No," said Adele. She didn't add, "For the same reason that I don't have a camera in there." She even kept the irritation she felt at a silly question out of her tone. Well, mostly out of her tone. "And a parabolic microphone wouldn't help while he's facing away from us."

There'd been a signal of some sort, though it might've been merely the clink of the metal stands on the cavern floor. A figure appeared in the alcove on the other side of the sinkhole, then vanished for a moment. Mondreaux waited with his hands on his hips.

The second figure reappeared in the alcove, pulling a narrow structure. "It's a ship's ladder," Daniel whispered. "We use them for access to the holds."

Adele focused her camera on the face and dialed in maximum light intensification. Mondreaux bent to catch the end of the ladder being extended toward him. That gave the camera a good angle at the second person. The image was blurred and grainy, but it was Lieutenant Pontefract beyond question. He wore a 2nd Class uniform.

"Got him!" Daniel said. "Got him! Adele, are you storing the images for evidence so—"

He paused, frozen. Adele hadn't opened her mouth, but white fire licked her mind.

"I'm very sorry," Daniel said. He was squatting beside her. He didn't stand up, but his back stiffened as though he were at attention and his eyes locked on the infinite distance ahead of him. "Yes, of course you're storing the information. I beg your pardon."

"Your apology is accepted," Adele said. A tiny smile tugged the corner of her mouth. Everybody makes mistakes. It's what you do next that separates the men from the weasels. . . .

The ladder slipped from the hands of one man or the other, raising a tinny *cling-g* as it hit the rock. Mondreaux walked across, his arms spread for balance. He wobbled slightly.

"Well, at least we know he's not from Alliance *Fleet* Intelligence," Daniel said, the hook of a sneer hidden in his smile. The RCN trained its midshipmen to the same standards as riggers: Daniel could've danced across that ladder blindfolded while carrying another man.

Which Adele certainly couldn't do. On the other hand, Master Mondreaux's professional skills appeared to be quite respectable, even if he didn't have a gymnast's sense of balance, or a rigger's.

Bending low, Pontefract and Mondreaux disappeared around the angle of the passage on the other side of the sinkhole. They left the ladder in place behind them. Adele let out her breath.

"Mundy, would you show me the plan of the cavern's extension, please?" Daniel said formally. "The part we can't see."

"Yes," Adele said simply. She hadn't been expecting that particular request, but she'd queued for immediate access all the files she'd used during their operation. She brought up the sonogram with a twist of her wands, then shrank the image area to limit it to the pigtail leading toward the Admiral's Mansion.

"All right, Hogg," Daniel said, using a stripped twig as a pointer. Adele noticed that he didn't stick the tip *into* the hologram but rather indicated his subject from outside where he didn't disrupt the image. "The neck just across the ladder is the narrowest point, but then the cavity swells out considerably before shrinking again. If we wait in the neck, we can prevent Mondreaux from escaping back into the mansion. And if he somehow gets away in the other direction, I think we can be confident that Mundy and Tovera will stop him before he leaves the cavern."

He gave Adele a smile that had only a perfunctory dash of humor. "By shooting him in the kneecap, if necessary," he added.

"I don't guess he'll get that far," Hogg said. His words were neutral; their implications were not.

"Any comments or questions, Mundy?" Daniel said, with the professional formality he affected when they were discussing RCN business.

Adele thought, then shrugged. "No," she said. "Since they've left the ladder in place, that appears to be the safest plan. Tovera and I will wait just outside the gallery's entrance and act as the situation warrants."

Things could still go wrong. Things could *always* go wrong. But all four of them had a demonstrated ability to act with intelligent dispatch in a developing situation. With dispatch and—Adele's smile was dry—with ruthlessness. She'd have her belt ready to use as a tourniquet in case she or Tovera blew Mondreaux's leg off at the knee.

She thought she heard a faint thump from the direction of the cavern. It could've been a door closing at the end of the passage; alternatively her mind might've invented the sound. Still, it was about the right length of time for Pontefract and Mondreaux to have reached the Admiral's Mansion.

Daniel and Hogg must've come to the same conclusion, because they both rose to their feet and looked toward the gallery. "One thing before we get into position, Hogg," Daniel said. "Are you carrying a gun?"

"If I was," Hogg said in low-voiced belligerence instead of answering, "it'd be only common sense, wouldn't it? I guess our boy Mondreaux is packing one, ain't he?"

"I don't know whether he is or not, Hogg," Daniel said calmly. "I *am* sure that I'd rather be killed myself than to survive to explain to Admiral Milne how I accidently killed her Flag Lieutenant. Leave the gun behind, please. Officer Mundy will take good care of it."

"Master, you know I won't use it unless—"

"I know things go wrong," Daniel said, not sharply but as relentlessly as a hornet. "I know mistakes occur. I try to minimize the possibility of irremediable mistakes."

"Master—"

"Leave the gun, Hogg," Daniel said, "or stay here with it. *Now.*"

"Aye, young master," Hogg mumbled, reaching into a pocket of his baggy jacket. He withdrew a squat, massive pistol which he handed to Adele. She eyed it, then slid it beneath her waistband.

Hogg's pistol threw a slug several times the weight of the tiny pellets from Adele's weapon. If you chose your target properly—an eye, a temple, the soft flesh at the base of a throat—the extra mass was unnecessary and the smaller projectile's reduced recoil let you swing onto the next target more quickly; but each to his own taste. Hogg could be depended on to get the job done, no matter what tool he was using.

"Good hunting, then, Mundy," Daniel said, smiling brightly. "Let's hope the morning finds us heroes instead of goats, eh?"

"Let's just hope the morning finds us alive, eh?" said Hogg. "I'll settle for being a live goat."

"Yes, well," said Daniel, setting off toward the Grand Gallery. "Adele, if Mondreaux kills me and Hogg, please shoot him in both knees, if you would."

"Yes, Daniel," said Adele Mundy.

And then I will shoot him in the back of the neck, before deciding whether to shoot myself as well. Because life really won't have much of value if anything happens to you.

※※※

Daniel used his helmet's light-amplification to study the cavern's wildlife while he waited for the spy's return. The mode was passive, just a matter of increasing the energy of every photon which struck the visor to the equivalent of many photons. It could be detected, but not as easily as Daniel's body heat could.

The chamber in which he and Hogg squatted was six or seven feet wide and ten in length. Rocks that'd scaled off of the roof and sides littered the floor. There must've been more debris in the recent past, but somebody'd cleared a path down the center.

Pontefract wouldn't have dared to delegate that task. Daniel smiled, amused to think of Milne's elegant Flag Lieutenant lifting rocks like a navvy.

His smile faded. This was going to be a very bad thing for Pontefract who, by everything Daniel had seen, was a perfectly decent fellow. His Academy scores were good—Adele had checked, of course—and one of his grandfathers had been an admiral. Admiral Pontefract had passed away years ago, but not before he'd nurtured a number of officers currently holding high rank in the RCN.

Pontefract should've gone far. Because of bad judgment in what he'd thought was a purely private matter, he'd be lucky if he was allowed to resign his commission instead of being court-martialled as a traitor.

An *eep-eep-eep* echoed through the passage. Daniel and Hogg both tensed for a moment, then relaxed. The sound could've passed for mechanical, but it was really an insectoid which'd been calling at eleven minute intervals ever since they'd entered the cavern three hours earlier.

Daniel wondered if the squeal of the door into the mansion a quarter mile away had brought the little fellow to this cave. Nothing seemed to be answering him, so he must be pretty frustrated by now.

He grinned, thinking of Ginny Raynham. No matter how things went tonight, he'd been luckier than the bug.

He and Hogg had gotten here through the slit connecting to the Grand Gallery. The passage twisting northward out of the chamber narrowed but never to the tight crawl in the other direction. The last fifty feet were saw-cut, ending at an armored door with a keypad lock. The inertial navigation system in Daniel's helmet proved the obvious, that the basement level of Admiral's Mansion was on the other side of that door.

The plan Daniel had made on the basis of the sonogram was still the correct one, though. There wasn't a better place than this chamber in which to wait for Mondreaux's return.

Hogg reached into a pocket and brought out a flask. He handed it to Daniel, who took another swig of the brandy. When he returned it, Hogg drank in turn.

"Looks like I should've brought the whole keg," Hogg said morosely.

"I don't imagine Mondreaux is going to sleep overnight in the mansion, Hogg," Daniel said. "Apart from anything else, Captain Molliman tells me that Milne spends quite a lot of time there herself. Keeping clear of her husband, according to rumor."

He wondered where Hogg'd come by the liquor. It was excellent stuff—certainly better than anything aboard the *Hermes*.

He didn't *ask* where the brandy came from, of course. Either Hogg wouldn't tell him; or worse, Hogg might. Knowing Hogg, that would probably make Daniel an accessory after the fact.

You wouldn't have thought enough light penetrated this deep in the cave for algae to grow, but the wet rock had blotches of it—pink rather than green when Daniel had examined it with his hand lamp earlier, though simply dark against lighter stone now. His visor's light amplification would show shapes and textures, but not colors.

Adele had downloaded part of Nikitin's natural history database into Daniel's helmet on her own initiative, so he'd had something to occupy his mind while he waited. Larval insectoids, slowly wriggling worms with a myriad tiny legs, were browsing the algae. They were relatives of a finger-long hopper that chirped in the surface forests, but this species was neotenous: the larvae bred and died without ever metamorphosing into adult forms.

A *clink!* echoed down the long passage, followed by *clink-clink*. Hogg grunted and straightened to his feet like a dog rising as his master appears. Daniel had offered him a helmet or RCN goggles with the same range of optical enhancements, but he'd refused.

That wasn't simply braggadocio. Hogg had hunted and snared for close on fifty years using the senses he'd been born with. Electronic "improvements" risked masking sensory inputs that'd meant success in the past.

Daniel rose also, stretching limb by limb. There was no need for haste. Mondreaux and Pontefract— who had to come down to pull the ladder back into hiding—couldn't get to this point in less than three minutes, and they had no reason to hurry.

Algae and insectoids had kept Daniel calm during the long wait, but now he had something else to occupy him. He spread the six-foot minnow net to make sure it wasn't knotted, then brought his hands together again. The net had a weighted rim and a drawstring to pull it closed.

It was intended for catching bait, but instead of casting it Daniel intended to drape it directly over Mondreaux's head and torso. He'd thought of bringing some sort of club—a wrench or a length of high-pressure tubing like Woetjans carried—but the net would keep the fellow from pulling a weapon. A good whack with a club risked turning him into a vegetable who couldn't answer questions.

Daniel heard feet shuffling down the passage. There were two people, as expected, talking in low voices. He couldn't make out their words. The entrance to the chamber brightened perceptibly; one or both men were lighting their way with hand lamps at minimum output.

Portions of the passage were wide enough for two men to walk abreast, but the slot into this chamber was not. Daniel, standing beside the entrance, spread the net before him with his arms raised. If Pontefract was the first through the opening, they'd have to hope that he was too focused on the narrow cleared path to notice the men poised to either side.

Mondreaux came through first. He didn't have a light, so the faint glow of his companion's lamp threw his shadow into the chamber.

"Next Thursday, then, dear—" he was saying over

his shoulder. Daniel stepped toward him, whipping the minnow net forward and down.

Mondreaux ducked, raising his left arm as his right hand snaked toward his hip pocket. He was *very* fast. Daniel kicked, the toe of his boot meeting the gun as Mondreaux brought it out and sending it clattering down the passage.

Somebody shouted. Mondreaux's companion flicked the lamp to maximum output. Daniel's visor went black momentarily to save his retinas. Mondreaux, lizard-quick, kicked Daniel in the ankle and darted past him through the chamber. The minnow net still dangled from his head and left shoulder, but he had his right arm free.

Daniel leaped for Mondreaux. Fallen rock skidded under his right foot. He caught the spy's sleeve rather than the cord of the net; Mondreaux twisted and jerked hard. Daniel crashed to the cave floor on his left side, clutching the torn-off sleeve.

Hogg's weighted fist smacked something hard. The shouting stopped. The hand lamp turned to light the ceiling instead of glaring at Daniel and Mondreaux.

Bent double, the spy dodged into the narrow throat between this chamber and the Grand Gallery. Daniel threw himself after the man. His left wrist was a mass of stabbing needles, but the pain didn't matter now. He ducked but he didn't duck low enough, and his head smacked the ceiling.

Daniel slid face-forward. The helmet had kept him from a concussion, but maybe if he hadn't been wearing the bloody thing he wouldn't have hit the rock in the first place. It was askew now. He flung it behind him and scrambled the rest of the way out of the throat.

Mondreaux was already across the sinkhole. "Don't shoot!" Daniel shouted and stepped onto the ladder. Neither Adele nor her servant was likely to blaze away without being sure of her target, but Hogg had drilled it into his young master that your fellow hunters were likely to be more dangerous than any animal you were after.

Mondreaux bent and grasped the ladder. He jerked it toward him, twisting it on edge at the same time.

Daniel was midway across the sinkhole. He jumped, not forward or back but to the exiguous ledge along the wall of the cavern to his left. Without his weight to anchor it, the far end of the ladder slid into the sinkhole.

Mondreaux screamed. He tried to fling the ladder away, but he'd already overbalanced. He teetered on the edge, his arms flailing in circles.

Daniel's ledge was less than a hand's breadth wide and generally only half that. He couldn't have stood still on it, because the arch of the wall pushed his center of mass out beyond his footing. The ladder sank into the pool beneath him with a bubbling splash.

As he'd found many times in a starship's rigging, speed could save you when nothing else would. Using the inertia of his sideways leap, Daniel sprinted along the curving ledge in two strides. The third put him into the floor of the cavern proper.

Mondreaux toppled forward with a despairing wail. Daniel grabbed his left wrist and pulled. Daniel's balance wasn't good enough to support his own weight and the spy's at arm's length; he went into the sinkhole also, still holding Mondreaux but catching the edge with his left hand. Gods! how his wrist hurt, it was burning in half and it didn't matter, not now.

"Adele, throw Mondreaux the rope!" Daniel shouted. Would the decorative cord support the spy's thrashing weight? Better than Daniel's own wrist would, at least. This couldn't go on. "I can't hold him much longer!"

The pool boiled. Bloody hell, the squid! There was Hogg on the other side of the sinkhole but he couldn't do anything, while Adele and Tovera had the whole length of the gallery to run.

Light leaking from Pontefract's lamp in the far passage glittered on the thousands of diamond points slashing upward, the tiny claws unsheathing as the squid reached for the struggling men. Mondreaux screamed like he was being gelded, and maybe he was.

Daniel felt his boots and trousers ripping downward. The pain in his legs was enough to make him forget his wrist for a moment.

Hogg leaned forward. Daniel twisted his face against his left shoulder as a tentacle curved toward his head. Six of the arms were longer than the others, the database had said. . . .

The pool lifted in a bubble of white light. The shock and roar were volcanic. Water spouted into the cavern's ceiling and sluiced along it toward the entrance.

For an instant Daniel hung in the air, several feet above the Gallery's floor. He'd have dropped back into the sinkhole, roiling and thundering as seawater rushed through the channel to refill it, but Adele twisted and threw him like a sack of flour to the wet stone.

"I have the other one!" Tovera said. Her voice remained emotionless but she spoke louder than Daniel had heard her before. "You can let go of him, Lieutenant."

Am I still holding Mondreaux? Daniel thought; and

he was, he had to consciously relax the fingers of his right hand and Gods! how his left wrist burned, it was a bonfire searing that whole side of his body.

"He's dead," Tovera said. "There's a compartment in his belt buckle, though. That's where the information will be."

She laughed—tittered would've been a more descriptive word—and added, "We were lucky it stayed attached."

Daniel rose to his knees and right hand, keeping as much weight as he could off his left side. Gods! but he hurt.

"Tovera, do you have bandages in your case?" Adele said. "Lieutenant Leary is bleeding."

Daniel looked at Mondreaux, sprawled on the stone beside him like a blood-soaked sponge. The spy had lost not only his trousers and shoes, his right arm had been ripped off at the shoulder and the grip of a hooked tentacle had flayed his face to the bare skull.

"I'll take care of him, mistress," Tovera said, handing Adele the belt and opening her attaché case. A small sub-machine gun was cradled in the center so that it presented itself to the hand of whoever opened the case, but around it were nestled a series of discrete compartments. Tovera took a spray flask from one, closed the case, and knelt beside Daniel.

He hadn't lost his hand lamp, for a wonder. He shone it down into the sinkhole. The pool had refilled, but the water thrashed and swirled with the rush of its flooding. The squid's body floated on top in a tangle of tentacles which the blast had torn off.

I didn't ask Hogg if he was carrying a concussion grenade, Daniel thought. *And a good thing I didn't. . . .*

"Hold still if you please, Lieutenant," Tovera said. The fingertips of her left hand touched his shoulder to keep his attention. "This is a styptic and antiseptic. I have something for the pain also, if you need it."

"I don't," Daniel said. His voice was harsh. A spray hissed prickly iciness down the back of his right calf, then the left one.

Daniel hadn't looked at his legs. He was afraid that they'd look like what was left of Mondreaux. He'd be able to handle that in a little while. If he was crippled, he was crippled; he knew the risks of his profession. Just at the moment, though, he was too close to slipping into shock to want to push himself in quite that fashion.

Hogg stood on the opposite side of the sinkhole. He'd brought his coil of deep-sea fishing line from his pocket and was swinging the weight on one end in the cavity. When it looped around the topmost rung of the fallen ladder, Hogg gave the line a quick jerk to set it, then lifted the ladder out hand over hand. The grenade had twisted the light metal badly, but it'd still do to cross the sinkhole.

The narrow throat leading from the Admiral's Mansion brightened as Mondreaux's companion squirmed through behind a hand lamp. Hogg glanced over his shoulder but continued to haul up the ladder; Tovera opened her case minusculely.

"Tovera, please take your hand away from that immediately," Daniel said quietly. He stood, putting himself between Adele's pale spider and the opening across the sinkhole. He couldn't feel anything in his legs, but they seemed to hold him upright. He felt as though he were balancing on very long stilts. Louder, he called, "Lieutenant Pontefract?"

Mondreaux's companion stepped into plain sight. It was Admiral Milne herself.

Nobody spoke for a moment. Daniel felt himself swaying.

Adele put a hand on his elbow and guided him back from the edge. "You'd better sit down, Daniel," she said. "I've only had time for a cursory examination of the material Mondreaux was carrying, but I believe on the basis of it I should be the one to discuss the situation with Admiral Milne."

"Good luck," Daniel said, bracing himself to sit down as directed. He'd stood up easily, but that was because he hadn't had time to think about it. "And I mean that very sincerely."

CHAPTER 14

Sinmary Port on Nikitin

"Through there, Leary," Lieutenant Pontefract said, opening the door. The lieutenant's face was impassive, but Daniel read in it a look of disgust. Perhaps that was a guilty conscience. "She's waiting for you."

"Thank you," Daniel said, walking stiffly into the enclosed garden behind the Admiral's Mansion. The door closed after him.

He didn't have any choice but to move stiffly: twelve hours in the *Hermes'* Medicomp, the tender's automated sick bay, had repaired much of the previous night's damage, but it'd be weeks if not months before Daniel would be able to move without twingeing reminders. His left wrist was in a brace, but his left elbow and shoulder joints jabbed him regularly also.

Milne's garden was small but more attractive than Daniel would've guessed. In the center was a paved patio with a square stone table. The benches on two sides were set at an angle rather than facing one another. The ends of the tract were shaded by a terran dogwood, at present full of white flowers, and a small tree with scarlet foliage. Shrubs—Daniel didn't recognize any of the half-dozen species—bordered the back wall, and a variety of flowers grew in discrete sections. Several were Terran hostas.

There were blue Cinnabar silkflowers as well. Daniel felt an unexpected pang when he saw them. His mother'd had a window box of silkflowers, so that even when she'd grown too weak to walk outdoors she had a reminder of the garden to which she'd devoted much of her life. An odd thing to remember now.

Admiral Milne stood in front of the table, her hands crossed behind her. To Daniel's surprise she was in civilian clothes, a suit of white-speckled brown. Makeup on her left cheek covered what must be extensive bruising despite treatments to dissolve the extravasated blood, but the side of her face was still swollen. She'd been very lucky that Hogg hadn't broken bones when he decked her.

Hogg, and more particularly Hogg's master, had been lucky as well. Adele had been able to fix matters as they now stood, but Daniel wouldn't have wanted to test how much farther her powers of persuasion went.

"You will *not* salute, Leary," the Admiral said in a tone that only charity would describe as a snarl. "And I'd rather you hadn't worn your uniform, so that I wouldn't have to be reminded you have a commission in the service to which I've devoted my life."

"Sir," said Daniel neutrally. He stood at Parade Rest, figuring that was the pose least likely to aggravate the already uncomfortable situation. He kept his eyes on the silver-barked shrub spreading beyond Milne's right shoulder.

"If justice were done, Leary," the Admiral continued, "you'd be on trial for murder. Yes, murder! The only reason that isn't happening is that your—I don't know what to call her!"

"Sir," said Daniel, angry to a degree that took him by surprise. "You may refer to her as Officer Mundy, or if you prefer her civilian title, Mundy of Chatsworth. A very noble house, as I'm sure you're aware; and one which is notably punctilious of its honor."

Milne blinked, suddenly wary. She looked like a toad realizing that the meal she's just swallowed might have a sting. "RCN regulations flatly forbid duels between officers," she said. "If that's what you're implying."

"Yes sir," Daniel said to the distant shrub. "But please keep in mind that the lady in question has been a Mundy all her life and an RCN officer for only the past few years. I assure you that *she* is aware of that."

"That's neither here nor there," said Milne, but the hectoring anger had gone out of her voice. Adele's reputation as a pistol shot had gotten around, and that the Mundys had tender honors was well known. So, of course, did the Learys of Bantry.

"Anyway," Milne continued, "you needn't worry about being prosecuted. *Officer* Mundy made it quite clear that such proceedings would lead to the scandalous blackening of poor Mondreaux's name. Better he be allowed to rest in peace as a victim of accident, which I suppose in a strictly literal fashion he was."

"Sir," said Daniel. Nobody'd intended Mondreaux to die, that was true; and Daniel couldn't imagine having an enemy whom he'd want to die in the particular fashion that Mondreaux had. It was Mondreaux's bad luck. *And* bad judgment, and perhaps bad karma—though that was a matter for priests and philosophers, not RCN officers.

The Admiral didn't say anything about what would happen to her own career if a court-martial heard the full story of what and why events had occurred the previous night. It was even possible that she wasn't thinking so much about her career as she was about her husband's reaction. "A tongue like a diamond drill," Captain Molliman had said, describing Master Milne.

"I dare say you understand, Leary," Milne continued, swinging her hands in front of her and then stuffing them clenched into her pockets, "why I don't want to look at you and your consort any more than I have to, though."

She paused. Daniel wasn't sure she wanted an answer—it wasn't a question, strictly speaking—and in any case the only answer he could've given was another place-holding, "Sir." He said nothing.

"Fortunately for both of us," Milne continued, "the needs of the service provide an answer. No doubt you've heard about the difficult situation on Yang?"

"Yessir," Daniel said. *Was Milne going to order the* Hermes *to Yang? Because if she did, Commander Slidell was going to be angry enough to chew hull plating.*

"The government of Yang has captured some two hundred mercenaries serving with the rebels," Milne said. "President for Life Shin has put them to hard labor, but I suspect that he'll have them all executed the next time he wants to give his supporters a little treat. Normally I'd say, 'Good riddance,' but it seems this particular lot is from the Burdock Stars, so they're Cinnabar citizens. It's my duty to procure their release and repatriation. Are you beginning to understand, Leary?"

Yes, Daniel thought. Aloud he said, "Sir, not at present."

Insectoids buzzed around the flowers. Daniel couldn't have told what they were without slipping his goggles over his eyes and dialing up the magnification. He'd wondered if these varied off-world plants had to be hand-pollinated, but apparently Milne or her predecessors had imported animals for the purpose.

Thinking about the garden was much less uncomfortable than imagining where the Admiral was going with this conversation.

"I'm going to send you to remonstrate with President Shin, Leary," Milne said. She grinned, then winced to have stretched muscles swollen from the wallop Hogg'd given her. "You and Officer Mundy. You've proven yourself such resourceful people that I'm sure you'll have no difficulty making Shin see reason. What do you think?"

"Sir," said Daniel to the bush. "The *Hermes* won't be ready to lift for some days, perhaps a week. Ah—"

"Who said anything about the *Hermes*, Leary?" Milne snapped. "I'm going to request that Commander Slidell send one of his cutters to deal with the situation on Yang. I can't tell a captain which of his officers to detail to a task, of course, but I'm sure the Commander will accept my friendly suggestion."

A cutter? To cow the Yang government into submission?

"They're all barbarians on Yang," Milne continued

cheerfully. "The government as surely as the rebels. After all, only a year ago President Shin *was* a rebel. That's why I think you and Officer Mundy are perfect for the task. You understand the minds of the puerile butchers you'll be dealing with!"

She laughed, then winced again. "At the very least," Milne added in a rasping snarl, "I think I can promise you an interesting time. Don't you think so, Leary?"

"Yes sir," said Daniel, even now managing not to meet the Admiral's eyes. "I do."

At least for as long as they survived. Which might very well be a matter of seconds after Lieutenant Leary delivered an ultimatum to President Shin with nothing but a cutter and her thirty-man crew to back it up.

Adele watched as Sun, lying on his back, spliced her specialized equipment into *Cutter 614*'s command console. The commo suite was quite sophisticated—virtually identical to that of the *Hermes* herself though without the redundancy—but there wasn't provision for anybody but the captain to use it: cutters didn't ordinarily carry their own signals officer.

Daniel, obviously thinking the same thing, said, "We'll weld you a jumpseat on the back of the console, Mundy."

He cleared his throat and added, "I regret this situation. That I involved you in it, particularly."

"There you go, mistress!" Sun said, starting to inch his way out of the very close quarters he'd been working in. No starship could be described as roomy, but cutters were tight even by the standards of a corvette like the *Princess Cecile*. "Want to test it now?"

"In a few minutes, Sun," Adele said. "Thank you

for your help. I don't have the expertise with tools to have done that myself."

"My pleasure," Sun said cheerfully. He got his head clear, glanced to either side, and then sat up carefully in the space between the console and the gunnery board. "I'll bring my duffel in, then. Captain, it'll be a pleasure to sail with you again."

"Are you assigned to *614*, Sun?" Daniel said in surprise. "I'd have thought . . ."

Sun grinned. "Every place in the cutter's crew went to a senior Sissie, sir," he said. "And it's not volunteers, though I guess we all would. Captain Slidell assigned us, just like that."

"Let's go out on the hull, Lieutenant," Adele said, closing down her personal data unit. She smiled. "I believe it's too early to watch the sunset, but I'm sure we'll find something."

"Eh?" said Daniel. His puzzlement warmed into a great, beaming smile. "Yes indeed, I'm sure we will. If I'm stationed on Nikitin for any length of time, I'd like to make a study of the seabirds. Do you know, I've already seen three off-planet species? I wonder if they're accidental or deliberate introductions?"

The cutter's single hatch for the present connected it to the tender. Going onto the hull required entering the *Hermes*' central passage, then exiting through one of the tender's hatches. With Daniel in the lead, they went out the same way they'd done a few days before.

Adele didn't have magnetic boots this time, but Daniel snapped a short safety line to her belt and attached the other end to his own harness. The worst her clumsiness was going to do was leave her hanging at the end of a six foot line. Unless Daniel's injuries—

"Daniel, are you physically fit?" she said sharply as she followed him up the ladder to the mast platform. "Perhaps we shouldn't—"

"Oh, heavens yes!" Daniel said, turning at the top and offering Adele his hand. "You mean from the squid? Yes, I need to use my legs or they're apt to swell and stiffen, but there's no better exercise than running up and down the antennas the way the crew has to do on a cutter."

He held up his left hand. "This wrist isn't quite right since I jammed it the other night, but there's nothing for it but exercise as well. I'll be fine."

Adele looked at her friend. He sounded both cheerful and pellucidly honest, but sweat beaded his forehead after the short climb and the muscles of his face were taut beneath the smile. To avoid pain Daniel would have to take enough drugs to turn him comatose. He wasn't willing to accept loss of function, so he was living with the pain.

Adele nodded in silent agreement. That was the same thing she'd have done, of course. No doubt the shared attitude was part of the reason they were friends.

"This is going to be a very dangerous operation," Daniel said quietly, his eyes on the birds circling overhead. It was obvious even to Adele that they weren't all native to the same world, since some had two wings but others four. "I don't mean difficult—frankly, it may well be impossible to achieve. President Shin won't surrender the captives unless he feels threatened, and a cutter is unlikely to threaten him sufficiently."

He turned his hands palms up and looked at Adele with a wistful smile. "The risk," he continued, "the danger, is that Shin will become so angry at the request that he'll massacre the cutter's whole crew out of hand. He'll view as an insult a ship that can't launch missiles into his palace from orbit. By foolish grandstanding, I've endangered people for whom I have high regard and a sense of responsibility."

"Daniel, that's nonsense," Adele said in honest surprise. "Mondreaux was a spy. Certainly I'm willing to let the Admiral wear a fig-leaf to save her retirement and I suppose her marriage, but you needn't be in any doubt about the contents of the recording chip that we took from Mondreaux's body. He was copying all traffic that passed through the console in Milne's office."

"I realize that," Daniel said, looking away again and crossing his hands behind his back. Though his face had seemed calm, he was knotting and unknotting his clenched fingers. "I realize that. But by deciding to capture him myself instead of taking my suspicions to the proper authorities, I created a real mare's nest. *And* got Mondreaux killed, which wasn't my intention."

"Daniel," Adele said quietly. "Look at me."

He met her eyes and nodded. "Yes?" he said.

"Daniel, I don't normally discuss this with you since I believe you'd rather not know, but I *am* the proper authorities," Adele said. She gave him a wry smile. "If you were wondering how this will affect your service record—"

"I'm not," he said. "That's the farthest thing from my mind."

"I know it is," she agreed. "But if you *were* wondering, I'd tell you that I will report to my superior that I requested the assistance of an RCN line officer to apprehend the spy whom I was sent to the Gold Dust Cluster to deal with; and my superior will speak a quiet word in the ear of Admiral Anston, who will offer you the Republic's discreet thanks at his next opportunity."

Daniel grinned, then shook his head in bemusement. "I swear to God," he said, "I never *dreamed* that Lieutenant Pontefract's duties as Flag Lieutenant extended to matters quite as personal to the Admiral as they apparently did. If I had . . ."

His voice trailed off. He was still smiling.

"If you *had* realized that Pontefract was a pimp . . ." Adele said. "Or if I had, which I did not—what would you have done differently?"

"Well, I'd have asked Hogg not to slug her with brass knuckles," Daniel said. "I'm not entirely sure he'd have obeyed me, but I'd have made the effort."

"Ah," said Adele. She cleared her throat, then smiled in turn. "Daniel, Admiral Milne won't receive any formal punishment. It'd embarrass too many people to publicize the business last night. Embarrassment to me in my future duties to the Republic, not least. Milne's folly, her stupidity—her thinking with her genitals—"

Daniel's face went watchfully blank. Adele had been a little too vehement, she supposed, in denouncing matters toward which others—Daniel certainly among them—took a more relaxed view.

"The Admiral's ill-judged actions," Adele continued in a calm, clinical tone, "caused injury to the Republic and very likely the death of Cinnabar citizens. If solving the problem she caused involved her being punched in the face, then I can only say I wish Hogg had hit her again."

Daniel's smile spread over his face again. "Well, just between us," he said, "Hogg feels the same way."

His chuckle built to bellowing laughter that bent him double. The riggers working on the antennas forward looked over at them, and the former Sissies began to laugh also.

CHAPTER 15

Sinmary Port on Nikitin

The captain's clerk, Orly, had been Slidell's clerk aboard the *Bainbridge*. He watched Daniel tensely over his console. The court-martial records showed he'd been heavily involved in the suppression of the mutiny.

From the scuttlebutt Hogg had gathered, Orly'd fired into the deck while arresting the bosun. He'd nearly blown his foot off, and the ricochet clipped the ear of a "trustworthy" technician behind him in the corridor.

"The Captain says you can go in now," the clerk said, his hand hovering close to the cloth-covered pistol on the stand he'd moved next to his console.

"Thank you, Orly," Daniel said, giving him a bright smile as he stepped to the hatch of the captain's day-cabin. He hoped the nervous clerk wouldn't decide he was baring his teeth in a prelude to a snarling attack.

On the positive side, Orly clearly didn't know much about guns. If he did cut loose in panic, he was at least as likely to shoot Captain Slidell as he was Daniel.

Though that didn't mean Daniel himself wouldn't be blamed for the result.

The whimsy made Daniel smile, which he realized instantly from the look on Slidell's face wasn't the expression to have worn on greeting his superior officer. This one, at any rate. Daniel braced to attention, saluted, and said, "Sir! I need to go over arrangements for *614*'s liftoff with you."

"Close the hatch, Leary," Slidell said. His tone had the calm of a dog straining at a leash. He didn't bother to say, "At ease," or return the salute; Daniel hadn't expected that he would.

Daniel pulled the hatch to, then dogged it on his own initiative. Slidell could snarl at him no matter which choice he made about dogging it—or if he asked direction. One learns very quickly in life, let alone in the RCN, that there are situations in which you couldn't win. You dealt with them and got on with your business.

"All right, Leary," Slidell said from his seat behind the console. "Nobody can overhear us now, so we don't have to lie."

"Sir," said Daniel carefully. If Slidell really thought nobody was eaves-dropping on them, he didn't know Adele very well . . . which was probably the case.

The day room was small but attractively appointed. The couch and two chairs, though bolted to the deck, were hand-carved wooden souvenirs of a previous appointment. On one bulkhead was a hologram of a smiling woman with two children whose features bore obvious resemblance to Slidell's. Across from the hologram were two rural watercolors, of a tile-roofed hut and of drystone fences snaking across a hillside. Slidell had a reputation as a skilled amateur painter.

"You're blackmailing the Admiral," Slidell said baldly. "She's furious, but she's giving you this new chance to make a hero of yourself anyway. No wonder you've got so many medals, Leary! I now see that you use not only influence but extortion to make sure that all the high-profile assignments are given to you!"

Daniel blinked. He was so nonplussed that he didn't even bother to deny the charge.

"Well, you've gotten what you were after," Slidell said. "And much may it profit you, Lieutenant! I've discussed the situation on Yang with people who know, and I don't mind telling you that *I* think you've overreached yourself this time. You may think you're Fortune's Favorite, but I think you'll find swimming in a cesspool like Yang leaves you stinking like the filth I know you are at heart!"

"Sir," said Daniel quietly. "I'm very sorry you feel that way. I assure you my only wish is to perform the tasks my superiors set me, according to the regulations and tradition of the RCN."

"Oh, don't worry, Leary," Slidell sneered. "It doesn't matter what I *feel* since I have my orders too. You've gotten the assignment you've connived for, and I've given you a crew of the most senior personnel who came with you from that corvette of yours."

"Thank you very much, sir," Daniel said, speaking as calmly and unemotionally as he could. Was Slidell literally insane? Hatred, even irrational hatred, was understandable, but coupling the hatred with the offer of the thirty best spacers in the RCN made the Captain's attitude completely beyond imagination.

"Oh, you needn't pretend to thank me, Leary," Slidell said with a tired sneer. "I'm simply watching my back. Do you think I hadn't realized how those people could sabotage the *Hermes* in your absence? Wouldn't that look fine? Not only does Lieutenant Leary pull off a brilliant coup, but while he's on detached duty Commander Slidell can't even manage to lift the tender from Nikitin! That's what you were planning, isn't it?"

"No sir," Daniel said. His voice rising despite his best efforts, he went on, "And if I may add, sir, that's a libel on some of the best and most loyal personnel who ever wore the uniform of the RCN!"

"You don't need to posture, Leary," Slidell snapped. "I told you we're alone here. I swear I'd send Pasternak with you, but I can't possibly put both my chiefs on the same cutter. I'm making do with getting Woetjans off the *Hermes*. Nobody's in a better position to lead a mutiny than the bosun, as I well know!"

He's a skilled astrogator, Daniel thought, straight-faced. *A beloved husband and father, and a very able watercolorist.*

And also more paranoid than most of the people in mental institutions.

"Sir," Daniel said, deciding to proceed as though none of the previous words had been said—which would've been a greatly preferable situation. "*Cutter 614* will be ready to lift in less than two hours. The crew's personal items are aboard and we're finishing loading stores. When will it be possible for the *Hermes* to lift us to orbit?"

"Not for a week, Leary," Slidell said, "though the work may go faster now that I've rid the crew of possible troublemakers. But in any case you won't be waiting for the *Hermes*. I'm ordering you to get under way immediately, based on the urgency which Admiral Milne attaches to your mission."

"Sir . . ." Daniel said, blinking again and swallowing. "Sir, we'll be extremely short of reaction mass if we have to lift to orbit ourselves. I realize repairs to the tender's rig won't be complete for several days at least, but I hoped you'd lift us to orbit, then land immediately to finish work."

"Did you, Leary?" Slidell said, sounding tired and disgusted rather than angry. "Then I'm afraid your hope has been dashed. Many of mine have been dashed over the years too. They tell me it builds character."

Daniel opened his mouth, then closed it again. What was he going to do, beg? Which indeed he'd have been willing to do for the sake of the crew, if he'd thought there was a chance of changing the Commander's mind. They'd be able to lift off and land, but they'd have to use the High Drive very sparingly during the voyage proper. That'd add days, possibly weeks, to the operation, though he wouldn't have the precise time until he'd revised his itinerary.

"Yes sir," Daniel said. He saluted again and opened the hatch without being dismissed. He doubted Slidell would have him court-martialled for the discourtesy, though you could never tell.

Sometimes you just had to deal with situations and get on with your business the best way you could.

Adele balanced her personal data unit on her lap, watching the *Garnet* lift in steam and iridescence on the left half of her display while she monitored port communications on the right side. She was coupled to

the cutter's main computer—there was plenty of excess
capacity—but only Daniel could use its display.

Cutter 614's outer hatch sighed shut, then automatically dogged itself—*cling-cling, cling-cling, cling-cling.*
Woetjans tested the closure manually, then stepped out
of the airlock and swung the inner hatch to.

The bosun wore her hard suit, as did the other
riggers in the cutter's single bay. Adele, hunching on
her jump-seat, had the feeling of being a small child
in a mob of adults. None of them wished her the
least harm, but there was a very real chance that she
was going to be trampled.

"*614* to *Hermes* Control," Daniel said. "We're closed
up and prepared to decouple. Over."

Adele would've heard the transmission anyway,
but he'd set the cutter's internal speakers to echo all
messages that went through the link to the tender.
If everything went right, most of a starship's crew
had nothing to do during liftoff. Daniel believed that
keeping his personnel aware of the ordinary exchanges
made it less likely that they'd use their free time to
invent extraordinary possibilities.

The high-pitched buzz of the *Garnet's* thrusters had
died away. The patrol cruiser's image changed from a
silvery cylinder to spots of plasma which themselves
merged into a bright single blur. Adele switched that
half of her display to a view of the *Hermes* from
scanners on the nearest vessel, the *Cutlass* in a slip
a quarter mile to the east.

"*Roger*, 614," Lieutenant Ganse's voice replied.
There was a loud double *clang* as the hooks locking
the cutter to the tender's hull released. "*I'm extending
the davits now, over.*"

The Second Lieutenant rather than Captain Slidell was taking charge of the cutter's liftoff. That was neither unexpected nor undesirable.

The cutter swung side to side as the telescoping davits extended, pushing her away from the *Hermes* so that she could light her thrusters without damaging the mother ship's hull and rig. The davits were hydraulic like the antennas themselves, but their seals shrieked like saws on steel as they rubbed.

The swinging motion intensified. Most of the crew was seated, though some were in the central aisle because the bunks/benches didn't have enough room when so many personnel were in rigging suits. Hogg and Tovera were in the back of the bay, making the close quarters closer yet.

Woetjans remained where she was. *Protecting me from being stepped on*, Adele suddenly realized. Sometimes she felt the crew—the former Sissies, at any rate—treated her like a mascot rather than a fellow spacer; but there was also the sort of unthinking respect that other members of the People's Party had shown toward their leader, Lucius Mundy. . . .

The bosun turned and looked down. "Ordinarily we'd lift from the davits," she explained. "If we was in orbit, I mean. Here Ganse's going to set us on the water. That's a bloody sight better than having to screw with the clamps releasing just so."

Adele nodded. The bosun meant clamps attaching the davits to the cutter—or vice versa—she supposed, but it didn't really matter to her. Woetjans, who could be expected to know, was pleased with the situation. In any case it didn't call for the involvement of a Signals Officer.

614's outriggers patted the water; then the vessel splashed hard with another double clang. On Adele's display a curtain of spray lifted and sank back to show the cutter bobbing. The imagery didn't look nearly as violent as the motion felt from inside. The davits shrieked again as they withdrew, but at least this time the sound wasn't transmitted directly through the cutter's hull.

"614, *this is* Hermes," Ganse said. *"You are cleared for liftoff. Over."*

"Roger, *Hermes*," Daniel said. "Break, ship prepare to light thrusters."

Adele echoed the command console as a sidebar over the left-side imagery. The four thruster icons were green, and the three High Drive motors were cross-hatched green on standby, showing that the pumps were cycling reaction mass though their converters weren't breaking it down into anti-matter as yet.

Sentino, the Senior Motorman in the seat to the left of the command console, waited nervously. Sun, at the gunnery board, had the thruster data up also; though a Gunner's Mate, he also had a Power Room rating, Adele recalled. That might come in handy. . . .

"Lighting thrusters," Daniel said, stabbing an index finger into his virtual controls. The cutter shuddered as though a giant pillow had struck the underside of the hull; the whine of the pumps picked up to meet the demand. Steam gushed on the imagery, completely hiding the hull.

"Liftoff in three seconds," Daniel said. That was much less time than he'd usually have given the nozzles to warm up before raising them to full power. "Liftoff!"

A roar echoed from the slip as plasma jets flash-heated divots of water into steam. For a moment *614* trembled as thrust struggled to overcome inertia; then the vessel began to rise.

Sentino said, *"Three's down by twenty percent!"* on the command channel. The words didn't mean anything to Adele, but Daniel had already taken the thrusters out of automatic mode and was adjusting them individually. A line of numbers cascaded on Adele's sidebar. Though the fringes were gibberish to her, she noticed the cutter leveled from what'd been a slightly nose-down attitude.

"Hold them there if you please, Sentino," Daniel said, using the intercom because no one could shout over the thunder of thrusters at maximum output. *"I judge it'll take some three minutes from commencement of lift before we can switch to the High Drive."*

Adele wiped the image from her display and got to work locating the *Garnet*. Captain Toron wasn't masking his vessel's emissions—he had no reason to—but through bad luck the patrol cruiser was on the other side of the planet when *614* lifted off. It took her nearly a minute to locate the other vessel, lock a laser communicator on it, and call, *"RCS Garnet,* this is RCS *Cutter 614.* Please reply by laser, using a reciprocal of this signal. Over."

It took a moment. *If Hernandez were under me—* Adele thought; and as she formed the words, the communicator crackled, *"Garnet to 614, hold one for the First Lieutenant."* Then in Zileri's voice it resumed, *"Mundy, this is* Garnet. *Why on laser? Is your microwave out? Over."*

"Garnet," Adele said, *"laser is more secure. I thought*

it as well that we not confuse Port Control. Are matters in hand from your side? Ah, over."

Zileri laughed. "*Commander Slidell would have kittens, you mean?*" he said. "*Well, I've run worse risks and the Skipper says he has too. But put Danny on and I'll tell him we're ready to pump. Over.*"

"I'll put you through to Captain Leary," Adele said. "He does not, I repeat does not, know anything about this. I, ah, didn't want to get his hopes up in case things didn't work out. Over. Ah, break. Captain, Lieutenant Zileri of the *Garnet* wishes to speak with you. May I put him through? Over."

She was sitting back to back with Daniel in the command console, but she had a thumb-sized image of his face at the top of her display. Daniel looked up in surprise from the astrogation layout on which he was concentrating and said, "*Paolo? I suppose he wants to wish me a safe voyage; we were friends in the Academy, you know. Sure, put him through.*"

"Lieutenant Zileri," Adele said, "you may go ahead. Over."

"*Danny boy,*" Zileri said, almost before the words were out of Adele's mouth. "*My Skipper tells me we've got a problem. We're up here in orbit with full tanks of reaction mass and we'd like to get rid of some of it before we land back in Sinmary Port. Is there any possibility that we could offload some to you? Anything up to a thousand tons, brother. Garnet over.*"

Daniel's image blinked like a small animal in the headlights. "*Paolo, is that you?*" he said. "*Good God, man, Admiral Milne'll skin you alive if she learns you've been helping me! I don't know what you've heard, but I'm not her fair-haired boy. Over.*"

"*The Skipper says he can live with that,*" Zileri replied. "*He says the only thing is, if you retire from the RCN, you have to will us your signals officer. You got that, Danny? Over.*"

"*You get Officer Mundy over my dead body,*" Daniel said cheerfully. "*Which probably means her dead body too, so I'll try not to let that happen. Now, if you're really willing to top off 614's tanks, let's plot a rendezvous and get on with it! 614 over.*"

Adele noticed that even as he spoke Daniel had switched his display to a Plot Position Indicator that gave the relative locations of the *Garnet* and *Cutter 614*. His image was grinning like a child on Christmas morning.

CHAPTER 16

Over Yang

"Here's Heavenly Peace, the capital of Yang," Adele said, placing the image on a quadrant of Daniel's command display. The crew could view it on their visors or goggles if they liked, though she'd learned that few spacers were interested in anything about landfalls except the harborfront dives. "Ships land in Sunrise Bay, but there's half a mile of marshes between the harbor and the city proper . . . here."

As Adele spoke, she highlighted first the broad body of water opening to the sea through a neck only three hundred yards wide; then the band of marsh surrounding the bay; and finally the city itself. Heavenly Peace straggled in much the same undisciplined fashion the marshes did.

So far as Adele was concerned, planets tended to be pretty much the same from orbit. Yang was mildly unusual: the native vegetation was reddish, almost purple, so the patches humans had hacked out of the forests to grow Terra-derived crops looked like green mold on fresh meat.

It was also unusual that a great deal of up-to-date imagery was available for Yang, permitting Adele to sharpen her real-time display for this briefing. *614* was half a million miles out from Yang, too far for a cutter's optics to get real detail. Daniel could've brought them much closer—and no doubt would after he'd gotten a look at the situation—but the rebel base on Big Florida Island had ship-killing missiles, and it was at least possible that the planet had sprouted other serious problems.

The imagery was available because over the past several years RCN vessels had been arriving on Yang with the regularity of a courier service. They'd carried— Adele had skimmed them all—Remonstrances, Protests, and occasionally Collegial Greetings.

Those last occurred when the Republic of Cinnabar addressed the new president of its sister republic, Yang. Often the Greetings were coupled with Remonstrances or Protests, however, since governmental change on Yang was a robust activity that not infrequently swept up Cinnabar citizens. As had happened this time, come to think; though the government hadn't changed quite yet.

"This is the Presidential Palace," she went on, increasing the magnification and highlighting a cluster of buildings. "It's in a walled and moated compound enclosing a total of three or four acres. We'll have to go there to see President Shin, since he rarely goes out. Also the prison where the Burdock mercenaries are presumably held is part of the same complex. We won't know their location for certain until I've spoken to the Consular Agent here, Mister Kwo."

She pursed her lips. "Unless they've already been shot, of course," she added.

"Hell," called Dasi, one of the senior riggers. "Me'n Barnes'll shoot 'em ourself if it means we go straight back outa here. We heard stories about this place on Sinmary, and *that's* no paradise port neither."

There was general laughter. Dasi was joking, of course; but if Daniel'd asked them to, he and his partner Barnes would probably have done just that. They were hard men in a hard line of work. They trusted Captain Leary, and they didn't worry much about things they figured were officers' business.

Daniel would never give such an order, of course. Several of those aboard *614* might carry out such a massacre without orders or even against orders, however. Hogg would beyond question kill any number of people if he thought it'd keep his young master safe.

And so, Adele supposed, would Signals Officer Mundy. She wouldn't like herself afterwards; but she didn't like herself anyway, so saving Daniel by slaughtering innocents wouldn't have a real cost for her.

"And where is Big Florida Island, if you please, Mundy?" Daniel asked with his usual public formality. "Since we're to avoid it on pain of being blown out of the sky, everyone tells me."

"It's here, a hundred and seventy miles north of Heavenly Peace, just off the coast," Adele said. She drew the image back considerably to bring Big Florida into the frame with the capital, then shrank the scale again to focus on the rebel stronghold. "The *Chrysoberyl* made a low-level survey of the island seven months ago, before the missile batteries arrived, so we know the layout very accurately."

The island was heart-shaped and about a mile across in either direction. The point was to the south, and on the heart's seaward lobe were something over a dozen sheds and buildings. A starship rested on the other lobe. The ground around it must've been soft, because a corduroy road—a track of tree boles laid side by side—had been built out from the center of the island to the vessel's main hatch.

"The missile batteries are here . . ." Adele said, putting a red caret at the point of the heart. Her wands flicked two more carets to life, on the shore of each lobe. "Here, and here. We don't have closeups of them, of course."

"One moment," Daniel said. "According to what I heard, the missiles are first-class weapons. The round that was fired at the *Cutlass* four months ago would've been fatal if it'd struck the center of mass instead of being decoyed above the hull because a jammed antenna hadn't folded properly."

"Yes, that's right," Adele said. "The missiles appear to be recent manufacture from one of the industrial worlds of the Alliance, Gransby or DeLoit."

"Why?" said Daniel. "Hypervelocity missiles cost a fortune. You could buy another junk courier ship—" he gestured "—like this *Beacon of Yang* for less than any one of those batteries cost, so what are the missiles intended to protect?"

Adele cleared her throat. "I don't know," she said. "I'll . . ." She'd have continued, " . . . try to find out," but as her mind formed the words she realized she didn't have any idea where to begin researching the question. Instead she added, "I'll keep that in mind."

"Switch back to the harbor, if you would," Daniel said, "and then return control of the imagery to me."

"Yes of course," Adele said, shifting to a display

in which the harbor filled half the image area. Ships winked like bubbles on a cup of hot cocoa. Most of the remainder was marsh, but she'd deliberately chosen a scale in which the edges of the city appeared as well.

She wondered about his comment. Adele hadn't locked Daniel out of his own display—though she could've done so easily if she'd had a mind to. She wasn't sure whether he really thought she'd been that discourteous, or if he were instead delicately asking her not to interfere with the display while he was working with it.

Using his virtual keyboard, Daniel ran a cursor across each ship in the harbor. They were mostly small freighters carrying plasma cannon for short-range self-defense. None had missiles nor the rocket batteries that were a pirate's favorite weapon. The only moderately large vessel, a 6,000 tonner built originally as a livestock carrier, had been a hulk for a decade.

Each time the cursor touched a ship, a sidebar including name, registration, and officers, appeared at the side of his display. Adele smiled faintly. Did Daniel realize that this information came from his Signals Officer's digging rather than some piece of software installed on the equipment?

Yes, probably he did. Daniel noticed things. When he got a moment, he'd even thank her for it. Now he had other matters to attend to.

"How do people and cargo get from the harbor to the city proper?" Daniel said, reducing his field and shifting it around the belt of marsh. "There aren't any roads that I can see, and the port facilities don't seem to be operating either."

"There's been no maintenance on the quays and slips since the Alliance left Yang eighty years ago," Adele explained. "There's no port control either, though I gather there'll be what call themselves customs inspectors coming aboard and demanding fees. Previous RCN vessels have sent the inspectors away with scant respect, though if I read the records correctly, a few years ago the *Bayonet* did make a payment. Her captain hoped the bribe would ease his way with the government."

"Did it?" said Daniel, raising his eyebrows in wonder. "I suppose we could find a reasonable sum if . . ."

"No, of course it didn't," Adele replied tartly. "There's very little connection between the various bureaucracies and whoever's President for the moment. Certainly no connection that works from the bottom up. Bribe President Shin if you like, but don't bother with the small fry."

"Ah," said Daniel agreeably. "And the question of transport? If we don't choose to hijack the customs boat, I mean."

Adele grinned. "I haven't ruled that out," she said. "The larger RCN vessels which've called here in the past carried aircars. We don't and couldn't have because of available volume. Freighters are met by barges from commercial houses in the city, either factors they already have an arrangement with or otherwise a mob struggling for the pick of the cargo. A warship won't have that option. I presume we can hire a barge after we've landed, however."

"That's one possibility," said Daniel in a detached tone which Adele took to mean, "That's not going to happen." He moved his image field onto the Presidential

Compound, still at the large scale with which he'd been searching for routes from the harbor.

Daniel's dismissive attitude irritated Adele a trifle. Well, it irritated her a good deal, but without any justification. The decision wasn't one for Signals Officer Mundy—and it certainly wasn't one for Mundy of Chatsworth, which is how she'd been unconsciously viewing herself in her mind as she lectured the crew.

"Do we have any information on the palace defenses?" Daniel asked, increasing magnification on one of the guard towers built onto the compound wall. "It looks to me like an automatic impeller here. Are the rest the same?"

Adele's wands sorted data. She had the answer, but she hadn't expected to need it above any one of a thousand other bits of information about Yang, its government, and its foreign relations, so it took her longer to find than she'd have liked. As data poured across her display she saw on the quadrant echoing the command console that Daniel was working his focus around the walls. He stopped at each tower to make his own assessment.

"There're six automatic impellers," Adele said sharply to draw Daniel's attention to her. "There's a three-tube laser in the northeast tower, but it was installed thirty years ago and wasn't used when President Shin—"

She paused for a smile of sorts.

"—Field Marshal Shin as he then was, when his forces stormed the Presidential Compound a year and a half ago. And there's a twelve-rocket launcher stripped from what'd been the Yang Navy before it sank in harbor. It's somewhere in the compound but apparently in storage."

"That's good to know," Daniel said, shifting his image to examine the moat surrounding the compound. "Mind, an automatic impeller can put enough holes in a cutter's hull to make it unflyable."

He slid his frame counter-clockwise, keeping the outer wall on the left of the image. Two keystrokes overlaid the moat with a scale ticked at one-foot intervals.

"Sir?" said Sun, watching Daniel intently from the gunnery board. "If you just lift high enough above the harbor to give me a line, I can take out all three towers on the facing side with pairs of rockets. Then we can assault easy."

"Come now, Sun," Daniel said with a broad smile. "We're not assaulting anybody. We're diplomats in uniform, come to clarify an unfortunate circumstance with the president of an independent world. Is that the correct terminology, Officer Mundy?"

Adele shrugged. "I think we're permitted to remonstrate," she said. "Since President Shin admits that he's holding Cinnabar citizens, but he hasn't freed them on his own account."

"Remonstrate, then," Daniel said, nodding cheerfully, "but not to the point of blowing a hole in his little fortress. At least until after we've tried other forms of reason."

He highlighted the moat on his display. "Fellow spacers," he said, raising his voice but not keying the intercom, "give me your attention. We'll be making another hop through the Matrix to bring us to within five thousand miles of Yang's surface."

"Woo-*ee!*" called Barnes. Woetjans, standing before the hatch, shouted, "That's our Mr. Leary!" Captains who trusted their extra-sidereal navigation to within five thousand miles, even at intra-system distances, were rare even in the RCN. Crews who trusted their captains to be that accurate were even more rare.

"Yang has no planetary or port control, so I don't intend to give the people on the ground time to wonder what we may have in mind," Daniel explained. "We'll go straight in. Rather than landing in the harbor—"

His orange highlight pulsed. This was an informational briefing, Adele realized, but it was also a pep talk. *614*'s crew would follow their captain wherever he led, but they were all experienced enough to understand the risks in the present situation. Daniel was showing them that *he* understood the danger—also firing them up so that their obedience would be not only willing but enthusiastic.

"—we're going to land here beside the palace. The moat itself isn't wide enough even a cutter can fit into it. We can straddle it, though, and it'll soak up our exhaust just fine. We can even refill our reaction mass when things quiet down. I know this'll be tricky—"

"Not for you it won't, sir!" cried Raymond.

"Yes, even for me," Daniel said, his smile spreading again. "But if I didn't expect to succeed, I'd have made a different plan."

He sobered. "Now," he continued, "that leaves the problem of the guns in the towers. I don't expect the sort of guards President Shin has around him to be exceptionally alert or courageous, either one, but there's a risk nonetheless."

"I can take care of them, sir!" said Sun.

"Land with the outer hatch open and facing the place," Hogg called from the back of the cutter's bay.

"Leave me in the lock with an impeller. A little steam and sparkling isn't going to keep me from making those towers real unhealthy for any wog who points a gun at us."

Adele had been going over the list of electro-optical transmitters within the Presidential Compound. Earlier RCN vessels had recorded that information along with reams of other data that no one had looked at until she did just now. Gathering data was much easier than retrieving and analysing it.

"I think," said Adele, "that I can clear the towers as we come in. Though I have no personal objection to having Sun and Hogg ready to act if I fail."

"Ma'am," said Hogg. "If you say you can do it, then I'll take that to the bank. But I'll still be watching through my sights, because *nobody*'s a problem when seventy grains of osmium've splashed their brains across an acre or so."

Adele joined the general laughter. Her RCN family had a sense of humor that wouldn't have done at meals in the Mundy household, but Adele found that it suited her very well indeed.

Landing a starship in an atmosphere was always a tricky business, and Daniel found that despite his care *614* was buffeted particularly badly. A cutter's four thrusters had plenty of power, but they didn't give the captain the delicacy of control available from the *Sissie*'s eight nozzles or the much greater arrays of large ships.

Keeping *614* from shaking herself apart—or flipping on her back; the cutter had so little mass that a thruster could be misaligned badly enough to do that—gave Daniel something to do rather than worry about what was going to come next, but he'd never been one to worry once he'd made a plan. As he'd told the crew, if he hadn't thought he could pull this off he'd be trying something else instead.

Though Daniel had to admit that if people told him that he was out of his mind and doomed to failure, he'd have agreed that they might have a point. What Daniel *knew* on the basis of this crew, the nimbleness of the cutter, and his own confidence in himself, was that they were going to come through at least the first part of the operation in fine shape. For the rest, well, they'd deal with it as it developed.

The ship's computer had picked the point at which they'd entered Yang's atmosphere and had controlled most of their descent. At ten thousand feet Daniel took over, mostly to get a feel for how *614* behaved on the way down. He'd been pleased with the way she'd climbed from Nikitin; going the other way she was skittish but instantly responsive. That was good to know, though in ordinary circumstances a cutter had little cause to land under its own power.

Heavenly Peace was in sight so Daniel expanded the image to cover the main part of the command display. The thruster data—output, flow, temperature, erosion, and reaction mass remaining—became a sidebar, balancing the flight information—air speed, speed over ground, location, and attitude—on the other side. If something went badly wrong—if a nozzle fractured, for example—the thruster data would fill the display again, though in that case Daniel would be concentrating on the feel of the ship in his hands rather than figures.

Along the bottom of the display crawled a block of text, the message that Adele was broadcasting through every medium available in the city below: MISSILE ATTACK! GET TO SHELTER. MISSILE ATTACK! GET UNDERGROUND OR YOU'LL DIE. She'd explained that every radio, telephone and computer, especially the National Command Net, would be shouting the same panicked warning.

614 approached from the southwest, thundering over natural vegetation and the farms of peasants who harvested bark but also grew their own food. At low level Daniel could see that each dwelling was a fortlet, and the small towns where the local magnate processed the bark into hallucinogenic drugs were fortified on a larger scale.

Occasionally somebody'd shot at *614* on the way down—the cutter's sensors could pick up the RF discharge of an impeller—but those appeared to be the ordinary vandalism of louts with guns rather than serious attempts to harm them. Nothing had pinged on the hull, at any rate.

Daniel'd chosen this approach because it didn't bring them close to Big Florida Island northwest of the city. The *Cutlass* had started a low-level pass to see just what was happening on Big Florida. They'd been rather too successful in learning, and in fact had been extremely lucky to survive.

The rebels' missiles could engage any vessel in orbit, and during its descent the cutter remained in range until it was within a mile of the surface. Daniel assumed that the rebels didn't waste missiles against ships that didn't look like a threat, so he'd plotted the course to be non-threatening.

Daniel didn't care about who ran—or claimed to run—the government of Yang. He had enough problems with the current president that he didn't need to bring in his enemies.

614 was coming in over the city proper, which Daniel hated to do—the citizens of Heavenly Peace might be individually reprehensible but as a group they were human beings even if they had a terrible government. There was no choice, though, since the palace was right in the middle of the built-up area.

When they were only a thousand feet above the surface, Daniel started braking at nearly 4 gravities. A larger ship couldn't have sustained that deceleration without breaking up. He didn't dare hover to a landing in normal fashion, but neither did he want to come in like a meteor. Four lobes of rainbow thruster exhaust bathed the cutter, curling over the hull to merge some distance back along their track.

The ground swelled abruptly. Daniel trusted his judgment. He'd calculated the burn and in addition to the figures the deceleration *felt* right, but despite that it never looked right at this stage of a descent.

It was bad enough when there was only water beneath, beginning to sparkle under a gust of ions. This time people ran screaming in the streets or threw themselves flat on the roofs of three-story buildings. Daniel'd known *614*'s passage would do some damage, rattle dishes and maybe singe clothes drying on the parapets of the houses closest to touchdown, but until this moment it hadn't occurred to him that folks might break their necks fleeing from the thundering apparition.

Death by violence was probably common in Heavenly

Peace. The thought that he might be accidentally increasing the risk bothered Daniel, though.

The wall of the palace compound flashed by to port. The guard towers were empty. Daniel didn't see even the backside of one of Shin's gunmen abandoning his post. Apparently Adele's warning had taken effect as *Cutter 614* plunged toward the city.

Which was just as well for the gunmen. Hogg was in the airlock, just like he said he'd be. Daniel was sure he'd have been able to nail his target despite buffeting, the goggles he wore to protect his eyes, and the sting of plasma wherever it touched his unprotected skin.

The cutter squelched down in an enormous plume of steam. The feel was completely different from either a conventional water landing or the more dangerous set-downs on hard ground where reflected exhaust was likely to unbalance the vessel in the last few feet of descent. The moat's muddy banks gave under the cutter's weight initially, then baked firm and held the vessel without the usual bobbing. The water flowing through the channel directly beneath the vessel continued to dissipate the plasma for the several seconds it took before Daniel was sure that they were safely on the ground.

"Visors down, people!" Woetjans bawled as she swung open the inner airlock hatch. "Try not to drown yourselfs, because the rest of us are likely to be too busy to fish you out!"

Steam swept into the cutter's bay, mixed with ions dancing like miniature rainbows as they absorbed electrons to merge with the atmosphere. RCN commo helmets had filters that slapped in place at need when the visors were down. They weren't gas masks, but they removed particles and anything active enough to be trapped in a ceramic that mimicked the convolutions of natural charcoal.

"Remember you're a guard of honor!" Daniel said, bellowing but using intercom as well. The ping of cooling metal and the bubbling rush of water replacing what'd been boiled out of the moat might overwhelm even his unaided lungs, especially when the spacers were so keyed up. They filed out carrying sub-machine guns and stocked impellers. "Don't shoot till I order you, I don't care what the wogs are doing!"

RCN vessels had external speakers to allow those inside to reach work parties outside on the ground who might not be wearing radio helmets. *Cutter 614's* speakers began playing brassy music, startling Daniel as he put his hand on a spacer's chest in order to make a place for himself in the line of those leaving through the airlock.

"*It's 'The Song of the Liberator Hwang,'*" Adele explained on their two-way link. "*It's the national anthem.*"

I suspect there're two people on the planet who know that, now that you've told me, Daniel thought. But it was the sort of detail he'd come to expect from Adele, and who knew? It just might help.

A short ramp connected the hatch to the port outrigger. Normally in port there'd be a temporary ramp from the outrigger to the quay or shore. There was no need of that here, so the twenty spacers Daniel'd picked to escort him were jumping to the ground to face the wall of the palace compound ten feet away.

Hogg waited for Daniel on the outrigger, the stocked impeller cradled on his left elbow. He looked worse for wear, but by no means as bad as he sometimes did after a night of partying. The goggles were up on his forehead now, but the kiss of the plasma had inflamed his cheeks and the backs of his hands.

"There's no fight in this lot," he said disgustedly, indicating the palace with a twist of his right thumb. "Dunno what I was so worried about. Mind, it's the sort of place you go whoring with a buddy so that her pimp don't scrag you from behind while you're anchored."

Nobody'd returned to the guard tower frowning down above the gate. That might be connected with the fact that Sun had aimed the cutter's twelve-rocket dorsal launcher straight at the tower. The warheads wouldn't have time to arm in the short distance they'd travel, but the impact of just one or two rockets would smash the yellow brickwork like so many wrecking balls.

Yang stank. Heavenly Peace stank, at any rate. It stank like a cesspool rather than with the normal swampy odor of decaying vegetation that landings on primitive planets usually brought.

The buildings across the moat from the palace had originally been of three or four stories, high enough to look down on the compound. In some cases portions of the walls still poked up fingers of masonry or wooden posts with rags of wickerwork remaining, but all floors above the first had been hacked or blasted away. Only at a quarter mile or so from the palace were buildings habitable to the original rooflines.

Habitable was a flexible concept, of course. From the look of the rickety structures, they'd be unsafe and uncomfortable even by the standards of spacers crammed aboard a starship.

The gate leaves were frames of angle iron wrapped with barbed wire. The mass was badly rusted, but fresh wire had been woven into it in the past month or so. Through the openings Daniel saw sheds straggling along the walls of the compound; in the center was a colonnaded building with stuccoed walls and a gilt dome. People were looking back at him through the pillars; they ducked out of sight when they caught his eye.

The national anthem cut off in the middle of the phrase, *"To die is a fine thing!"* In Adele's voice the speaker called, "The Republic of Cinnabar sends greetings to its respected brother, President for Life Shin!"

Eyes poked out from around pillars, then disappeared again. Was one of those nervous peepers President Shin himself?

"Adele, can you cut me into the loudspeakers myself?" Daniel asked.

"Done," Adele replied a heartbeat later. *"Toggle it by saying, 'speaker.'"*

"Speaker," said Daniel. In a thunderous voice he continued, "President Shin, if you're all right, please admit us to your compound. Otherwise we'll have to attach a grapnel and line to your gates and pull them open with our winches so that we can bring aid to you if you're incapacitated. Speaker."

"Hell, we don't have to do that, sir," Woetjans growled from Daniel's left side. "I can shin up that and open the gate from the inside. It looks like just a bar to pull outa the staples."

"I think we'll wait a moment for our host to admit us properly, Woetjans," Daniel said mildly. He didn't add—because Woetjans would've taken it as a challenge—that if she started climbing the latticework, she was likely to draw fire from the darkened interior of the palace. Daniel neither wanted to lose the bosun on whom he depended nor to start a full-scale war—which that would do, since if anything happened to Woetjans he'd order Sun to put the whole sheaf of rockets into the palace facade.

Armed men and a few women—also armed, and with the left side of their faces painted red—began to appear from the palace, taking a few tentative steps beyond the colonnade. Daniel waited, wearing a false smile and gleaming Dress Whites with all his medals. It'd been hard to carry the uniform on a cutter without getting it soaked with oil, and he knew it'd be the worst possible costume if the negotiation turned into a gunfight. It was necessary, though, if the mission were to have any chance of success.

The soldiers came forward in a tight, chattering group, reminding Daniel of a flock of chickens rushing toward grain spread on the ground. They wore khaki uniforms, though different dye-lots gave them a motley appearance. Well, many things gave them a motley appearance. Their weapons were a mix of electromotive and chemically fueled types. Some of the latter were so new that splotches of packing grease still blackened the receivers. Daniel wondered if the bores were clear.

The woman in the center had gold rings with bangles the length of both forearms; she wore a bicorne hat covered with gold braid. Daniel would've thought of her as ridiculous despite the sub-machine gun and the half dozen long knives stuck through her belt if it weren't that he noticed her three-strand necklace was of human teeth.

"I'm Captain Ding-wei!" she said in an angry sing-song. "You got no right coming to Yang and giving us orders! Go away back to Cinnabar!"

Daniel saluted. "We're not giving orders," he said calmly. "We're here to greet our brother President Shin. The rocket launcher—"

He gestured.

"—is locked in that position. We have no intention of blowing the palace off the face of the planet with it."

"Now that we've made nice-nice, Captain," Hogg said loudly. He rapped the gate frame with the muzzle of his impeller. "How about you get this open so we can come in and all have a nice civilized drink? Eh?"

The iron continued to ring off-key. Ding-wei scowled, then noticed that the impeller was now aimed up her left nostril. She cried, *"Wau!"* and jumped back, colliding with one of her coterie. He dropped his automatic rifle with a clatter. It didn't fire. Judging by the rust on the bolt and receiver, it might not be *able* to fire.

"Captain Ding-wei," Daniel said in a stern voice, "the sooner you do your duty and take us to see the President, the better off we'll all be. There could very well be an accident out here!"

He rather wished that weren't so true. Some members of his escort were good shots, but even they were spacers carrying powerful weapons instead of soldiers who'd been trained in gun safety as well marksmanship. It'd be very bad if one of Daniel's escort blew a guard's brains out accidentally. It'd be even worse, at least from Daniel's viewpoint, if one of them blew *his* brains out—and that could certainly happen.

"Corporal Jing!" Ding-wei snapped. "Open the gate at once. Now! Now! Now! you dirty little man!"

That was a fair description of Jing, who looked at the captain in terror before jumping to the gate and sliding the bar from its staples. His khaki trousers had been cut into shorts with the left leg six inches longer than the right, but Ding-wei wasn't anything to brag about either. She must've been eating when she ran outside, because her face and both hands were greasy. Her hair was a mat of its own oils and the dull yellow dust blowing along the city's streets.

As soon as the bar dropped clear, Barnes and Dasi shoved the leaves open with the soles of their boots. The hinges protested shrilly, but the riggers were big men and determined. They strode on, their impellers pointed forward. The remainder of the escort followed, driving the Presidential Guards before them like wind-blown thistle-seeds.

"Captain, lead us to President Shin, if you would," Daniel said. He made a shooing motion with his left hand. He'd have taken Ding-wei by the shoulder and turned her around, but her tunic looked like it'd been used to swab out an abattoir.

The captain flinched from the almost-contact and moved back into the building at a quickening pace. Daniel and his spacers followed closely, while the remainder of the guard detachment seemed to melt into the shanties to either side of the courtyard.

The hallway was covered with ceramic tiles whose glazing formed murals. Oversized figures led armies or addressed crowds of people only half their size. The giants had been defaced: gunfire had erased their heads and blown craters in their groins. The underlying walls were reinforced concrete, but in several places the shots had smashed through into the next room.

"What the Hell's that?" Hogg muttered, elbowing Daniel and nodding to the damaged murals.

"A political statement, I presume," Daniel murmured. "I'm as glad I wasn't here when it was happening, though. The ricochets would've terrified anybody who wasn't crazy. Or crazy drunk, of course."

Ding-wei gestured to a door of bronze filigree over velvet in a tall archway, then stepped out of the way. "Through there," she muttered. She wiped her face with her left hand, smearing the red paint. "He's in there. Go on, then."

"Right," said Daniel, striding forward. Hogg grabbed the vertical handle and dragged the door open, but Daniel stepped through first. He wasn't sure what he'd find on the other side.

The reality was a hall sixty feet high to the top of the palace dome, filled with several hundred armed women painted the same way as the captain. Sunlight coming through dome and clerestory windows slanted across their grotesque faces and made the scene look like the throne room of Hell.

The only man in the hall sat on a high dais in the center. He wore a purple robe and a chaplet of gilt flowers bound his hair.

The man called something but his words were lost in the cries of the women, a snarling, squealing surf of noise. Those nearest the door pointed their weapons at Daniel; at his side Hogg, his sub-machine gun slung, reached into a pocket and came out with another concussion grenade.

The smell of anger, sweat, and female hormones filled the crowded hall. Daniel blinked, but there was no help for it. With his left hand he pushed away the muzzle of the impeller aimed at his Kostroma Star, pointing it toward the ceiling instead. He bellowed, "Make way so that the Republic of Cinnabar may greet his excellency President for Life Shin!"

He doubted many of the women could hear him, but affecting those to his immediate front would help. "Woetjans, Hogg," he said. "Start forward. We don't want a brawl, but get the mob moving aside."

"For the honor of the Democratic Republic of Yang!" shouted a public address system so crackly that it was a moment before Daniel recognized the voice as Adele's. He hadn't been sure the hall had a PA system, and from the sound of this the speakers were in doubt themselves. *"Make way for the respectful envoy of the Republic of Cinnabar! Make way for the envoy to greet his excellency President for Life Shin!"*

The women between Daniel and the throne seemed more startled than obedient, but at least they didn't actively object when Daniel's escort began shoving them aside. He felt a little embarrassed to be carried through the crowd like a doll in tissue paper, but neither his uniform nor his pose as the plenipotentiary of a great power would survive the scrum.

Besides, the spacers were having fun. The smallest of them were bigger than all but a few of the painted women, and those few were fat, not large. The opportunity to push around obnoxious little people might be morally questionable, but beyond doubt spacers

as aggressive as those Daniel'd picked for his escort
found the activity spiritually fulfilling.

As the spacers advanced Woetjans stepped aside and
let Barnes take her place at the point of the wedge.
She leaned close to Daniel and rasped in a voice that
probably wouldn't be overheard in this cacophony,
"Hey, Cap'n? You know, if this lot's the royal guard
or whatever, we don't need to talk to anybody. If we
go back out in the hall and toss a few grenades in,
the ones that're left'll likely keep outa the way while
we get the prisoners out. They're supposed to be
here too, right?"

*That'd mean slaughtering hundreds of people out of
hand!* Daniel thought. But the bosun knew that too,
so rather than state the obvious Daniel said, "We'd
have to march the prisoners through the city, I suppose
to the harbor, Woetjans. Then we'd have the further
problem of what to do next, because *614* can't carry
two hundred extra bodies to Nikitin."

He smiled, adding in an understatement that Woetjans certainly wouldn't understand, "And there might
be political problems also. With Admiral Milne."

And with Admiral Anston. And with some three-
quarters of the Senate, though Daniel knew from
comments his father had snarled when he was Speaker,
there were Senators whose view of foreign relations
was just as simplistic as the bosun's.

*"The respectful envoy of Cinnabar brings greetings to
his excellency President Shin!"* the PA system shouted
through its pops and sizzles. The single working speaker
seemed to be on the dais with the President. He'd
jumped to his feet and was staring at it in frightened
anger with his hands over his ears.

Shin's chaplet was disarranged. Daniel's helmet damped the sound down to safe levels, but it must've been very uncomfortable for the locals who didn't have similar equipment.

One effect of the snarling racket was to move the female guards away from the dais. Daniel stepped into the cleared area and saluted the President. He made a better job of it than usual, but Shin probably wasn't a good judge.

"Your excellency!" Daniel said brightly. "I greet you in the name of the Speaker and Senate of Cinnabar. May you reign long in the friendship of the Republic!"

Shin was in his late thirties. Though he was getting soft he remained a handsome man except for a broad pink scar starting at his right eyebrow and trailing diagonally into his scalp. His chaplet now hung from his right ear, and he wore an expression of petulant disgust.

"Why are you here?" Shin demanded. "And why are you shouting like that? You know, I could have my Death Virgins kill you all! I could have them kill you with their teeth!"

"Your excellency," Daniel said with a broad smile as though he thought the threat was a joke between friends. "If you mean, 'why is your own equipment behaving like that?', I'm sure I don't know. And as for why the Republic sent me, I'm here to arrange the repatriation of the Cinnabar citizens you gathered up for us. I believe there's about two hundred of them? We'll get them off your hands at once and send them back to Burdock where they belong."

President Shin sat down again. He tried twice to

straighten his gilded chaplet, but it slipped off each time he removed his hands. Perhaps it'd originally been held in place with a hairpin which he'd lost in covering his ears. He flung the ornament to the floor.

"Send them where they belong?" Shin said in a high, angry voice. "I'll send them where they belong, never fear. They were fighting me! I'll burn them all alive in Shin and Hwang Stadium on Liberation Day next week!"

"Personally I share your sense of humor, your excellency," Daniel said, continuing to smile, "but I'd greatly regret if some of the hotheads in the RCN heard you say you were planning to murder Cinnabar citizens. Why, the very commander of my squadron, Admiral Milne, would insist on blasting Heavenly Peace to a glowing crater. Such a terrible thing to happen simply because a woman didn't understand that you were making a joke."

"They were fighting me," Shin said indignantly. "Fighting *me*."

"Yes, your excellency," Daniel said. "They'll be punished for their interference in Yang's affairs. But they're Cinnabar citizens, so the Republic will punish them."

In all truth, he suspected the mercenaries *wouldn't* be punished; that was at the discretion of the Civil Administrator of the Burdock Stars. They might even be allowed to hire a transport to Yang and rejoin the rebels on Big Florida Island. It wasn't fair or proper, but that wasn't the business of an RCN officer.

Daniel rather doubted that "fair" and "proper" were concepts that President Shin thought much about either. Perhaps the universe was displaying a certain rough justice.

Shin stared at Daniel, his expression suddenly calculating. He bent and picked up the chaplet, toying with it as he continued to watch and think.

Daniel waited, his back straight and a friendly smile on his face. That was his usual expression, and it did as well in this place as any other would.

He didn't press for a reply. Judging from what he'd seen of Shin, the fellow's reflex was probably to order his Death Virgins to murder the Cinnabars out of hand. Anything requiring more thought than that was a good result. The result might not please Admiral Milne, but that was a matter to sort out weeks and light years away.

Shin's female guards were pressing closer, forcing the spacers into a tight arc around Daniel and the edge of the dais. The women weren't hostile, at least overtly, but there were too many of them for the space and they wanted to hear what was going on.

They couldn't *possibly* hear over their own echoing shuffles, whispers and clinking equipment. The smell of the hall was overpowering.

"You came to save Cinnabar citizens, that's what you're telling me?" Shin said, spinning the chaplet on his joined index fingers. He didn't look angry any more. Daniel had a suspicion that the President for Life wasn't the stupid savage he'd assumed.

"That's correct, your excellency," Daniel said. He had to raise his voice to be heard, even as close as he stood, but he tried to pitch it so that the volume didn't make it threatening. "It's a principle of the greatest importance to my republic."

"If you want to save Cinnabar citizens," Shin said, "then you can save my great friend Maria Mondindragiana. The rebels captured her in her villa and took her to Big Florida Island. You bring back Maria and I'll give you my prisoners. There!"

Shin straightened, looking smug.

Daniel kept his face blank for a moment as he thought. "Your excellency," he said, "do you mean that Mistress Mondindragiana is a Cinnabar citizen?"

"Of course she is!" said the President. Daniel could barely hear him. "She comes from Waystation. That makes her a Cinnabar citizen."

It certainly does not, Daniel thought. Waystation was a Cinnabar protectorate, but only a quarter of the residents were actually citizens of the Republic. This wasn't the time to halt negotiations for a records search, however.

"We'll operate on the assumption that she's a citizen, then," Daniel said aloud. "What else can you tell me about how the lady's being held?"

"She's on Big Florida Island!" Shin said, petulant again. "What do I know about what goes on there? The rebels stole her and I want her back, that's all that matters. You bring her back, all right?"

He set the chaplet on his head. This time it remained balanced.

"And one more thing," the President said. "You bring her back before Liberation Day, you hear? That's a week. Because if you don't, I burn those dirt in the stadium to teach other dirt not to fight against me!"

Daniel saluted again. "Very well, your excellency," he said. "We'll proceed immediately with our preparations. Good morning to you!"

"*Make way for the respectful envoy of Cinnabar, leaving to carry out the instructions of President for Life Shin!*" the loudspeaker shouted. "*All hail the friendship between the Democratic Republic of Yang and the Republic of Cinnabar!"*

A surge trembled through the packed hall. The women gave way minusculely, enough for the spacers at the key of the arc to start advancing toward the door.

The motion reminded Daniel of the times he'd watched a startled snake regurgitate recent prey. This was better than some outcomes.

Though he had to admit that the thought of attacking the rebel stronghold with thirty-odd spacers and a cutter didn't seem a *great* deal better than being chewed to death by hundreds of crazy women.

CHAPTER 17

Heavenly Peace on Yang

Adele and her escort picked their way through the streets of Heavenly Peace. Daniel had offered as many armed spacers as she wanted, but that would be threatening in the wrong way. For Adele's purpose, the two servants were better.

Hogg led by three paces; Tovera trailed by the same distance. The premises of Acme Trading Company were within a few blocks of the palace—to the extent that "blocks" were a real concept in this twisting warren—but the state of the streets made the journey seem longer.

Filth wasn't the problem they'd expected: spring tides scoured the streets. The high water marks on the buildings were above what Adele could reach with her arm outstretched. There were more substantial barriers, though: burned-out vehicles, tree trunks swept in on the tides that took out the garbage, and the rubble of a collapsed building. That last had been blown up from the inside, and from the smell there were still human bodies buried in the ruin.

"There it is," Hogg said. "I've seen prisons I liked the look of more."

He carried a stocked impeller ready to use; Tovera held her sub-machine gun openly instead of concealing it within her attaché case. The problems of getting from *Cutter 614* to here didn't include the local residents, all of whom had fled or at least hidden at the approach of murderous looking strangers.

Acme Trading Company was a fortress with a walled compound at the left side and to the rear of the main building. The cast-concrete walls hadn't been painted, but the yellow dust of the city'd weathered into their pores. There were no windows on the building's two lower stories; those on the topmost were small and covered with heavy grates.

"Maybe it's a prison for the people outside it," Tovera said. She made a sound like a small reptile laughing. "That would seem justified."

The compound backed onto one of the channels that meandered through the swamp to the harbor after. A barge was tied up there now, under the automatic impeller in the tower above the gate on the water side. A similar gun pointed at the trio from the top of the main building. They tramped on stolidly toward the street door, which put them too close for the gun to bear on them.

A pair of rats—huge things, dappled brown on fawn and weighing at least a pound and a half apiece—were bickering over a rib bone in the door alcove. It was too big for a human rib, Adele thought, though she didn't suppose that mattered.

The rats turned at the approach of Adele and her companions. Instead of fleeing, they hunched down and bared their long chisel teeth, clicking them together.

"Stand aside," Tovera warned quietly.

"Don't shoot!" Adele said over her shoulder. The crackle of the sub-machine gun could bring any kind of frightened response, including a grenade from the guards on the roof of the building.

Hogg had balanced his heavy gun in his left hand. His right made a sidewise motion, snapping out a four-ounce sinker on the end of monocrystal fishing line. He jerked it back as though it'd been a yo-yo. The line curled around the neck of one rat and decapitated it neatly. The blood-spouting corpse sprang in one direction while the living rat ran the other way.

"Well, I guess the bone's ours, Hogg," Tovera said.

"I'm a captain's servant now," Hogg said, dropping the weighted line back in a pocket, but he continued to wear the mesh glove that let him handle the monocrystal without cutting off his own fingers. "I eat better'n that."

Adele smiled faintly. "I wish I could say I always have," she said. "But there've been times I was very poor and very hungry."

And I may be both those things in the future, Adele thought, *but I'll never again be without friends. Since now I know what it's like to* have *friends.*

The door was metal and opened outward. The upper hinge sagged, so at some time in the past Acme had had to grind down the stone lintel and dig a trench in the street so that the door's lower edge cleared. There'd once been a peephole, but a thick plate had been welded over it; instead, a video camera was glued to the jamb and connected to the interior with a length of flex snaking up to the third-story window.

"I'm Mundy of Chatsworth," Adele said. She was wearing RCN utilities—she hadn't brought civilian clothes with her on the cutter—but her present business wasn't, strictly speaking, that of a signals officer. "You've been informed that I'm coming. Open your door."

Nothing happened for a moment. Hogg fingered a dimple in the face of the door that a bullet had made; the fragmented projectile had splashed a star around the impact. "What d'ye think, Tovera?" he said. "This must've been a pistol. Would one of these—"

He patted the butt of his impeller.

"—punch clear through, d'ye suppose?"

"I doubt it," Tovera said, giving him a thin-lipped smile. "But you could certainly shoot the hinges off."

They both laughed. *What are the people inside thinking?* Adele wondered, but that was merely an idle thought: she didn't care, not really, about the opinion of Masters Bonn and Herbrand, late of Xenos on Cinnabar but now doing business on Yang as Acme Trading Company.

The door creaked open. Behind the two beefy locals who were doing the considerable labor of pushing it stood a plump, frightened looking man whom Adele recognized as Tre Herbrand from the image in his citizenship file. He was a Lantos native but he'd been granted Cinnabar citizenship by the governor of his home district, the Queen's Globe.

"How are you doing that to our console?" Herbrand demanded. He had rounded features with eyes as close set as a pig's. Adele suspected it wouldn't make her happier to learn what personal services this man had provided the district governor to gain citizenship. "How are you making it play your message? It's shielded!"

"Not very well," Adele said coolly. "Take us into your office and I'll break the loop. It's served its purpose."

She gestured him back with the fingers of her right hand; not the hand resting near the pocket holding her pistol. That was merely habit. Herbrand was no threat and his two laborers were unarmed. A man with a sub-machine gun waited a little way down the hall, but that must be a normal precaution against rats that might come in when the door was open—four legged and two legged both.

"You can't order us to help you," Herbrand said, shuffling quickly down the passage ahead of them. The laborers were squealing the door closed again; the gunman stayed where he was but dipped his head in acknowledgement as they passed. "I wish Bonn was here. He has influence in Xenos, you know. Real influence!"

Boxes and bales were stacked ceiling high on both sides of the room. Along the back wall were a circular staircase, a freight elevator and—partitioned off from the remainder of the volume—an office from which Adele could hear her imagery blaring at high volume. She didn't see anyone else on this floor, but voices echoed down from the upper stories.

"He has no influence with my commanding officer, Speaker Leary's son," Adele said, walking in and seating herself at the merchant's console without asking permission. The machine was some twenty standard years old, obsolete by Xenos standards but quite adequate here. "And more to the point, Master

Herbrand, he has no influence with me and it's me that you're going to have to satisfy."

She'd looped an image of President Shin directing Daniel to recover his mistress from the rebels, using video taken from Woetjans' helmet so that Daniel himself in uniform would be visible. At the end she'd cut in a clip of herself telling the proprietors of Acme Trading to expect her within the half hour. She'd entered the fortress through the microwave antenna on its roof. Her feed claimed to be from the Harbormaster's office with information on recent arrivals—information for which the company paid a regular bribe.

It was a neat job, but nothing Adele would get a swelled head over. A proper Alliance military target was better protected by an order of magnitude, and—

Adele allowed herself a satisfied smile as she typed in the code series that returned the console to its owner's control. She didn't even bother to couple her own data unit to do the job.

—she'd penetrated those targets too.

"Well, you still can't threaten us," Herbrand muttered in a despairing attempt at bluster. "Yang is an independent state. You have no authority here."

Hogg chuckled. He took his throwing line from his pocket and used the seat of an upholstered chair for a towel to wipe the monocrystal clean of rat blood. Bits of stuffing flew out and drifted around the room.

"Leaving that question for the moment," Adele said, turning to face the merchant, "I think you should be asking yourself how President for Life Shin will react to hearing that you refuse to help us carry out his request. Given that I'm offering you payment at the rate you'd expect from commercial captains, I'd be surprised at your refusal as well."

"Payment?" Herbrand said in amazement. He stood nervously in the middle of the office. Adele's companions lounged against the walls on either side of him, and Adele remained seated in sedate comfort at his console. "At commercial rates?"

"That's right," Adele agreed. "The transfer will be made from the Gold Dust Cluster secret account to whichever correspondent bank you use on Nikitin. This is public business, you see."

"Oh," said Herbrand. "*Oh.*"

He sat on one of the chairs beside the console and said, "What is it precisely that you'd like from Acme Trading Company, Mistress Mundy? I assure you our rates are competitive with any you'll find on Yang."

"I assure you that's correct," Adele said with a faint smile. "Because I've checked your records for the past three years to determine what those rates are. I'm not here to haggle, sir. But you *will* be paid."

Herbrand nodded, making a steeple of his hands on his lap. "I'm very pleased to hear that," he said. "In the past, you see, the Admiral—who I know is the only person authorized to use the secret fund—hasn't taken such an interest in affairs on Yang."

"On my honor as a Mundy, the payment will be made," Adele said.

And so it would, though it'd come as rather a surprise to Admiral Milne when she learned that it had. This was an absolutely proper use of secret funds, precisely what the funds were meant for in fact. But had Adele—or worse, Lieutenant Leary—requested a line of credit from them for this mission, the Admiral would've refused angrily.

Adele wouldn't use her information skills to steal any more than she'd use her pistol to rob people in the street. Putting those skills to the purpose of causing others to act as they ought to, however—well, what could be more proper than that?

"As for what we need," Adele continued, "the immediate requirement is for an aircar."

"All right," said Herbrand, nodding and now rubbing his hands together. "Acme has three aircars, there's one that we can lease to you—with proper indemnification against loss, of course."

"You have one aircar that has a reasonable chance of making it to Big Florida Island and back," Tovera said. She giggled. "The twelve-place Metrolight. And I'll try not to lose it."

"Hey, how come you get to drive the aircar?" Hogg said. "I know how to drive one too. We'll roll dice for it."

"You *don't* know how," Tovera said, "but I learned on Todos Santos while you were partying after we got back from Radiance. And I'd rather bet on the sun rising in the west than against you rolling your own dice."

Herbrand pursed his lips. "Well," he said, "I'm sure we can accommodate you, though with not the Metrolight—not for a trip to Big Florida, especially. The—"

Hogg snicked his folding knife open and stepped closer to the merchant. "You wasn't listening," he said. "The mistress told you we wasn't here to haggle."

"Hogg is quite right, Mister Herbrand," Adele said coldly. "My expert—"

She'd had no idea that Tovera knew how to fly an aircar. She'd been expecting to use Barnes for a driver, hoping against hope that his skills would've improved since the most recent time she'd seen them demonstrated.

"—has chosen the Metrolight, so that's what we'll have."

She coughed slightly, then resumed, "You can think of this as an exercise in eminent domain, if you wish. It's immaterial to me whether you feel the taking is by the government whose citizen you are or that of Yang where you reside, but—"

Adele smiled, very slightly.

"—since we'll pay you and we intend to return the vehicle, I think the situation better fits an action by the Republic of Cinnabar."

"All right, all right," Herbrand said, seemingly more resigned than angry. Hogg closed his knife but didn't move away from the merchant for the moment. "You have no idea how hard it is to get a working aircar to Yang, but all right. Is there anything else you need?"

"Yes," said Adele. "The Republic will use you as our agent to arrange transport for some two hundred Cinnabar citizens back to one of the Burdock Stars. I'm not fussy about which planet they land on. I want them to arrive alive and in good health, but this isn't a luxury cruise. Anything suitable for cattle will be good enough for this purpose."

"Just as well you don't want luxury," Herbrand said, "since I'm a businessman, not a wizard. Does it have to be one hull?"

Adele thought. "Yes," she said, "though if there's

a significant price difference we'll consider alternatives."

She wished Daniel's sister Deirdre were here, a banker and heir apparent to Corder Leary's business interests. Adele didn't know and didn't *care* about things like rates and discounts. She knew the words, though, and she knew to use them now because if she didn't Herbrand would sense weakness. Then, because he was . . . not a fool, not exactly, but because he was completely unfamiliar with who he was dealing with, he'd attempt to cheat her.

She was Mundy of Chatsworth. Disrespect for a Mundy would not go unpunished.

Adele rose. "Mister Herbrand?" she said. "A piece of advice for you. I've come to do business in a fashion that provides a fair profit for Acme Trading Company, including an indemnity for replacing your Metrolight if things develop badly. I do not wish to shoot you. But be very clear that I *will* shoot you if you insult my honor. Do you understand?"

"Don't dirty yourself, mistress," Hogg said, grinning. "Let me'n Tovera take out the trash. She likes it, and I don't mind."

Tovera's laugh didn't sound like it came from a mammal, let alone a human being.

"I hear you," Herbrand said. His voice was quiet and the way his eyes flicked from one servant to the other suggested that he meant what he said.

"We'll return to the cutter now," Adele said. "A party will pick up the aircar in an hour's time. I'll have sent you the necessary credit information by then."

She walked out of the office. This time Tovera was leading while Hogg brought up the rear.

"Mistress Mundy?" Herbrand called.

Adele looked over her shoulder. The merchant stood in the doorway. "Yes?" she said.

"You might be able to come back alive from talking to Generalissimo Ma on Big Florida," Herbrand said. "And I'm more than willing as a businessman, as well as a loyal Cinnabar citizen, to take the Admiral's money for chartering a ship to the Burdocks. But mistress, do you honestly believe you're going to get the President's fancy bit off the island and trade her for those Burdock mercenaries?"

"Yes, I do," Adele said. "I'll admit that I don't know how, but I don't need to know."

She smiled. "I *do* know Lieutenant Leary," she added as she walked toward the outer door.

614 rested on a sandy islet just within the jaws of Sunrise Bay. Daniel, on his back in an inflatable raft beneath the cutter, felt the low-frequency thrum through the water. Seconds later Claud at the gun on the top of the hull shouted, "Incoming aircar! It's headed straight for us!"

"*Do not shoot!*" Adele's voice snapped through the intercom channel and the outside speakers both. "*The vehicle's ours with only our people aboard.*"

"Carry on by yourself while I go ashore, Sentino," Daniel said to the motorman in the raft with him. He tugged them over with the tether, then clambered up onto the port-side outrigger. "I think this needs me more than the thruster nozzles do."

The truth was, neither activity needed Daniel very much. The two nozzles they'd checked were good for another six hundred hours of continuous service, and there was no reason to expect the stern thrusters to be in any worse shape than the bow pair. Similarly, the only business he had with the rented aircar was to ride in it to Big Florida Island and, if things there went at least moderately well, to ride back.

Daniel smiled brightly to the spacers who'd been watching the approaching vehicle with concern. He was the captain. His only important job at the moment was to show his crew that he had matters under control, but there *was* no more important job than that.

Adele came out of the hatch, bending lower than the opening required. Daniel gestured her to join him as he walked to the end of the outrigger where they could speak privately despite remaining in plain sight of the crew.

The aircar was mushing along at no more than thirty miles an hour. Adele made a slight gesture toward it and said, "Tovera's obviously at pains not to look threatening. Mind, if somebody does shoot at her and miss, she'll probably respond."

"I don't think Barnes and Dasi would be pleased about it either," Daniel agreed mildly. "To be honest, I hate to issue weapons to spacers. They're good people, absolutely the best, but I *don't* think they're safe with guns, most of them."

Barnes and Dasi were journeyman mechanics and strong enough to manage repairs that'd normally require heavy equipment. He'd assigned them to accompany Tovera in the aircar while he moved *614* out of the city proper.

The two men could also break heads in situations which Tovera would solve by shooting whoever was in the way. Tovera doubtless preferred her own methods, but Daniel didn't.

"I don't think safety has a high priority on this mission," Adele said. She looked at him and quirked her minuscule smile; it made her look ten years old. "I don't think it ever has with you, does it, Daniel? And the rest of us have all volunteered to serve under you."

"Well, there's risks you can't avoid," Daniel said. "But really, I think we have a very good chance of coming through the operation. It's not a suicide mission."

He felt his face shift into harder planes than usual. "Adele?" he said, his voice pitched very low. "I wouldn't throw away this crew just to keep Shin from burning some gutter-sweepings from Burdock. If that were the choice, I'd light the pyre myself. Duty, yes; and RCN personnel have to be ready to die for the Republic. But my crew are citizens as well, so *I'll* make the decision as to what's worth them dying for."

"Yes, of course," Adele said. She smiled faintly at him. "The Learys always treated their retainers well."

Daniel laughed. "So you think I'm acting like a Cinnabar nobleman instead of an RCN officer?" he said. "Well, you may be right."

"I don't think there's a great deal of difference," Adele said, her attention back on the aircar as Tovera brought it in for a landing. "Not among the good ones, that is."

"*Or* the bad ones," Daniel said with a momentary frown. There were officers who treated their spacers much the way callous nobles treated their dependents. They tended not to be fighting officers, however, if only because dangerous situations gave aggrieved underlings opportunities for redress that'd send a house servant to the execution dock.

The aircar landed ten yards up-beach from *614*. The stern was high and therefore slammed hard after the bow hit. The sand the fans kicked up blew away at a slant instead of flaying the spacers outside the hull.

That was typical of Tovera's calculated handling. Her driving was skillful in a cold fashion, but she had absolutely no aptitude for the business. She hadn't realized till she touched down that one of the bow fans was badly misaligned.

Daniel grinned, amused that the insight made him like Tovera a little better than he had. He'd thought of her as a machine that killed, a creature with no more personality than a poisonous reptile has. Seeing her struggle to do something that she found so uncomfortable made her human in a way. Made her the sort of human Daniel respected, because by God! she *was* driving the vehicle.

"Daniel?" said Adele, who'd been watching his expression.

"I was thinking," he said, shading the facts slightly. The Mundys treated their retainers responsibly also, and he had no wish to seem insulting. "I'd rather be driven by somebody who knows what she's doing despite her awkwardness executing it, than by Barnes who has a real instinct but . . . well, if he behaved that way when he was out on the hull, I'd ground him. If he survived his first climb up the rigging."

"I suppose that's what Tovera thought also," Adele said, smiling faintly. "I'm surprised that she isn't better at it, since she's such a good shot. A lack of practice, I suppose."

Daniel looked at her. "I think a lack of aptitude, rather," he said. He thought but didn't add, *Perhaps if we mounted scythes on the car, Tovera might improve.* Instead he went on aloud, "She's competent, though, which is a considerable improvement on what the *Sissie*'s had in the past."

He heard what he'd just said and chuckled. "Or *Cutter 614* has had, which is what I ought to have said, I suppose."

The two riggers waited by the aircar while Woetjans and six more spacers, two of them carrying a heavy toolbox, joined them. Tovera walked back to the cutter. She nodded to Daniel and Adele as she stepped through the hatch.

"She's getting the equipment she'll install on the vehicle," Adele explained quietly. "The others will remove body panels and do other heavy work necessary."

"Should you be there?" Daniel said, afraid that he'd been taking Adele from her duties.

She shook her head. "I'm not a technician, Daniel," she said. "I use the equipment, but Hogg would do a better job installing it than I would."

Daniel laughed. "If it's at all similar to rigging a wire snare," he said, "I'm sure Hogg would do very well indeed. But I take your point."

The cutter's centrifugal pump had been purring at low volume as it filled *614*'s tanks with reaction mass. The high volume setting would've accomplished the task long since, but Daniel hadn't felt the loud whine and vibration were required.

He cleared his throat and went on, "I don't want to seem anxious, but do you have an idea of how long the modifications are going to take?"

"There're six separate sensors," Adele said, "but they can be glued in place. The body panels are plastic and transparent on most of the wavelengths we'll be using. The only delay will be disguising the installations. Since you're penetrating a rebel base on Yang rather than an Alliance Fleet anchorage, I don't expect that will require much effort."

She paused in startled concern. "Ah—that is, unless you think we *should* spend the effort, Daniel," she said. "Your opinion of the danger is paramount, of course."

"Oh, good God!" Daniel said. "Adele, why in the name of heaven would I worry about some drug-sodden wogs finding equipment that you and Tovera feel is adequately concealed? Her life's at much at risk as mine is, you know."

Adele smiled. "Yes, Daniel," she said. "But Tovera doesn't really care, you know. And I do care about you."

Hogg and Tovera had joined the spacers at the aircar. At Woetjans' command, riggers on the cutter's hull were running a mast out parallel to the ground. It'd act as a derrick in case they wanted to lift the big car, Daniel supposed.

"If the work's done within the hour," he said, thinking aloud, "we'll set off this evening. Two hours to get to the island, plus however long Generalissimo Ma spends talking to me. Not long, I would expect."

He grinned. Adele nodded but didn't grin back.

"And then two hours back. With any luck we'll have returned before nightfall."

"There's been one change of plan, Captain," Adele said. "In accordance with my authority as granted by officials of the Republic—"

She means her spymaster, Daniel thought. He looked at Adele sharply. She was staring in the direction of the aircar. Two body panels lay beside the vehicle, and Tovera was squirming into the cavity.

"—I've determined that you'll pilot the cutter to a place named Fishhead Cove, on the mainland three miles south of Big Florida Island. It's generally uninhabited and at any rate doesn't have a garrison from either the rebels or the government army. Tovera in the aircar will join us there. You and Tovera will then fly to the island proper. The cutter will be in position to make an immediate attack if the rebels—"

She shrugged.

"—behave badly. Behave like a gang of drug-sodden wogs, in the words of a friend of mine."

"Oh, I can't allow that," Daniel said, shaking his head in disbelief. "Adele, a direct attack doesn't have any chance of success. If the rebels cut up badly, I've given Woetjans orders to return to Nikitin. It's a matter for Admiral Milne, then."

"Lieutenant Leary," Adele said, her tone as cold as Daniel had ever heard it, "I assure you that my authority in this matter supercedes yours. If necessary I'll remove you from command and place the cutter under the bosun until we've reached the cove."

Her smile, minute but warm despite that, flashed again. She added, "Though I hope you won't force me to do that. Woetjans says that because of the missiles on Big Florida Island, we can't rise more than ten feet above the sea throughout the approach. She thinks we'll be much safer with you at the controls."

Daniel looked at the aircar. Only Tovera's feet were visible. Hogg, squatting beside them, took a thumb-sized bead from a carrying case and reached into the vehicle.

He cleared his throat and, without turning his head, said, "I don't think Woetjans could keep the cutter within the necessary parameters. That's my duty and I'll take care of it."

Hoping that he had the stinging in his eyes under control he faced Adele and went on, "I honestly don't believe attacking with *614* has any chance of success. With me in charge or with anyone. I really wish you'd scrap that plan and simply go back to Nikitin."

"Daniel," Adele said with a shrug, "there's not a person in this crew who'd leave you to die in order to save his own life. Not one."

She gave him a broad smile, an expression as unnatural to her as religious ecstasy would've been. "So as the same friend said," she went on, "'There's some risks you can't avoid.'"

CHAPTER 18

Fishhead Cove on Yang

Adele watched the aircar rise vertically, or as close to vertically as Tovera could manage; it listed to port and was drifting downwind—though not badly. The driver finally got her vehicle level and headed toward the island three miles to the northeast.

Daniel, on the second of the car's four benches, had his arms spread over the seat back and looked completely at ease. He was in his Whites with full medals, but his saucer hat sat upside down on the seat beside him with a dead impeller battery to weight it. The aircar was open-topped, so the hat would certainly blow away if he tried to wear it.

The bow pointed two points to the right of its course. Hogg, standing beside Adele on the outrigger, spat into the water and muttered, "Anyhow, they don't give points for style."

He sounded angry, which meant he was worried. Adele wasn't sure she'd ever seen Hogg angry in the normal sense. Where somebody else might've frothed with rage, the plump countryman would smile as he snicked his knife open or aimed a boot where he thought it'd do the most good. Watching the young master go into a dangerous situation without him made Hogg snap and snarl, because he had nothing else to do.

"I suspect that for Yang, Tovera is an exceptionally good driver," Adele said in a calm voice that she hoped would be soothing. "Do you suppose Daniel is really that relaxed?"

Hogg grinned approvingly. "Oh, he knows that if you put on the face, the feeling comes along after," he said. He gave Adele a speculative look, adding, "I figured you did the same, mistress. That or you're an ice queen and no mistake. I never seen nothing faze you."

"Don't confuse calm with resignation, Hogg," Adele said, feeling the corners of her mouth lift in the hint of a smile. "Though I suppose they have the same effect."

The aircar had disappeared over the spit of land framing Fishhead Cove to the north. The burr of the fans remained faintly audible, unless that was Adele's imagination.

The cove was black with vegetable matter from the creek feeding it. Dust and pollen formed whorls on the surface, with leaves and occasionally a floating branch to vary the pattern. The banks were six to ten feet high, steep and rocky, and the forest marched to the edge of them on both north and south. A scum of algae floated on the margins and gummed the shore where the tide had lifted it, tying together land and water.

Though the Mundys had a country estate, Adele had grown up at Chatsworth Minor, the townhouse in Xenos. To her this landscape didn't seem so much wild as it did untidy.

"Pretty place," murmured Hogg. He was cradling an impeller in the crook of his left arm. With his right hand held out horizontally he indicated the shore of the cove. "See them burrows down at the water? If we was going to be here overnight, I'd run snares and see what it was dug there."

Adele didn't even see the burrows—or see them for sure, at any rate. She could pick out changes in color and texture, but she wouldn't have thought any of them were holes if Hogg hadn't told her some were present.

He looked at Adele, his face twisting with pain and disgust. "I wish he'd of took me," he said unhappily. He wasn't changing the subject, just admitting what in his heart the subject had always been. "Look, I'm not saying anything against your Tovera, mistress. She'll take care of the master if anybody could, I don't doubt that. But he's *my* master."

Adele shrugged. "Tovera can drive an aircar," she said simply. "You can't. All the force at our disposal couldn't protect Daniel if Generalissimo Ma decided to kill him. His only safety's in looking like a well-born but dim-witted officer and his civilian driver, neither of them armed. They'll be safe so long as they're harmless."

Unless the rebels decide to kill them for the same reason boys throw rocks through the windows of abandoned buildings, Adele thought. *For the sheer delight of destruction.*

"Tovera didn't take a gun?" Hogg said in amazement. "Bloody hell. That must've been hard on her."

"Guns wouldn't help, Hogg," Adele said gently. "Looking innocent and a little stupid is their best defense."

Hogg shrugged his big shoulders, loosening them. "Guess I'll go up on top of the rock and find a soft spot to wait and watch where they won't be seeing me back," he said, nodding toward the spit of land. "I can crank up the sights on this thing—"

He jiggled the impeller.

"—to plus one-twenty-eight. That's enough to get a good view if I keep it steady."

Adele frowned. "Big Florida Island is miles away, Hogg," she said. "Can you really hold your sights that steady?"

"Aye, with a rest, mistress," he said with a bearlike grin. "And I trust what you say, that guns won't make the young master safe. But if them wogs start shooting, they're going to learn what *real* shooting is."

He crossed the catwalk to the shore. A dozen spacers sat there cooking on a small fire. Adele watched Hogg for a moment, then went back into the cutter to check her equipment. The radio was sending a looped message to Generalissimo Ma, informing him that Lieutenant Leary was coming to treat for the release of a prisoner; that the lieutenant was unarmed but had the whole weight of the RCN behind him.

Those were fine words. Adele desperately wished they'd been true.

Daniel jerked forward suddenly as he saw the construction on the far side of Big Florida Island, then remembered he was supposed to hide the fact he cared about anything but Maria Mondindragiana—and something to drink. He leaned back in his seat again, but he cranked up the magnification of the goggles he wore against the windrush to plus sixteen.

"They're building a starport, Tovera," he said. "Good God, it's the size of Harbor Three! They're extending those sandspits to the north with concrete pilings to anchor breakwaters!"

Because no one but Tovera was in the car with him, Daniel had perforce to treat Adele's servant as though she were human or else hold his tongue. This was so unexpected—and important—that he'd have blurted something to the dashboard if he were alone.

"Sir," said Tovera, an emotionless acknowledgment. "Will the additional laborers affect our plans to retrieve the woman?"

"I doubt it," Daniel said. "But they're not building this for commercial purposes, not here on Yang. While I don't know the minds of the people in our Navy Office, I'm pretty sure your mistress does. Since she didn't tell me there was a new RCN base going up on Big Florida, I think we can be confident that it's an Alliance project."

The aircar was fully visible to the rebels. They flew at 30 mph and stayed a hundred feet in the air, holding a straight course. If the guns trained on them opened fire, even with the bad marksmanship to be expected on Yang, they'd almost certainly blast the vehicle out of the sky before Tovera could take evasive action.

Well, if it happened, it happened.

A dozen prefab barracks, basically shipping containers with doors and windows cut into the sides, clustered just south of the bay where the construction was going

on. The island's earlier structures, a fortified mansion
and its outbuildings, were some distance away in the
center of the island. They'd been falling to ruin for
decades, but they were now being repaired with poles
and plastic sheeting.

The vessel the rebels were converting to a warship
was on the north side of the mansion. Half its antennas were missing, but it still had a turret with two
plasma cannon on the dorsal bow. A 12-tube rocket
launcher had been added astern.

"*Daniel?*" said Adele in a tinny voice through the
miniature radio she'd clipped to Daniel's epaulette
like a fourth rank tab. He'd never have worn such
an item with his Whites at a Cinnabar function, but
he doubted Generalissimo Ma was an expert on RCN
uniforms. "*The rebels are hailing you, but they're on
FM and your vehicle has only AM radio. I'm patch-
ing them through.*"

Instantly someone else snarled, "*Land that car!
Land at once or we'll shoot you down, I don't care
if you're the whole Cinnabar Senate!*"

"Roger, Big Florida Base," Daniel said, dropping
into proper communications protocol by reflex. "This
is RCN aircar 5063—"

He had no idea what the number painted on the
vehicle's bow meant. He needed to identify himself
some way, though.

"—approaching Big Florida for negotiations. We'll
land at the entrance to the large stone building, over."

Tovera glanced at him over her shoulder. He nodded.
She slanted the aircar's bow down instead of tilting the
fans toward vertical while throttling back as a more
skilled driver would've done. Gravity accelerated them

into a dive toward the mansion rather than them sloping slowly down for a landing as intended.

That was almost fatal: they flew into a burst of sub-machine gun fire that'd been aimed to miss them ahead. Three pellets popped on the car's underside. One must've hit a fan blade before it sang away.

"Land at once!" the rebel shrieked. *"Land or we'll kill you!"*

"Tovera," Daniel said, "drop her fast but aim for the mansion still. Break—"

Not strictly correct, but he had to cue Adele as he went on, "Roger, Big Florida Control. We're landing immediately. Please stop shooting at us. RCN aircar out."

Twenty or thirty people stood outside the mansion and looked up at them. Most of the spectators were armed. More were sauntering from the building or pushing aside the walls of sheeting to look out.

The aircar plunged downward. Tovera jerked the yoke toward her, then realized she had to add power fast instead of throttling back as she'd started to do. Rebels bellowed and jumped out of the way, some of them dropping their guns.

Tovera avoided a smashup, but the aircar pogoed upward again instead of settling. She caught the vehicle twenty feet in the air, achieved wobbly balance, and lowered them to the ground in a series of ratchets. The bow dipped first, then the stern.

"Thank you, Tovera," Daniel said, rising to his feet before he stepped out of the vehicle. He set his hat on his head and straightened it by feel. "That was more than good enough."

Which was true. Tovera'd been thrown out of her

planned approach by the radioed orders and hadn't managed a smooth transition to the change. Nonetheless they were safely on the ground, which is all that was required. Barnes would likely have landed on the first pass, but in a doughnut of grit and with a bang that'd threaten the frame if he didn't break it.

Tovera didn't reply. Daniel looked at her. She was white with fury—at herself, apparently. She hadn't met her own standards, even though she'd exceeded his.

An extremely tall man with pale skin and blond hair ran toward them from the mansion. His uniform was as ornate as Daniel's and a great deal more colorful. He was dressed all in orange, but each garment—tricorne hat, tunic, sash, trousers and dyed leather boots—was a different *shade* of orange.

Daniel blinked at the fellow. *Hogg would be envious*, he thought, but that was a warning as well. Hogg's flamboyant taste didn't make him a harmless buffoon, so the same might be true of this fellow.

"You Cinnabar goat-fuckers!" the blond screamed. He wasn't a Yang native, obviously. "Didn't you hear me tell you to land at once? By God, you'll know to do what I tell you the next time!"

He lifted his right hand for what was obviously intended to be a full-armed slap. He was rangy rather than bulky but he was also six-eight or nine, a good foot taller than Daniel.

"Pardon me, sir," Daniel said in a voice loud enough to be heard. "I'm a Cinnabar gentleman and an RCN officer. Don't presume—"

The blond swung. Daniel caught his wrist with his right hand and stopped the blow in the air.

"I say, this behavior isn't—"

The other rebels were watching, jabbering among themselves more in interest than anger. The blond was obviously a leader of some sort, but he was also a foreigner.

The fellow drew back a leg to kick. *Act harmless and a little stupid*, Adele had said. Daniel could see the logic of that, but he *was* a Leary.

He still held the blond's wrist. He let go of it. The fellow'd been straining to pull out of Daniel's grip, so he jerked himself off balance. Daniel grabbed the blond's raised boot with both hands and twisted hard. Because of the considerable leverage, the knee popped before the ankle did. He toppled backward, screaming.

Daniel bent to open the flap of the fellow's cross-draw holster. He grabbed Daniel by the shoulders. That might've been a response to pain rather than from a desire to continue the fight, if you wanted to call it a fight. Daniel backhanded him absently and tossed the fellow's small pistol into the aircar without looking behind him. That motion only *looked* accidental.

"There, that's all right, then," Daniel said, straightening to smile brightly at the circle of watching rebels. *Bloody hell, he'd burst the left shoulder seam of his tunic. Thank the good fortune of the RCN that the sash of the Order of Novy Sverdlovsk would conceal most of the damage.* "Will one of you gentlemen—or ladies, that would be fine—please take me to Generalissimo Ma? We have an appointment."

A husky male rebel with a rocket launcher stepped to the fallen blond and jabbed bare toes into the injured knee. "What price your pretty clothes now, Platt?" he said over the victim's screams.

Tovera switched off the aircar's fans. She sat primly

with her hands on the steering yoke instead of reaching for the pistol on the seat behind her. She hadn't shut down before: even without scythes, the vehicle was a weapon. Sweeping unexpectedly into the arc of spectators, it could've been a very effective one.

"Really, can anyone help me?" Daniel said, looking hopeful and innocent. "Then shall I just go in by myself?"

"I'll take you to His Nibs," said the man with the rocket launcher. "Say, it was a treat watching you break Platt's leg. You want to break the other one before you go?"

"I hardly think that'll be necessary," Daniel said, dabbing at his medals as if to dust them. He wanted to suck air through his open mouth, but for the sake of appearances he was forcing himself to breathe normally.

He followed the rocketeer into the mansion. The rough stone interior walls made it look like a prison, but it must've been a very fancy place in its day. The plaster that'd fallen to litter the floor—nobody'd bothered to sweep it out during the current reoccupation—had been frescoed.

Light sockets were spiked into cracks in the walls and connected by wire that hung in swags between them. They threw harsh shadows across what would've been ugly enough even with soft lighting.

Most of the other spectators trooped in behind Daniel and his guide. He was apparently the best entertainment on offer this evening. None of the rooms they passed had doors, but quick glances to either side showed only tangled fabric—clothing, bedding; who knew?—and not infrequently sprawled people.

The place stank. Most if not all of the hundreds of

inhabitants were using the nearest corner as a latrine instead of going outside to void their wastes against the exterior walls as the better classes did on Yang.

The rear of the original building had been a garden enclosed in a pillared court. It'd been covered with plastic panels and turned into the Generalissimo's headquarters. Fifty or more armed people stood about, while Ma filled a raised stone bench that would've held three men Daniel's size. A woman, striking though she wasn't in her first youth, sat on a stool at the Generalissimo's feet. She had an olive complexion and lustrous, curly hair the color of polished coal.

In one corner of the garden was a modern communications console. The technician sitting at it looked over her shoulder at Daniel with an unreadable expression. She wore a one-piece beige garment, possibly a uniform though it had no insignia and Daniel didn't recognize the cut. If—as seemed likely—she and Platt had come with the console to handle the rebels' information services, she was going to be working a double shift for the next long time.

"Why are you here, Cinnabar?" the Generalissimo squeaked. "Go away now! You have no business with the Light of Free Yang movement."

Daniel had the odd feeling that Ma's rolls of fat were squeezing his voice into a high-pitched chirp. He didn't suppose human physiology worked that way, but the notion had the seductive plausibility of a good urban legend. . . .

Aloud he said, "Sir, I'm here as representative of my republic. I understand you're detaining one of our citizens, Mistress Maria Mondindragiana. I've come to request her release on behalf of my people."

The pretty woman at Ma's feet had been watching Daniel in a speculative way that he was familiar with; so familiar, in fact, that he'd been sucking in his gut in what was closer to instinct than reflex. When he spoke, her face went completely blank, as still as a bust stamped onto a coin.

"My Maria, detained?" Ma giggled. "What a joke! She's with me because I'm six times that man that eunuch Shin was. Maria loves me and loves my loving! Tell him so, Maria."

That last was beyond any question a command. The woman formed her mouth into a professional smile and said, "Me want to get out of here? What reason could there possibly be that I'd want to get out of here, Mister Cinnabar Officer? The Generalissimo's troops came to my villa, and I never had any thought but to go with them."

So she really did want to leave, Daniel thought. He hadn't been sure till he heard her carefully worded response. In a way that was a pity, because part of him would much prefer to lift from Yang at once and head straight back to Nikitin with word of what was happening on Big Florida Island.

"Very well then, Generalissimo," Daniel said. Instead of saluting, one military officer to another, he made a bow so low that it was just short of an obeisance. *This was the tricky part.* "I'll tell you frankly that from the very beginning I was more than a little doubtful about what President Shin claimed. Between us as soldiers, I'd be doubtful if *that* fellow walked in the door wet and told me it was raining."

Ma piped like a teapot at a hard boil. His eyes were closed and waves rippled through his fat from his

calves to his swollen jowls. It was only by deduction
that Daniel was sure the Generalissimo was laughing:
if it'd been having a fit or in a rage, his retainers
wouldn't still look bored.

Mind, Generalissimo Ma could have a fatal stroke
while laughing. Although Daniel didn't think the universe in general would be worse for that occurrence,
it'd make his own task even more complicated than
it already was.

"Since that's the case . . ." Daniel continued when
he thought the squealing laughter had dropped to a
point that the Generalissimo could hear him again.
"I'll go straight back to the city and give that Shin
a piece of my mind. I'll show him that he can't lie
to a Cinnabar officer and get away with it! If he
doesn't turn over his prisoners to me at once, he'll
live to regret it!"

It was obvious—and inevitable—that the rebels had
spies in the Presidential Palace. By telling Ma what
he already knew, that Shin had sent him, Daniel could
look like a dimwit who blurted secrets—without in
fact giving anything away.

It was very important that he seem to be a dimwit,
because any visitor with half a brain must inevitably
know too much to be allowed to live. The only reason
the rebels had allowed Daniel to approach was that
shooting an RCN officer really would bring massive
retaliation. Admiral Milne might be delighted with
the result, but she wouldn't let it go unpunished; *no*
Cinnabar official would. Since he'd come in unexpectedly high, they might decide they had to shoot
him anyway.

The information would reach Milne regardless,

through the data the car's spy suite had already transmitted to Adele aboard *Cutter 614*. Daniel, giving the
Generalissimo a sappy smile, had personal reasons to
want to bring it back himself. It was nice to know
that he'd be avenged, of course, but that wasn't his
first choice of outcomes.

Ma grew still. He looked around the room. "Where
is Platt?" he said in dawning irritation. "Is Platt not
here?"

"Naw, he decided to take a lie-down outside, boss,"
said the rocketeer who'd brought Daniel in. "You know
them stuck-up foreigners."

The rebels who'd come in with him laughed. Ma's
frown turned to puzzlement, then back to anger before
blanking again. He fixed Daniel with his eyes. In a
falsely jovial voice said, "I wonder, Lieutenant . . . I'm
building a new fort on the north of the island. Did
you notice it, perhaps?"

"Haw!" said Daniel, wondering if he was overdoing
it. "I'm not much for architecting, your lordship. I
leave that for the other chappies, the Land Forces of
the Republic we call them, you know. Mind, I like a
spot of hunting and fishing when I'm on leave."

"Too bad," Ma said. "I'd have been pleased to give
you a tour if you wanted one. Well, you'll want to
be getting back to that traitor to Yang in Heavenly
Peace, won't you? Only one thing, Lieutenant—stay
low when you leave here. Very low. As if you were
a boat on the water. Otherwise there might be an
accident."

Daniel gave him a goggle-eyed stare. "Ah?" he said.
"Right, right, whatever you say, your lordship. The girlie
driving me said we should stay high so we didn't look

like we were sneaking up on you, you see. Might've known whatever a girl said was wrong, what?"

He bent over with laughter. Ma squeaked companionably for a moment, then fell silent.

Daniel turned, called, "Cheerio, then," over his shoulder, and sauntered back down the hall. The rebels standing there made way for him. He thought he heard his guide say, "Remember, break the other one!"

He walked from the mansion without challenge. Platt had disappeared. A few rebels stood outside, chewing and spitting what was probably a drug. They paid Daniel no attention.

He got into the car. The pistol wasn't on the seat any more. In a low voice he said, "Head due south, keeping the headquarters building between us and the construction to the north. And stay right on the surface. That's very important."

Tovera had switched the fans on when Daniel came out of the building. She slid the car forward under power, scraping the underside along the pebbly soil for the first twenty feet. She started slowly, but as they crossed the margin of the island she increased power so that the occasional waves they touched gave the car solid slaps.

"You succeeded, then?" she said.

Daniel had been lost in his thoughts. "What?" he said. "Yes, I think I did. Even if the sensors you installed on the vehicle fail, I believe I have enough information to create a workable plan."

"The sensors won't fail," Tovera said. She glanced back at him and smiled. Daniel had seen bare skulls with more humor on them than this woman's expression.

"I succeeded too," she said. "I've learned which of those people it was who shot at us on the approach. I'll make it a point to meet him again."

Tovera laughed. Daniel kept his face blank. She had a right to be angry about being shot at, but he'd rather that she didn't make her intentions so clear in the sound of her cruel laughter.

CHAPTER 19

Fishhead Cove on Yang

Daniel stood on the cutter's port outrigger, just to the right of the hatch. "Well, fellow spacers," he said to the crew gathered in an arc on shore facing him. "We've got our work cut out for us this time."

Insectoids whirred in the darkness, and occasionally something larger swooped over the cove with a *whick-whick-whick* of wings. Yang had no visible moon, but the system was located in the center of a globular cluster that turned the night sky into a milky haze.

"We're going up against hundreds of rebels," Daniel said. He paused deliberately before going on in a dead-pan voice, "The best soldiers Yang has to offer."

Woetjans guffawed. Harsh, delighted laughter rang from the assembled spacers.

"Not only that," Daniel continued in feigned portentousness, "but there's an Alliance naval base going up in the north bay of the island. From the look of it there's probably a hundred or so people in the construction crew, and they may be from Alliance planets."

There was more laughter. Daniel had always hated politics: the deals, the lies, and so often the truth stated in a false way. That's what he was doing here, setting out the dangers "honestly" but making a joke of them.

Speaker Leary would be proud of his son. Well, it had to be done.

A hologram ten feet in diameter hung in the air over Daniel's head. It showed a direct overhead view of Big Florida Island, corrected from the slant image recorded by the aircar's sensor suite as Tovera approached. A saffron highlight now pulsed over the jaws of land and the water beyond where the pilings were going in.

Harrison and a team of riggers had shifted *614's* console into the airlock so that Adele could project images that the whole crew could see without depending on their helmet visors. That'd be perfectly adequate in a technical sense, but it'd mean an additional distance between Daniel and the crew when he wanted—*needed*—to fire them up for a very dangerous mission.

The down-side was that Daniel couldn't lift the cutter until the console had been returned to its normal position in the bow; indeed, they couldn't *board* the cutter until they'd shifted the console so it didn't block the hatch. That was a chance Daniel was willing to take, because the operation he'd planned was going to need all the verve and enthusiasm his crew could muster.

"We're doing this to rescue a girl from Waystation . . ." he continued. An image of Maria Mondindragiana appeared above him. Daniel had no idea how Adele had gotten that visual, since there'd been stone walls between the woman and the aircar's sensors all the time that he knew of. "And she's not even my type!"

This time the laughter redoubled. And it was all true, every word of it. . . .

"You mean she's grown shut, Captain?" Sun called.

"I bet that wouldn't stop our Mister Leary!" Enescue put in, rousing another gust of laughter.

"The rebels have a three-thousand ton packet that used to be on the Cinnabar to Baltoon run," Daniel continued. Adele responded promptly with visuals of the *Beacon of Yang*, rotating her first on her horizontal, then on her vertical, axes. "They're trying to convert her to a warship. I don't think they're going to succeed in my lifetime, but there's still the bones of a ship there. Her fusion bottle works—"

He'd queued the series of highlights, just for color since the spacers didn't need help locating the basic elements of a starship. Adele brought them out on call.

"—her dorsal turret works though it can't be retracted, and about a third of her thrusters work. I wouldn't be surprised to learn that some of her High Drive motors work too, but since she doesn't have enough thrusters to reach orbit, that doesn't matter."

A creature in the cove slapped the water three times, with about thirty seconds between one *whap* and the next. The first time Daniel'd heard the sound he'd thought it was a fish jumping to avoid a predator. It was too regular, though, and always from the same direction; probably it was the mating call of a creature whom he'd never have a chance to identify. That'd remain one of his lesser regrets, he supposed.

"We'll put off for the island tonight at oh-three-hundred hours local time," Daniel said, no longer pretending to joke. "I'm leaving Whitebread and Racine as anchor watch in the cutter—"

"But sir!" cried Whitebread. The spacers to either side of him drew back as if he'd been declared contagious.

"All of you!" Daniel shouted. He wasn't using a loudspeaker, but his voice was pitched for command and the cutter's hull acted as a sounding board. "This is the RCN and I'm your captain. Shut up and follow my orders, or by God! you'll never ship with me again."

If you survive and I do, he added in his mind. But they were all operating on the assumption that would happen. Aloud he went on, "*Do* you understand?"

Whitebread didn't speak. Racine muttered, "Aye aye, sir, but I wish you took me too."

"Right," said Daniel, "Whitebread and Racine on anchor watch, so we don't get back and find some fisherman has managed to lift the cutter while we were gone. Or lock us out, that'd be as bad. The rest of us'll be in the aircar, heading for Big Florida to land at the point *here*."

The terrain image reappeared above him. This time a red bead pulsed at a notch on the southwest shore. A fold of land ran up from it till it was nearly parallel to the *Beacon*'s port side. It'd be scarcely noticeable to a person standing at a moderate distance, but it was nonetheless sufficient to conceal someone moving on all fours.

"In ground effect, the car should carry thirty," Daniel added. "If there's any doubt, we'll tow the life raft with a few of you in it. We'll be going in slow anyway so we don't arouse attention. Are you all clear so far?"

Nobody asked questions. Daniel would've been surprised if they had. This was all new to the spacers, but the plan was simple enough in outline. They weren't talkers, and asking questions wouldn't make the operation easier to execute.

"Now the ship, the *Beacon of Yang*," Daniel said. "It isn't properly manned, but a number of the rebels are living in it. Hogg and I, and Portus with Tovera, will go in ahead to secure the bridge and power room without noise. When we've accomplished that, we'll summon the rest of you."

Easier said than done, of course. But possible for fast, ruthless people who knew what they were doing. Portus was a crag-featured countryman who'd done his share of poaching. Hogg vouched for him.

"According to our information," Daniel said, "Generalissimo Ma is using Hold One on F Deck—"

The lowest of the *Beacon*'s six decks.

"—as a suite for himself and the prisoner we've come to rescue, Mistress Mondindragiana. He apparently finds it comfortable, and by Yang standards I suppose it is. His bodyguard company is quartered in Hold Two, just astern. Ma apparently thought that because a starship's hull's very thick and that nobody can approach him without going through the guards, he'd be really safe."

Daniel paused, grinning. "It doesn't seem to have occurred to him," he added, "that whoever controls the bridge can close the hatches on him and his guards both. As I intend to do."

This time the laughter was mixed with cheers and catcalls.

"That leaves us the problem of how to get them

out, of course," Daniel continued. "I propose to do that by bringing the ship to this cove, skating it across the strait, and opening Hold One's main hatch."

He shook his head in amusement and added, "I'm afraid the Generalissimo isn't much of a naval architect, since he doesn't appear to have known that the side of a bulk storage hold hinges down."

Daniel wasn't worried about getting Maria out unharmed, since Ma didn't look the sort to fight a battle to the death in which his prisoner might catch a ricochet. There might be a few guards or attendants in Hold One with the happy couple, but Daniel planned to have the cutter's rocket launcher aimed into the opening as the hatch lowered.

He wouldn't use it, of course; in the worst case, single shots by Hogg or Tovera would end the problem without danger to anything but whoever was resisting. It was very unlikely that anybody *would* resist when they found themselves staring at the business end of a dozen rockets, however.

"Now, I want to warn you," Daniel said. "According to the *Beacon*'s gauges, she's got plenty of reaction mass in her tanks to get us here, and according to my calculations the five thrusters she's still got are enough to move her in ground effect. There were more when she landed on Yang, but the rebels robbed three of them to outfit a cutter they were using to boost their income by piracy."

That venture'd failed three months earlier when the entrepreneurs met the *Cutlass*. So small a vessel wasn't really worth a missile, but she'd gotten one anyway when her captain unwisely tried to flee instead of surrendering.

"I trust my calculations farther than I trust the

Beacon's gauges, but I could be wrong and they could *sure* be wrong," Daniel said. "I'd still rather have a starship's hull plates rather than an aircar's between me and whatever the rebels get around to shooting as we leave."

"Sir?" called Sun. "You say the dorsal turret works?"

"As best as we can tell from the ship's internal diagnostics," Daniel said. "And the rocket launcher they mounted astern also. You'll get a chance to see as soon as I light the thrusters, Sun."

The gunner's mate patted his hands together in enthusiasm. *One* crewman was sure ready for this operation.

Actually they all are, Daniel thought, looking around the arc of faces illuminated by scatter from the big display above him. The crew he'd brought with him from the *Sissie* was used to ground operations that most RCN spacers would never dream of. That didn't make them a trained commando, of course, but they had the skill and lack of hesitation that past successes bring to a veteran.

"We'll have to play this by ear, I'm afraid," Daniel said. He felt a sudden warmth toward these spacers, his siblings in a sense that Deirdre could never have been. "The rebels aren't organized enough for me to make detailed plans. Chances are they'll be scattered all over the ship, in corridors and storage areas as well as the ordinary compartments. If they'll surrender, tie them with cargo tape. If there's any doubt in your mind, don't risk yourselves or your buddies."

"No fear, Captain!" Woetjans said. Even without the chorus of growls, Daniel wouldn't have doubted she was speaking for the whole crew.

He didn't look forward to the possible massacre he saw ahead of them, but this was war. The difference between victory and failure was very often the willingness to see what had to be done, and to do it instantly and with all the strength at your disposal.

"Apart from that," Daniel said, "be careful, especially those of you with stocked impellers. If a cutter's arsenal had enough sub-machine guns and pistols to arm everybody, that's what I'd issue. I don't want to lose half of you to ricochets, and that could happen."

Daniel cleared his throat. "Any questions before we put *614* back in shape and get some rest?" he added.

"Sir?" said Whitebread. "This is a big base the Alliance is building?"

"Yes, it is," Daniel said. Whitebread wouldn't have spoken if he weren't peeved at being left behind, but the question Daniel saw coming was a good one nonetheless.

"Sir, then why aren't we beating it back to the squadron soonest? Instead of grabbing up some bint like you could rent a hundred of on the Parade at Waystation?"

Yeah, that was the question.

Daniel could've lied. He could've said he wanted to get additional information on the status of the base, or that the rebels were obviously intriguing with Alliance envoys and it was therefore the duty of an RCN officer to punish them immediately to the extent of his ability.

Both those things were true, and there were other true things that he could also have said; and the crew would've believed him because he was Mister

Leary and they were his siblings and his children. But *because* he was their Mister Leary, he was unwilling to tell little truths in the form of a lie.

"Whitebread, you're quite correct as to where my duty as an RCN officer lies," Daniel said. "I'm willing to take this risk because the base is months from completion and I think we'll get away with it. But the *reason* I'm taking it is that I saw the girl, and I saw Generalissimo Ma. I won't leave her in his hands if there's a way to get her out."

There was dead silence on the bank of the cove.

Daniel took a deep breath. He was trembling. "I told you," he said, "that we're the RCN; but I've just admitted this isn't properly an RCN mission. *614* hasn't become a democracy, but this one time—if any of you want to opt out for tonight, you can stay with the cutter and no questions asked."

Whitebread looked around his fellows. "And if any of you does," he said loudly, "I'll take his fucking place, got that?"

From the cheers that went up in response, Whitebread and Racine were still on anchor watch.

By now Adele had been on enough planets to see the way people travelled on less developed worlds where vehicles were imported, expensive, and rare. There'd been a six-wheeled truck on Sexburga that must've held a hundred passengers, and on Falassa families of five and six rode to the port with their stock in trade—ten-foot lengths of sugar cane—sticking out to either side of scooters that looked small for a lone driver.

By those standards, the aircar she'd leased from Acme

Trading wasn't overloaded with thirty people clinging to it. By any other standard, this was insane.

To Adele's surprise the car actually had enough power to carry the load, though only with the underside of the vehicle so close to the ground that the fan thrust acted as an air cushion. The crew'd bolted two ladders to the body, crosswise on either side of the center of gravity. These provided seats of a sort for the people who couldn't by any stretch of the imagination fit into the passenger compartment.

Adele was on the front bench. Tovera was to her left, driving with an expression of frozen blankness quite different from her normal bland amusement at the world around her. Daniel was to Adele's right, holding a baton cut from two-inch high-pressure tubing. He was smiling, though his eyes weren't focused on the island just ahead.

To Daniel's right was Hogg, his left leg in the passenger compartment and his buttocks riding on the top edge of the door. The perch looked terribly uncomfortable, but Hogg seemed more pleased than not. He held an impeller with its butt resting on his right thigh, and he'd slung a sub-machine gun across his chest. That was probably for Daniel if they got into a situation where the baton wasn't enough . . . as they might, as they certainly might.

Adele's pistol was in her tunic pocket, as usual. On paper a heavy service pistol would've been a more reasonable choice, since they were going into action and had no reason to conceal their weapons.

Adele stuck with what she had. She was Adele Mundy, librarian, who carried a pocket pistol for defense as other Cinnabar nobles did—at least nobles from houses as pugnacious as the Mundys of Chatsworth, and there were many. The person who'd killed scores, maybe hundreds of people by now, wasn't *really* Adele Mundy. . . .

Most members of the raiding party hugged their weapons to them, kneading the grips or running their fingers caressingly over the receivers. In their hearts they hoped that the guns' power to destroy would somehow protect them against their own destruction.

It wouldn't, of course. There was always the chance of a terrified peasant triggering a shot into the night and snuffing out the life of someone as skilled as Tovera or as Adele herself. But even hardened spacers needed talismans against the uncertainties of life and the certainty of death at the end of it.

Adele's personal data unit was open on her lap. She doubted that she could use it because of how tightly the four of them were packed into the front seat, but it was there. Everyone needs a talisman.

The aircar ticked a ripple, then almost at once slammed hard onto the surface of the water. They staggered aloft again in a fine salt mist; Tovera's hands were rigid on the control yoke. Only the fact the strait was sheltered and the air was generally calm made this operation thinkable, but even so it was proving a near thing.

Adele swallowed and prepared to slide the data unit back into its pocket; the jolt had almost sent it sailing out of the vehicle. They were within half a mile of the shore anyway. Lights sparkled through the mansion's windows and open hatches on the *Beacon of Yang*.

"Bloody Hell," said Daniel in a low, urgent voice. "There's a starship landing! Hear it? Adele, do you know anything about this?"

She'd been wrong to think she couldn't use the data unit in these close quarters. She'd coupled it to *614*'s console and sensor suite, of course, and she scarcely had to move her arms at all to enter commands through her familiar wands. *There* the ship's identification code, *there* the conversion of that code. . . .

The data came off Adele's tongue at the same time it touched her own higher faculties: "Daniel, they're Alliance Fleet Ship *Greif*, a twelve-hundred tonne courier vessel. They've announced they're landing, but there's been no reply from the ground that I can find."

Adele could hear the thrusters now, the thrum at high altitude. If she'd looked toward the western sky she'd probably have seen the pulse of plasma growing brighter with the vessel's swift approach.

"Lieutenant?" Tovera said without turning her head. "Do we return to the ship?"

"Crew," said Daniel, keying his intercom instead of answering Tovera alone. *"An Alliance courier is landing on Big Florida. They'll touch down about the time we reach the Beacon. We're continuing the operation. I hope and expect the courier will provide a diversion for us. Break. Adele, I sincerely hope that they don't land on top of the swale where we're making our approach. Any way to check that, over?"*

Adele copied the image from the *Greif*'s command console onto Daniel's visor. It meant nothing to her.

"Good, good!" he grunted. *"They're putting down beside the headquarters."*

The aircar burped over the muddy shallows, then grounded with a heavy shock that would've thrown Adele into the wind screen if Daniel hadn't placed his left arm across her chest like a padded restraint.

His feet, she noticed as she grabbed her data unit with both hands to keep it from sliding forward, were braced against the front of the compartment.

Tovera shut the motors off. The feathered fan blades continued to spin down in a deepening whine. The riggers on the ladders had sprinted clear before the car'd fully bumped to a halt, and the larger number of spacers wedged into the passenger compartment were jumping out now.

The courier vessel's exhaust was a wavering flare in mid-sky, throwing distorted shadows at the spacers' feet. Blotches of light brightened on the mansion as the rebels quartered there pulled tarpaulins aside to see what was happening.

They'll burn their retinas out if they do that for long, Adele thought as she climbed out of the aircar after Daniel. That would make the raiders' job easier.

"Get down, you bloody fools!" Hogg snarled. He'd already started up the swale, cradling the big impeller on his forearms as he crawled forward on elbows and the inner edges of his boots.

Daniel was immediately behind him, staying equally low. The length of tubing was thrust under the back of his belt; it wobbled behind him like a stiff tail but didn't get in his way as he crawled. The mottled utility uniform blurred his outline, but the yellow commo helmet winked in the glare of the descending exhaust.

Portus followed Daniel. He'd slung a sub-machine gun over his back so that the muzzle would hang down when he stood, but for now he too was worming up the swale on knees and elbows. There was a large knife strapped to his right calf; the tip of the sheath was down inside the boot.

Hogg was already out of sight. Shutting down the aircar had slowed Tovera, but she was right behind Portus now. Her sub-machine gun, smaller than the RCN weapons, was holstered on her right hip since she wasn't carrying the attaché case in which she normally concealed it. A square container on her left balanced the weight of the weapon. It was of a size to be a first aid pack, but knowing Tovera it was something quite different.

On the shore, Woetjans was organizing the crew to follow when Daniel gave the word. The spacers were squatting with their weapons pointed in all directions, including one fellow whose impeller bore was a black hole if Adele glanced in that direction.

She didn't move for a moment. She'd intended to be the last person moving toward the *Beacon of Yang*, but . . .

Adele got down on her hands and knees and started upward. She wasn't able to stay as low as the hunters ahead of her, but her hips were still below the edge of the swale. She didn't really have a place in an assault, so she might as well be close to the front.

The courier vessel had slowed its descent almost to a hover, preparing to land between the *Beacon* and the rebel headquarters. Its exhaust hammered downward and made the ground shake.

Adele smiled faintly. She *was* a librarian; but she was a crack shot as well, and right now her friends were likely to need that skill more than they did information services. Close to the front . . .

CHAPTER 20

Big Florida Island on Yang

Daniel crawled with the diligence of a turtle plodding up a beach to lay her eggs. The most difficult thing was to force himself to keep his eyes raised instead of crunching onward with his nose down as though there were nothing on Big Florida Island that might be dangerous. The back of the thermoplastic commo helmet gouged him between the shoulder-blades, but that was better than a shot in the same place from a wog standing unnoticed on the edge of the gully.

The island's soil was pebbles in coarse sand. Except where bound by the roots, run-off quickly eroded it when storms swept in from the sea. The gully was bordered by fibrous-stemmed bushes with small leaves, and squat plants which spread up-slanted foliage to catch rain; their rootlets fuzzed the sides where freshets had scoured the ground away despite them. Daniel's shoulder had brushed one patch as he started upward. The touch had seared him like fiberglass, and tips broken off in his skin continued to itch.

The courier vessel had roared while descending; now it snarled in a hover, its eight thrusters scooping out the soil and flinging the debris in all directions as molten glass. With all that happening on the other side of the *Beacon of Yang*, there was no longer any point in creeping around.

"Cinnabars, up and at 'em!" Daniel called, rising as he spoke and leading Hogg for the last twenty feet to the *Beacon*'s port outrigger.

The partly converted freighter wasn't a large ship in absolute terms, but she was enough bigger than *Cutter 614* that it was a momentary shock to see her up close. That was particularly true on land; in the water the pontoons would be almost submerged, but now they loomed as walls of rusty steel.

There was a ladder at the wedge-shaped tip of the outrigger where it could rise straight to the top instead of following the curve of the sides. Daniel took his sub-machine gun from Hogg, slung it, and continued to lead up the ladder. He knew the interior of a starship better than his servant did.

The rungs quivered as though the rebel vessel was alive, but Daniel knew that was an illusion caused by the *Greif* landing close by. The *Beacon* had electricity because, so long as it got water in sufficient quantities and the bottle itself remained intact, a fusion power plant was nearly as stable as a magnet. Thus far the rebels had met both requirements.

Nobody'd tested the thrusters in the past nine months, though, so Daniel knew there was a real chance that the reaction mass lines were clogged with debris or corroded shut; the instruments wouldn't indicate that until water began to flow—or didn't. If worse came to worst, he and his crew would have to escape on the aircar that'd brought them. That'd be very dangerous, though there'd probably be less of a load going back.

Daniel reached the top of the outrigger. Lights shone through a score of hatches that were either open or askew. The air circulating system had broken down; rather than repair it the original owners had sold the vessel to Generalissimo Ma and made delivery to Big Florida Island with a minimal crew who'd worn air suits for the whole voyage. Here on the ground, most of the hatches were open for ventilation.

That made Daniel's plans easier, though if necessary he'd have taken his party up the boarding ramp on the other side and in the main hatch. Everything depended on the rebels being unprepared and incompetent, but Daniel was willing to count on that in much the same way as he'd have counted on dawn.

With the sub-machine gun in his hands and Hogg beside him, Daniel trotted along the catwalk running the length of the outrigger. He glanced over his shoulder. Portus was leading Tovera onto one of the horizontal hydraulic struts that advanced and retracted the outrigger. The tube was a meter in diameter, an easy path for Portus, but it wasn't meant for pedestrian use. Adele's servant followed the rigger without hesitation, as she'd said she would.

Daniel smiled without humor. There was a carrot for Tovera at the other end, of course: as soon as she entered the hull through the service port above the strut, she could begin killing people. Daniel wasn't going to complain. Having Tovera with them would save the lives of people he cared about much more than he did any of those at present aboard the *Beacon of Yang*.

The power room was in the stern on E Deck, just above the bulk storage holds. Daniel needed to get to the bridge, forward on A Deck and sixty-five feet above the ground. The external bridge hatch had been lifted upward. Its opening was large enough to pass navigation consoles and similarly bulky electronics, but there was no direct way to get to it from the ground. Daniel and Hogg would enter from the other direction.

The courier vessel had shut down, so its thrusters no longer backlighted the *Beacon* with an actinic glare. The visors of RCN commo helmets had darkened to block the dangerous UV. None of the rebels Daniel'd seen when he met the Generalissimo had similar protection, so there was a good chance that anybody who'd been sober enough to awaken was at least temporarily blinded by the exhaust.

Daniel slung the sub-machine gun and started up the angled strut. It was butted into a great socket on B Deck which, according to the plans Adele had provided, ran transversely through the hull to the starboard socket. A tensioned cable paralleled the strut so that the crew could inspect and repair the hydraulics while the vessel was in vacuum. With the line for a handhold, Daniel and his servant trotted up the tube as if it were a steep hillside.

People were shouting in the night. Daniel couldn't understand the words, but he suspected there was probably nothing to understand so that didn't matter. Rebels were trying to get the attention of the *Greif*'s crew, but those aboard would keep their vessel closed up for several more minutes against the heat and residual plasma of the landing. The ground directly beneath the thruster nozzles would be molten glass.

A ladder circled the hull just aft of the socket. Daniel paused to eye the gap, then half-jumped and half-stepped out, catching rungs with his right boot and both hands simultaneously. He scrambled upward quickly, feeling a double clang as Hogg grabbed the ladder below him. It sounded loud, but reason told Daniel that it was very unlikely those aboard the *Beacon* could tell the difference between the noise they'd made boarding and the pops and pings of the courier vessel cooling nearby.

He reached the walkway running the length of the dorsal spine and started forward, glancing over his shoulder to make sure that Hogg was following. Hogg was, of course.

Daniel's right foot stepped onto what should've been a section of plating dimpled with non-skid rosettes. It was empty air instead.

"Bloody Hell!" he shouted, turning a stride into a leap off his left leg and grabbing a hawser on the dorsal antenna folded overhead. Working in a starship's rigging makes a man subconsciously aware of all nearby lines, just in case—as now.

He dangled for a moment, taking a good look at the footing as he ought to have done before. "Hogg," he said, "there's a section of catwalk missing. If you're using light amplification, you may not see it."

Daniel twisted back, then threw himself forward to the other side of the gap. Under his breath he muttered, "Since *I* obviously didn't see it."

There was plenty of starlight for the helmet visors to amplify into clear images, but it placed those images without relative distances. The catwalk showed almost the same as the hull plates that curved outward six inches below. Daniel knew he should've been more careful, but a careful man wouldn't have been here in the first place.

Daniel expected Hogg to use the hawser to swing hand-over-hand across the two-meter gap; instead the servant simply waited for Daniel to get clear, then hopped over. That way he continued to cradle his impeller, ready to shoot.

Hogg carried a coil of quarter-inch line, too thin to climb for any distance without gloves but easy to carry and sufficient for swinging down through the bridge hatch. He tied it off to a strut supporting the catwalk and handed the rest of the coil to Daniel. They could hear voices from below.

"How we going to handle this, master?" Hogg said quietly. If he was worried about anything, that fact didn't show in his voice.

Daniel handed Hogg the sub-machine gun and slid the baton around so that it was in front of his chest with only the bottom three inches under his belt. "I'll go in," he said. "You follow me with that—"

He nodded to the sub-machine gun.

"—but only shoot if you have to."

"Figured you'd do it that way," Hogg said morosely. He slung the impeller behind him. "I never could get you to understand that a soft heart generally amounts to the same thing as a soft head."

"Regardless, we'll do it my way," Daniel said, shrugging. "Anyway, remember that we need at least one working console in order to get out of here. A bullet in the wrong place and we're walking back to the aircar."

"These won't penetrate to the other side of a body," Hogg said, thumbing the raised pin on the receiver

that indicated the weapon was charged. "And I don't
figure to miss."

"Ship," said Daniel, keying his helmet. "Team One
is in position. Team Two, report. Over."

"Team One, this is Two," said Portus. His voice was
unexpectedly breathy. *"We're in position. We had a
bit of trouble, but there's no alarm. Over."*

Daniel stepped onto the top of the raised hatch,
the coiled line in his hands . . . *a bit of trouble.* . . .
Somebody'd been sleeping in the compartment which
Portus and Tovera entered or had challenged the pair
when they passed down a corridor on the way to
the power room. Somebody was dead, maybe a lot
of people were dead, but Daniel's plan and Daniel's
crew were intact.

So be it. He grimaced, but he knew where his
duty lay.

Daniel gripped the coil firmly. "Team Two, execute,"
he said. He jumped outward, letting gravity and the line
on the fulcrum of the hatch coaming swing him into the
bridge. He'd dropped the line and had the cudgel out
in his right hand before his feet hit the deck.

Only three of the ten illumination panels in the
compartment's ceiling still worked, but they were a
brilliant improvement on starlight. There were six
people present—no, seven, the last bending over to
pull on his trousers behind the command console.

Daniel swiped the nearest man across the temple;
the tubing made a sound like wood striking wood.
Half-recovering the cudgel, he belted the fellow turning to gape, flinging him back spraying blood from a
pressure cut in the middle of his forehead.

All of the men were armed, but they weren't thinking

first about their weapons. Daniel kicked a screaming woman into the path of the bulky fellow running for the corridor, then stepped forward and knocked the fallen man's face back into the decking as he tried to get up.

The man on the other side of the console had let his pants go to snatch up a wide-mouthed mob gun; its spreading aerofoils could clear a room. Daniel had him, had him *sure* before the muzzle came up, but the woman he'd kicked lunged for him with a stiletto. He broke her nose with a straight thrust as though the tubing were a rapier.

The man coughed blood and dropped the mob gun, pitching forward onto his face. Daniel hadn't heard Hogg shoot, but the air of the compartment stank of ozone and vaporized aluminum driving bands. Hogg's burst had punched four holes in the rebel's bare chest, all of them into the mass of blood vessels rising from the heart. Daniel didn't like killing, but anybody who carried a mob gun knew what the rules were.

That left a woman making bubbling screams with both hands over her face and two more unharmed for the moment. One was curled up in a ball under the seat of a non-functioning console that'd been cannibalized. The third woman was digging for what was probably a weapon in a pile of clothing.

That one backed against a bulkhead and raised her hands when she saw Daniel turn toward her. After a moment's consideration, she put on a broad professional smile and tugged her blouse down to bare her breasts. Daniel wasn't even slightly tempted, but he did admire the lady's spirit.

"Crew, everybody aboard ASAP!" Daniel said as he sat down at the command console. He was using the command-only channel, so he didn't bother with identifiers. "Break. Hogg, close the hatch."

Instead of obeying, Hogg stepped to the side of the console with the sub-machine gun raised to his shoulder. He kept both eyes open while looking through his sights, so from that position he could watch the corridor while keeping the women within his peripheral vision.

One of the men was moaning, but none of them were going anywhere. Daniel'd struck with his full strength, so the rebels almost certainly had fractured skulls or worse.

More Cinnabars were swinging in through the hatch. The third or fourth stumbled, jerking Daniel's attention away from the display that was forming much slower than he'd have liked. Adele was there, wriggling out of Woetjans' grip; the bosun had snatched her off the line so that Barnes could follow.

Dasi knelt with a roll of cargo tape, trussing the living rebels with the quick brutality of a butcher jointing carcasses. He'd started with the women.

Hogg fired a short burst down the corridor. Daniel heard the pellets whop into a target rather than the sharp crack they'd have made against steel; nobody screamed, which meant the target couldn't scream. That was why he'd brought Hogg with him, after all. . . .

He could hear other shots, now. A projectile whanged against the outer hull and howled off into the night, a very different sound from the echoing *brap/brap/brap* of one hitting the interior of the vessel.

"Sir, I'm here!" Sun shouted. Hogg and Woetjans were leading a squad down the corridor but other spacers continued to enter through the hatch. "Where's the gunnery controls?"

"They must be in the turret!" Daniel said as his fingers hammered commands into the keyboard. "If you can get the guns working, take out the Alliance courier first and then work over the headquarters building!"

Images on the display coalesced enough that Daniel could find the propulsion icon and bring up the plasma thrusters. He switched on the pumps and felt a wash of relief as the *Beacon* begin to vibrate to their deep, familiar rhythm. He wouldn't have trusted the display, but now he knew in his bones that reaction mass was cycling through the system.

Next Daniel called up the *Beacon*'s emergency schematics. He'd looked for a damage control display, but there wasn't one—of course, he realized, because this wasn't a warship. Any vessel was liable to a hard landing or a botched orbital docking maneuver, so there *was* a plan of the internal subdivisions and a way to close them from the bridge as he'd so confidently assured his crew before they set off.

Daniel hammered the keyboard with the sequence of commands that'd dog Holds One and Two. The icons would switch from red to green while the sound of metal butting into metal rang through the ship. He shrank the emergency display down to a sidebar and prepared to light the five thrusters.

The icons stayed red. He'd have been willing to believe that was a sensor error, but he couldn't have missed the quiver of the dogs seating even five decks below. The holds were still open.

"*Members of the Light of Free Yang!*" the public address speaker in the ceiling crackled. "*You are in the hands of the Republic of Cinnabar Navy. Throw down your arms. Leave the vessel unarmed or wait for RCN personnel to take your surrender. Those who surrender will be freed shortly, but those who resist will be classed as pirates and hanged. Throw down your arms!"*

Daniel jerked his head around. Adele was seated at the cannibalized console with the little personal data unit on her lap. She'd apparently coupled it to what remained of the console and was using its hardwired linkages to access the command unit without displacing Daniel.

The *Beacon's* systems didn't work worth a damn. Her new RCN crew made up for that, though.

A ringing clang started Daniel. *We've been hit!*

But they hadn't: the personnel hatch of Hold One had dogged shut at last. The guards in Hold Two could still get out, but there was more than one way to skin a cat.

Grinning broadly, Daniel fed in the commands that lowered the starboard exterior hatch of Hold Two into a full-length ramp. The vessel rocked as corroded seals broke free, then trembled as gears began to pull the hatch down.

The *Beacon's* external video worked considerably better than most of her electronics, but Daniel had left the image as a thumbnail on his display. Now he expanded it.

As he'd expected, guards were crawling out of the hold before it was more than half open. They dropped to the ground, then scrambled off in the direction of the headquarters building. A few were armed, but most had left their guns in the hold or lost them when they fell out of the ship. They were welcome to go.

To Daniel's amazement, the Generalissimo was one of those fleeing: there was no mistaking his 400-pound body. He must've escaped before Hold One closed. Mondindragiana didn't seem to be with him. God only knew how they'd have found her again if she'd gotten out.

The *Beacon of Yang* rocked with a controlled thermonuclear blast: Sun had fired one of its 10-cm plasma cannon. His bolt hit the Alliance courier forward, in line with where the bridge was on most commercial vessels and almost all warships. Even with an atmosphere to dissipate the stream of charged particles, the short-range impact dished in the hull plating and punched a glowing cavity in the center.

Steel flashed outward as a vivid red fireball, scattering molten droplets from the edges. The *Greif* rang like a thousand-tonne anvil struck by a hammer of ions driven at light speed. The piercing sound made Daniel's bones quiver aboard the *Beacon of Yang*; what it must've been like to those on the ground where the shock waves echoed between the two starships was beyond his imagination.

Rebels fell flat. Some tried to cover their ears but others had been knocked unconscious. Lines of dust lifted from the gritty soil, collided with one another, and hung dancing in the air.

Daniel lit the thrusters. The three remaining of the six originally mounted in the bow came to life instantly.

Daniel flared the nozzles to dissipate the energy until he was ready to move. They threw loose rainbow banners, searing the soil but unable to scoop it out. Light flickered through the open hatch. Daniel felt his skin prickle at the touch of particles that drifted up to him, and his helmet filters slapped down to protect his lungs from the ozone.

Starboard Six in the stern was firing; Port Six was not. Daniel opened the starboard feed wide, acting with cold decision as his mind processed an unacceptable situation and provided a response that would've caused his immediate court-martial if he'd ever done it in front of a senior officer.

Reaction mass to the working stern thruster increased from the 20 percent idling flow to its maximum, some 79 percent. The pump was shot and the feed line was clogged, but it ought to be enough.

"Ship, hang on!"

A roaring plume lifted like a geyser about the *Beacon*'s stern. The ship shook even though the nozzle was wide open. When the flow had stabilized, Daniel irised the nozzle aperture to the tightest setting, providing full thrust.

The stern rocked on asymmetric thrust that raised the tip of the starboard outrigger off the ground though it couldn't lift the whole vessel. Daniel flared the nozzle again. When the power dropped, so did the *Beacon*'s stern—with a bone-jarring, mind-numbing crunch into the hard ground.

The shock bent the aft outrigger struts and strained every frame from the midpoint sternward. Daniel'd been waiting for it, but he bounced against his seat restraints. It threw everybody else aboard off their feet.

And it jarred loose whatever was blocking Port Six. The thruster lit and after a moment settled into the same rasping vibration as the other four working units.

The courier vessel's turrets had been withdrawn into the hull for landing. Now the upper one began to rise, controlled from the Battle Direction Center aft or perhaps at the turret as the *Beacon*'s was. It mounted standard Alliance 10-cm weapons; they'd rip the converted freighter's thin plating like flames flashing through muslin.

The *Beacon*'s turret was on the dorsal centerline, directly over the main A Deck corridor. The turret hatch was open and the short access ladder hung down. The twin plasma cannon were supposed to fire alternately at a combined rate of two hundred rounds per minute as long as the gunner kept his foot on the firing pedal.

Daniel heard Sun screaming curses within the turret; suddenly the gun fired twice. After the second round, something *crack*ed and flooded the open turret hatch with the blue-white sparkle of a short circuit.

Sun dropped to the deck, still cursing and now trying to beat out the flames on his trousers. Miquelon kicked his feet out from under him and covered him with a quilt from the bedding that'd lain piled on the bridge. She had to fight to keep the panicked gunner from throwing her off before she'd smothered the flames.

The second pair of bolts hit the *Greif*'s turret and the hull immediately below it. Deuterium pellets in the Alliance loading tubes, ready to be compressed by laser arrays, detonated instead at the touch of the *Beacon*'s plasma. A scallop of hull around the turret vaporized.

Daniel raised his mass flow to 60 percent for the bow thrusters, 75 percent for the stern pair. He knew they wouldn't stand 75 percent long, but he had to break the grip of gravity. He shrank the nozzles.

Rocks and gobbets of glass fused from sand splattered the underside of the hull moments before the ship started to rise.

But she did rise, only a few inches but that was enough. He angled his thrust minusculely and the *Beacon of Yang* slid forward. He didn't have to turn her because the imbalance forward made her drift starboard toward the single bow thruster. The stern dragged, adding the shriek of metal scraping rock to the snarl of the plasma jets.

That was all right. Even if they ripped the bottoms off both pontoons, they'd be able to skate over the strait on thrust alone.

A rattle of slugs pelted the *Beacon*'s stern quarter and howled away in the night. An automatic impeller was shooting at them from the top of the Generalissimo's headquarters. On the video display the osmium projectiles scored the night in neon streaks as they ricocheted. The light quivered through the bridge hatch as well.

"Ship, this is Six," Daniel said, hearing his voice echo through the public address system. There were scores, maybe hundreds of rebels still aboard, but the *Beacon of Yang* was an RCN warship nonetheless. "We'll transfer immediately to *Cutter 614*, then lift for Heavenly Peace where we'll wrap up a few details. After that, fellow spacers, we head back to Nikitin by the quickest route your captain can plot. Six out!"

He heard the cheers, spreading faintly against the roar and shriek of the vessel's passage. They reached the strait, shrouding themselves in a blanket of steam and broiled sea life.

Snarling thunder astern twisted the hull, then

subsided. Daniel balanced the controls with one hand while checking the emergency schematics with the other. Nothing had changed for the worse. If the rebels'd hit the *Beacon* with a heavy weapon, they'd failed to do serious damage.

On the external video a score of bright sparks snapped into the rebel headquarters. The building swelled outward in a red flash, then collapsed on itself.

"Six, this is Sun!" Daniel's commo helmet chirped. Adele must've passed the message after blocking all those before it. *"The rockets work! The rockets work!"*

A mushroom of dust rose from where the headquarters had been. It stood as a marker when the rest of Big Florida Island slipped below the horizon.

Adele could generally work through whatever was going on around her, and her helmet's noise cancellation system prevented the deafening racket of the *Beacon of Yang*'s progress from being a problem. The vibration, though—the high frequency buzz of five unsynchronized plasma thrusters, punctuated randomly when one or both outriggers scraped the surface—was a different matter. That kept jouncing the data unit off her lap. Every time she had to grab it, she lost the display on which she'd been working.

The roar of the thrusters increased. Adele's body shifted sideways as the starship decelerated; steam curled through the open hatch. They were settling into the exhaust which they'd outrun while they were proceeding at a steady rate from Big Florida Island.

"Ship, this is Six!" Daniel's voice ordered. He was sitting at the command console, close enough to touch, but reflexively Adele glanced instead at the image she

kept at the top of her screen. "*Ferguson and Sun, get to the cutter and bring up your systems. Woetjans, make sure the corridors on every deck are open to the outside. Don't trust the powered system or the schematics, I want each one of those doors open if you have to blow it clear! Six out.*"

The *Beacon* quivered, then burped air loudly. The ship rocked deeper than a moment before, then shook with a sizzling crash.

"Bloody hell, the thrusters are starting to go under already!" Daniel said, this time speaking normally instead of using the intercom. "Bloody *hell*, but we can't leave the poor wogs to drown just because they're too bloody ignorant to get out before this sorry excuse for a ship sinks or turns turtle. Adele, can you make it to the cutter on your own?"

"What?" said Adele, lost for a moment. She'd heard her friend speaking, but she'd been too busy with the data she'd snatched from the *Greif* to process his words. "To the cutter? Yes, I suppose so—down to the entrance gallery and across the ramp, you mean? Or do I need to go—"

She nodded toward the hatch by which she'd entered the bridge. The line still dangled there, but she doubted she could pull herself onto the dorsal spine. Even if she did, she'd probably need as much help climbing down the outrigger strut as she had coming up.

"The ramp will be fine," Daniel said, a small smile quirking the corner of his mouth. He turned and started out of the bridge; Hogg waited in the corridor. "I'll check the corridors and join you in the cutter as soon as I can."

"Daniel?" Adele said, speaking loudly in her need

to stop him before she could ask her question. "Do I have to leave immediately? I have some work."

Daniel's face went professionally blank. "You can take five minutes," he said. "No more, it's not safe. Tovera—"

Adele followed his shifting eyes. Tovera stood just behind the partial console. The three of them were alone on the bridge. The captured rebels were gone, though the corpse was still sprawled against the forward bulkhead. The prisoners had been trussed like poultry going to market, so somebody'd either cut them loose or carried them away without Adele noticing.

"—make sure she leaves in five, all right? I don't want something to happen."

"I'd rather die," said Tovera; and smiled. Daniel grimaced at the joke—because to Tovera, it *was* a joke—and left the bridge. He was talking over the intercom.

Adele went back to her data. She'd gotten into the *Greif*'s computer easily during the several minutes the Alliance courier vessel lay alongside the *Beacon of Yang*. Though the dispatches were in a separate electronic compartment from the ship's own working files, they were nonetheless housed in the main astrogation computer. Adele had penetrated that compartment—Alliance Fleet Command used twelve formats for the purpose; she had the keys to all of them on her data unit—and downloaded the files.

But that was as far as she'd gotten, because, she hadn't been able to break the encryption. The software and devices coupled to Adele's console on the *Hermes* would make short work of the problem, but the tender was weeks distant.

She was *sure* that she could obtain by finesse what

she couldn't at this moment get through brute force, if she could only view the problem from just the right slant. If she concentrated, she could—

"Ma'am?" a voice said. Then, louder, "Mistress Mundy, please?"

Adele jerked her head around, the sequence of numbers in her mind raining down like glass from a shattered mirror. Dasi was peering at her with a worried expression. He held an impeller at the balance; it'd been fired recently because the barrel, a tube of synthetic diamond wrapped with coils of fine wire, was still hot enough to distort the air above it.

Dasi's big left hand held the wrist of Maria Mondindragiana. If Adele hadn't been seeing the woman only inches distant, she'd have thought there was something wrong with the image.

The rebels aboard the *Beacon* had been disheveled or worse—wakened from drunken sleep and then sent scattering by the fear of death. Mondindragiana by contrast wore a dress of natural fabric and a gleaming fur stole. Her jewelry was massive and brilliant, and she'd applied makeup with more taste than Adele would've given her credit for. She looked like a queen, not a refugee.

"Mister Leary said bring the whore to 'im," Dasi said, "but he's gone off, and—"

"I am not a whore, you Cinnabar nancy!" Mondindragiana shrieked.

Dasi's face flushed. His right arm went back, lifting the impeller and positioning the butt to smash the woman's face through the back of her skull. Dasi was a man by almost any standard you cared to apply, and perhaps for that very reason there were subjects on which he was sensitive.

"Dasi!" Adele shouted, jumping to her feet. Tovera had her sub-machine gun out, but that wouldn't necessarily keep the big rigger from acting. By putting herself between the gun and its target, Adele made Dasi jerk away.

Dasi's eyes cleared; he lowered the impeller and flung the woman's arm away from him. "Look," he said in a husky voice, "you take care of the bitch for Mister Leary, all right, ma'am?"

"Yes, all right," Adele said calmly. Dasi had already turned to stride from the bridge. He probably didn't hear.

Mondindragiana straightened her garments. "Men!" she muttered, then looked shrewdly at Adele. "So," she went on. "You are who? You are the wife of Captain Leary, is that so?"

"It is not," Adele said as she placed her data unit in its pocket and looked around the compartment to see if there was anything else she should be taking. There was obviously no point in continuing to struggle with the encryption. "I'm the signals officer of *Cutter 614* which Captain Leary commands."

"Just so there's no confusion . . ." Tovera said. It was always a shock when Tovera spoke in company. "My mistress is *also* Mundy of Chatsworth. I'm the servant who kills people for her."

Tovera giggled as she replaced the sub-machine gun in its holster.

"When she doesn't want to bother killing them herself, that is," she added. "I wouldn't want you to be surprised at what happens to you if you decide a whore from Waystation can insult a Cinnabar noble."

Adele looked at her servant. *How very odd: Tovera*

is reacting to the insult to Dasi in just the way another Sissie might do. Tovera's behaving like a member of the crew, of the family, of spacers serving under Captain Leary.

Tovera was a sociopath, of course, but an intelligent one. She adapted by mimicking the behavior of successful members of the society to which she'd associated herself. At the moment, she appeared to be mimicking Adele Mundy. Given their mutual proclivities, that wasn't a bad choice.

"Yes, that's substantially correct," said Adele, straightening to really observe Mondindragiana for the first time. "I hope you'll keep it in mind, because there's been quite enough killing today already."

She glanced at Tovera. The servant kept a straight face, but Adele gave her a tiny grin. "Enough for some of us, anyway," she added. "We'll return to Heavenly Peace and deliver you to President Shin. A cutter's crowded at the best of times, and I presume we'll skim the surface to avoid attack by the missiles on Big Florida Island; that'll mean a rough ride. Keep quiet and as much out of the way as possible, and you'll shortly be back where you belong."

"But I don't belong there," Mondindragiana said.

The *Beacon of Yang* gurgled loudly. The deck had been slanting slightly to starboard. That side lifted noticeably, then sloshed down to a slope of fifteen degrees as another compartment flooded. Tovera raised an eyebrow and glanced toward the corridor.

Adele grimaced. *Why does everything become more complicated than it ought to be?*

"Yes, well, I'm sure you can work that out with the President after he's released his Cinnabar prisoners,"

Adele said. "Tovera, if you'll lead the way, we'll get out of here more quickly than if I do."

She smiled wryly. "And since it seems that Daniel wasn't exaggerating the danger of sinking," she added, "that would be just as well."

"Signals Officer Mundy," Mondindragiana said in a calm, steely voice. She hadn't followed Tovera and Adele toward the hatchway. "I can't claim to have been born to one of the great families of the Republic, but Procurator Vorga granted my citizenship application twelve years ago for reasons that seemed good to him. If you like, you can shoot me for telling the truth, but I *am* a Cinnabar citizen."

Tovera turned and raised an eyebrow again. She touched her weapon.

The woman really does look like a queen, Adele thought. *For all that she was born in a slum on a gutter planet and crawled up from there on her back.*

Ignoring further rumbling from the bowels of the ship, Adele said, "Mistress, we believed that Generalissimo Ma was holding you against your will. If this isn't the case, you have my sincere apologies and I'm sure those of Captain Leary. We'll leave you—"

"Faugh, Ma is a pig," Mondindragiana said, flicking her beringed left hand to dismiss the thought. "He's a pig and he and his men live like pigs. He didn't care about me as a woman—what would that one do with a woman, eh? Just a trophy, a thing he'd taken from Shin."

"Well, then," Adele said, "we've freed you and—"

"I'm not free if you give me back to Shin," the woman said harshly. "Yes, I know, I came to him of my own choice, but he wouldn't let me leave. And he's worse than Ma. Shin can't use a woman in the normal ways either, so he does other things. Shall I show you the scars?"

She pinched a fold of her long skirt and began to draw it up.

"No!" said Adele, her nostrils flaring. In a more settled tone she went on, "No, that won't be necessary, mistress."

Two more thruster nozzles dipped into the cove, one and then the other. They shattered with piercing *crack*s. The *Beacon of Yang* lurched further to starboard.

"Mistress?" said Tovera. "It's your decision, of course, but . . . ?"

"Yes, of course," Adele said. "Come along, Mistress Mondindragiana, we'll discuss this on the way. You see the problem is—"

They followed Tovera into an armored stairwell, a companionway. None of the lights that should've illuminated it were working, but Woetjans' crew had locked open the doors onto every deck. The corridors beyond were bright enough that Adele didn't even switch her visor to light enhancing mode.

"The problem is," she continued, raising her voice to be heard over their echoing steps, "that President Shin has demanded your return in exchange for his release of two hundred other Cinnabar citizens. I can't speak to your relative value to the Republic compared with that of the other citizens, but Captain Leary was sent to procure *their* release. I don't wish him to be put in a position of explaining his failure to an admiral who isn't best pleased with him already."

"Out this way, mistress," Tovera said, standing in a hatchway and looking down the corridor beyond. She held her sub-machine gun ready.

"I have seen this Daniel Leary," Mondindragiana said calmly. "He's a man, that one. *He* won't leave me to that impotent scum Shin after I explain."

You've certainly sized Daniel up accurately, Adele thought. Aloud she said, "Mistress, if you don't return to President Shin when we arrive in Heavenly Peace, it's very possible that he'll order an attack which will destroy our cutter."

"Captain Leary won't be afraid," Mondindragiana said stolidly.

Three Cinnabar spacers were in the corridor, chivvying rebels—former rebels?—toward the opening brilliant with floodlights from outside. The last man, Merlati, waved toward Adele and called, "Better move it, sir! She'll go over before long or I'm a priest!"

"I dare say the captain would do much as you suggest," Adele agreed, "but I'd like to spare him the risk. Mistress, if you will go back to the Shin with apparent willingness, I'll attempt to get you out again before *Cutter 614* lifts from Yang. I don't know how yet; I'll need to discuss the business with others—"

Particularly with Hogg. Hogg by now would've learned the ways in and out of the Presidential Palace. Doubtless he had plans for turning the knowledge to a profit.

"—but I'll try. And I'll succeed or die trying."

They'd reached the entrance gallery. The cutter's lights were trained on the opening and ramp. They were so bright that Adele slitted her eyes and considered darkening her visor.

"So," Mondindragiana said. "There are possibilities on Nikitin, yes."

She looked at Adele. "You swear that on your honor as a Mundy?" she said.

"Yes, mistress," said Adele. "I do."

Mondindragiana shrugged. "Then I accept," she said. "Who could doubt the word of a Mundy of Chatsworth?"

Adele didn't like the woman; she couldn't imagine circumstances in which she *would* like the woman.

But she certainly respected Maria Mondindragiana's intelligence.

CHAPTER 21

Sunrise Bay on Yang

Adele clucked her tongue against the roof of her mouth in surprise and delight; anybody else would've been dancing about the room. Well, dancing to the limited extent that the interior of *Cutter 614* permitted it. The dispatches were beyond her, but she'd decrypted the *Greif's* log.

"Ma'am?" said Sun, seated at the gunnery board with a real-time panorama of the harbor of Heavenly Peace up on his display. "Mistress Mundy? Hogg's coming back, and your Tovera too."

"Ah?" said Adele. Because of who she was, she instinctively switched to the cutter's external sensors instead of saying to Sun, "Is Mistress Mondindragiana with them?"

It was a considerable surprise to see that the two servants were alone. Hogg was rowing the rented skiff—a small part of the considerable profit Acme Trading Company was making from *614's* visit, and in Adele's opinion well worth the money. Tovera sat in the

374

bow like a figurehead without character, her attaché case part-open in her lap and one hand inside it.

Adele's face went blank. She hadn't considered the possibility that Hogg and Tovera would fail. She'd asked if she should accompany them; Hogg had been adamant that Adele's presence would merely rouse unwelcome attention which they'd avoid if they were alone.

Adele knew that what he really meant was that she mightn't approve of some of the actions they'd have to take to accomplish the task she'd set them. Either way, she'd let them get on with it. The job had to be done.

It still had to be done, by Adele herself since her agents had failed. She'd given the woman her word as a Mundy, after all.

Adele smiled wryly. She was pretty sure that Mondindragiana didn't know anything about the great houses of the Republic: the Mundys, the Learys, or any of the rest. But she knew people, and her assessment of Adele had been just as accurate as the one she'd made of Daniel.

"*Base, this is Six,*" Daniel's voice crackled in her ears. Adele was using the Acme Trading Company systems to relay transmissions, since the commo helmets' maximum range was under a half mile. "*We've delivered our packages and on our way home at the best speed this barge can manage. Which isn't fast enough to suit me, but we should arrive in a few minutes. How's your situation? Over.*"

"Ah," Adele said. Apart from the fact Mondindragiana wasn't coming aboard, a possibility that Daniel hadn't been apprised of, everything was as it should be. "Ah, well enough, Six. Ah, Base out."

There was nothing more she wanted to say until she'd learned the particulars of the situation from Hogg and Tovera. She didn't know what this meant. . . .

"The Captain on the way back, mistress?" asked Ferguson. He and Sun were aboard because of their specialties: if necessary they could lift and fight the cutter by themselves. Three crewmen who'd been injured aboard the *Beacon of Yang* were here also: a broken leg, a crushed hand, and severe lacerations caused when a spacer fired his impeller into a bulkhead. The slug hadn't penetrated, but it'd blasted fragments of steel off the opposite side, hitting a comrade in the next compartment.

A fourth crewman, Tomms, was dead. He'd tripped going up a companionway and fired his sub-machine gun. The ricochets had killed him.

Daniel and the remainder of the crew had escorted the former prisoners to the ship that would take them back to the Burdock Stars: the *Armitage 8*, floating not far off in the harbor but hidden by a stand of trees rooted in the shallow bottom. Acme Trading had supplied a motor barge and a three-man crew for the purpose. The Cinnabars had gone along armed to the teeth to keep the locals from massacring the people who were supposed to have been the entertainment for Freedom Day.

A starship lighted its thrusters. The pulse of static from ionized exhaust scored Adele's display a fraction of a second before the sound reached the cutter: first a high-frequency chop in the water, then the air-borne snarl.

Glowing steam rose from the other side of the wooded spit; a medium-sized freighter slowly climbed out of the plume. The *Armitage 8* had gotten away, so there was now no reason for *Cutter 614* to remain on Yang.

Tovera entered the cabin and nodded to Adele. Her face had gotten more sun than was good for her. Cutters were too small to carry Medicomps; the tender was expected to supply the crews' medical needs along with everything else beyond the bare minima for survival. A bad sunburn could be just as disabling as a crushed hand.

Adele smiled faintly. In the particular case it probably wouldn't matter. She didn't imagine anything short of a full-body cast would disable Tovera.

Hogg came in behind the other servant. "What do we do with the boat?" he asked. "I left it tied to the outrigger for now."

"Captain Leary's returning with the barge," Adele said. "Its crew can carry the skiff back with them. Tow it, I suppose."

Adele had seen people in almost any sort of garment in Heavenly Peace, mostly in bits and pieces. To the degree there was a national costume, it was a broad-brimmed straw hat and a thin cotton wrap of brown or muddy blue.

Tovera wore only the wrap, but Hogg had the hat as well. He sailed it out the hatch into the harbor, then shrugged off the wrap and balanced it in his hand. "Do for wiping rags, I guess," he muttered. "I won't be sorry to look down on this pisspot world, though."

Adele cleared her throat, considering. No place aboard a cutter could be called private. Though the three wounded spacers had gone out to watch for the barge, Sun and Ferguson were in arm's reach at their stations.

But there was no need for secrecy. Going outside with the servants to whisper would cause distrust and unease for no benefit.

"Where's Mistress Mondindragiana, then?" Adele said calmly.

Hogg laughed. "At about a hundred thousand feet and rising, I guess," he said. "Things couldn't have gone better, eh, Tovera?"

"There was no trouble," Tovera said with a faint smile. Her words weren't necessarily agreement, since the pale woman tended to view as entertainment what was trouble to other people. "I went inside and escorted the woman to the kitchens. The cook's helpers put her into a garbage container and carried her to the canal where Hogg was waiting with the boat."

"Oh, don't let me forget," Hogg said, reaching into one of his voluminous pockets. He came out with a handful of coinage, a mixture of Cinnabar and Alliance issues that passed current on Yang. There was no local currency, not for anything more serious than buying a yam for dinner. "We spent some of your money, but we got most of it left. This is a cheap place to bribe, let me tell you."

"Yes, all right," Adele said, looking for the bag of wash leather in which Herbrand had provided the money in exchange for a further draft on the Secret Account.

"I have it, mistress," Tovera said and produced the bag. It clinked—she'd needed a portion of the money inside the palace, Adele supposed.

Hogg wasn't a conventionally honest man. Adele

suspected the only laws he hadn't broken were ones he hadn't gotten around to yet. He knew that he could've claimed twice the amount in bribes; he knew further that any money that returned to the Secret Account would probably be squandered by Admiral Milne on activities that did less for the Republic than Hogg financing a drunken celebration for *614's* crew in Sinmary Port.

Hogg was returning the overage anyway, because Mistress Mundy had given it to him. The money didn't matter to Adele, but it did matter to her that Hogg was a principled man.

She grinned slightly. They weren't a priest's principles, perhaps, but she'd learned as a penniless orphan that few enough priests *had* principles.

"Thing is, we didn't let her outa the can like she thought we would," Hogg said. "We hauled her down to the *Armitage* and told the Engineer not to open it up till they were in orbit."

"We'd made arrangements with him," Tovera explained. "He'll think he's gotten a pleasant surprise when he sees how pretty his new passenger is. Later on he may change his mind."

"Not between here and Lantos," Hogg said, chuckling. "No broad *that* pretty wears out her welcome in two weeks."

"That Maria was coming with us?" put in Ferguson. The two warrant officers had been listening intently. "Say, that'd have been something."

"Seemed to me she took a shine to Mister Leary," Sun said with a broad grin. "There isn't much room on a cutter, but Mister Leary can manage most anything if he puts his mind to it."

"Yeah, that's kinda how I felt about it," Hogg said, turning to eye the other men. "Which is why she's going t' Lantos on the *Armitage* 'steada Nikitin with us. The young master's got a head of his own, which is as it should be. And a dick of his own, the good Lord knows. But his mother didn't set me looking after him to so's I could drop him in shit he don't need to know about."

"Hey, Officer Mundy!" Kerman called through the open hatch. "We got 'em in sight. They'll be docking in five minutes, maybe less."

"Very good," Adele said, using the intercom instead of shouting. "Ah, carry on. Out."

Ferguson was technically the senior officer, but any time Daniel was gone the Sissies acted as though Adele was in charge. And therefore she was.

She cleared her throat. It was hard to know how to proceed . . . or even if she ought to.

"Ah, Hogg," she said. "I don't have any affection for Mistress Mondindragiana, but the conditions you're describing . . ."

"Are better than the ones *she* picked, selling herself to Shin," Hogg said forcefully. "We went to Big Florida and pulled her out, and you didn't hear me say a thing against it. That's the way the master is. It wouldn't have mattered if she was ninety years old and a pig besides, he'd get her out because she's a woman and he's Daniel Leary."

"Barge coming alongside," called a spacer on the outrigger.

"Here, Borney," Woetjans called from the near distance. "Take a line and tie it off to a strut."

Hogg paused, his eyes fierce, and mopped his

forehead with the local garment he still held. Tovera offered him a flask. He waved it away, but the thought brought a smile and broke his mood.

"And we got her away from Shin," he continued more calmly, "because you said to and that's good enough for me. But mistress, I don't need to hand the boy over to that one, not though she wants it and you want it and he wants it too, being the randy bugger he is. He's got enough trouble back on Nikitin, *I* say."

"I take your point," Adele said. "And whether or not the lady's happy with her present situation, you met the terms of my promise to her. She has no legitimate complaint."

Considering the matter dispassionately—which was usually easy for Adele, but in this case she was over-correcting for her violent distaste for the woman—Mondindragiana would probably do well in the Burdock Stars or anywhere else she found herself for as long as her looks lasted. Longer than that, Adele suspected. If one treated the situation in the way an RCN officer and an agent of the Republic's intelligence apparatus should, there was every reason Mondindragiana should be kept away from a major RCN base.

Adele laughed. Hogg blinked at her. "Ma'am?" he said. "I don't think I've heard you do that before."

"Well, Hogg, have you ever found yourself in a situation where the best and most moral action you can take is one that will make an enemy very uncomfortable?" she said.

Hogg grinned broadly. "Well, mistress, I wouldn't put it in those words, they're not, you know, the way I think," he said. "But I don't know I've *ever* doubted that doing down an enemy was the right thing to do."

Three crewmen ducked through the hatchway, laughing and chattering about something Adele couldn't follow out of context. One of them had a fresh gash on his right cheek. Their guns had been fired.

Daniel was the next into the cutter. "*Good* morning, Officer Mundy!" he said with a bright smile. "And it's a very good morning, because we're going to lift from Yang in a few minutes. If we're lucky the wretched place will've vanished into a black hole before we're again required to visit it."

He laughed, seating himself at the console with the easy grace he displayed in every physical arena. "I don't say I'm counting on that, but it seems a good place to display my natural optimism."

Adele switched to the two-way link even though they were sitting back to back. "You had trouble, then?" she said.

The cabin was filling with excited spacers, stripping off equipment and handing their guns to Rocker and Rosinant who acted as assistant armorers. For the most part the weapons had to be unloaded before they were clamped in place against the outer bulkheads aft. The racket was beyond what Adele wanted to shout through, even to someone as close as Daniel was.

"*Oh, not really trouble,*" Daniel said cheerfully. "*There was a bit of stone-throwing. We gave some houses a little extra ventilation at the roofline, and there may be a citizen or two with a sub-machine gun pellet in the calf.*"

He shrugged. "*It doesn't make me want to stay on Yang longer than I already did, but it actually went better than it might've done.*"

"Yes, well," Adele said. She fought the desire to

—

smile, though it wouldn't have mattered since Daniel couldn't see her face. "It went well here, too. I apparently won't be able read the dispatches from the *Greif* until we're back with the *Hermes*, but I have her logbook if you'd like to see it. I don't know if it's of any interest."

Daniel was setting up the astrogation display to check the course he'd already programmed. "*Yes, certainly,*" he said as he continued to slide through screens of data. "*It might be something to bring me back into Admiral Milne's good graces.*"

He frowned in concern, trying instinctively to look over his shoulder at Adele; and failed, of course, as she noted with amusement from the expression of the small image at the top of her display.

"*That is,*" he went on, "*if it's permissible to let her know something that you've, ah, uncovered. Instead of keeping it secret until you've carried it back to Xenos.*"

Adele sniffed as she transferred the files to the main computer. She inserted an icon on the corner of Daniel's screen so he could find them. "Daniel," she said, "I'm a librarian. My job is to disseminate information to anyone who might need it. If someone of superior rank doesn't feel that's how information should be handled, then he or she is welcome to dispense with my services."

Daniel chuckled and brought up the log. She was confident of her decryption, but the data remained unintelligible to her: a series of points and times with occasional notations involving the vessel's supply and maintenance status, as well as personnel matters in cursory form. Where other ships were noted by

pennant number, she'd bracketed in the name and
particulars from her database.

"*Umm, they made very good time,*" Daniel murmured. "*I couldn't have trimmed more than three
days off my . . .*"

His voice trailed off; he began to type. Adele thought
for a moment he'd lost interest and gone back to his
previous course calculations, but on checking she saw
that Daniel had shrunk those down to a sidebar. He
was working on a course, but a quite different . . .

Yes, that was it. She still didn't understand what
the points in the *Greif*'s logbook were, but she could
re-extract them from the course Daniel was now
plotting. He was simply back-tracking the Alliance
courier.

He paused. "*Mundy,*" he said to the display, "*so that
I understand this beyond possibility of mistake: the
information you gave me was the* Greif*'s own course,
not information from some other vessel that the* Greif
was carrying in the form of a dispatch?"

Adele frowned. "Yes, that's correct," she said. "I'm
unable to read the dispatches. This was the ordinary
log. Is it important?"

"*Yes,*" said Daniel. Switching to the intercom he
went on, "*Ship, this is Six. I know some of you were
hoping to get back to Nikitin shortly, but I'm afraid
we're going to rendezvous with the* Hermes *off Lantos
instead. We can get to her in three days, maybe less
if I'm lucky. I don't see it being fewer than eight to
Nikitin even if I strain our frames.*"

He cleared his throat. "*The courier we gave a
hard time to the other night had left an Alliance
convoy of twelve transports early last month, some*

twenty-one days ago," he continued. "*The convoy's being escorted by a modern heavy cruiser and two destroyers. I don't think* Cutter 614 *alone is going to be sufficient for the job of stopping them, and to tell the truth I'm not looking forward to attempting that even with the* Hermes's *whole flotilla. But I'm afraid that's what we're going to have to do, fellow spacers, because by the time the squadron could arrive from Nikitin, the Alliance will have a permanent base on Yang with an orbital minefield that'll make it impossible to remove. Six out.*"

"*By God, we'll kick their asses!*" Woetjans bellowed.

It was an absolutely insane thing to say, but just about everybody aboard shouted agreement.

Including Adele Mundy.

Daniel stood on the topsail yard of the Dorsal Forward antenna, drinking in the what for him was the most beautiful thing he'd ever seen: the universe itself, pulsing and shimmering about the cutter. To a layman the view was a wash of light painted with a broad brush. Daniel saw individual bubble universes and the interstices between them, and he judged their energy levels relative to that of *Cutter 614* by their apparent brightness.

He took his left hand away from the antenna and stood balanced on the spar alone. The only sound was the hiss of his breath within the hard outlines of his rigger's suit, but in Daniel's mind a great orchestra swelled and thundered. This was his ship and for the moment his universe; there was nothing greater.

The semaphore repeaters amidships at the dorsal and ventral positions flickered, indicating the coming course change to the riggers on the hull. There was no need for the crew to act if all the hydro-mechanical linkages adjusting the sails worked properly; and indeed, there were probably days when that happened, somewhere in the human universe. Daniel had never been on a ship where that was true, however, so the riggers were ready to unkink cables and release stuck catches with a wrench or a boot-heel.

A starship's sails were thin, metalized fabric carrying a minute, very precise charge determined by the astrogation computer. The sails acted to deflect a portion of the Casimir radiation which was the only true constant throughout the infinite bubble universes. The pressure of Casimir radiation didn't drive the ship, but it shifted it within the Matrix from one bubble to another. In each universe the local constants of mass, distance, and velocity differed from those of the sidereal universe—the only one in which human beings could exist.

The theory was simple; the practice required the greatest precision to which human beings could aspire. Any input—a low-power radio intercom, the magnetic field of an electric motor or even of a control cable—would distort the bubble the sails had formed and send the vessel—*somewhere*, elsewhere; probably distant, possibly distant beyond calculation. All the machinery on the hull had to be hydraulic or mechanical, and the riggers communicated by hand signals and semaphore rather than radio.

The yard beneath Daniel's boots began to rotate; it would move 15 degrees clockwise, as he knew from reading the semaphores himself. The gears rumbled at a low note with an occasional jerk.

Daniel sighed and reached for his safety line to snap it onto a nearby shackle. He shouldn't have been on the hull without a handhold or a coupled line, nobody should. He wasn't a rigger, and he wasn't just a midshipman either: he was captain of this vessel, and if he drifted away to spend eternity in a universe of his own, *Cutter 614* and its personnel would be put at risk.

And yet, and yet. . . .

He was Daniel Leary, an astrogator whose feel for a course was gaining him a reputation to rival that of his uncle, Stacey Bergen. That instinctive understanding didn't just happen; it came because Daniel made himself a part of the ship and a part of the cosmos through which the ship voyaged.

Daniel chuckled, alone in his helmet. Instead of fixing his line, he gripped an antenna stay and slid down it to the hull, still laughing. This'd be the last transit before the cutter returned to sidereal space in the Lantos System, so he needed to be at his post in the command console.

There was an intangible benefit to Daniel behaving as if the hull of a starship in the Matrix was no more dangerous than the Admiral's Cabin on a battleship: the riggers respected him. That wasn't a small thing, given the places he'd had to send those riggers in the past—and would send them again, for as long as he lived and served in the RCN.

The airlock was empty. Daniel spun the undogging wheel which slid a red indicator across a panel in the inner hatch, then stepped inside and closed the chamber. In larger vessels the airlock could hold eight or more hard-suited riggers at a time, but in the cutter there was room only for six—and that because they were willing to pack in tighter than was safe in event of a malfunction. If safety was your prime concern, you didn't become a rigger.

Air pressure was still building in the chamber when the cutter transited, slipped from one bubble universe to another. For a moment, Daniel felt as though his body'd been turned inside out—that his eyeballs were staring at one another and the outer darkness of the void pressed against his bone marrow; then the ship was through. The inner hatch opened onto the cramped, familiar cabin of *Cutter 614*, and he was grinning at the faces of spacers he'd served with for years by now.

"How's it look, sir?" Cadescas asked, looking up from the shell she was scrimshawing with a short-bladed folding knife.

Barnes took the helmet Daniel'd removed in the airlock and two other spacers of the starboard, off-duty, watch started throwing the catches of his suit before he could get to them himself. It wasn't necessary, but it made them happy so he didn't object. . . .

"Well, Cadescas . . ." he said, speaking to be heard by all those within the cabin. "If I'm reading the sky out there correctly, we've just beaten the record run from Yang to Lantos by a good six hours."

He grinned broader. "And a very good time for that piece of history, I'm happy to say."

Daniel settled into his console and began making notes that he'd forward to the Mapping Section of the Navy Office when the next dispatch vessel left for Xenos. Machines couldn't chart the Matrix—only human astrogators could, putting down their impressions of the streams and whorls of energy beyond the bubble which a starship's own sails formed about it. These observations made it possible to judge a ship's position relative to the sidereal universe without dropping into that universe to take star-sightings. The latter process required over an hour for a skilled astrogator with a crew that knew its business; less fortunate vessels might take the better part of a day.

By a combination of skill and art, Lieutenant Daniel Leary had shortened the run from Yang to Lantos considerably—if when they dropped into sidereal space shortly they found they really were in the Lantos System, of course. Since a few minutes remained before *Cutter 614* reinserted, Daniel would write up his observational notes in the hope that they'd prove accurate. If they didn't, well, he could provide later vessels with details of a course that'd led him astray.

He chuckled.

"*Daniel?*" Adele said over their two-way link. "*Good news?*"

"Ah," Daniel said in mild embarrassment. "Ah, please don't spread this around, Adele, but it just occurred to me that if I took us onto a false course and lost us time—possibly days or weeks of time—I'm actually more likely to survive to send the information to the Mapping Section. I'm not sure which I should hope for."

"*I see why you laughed,*" Adele said, meaning more than the words themselves. "*Personally I wouldn't bet against your navigation, nor would anyone else on the cutter. But is it certain that the* Hermes *will be on Lantos when we arrive?*"

Daniel shrugged, closing the file with his notes and bringing up a schematic of the Lantos System—six planets around a yellow sun. The fifth, Lantos itself, was inhabited, and there was a certain amount of mining for fullerenes occurring naturally in the asteroid belt between the fifth and sixth worlds.

More to the point, those asteroids provided bases for pirate vessels which could be supplied by intra-system traders who claimed to be servicing the miners. Because the Lantos System was roughly central among the Burdock Stars, both pirates and anti-pirate operations tended to concentrate there.

"Nothing's certain, no," Daniel agreed, "but Captain Slidell's a very punctilious man. The Standard Operating Procedure for anti-pirate operations here is for the tender to orbit Lantos, touching the surface as needed to replenish air and reaction mass. The cutters operate around Lantos and in neighboring systems—just as the pirates themselves do, of course—and rendezvous with the tender every week or so. It's a perfectly good plan, and I don't see Mr. Slidell varying it on whim."

He pursed his lips as he considered another possibility. "Now, it's possible that the *Hermes* won't have reached Lantos, that's true," he admitted. "Things can go wrong with even a well-found vessel. But Slidell's a very able officer, and he'll be on his mettle to prove himself after the problems with the *Bainbridge* cruise. I'd be very surprised if the *Hermes* hasn't been on station for at least three days."

A red starburst at the top of his display formed itself into the figures 30 and began to count down. "Ship, this is Six," Daniel said, his voice calm but anticipation making him grin broadly. "Prepare to extract from the Matrix in . . . fifteen seconds. Over."

Several spacers cheered. Daniel knew that

somebody'd cheer if he announced he was setting a course for Hell. It was good that his crew trusted him, though it concerned him that they trusted him so much farther than *he* thought was reasonable.

Cutter 614 dropped into the sidereal universe. The experience affected individuals in various ways and the same person variously on different occasions. This time Daniel felt for an instant as though he'd been compressed and shoved through a pinhole, then allowed to expand on the other side.

It was uncomfortable, but many things were uncomfortable. And it was over more quickly than, say, being caught by an autumn cloudburst when you're three miles from your hunting cabin.

Someone toward the rear of the cabin was retching. The cutter's crew were entirely veteran spacers, so there was nothing to be ashamed of. The next time it might be Daniel himself.

The cabin illumination was the same whether *Cutter 614* was in the Matrix or sidereal space, but the light looked, *felt*, richer than it had an instant before. Daniel brought up a Plot Position Indicator on his screen, but before he could more than begin to scan it Adele's voice said, *"Captain, I've identified the* Hermes *and am training a laser communicator on her. Do you wish to send a message? Over."*

A blue highlight pulsed softly over one of the blips on the PPI. He'd seen Adele do that before; she'd explained it was a matter of setting her equipment to scan for RF signals unique to a particular vessel, particularly the precise frequency at which that ship's High Drive motors cycled. It still seemed to him to be the next thing to magic.

"Yes, if you would," Daniel said, deciding what he needed to explain openly to Slidell before he and the Captain could discuss Daniel's proposed solution in private. He cleared his throat.

"RCS *Hermes*," he said, "this is RCS *Cutter 614*. We'll be making our final approach through the Matrix shortly and will dock as soon as possible. I recommend the entire flotilla be recalled immediately, as we've sighted the approach of a substantial Alliance convoy which will require immediate action. *614* over."

Daniel paused. Did that sound too directive? Well, it was no more than the bald truth.

His fingers began keying in the commands that would lift the cutter through the Matrix for most of the remaining 600,000 miles to the *Hermes*. It was a short hop; Daniel suspected he'd have it set up before Slidell decided how to reply.

It'd be a pity if Slidell was offended, but Daniel was nonetheless *quite* sure that this was no time for anything but the truth.

CHAPTER 22

Lantos System

Daniel'd donned his 1st Class uniform before boarding the tender, but he didn't need Hogg's clucks and grimace to tell him that what'd he'd put the garment through on Yang hadn't been to the white fabric's benefit. There was also the problem that the cutter didn't have bathing facilities, and Yang *certainly* wasn't a place to shower.

He'd thought of cleaning up aboard the *Hermes* before seeing Captain Slidell, but they really needed all the time they could get—and probably then some. Maybe Slidell'd make allowances for the fact that Daniel'd made himself as presentable as he could by wearing his Dress Whites.

He grinned despite his determination to maintain a serious mien. Probably not, but maybe.

"Welcome back, sir!" a Power Room technician said cheerfully as they passed in opposite directions along the A Deck corridor. The fellow's name was Melies; he was a former Sissie.

Spacers from the *Bainbridge* whom Daniel'd seen since his return were quiet and even worried looking. They dropped their eyes to avoid meeting Daniel's.

The one blessing in all this was that four cutters hung in their davits before *614* docked; *612* was the only one missing. The number of available cutters wouldn't matter if Slidell accepted Daniel's plan, or at any rate wouldn't matter to Daniel; but they provided more choices, even if none of those choices was a particularly good one.

The Captain's office on the *Hermes* was a two-cabin suite on A Deck, adjoining the bridge. There was a screened latrine in an inside corner and the desk folded down into a bunk so the suite could be used as a watch cabin when the captain expected trouble and didn't want to be too far from the bridge.

"One moment, Lieutenant," said Orly, seated at the desk in the outer office. "The Captain asked me to announce you. He's with Lieutenant Ganse."

He touched the commo switched and murmured something concealed by the cancellation field. Orly wore a vaguely hopeful expression rather than the nervous twitch he'd demonstrated when Daniel first met him in Harbor Three. Daniel wondered if he'd been talking to Sissies; that seemed more likely than that Slidell himself had begun speaking more positively about his XO to his secretary in the days since he'd sent Daniel off to Yang.

"Go on in, sir," Orly said after a moment, then flashed a sheepish smile.

Daniel was ready to accept anything he could as a good omen. He squared his shoulders and entered, pulling the hatch to behind him.

"Sir!" he said, with what might've been his best salute in the past year. "Lieutenant Leary reporting!"

"Then report, Leary," Slidell said in a grim voice. "Did you carry out your mission?"

Ganse pursed his lips and looked from Daniel to the Captain. He and Slidell were seated at the desk. There were two more chairs in the office, but Slidell hadn't told Daniel to take one.

"Yes sir, we did," Daniel said, shifting his right foot the regulation half pace to the side. He hadn't even been told to stand easy, but he decided that to hold the First Lieutenant at attention while the Second Lieutenant sat would be excessively insulting, even for Slidell. "The Cinnabar citizens are on their way here in a chartered transport. The particulars are in my formal report and can wait, but I'd like to tell you critical information that Signals Officer Mundy obtained in the course of gaining the prisoners' release."

"You did it?" Lieutenant Ganse blurted in amazement. "By God, Leary, that's good work!"

"You hired a transport?" Slidell said almost simultaneously. "How in blazes did you do that, Leary? If you've been exceeding your authority—"

"Not at all, sir," Daniel said, ignoring Ganse and deliberately misinterpreting the Captain's question. "A firm of Cinnabar factors on Yang was very helpful in effecting the release of their fellow citizens. But in the course of carrying out Admiral Milne's orders, we learned through captured communications that the insurgents on Yang are in league with the Alliance. They've a base under construction on Big Florida Island and—"

"How did you capture Alliance communications?"

Slidell said. He'd spread his hands with his arms forward on the desk like a cat tensing to pounce. "Good God, Leary, if this is some kind of jape I'll send you back to Xenos in irons!"

"Sir, there's a twelve-ship Alliance convoy heading for the base being constructed on Yang," Daniel said, keeping his voice calm. *Any* superior officer would've had difficulty assimilating this information. Slidell's active hostility was regrettable, but it changed only the tone of the briefing. "The logbook of the courier vessel we damaged there didn't have a manifest of their cargoes, but common sense suggests a shipment of that size includes a planetary defense array as well as a considerable garrison. The escort is the heavy cruiser *Scheer* with the destroyers *Z17* and *Z21*."

"Logbooks are in code, aren't they, Leary?" Ganse asked. He obviously couldn't understand how what Daniel was saying could be true, though he was trying to. "I didn't think they could be read until the boffins back in Xenos had been over them."

He frowned. "Or maybe Sinmary Port, I grant," he added.

"Captain," said Daniel, calmly but earnestly, "my Signals Officer has some experience with this sort of thing, as I believe you know. She was able to decode the material, though I should note that she didn't understand the significance since she doesn't have astrogation training. The courier left the convoy fifteen days ago, at an uninhabited system listed as CZ 486455 in RCN charts. If they—"

"Wait!" Slidell said, not raising his voice excessively but certainly making clear who was in charge. "You say your friend Mundy did this all by herself? Then it hasn't been checked. How do we know she's right? Or even that she hasn't made the whole thing up!"

Ganse drew in his breath. Daniel closed his eyes for a moment. He had to find the correct words or there'd be a bad result—for Cinnabar, for Adele, and particularly for Captain Slidell.

"Sir," Daniel said. Slidell looked slightly abashed, as though he hadn't known what he was going to say till the words rang in his own ears. "I'm an RCN officer first and foremost; the needs of the service are my main concern, as I know they are yours. But Officer Mundy . . ."

His tongue touched his lips. He was afraid the Captain might try to interrupt, but that didn't happen.

"She's a great asset to the RCN and the Republic, of course," Daniel continued, "but at core she's still Mundy of Chatsworth. She wouldn't hesitate a heartbeat to resign her warrant in order to pursue a matter touching the honor of her House."

Daniel hoped Slidell understood what he was saying. He hoped further that the Captain had heard enough about Adele's marksmanship to understand what a duel with her would mean.

Both those things were probably true, but from Slidell's sudden grimace Daniel suspected that it was the man's innate courtesy which caused him to say, "I misspoke, Leary. But the most scrupulously honest person may make a mistake."

"I agree, sir," Daniel said, taking a deep breath now that his chest muscles had relaxed enough to permit it. "Though as a personal observation I'd note that Officer Mundy makes fewer mistakes than most people. Be that as it may, the data themselves are too complex to be coincidental, and Officer Mundy doesn't have enough knowledge of astrogation to have unconsciously biased those data in the process of decoding."

Slidell clenched his right hand into a fist. "Yes, I see that," he said, glaring at his own knuckles. He raised his eyes to meet Daniel's. "You understand my disinclination to go haring off back to Sinmary Port crying 'Wolf!' and having the whole business turn out to have been a mistake, I'm sure?"

"The *Scheer* . . ." Ganse said in a tone of grim musing. "I wonder how quickly the *Cornelwood*'ll be able to lift? Not quickly enough, I'd judge. Even if the *Scheer* wasn't thirty years newer. Of course *we're* RCN."

"Sir?" Daniel said. "I believe there's an alternative to summoning the squadron from Nikitin. Well, an addition to that—obviously we need to inform Admiral Milne as well. I had an additional several days to consider the matter on the voyage from Yang, you see. Might I use your display, sir?"

Slidell glowered in a return to angry suspicion, then shook himself and said, "Yes, all right, use it, but don't be too long about the business."

He brought his display to life, a pearly shimmer above the desk, then tapped in the command which projected a virtual keyboard on Daniel's side. Though he didn't say, "Sit down," Daniel took the offer as implied and lowered himself into a chair to begin work.

"One of the Alliance transports, the *House of Zerbe*, is having trouble with her main computer," Daniel explained as he brought up data. "Because the *Greif* was the handiest vessel in the convoy, she was twice sent back to complete the *Zerbe*'s calculations so that the whole force could move on. The *Zerbe*'s problems delayed the convoy's progress at least ten days since it lifted from Pleasaunce."

The omnidirectional display now showed the convoy's course from the Alliance capital in red, followed by an extension in bright orange along the route the courier vessel had taken to alert Yang that they were coming. Daniel added a yellow underscore to the portion that the convoy had probably traversed after the *Greif* separated from it.

"Now, while we don't know that the main body is going to take the same course as the courier did," Daniel continued, "it's at least probable that it will. The gradients are lower along that route than for the two alternatives I plotted on the way from Yang—"

He could explain his reasoning, but he hoped Slidell wouldn't ask. He *knew* the convoy's commodore would follow the same route as the courier vessel, but that certainty was based on Daniel's reading of the fellow's choices during the earlier portion of the voyage from Pleasaunce.

Though Slidell was a skilled astrogator, his plots were too calculated for him to be able to get into the mind of an astrogator who was a hair quirkier. If he didn't believe Daniel without evidence, the evidence Daniel had available wouldn't convince him.

"All right," said Slidell with a wave of his hand. "Go on, then."

"The *Greif*'s third waypoint before arriving on Yang was the Vela Maun system," Daniel said, highlighting a section of the route and then switching to a plot of the system itself. "They're using the gas giant Marduk as their rendezvous, not Vela Maun itself. If they follow their practice during the voyage thus far, they'll make short hops as necessary to form within a hundred thousand kilometers of one another before proceeding."

Lieutenant Ganse had taken out a small astrogation computer and was plotting something on his own, though with frequent references to Daniel's display. Daniel rather liked Ganse—he was a keen officer and technically proficient, though he needed to fight the strain of indecision to which he seemed prone.

"Now, Marduk has a dozen real satellites," Daniel continued, "but there's also a certain amount of metallic debris captured from the asteroid belt. The quantity and location of those bits is constantly changing. My thought is . . ."

He swallowed and raised his eyes to Slidell's before going on, "The convoy won't be expecting attack. I believe a single cutter might escape detection among the debris. More than one ship would certainly arouse suspicion, but with all emitters shut down there's a chance for one."

"What good would a cutter do against a heavy cruiser, Leary?" Lieutenant Ganse asked with a puzzled frown. "Why, we don't even carry missiles."

"We wouldn't target the heavy cruiser, Ganse," Daniel said, nodding. "The transports will have their antennas extended and sails spread when they arrive. They'll make perfect targets for a cutter's rockets. With luck we'll be able to cripple half the convoy, perhaps more, before the escort can react."

What he meant was, "Before the escort blows us to glowing vapor," but RCN service had risks. Spacers wearing the uniform found companions in every port, looking for a hero to couple with. Those who served with Daniel Leary and survived had earned that adulation. . . .

"They'll be weeks putting the damage to rights unless they're willing to leave the cripples behind," he added. "And that'd mean splitting the escort, which would be even better for us when Admiral Milne arrives with the squadron."

Daniel lowered his eyes. "I'd of course command the cutter," he said quietly. "Since it's my plan. And call for volunteers, because obviously there's, ah, a great deal of risk involved."

Slidell's face hardened, not all at once but in a series of tiny increments. It was like watching a time-lapse image of a pond freezing in winter. *What in bloody hell did I say to make him angry?*

"So *of course* you'll command the cutter, will you, Leary?" Slidell said. He rose from behind the desk slowly, in barely controlled anger. "Are you captain of the *Hermes*, then, to decide what flotilla assignments are to be?"

"No sir," said Daniel quietly. He wanted to stand, but he was afraid that'd look challenging; to Slidell in his present mood, at any rate. "It was my plan, and—"

"And I'm still your captain, Leary!" the Captain said. "You're a clever devil, I'll give you that. But you're not clever enough to make me the goat while you play the hero again. Yes, it's a good plan. I'll see you get credit, because *I'm* an honorable man. But I'll be the one to execute it!"

"But sir . . ." Daniel said. That was his tongue moving before his mind caught up with it. He started to say a number of things, all of them wrong, and managed not to let them pass his lips:

"It's dangerous." Which would be answered by, "Are you calling me a coward, Leary?"

Slidell certainly wasn't a coward, but Daniel wasn't sure he appreciated just how dangerous the proposed operation was. Slidell hadn't been in that sort of situation before, while Daniel—and the spacers he'd take for his crew, because they'd *all* volunteer—had.

"The cutter will have to look like a rock." To which Slidell would reply, "Are you saying I don't know how to handle a ship? I was commanding cutters before you were born, you puppy!"

And indeed, Slidell's ship-handling was of the highest quality. The difficulty was that this wasn't a matter of greasing a ship into a dock or making a rendezvous with another vessel in orbit. The cutter had to look like a chunk of nickel-iron which'd been twisted from the core of a planet when it'd disintegrated, then was caught by the gravity field of the gas giant that would some years or decades in the future suck it to flaming immolation. Unless the cutter's motion was eccentric in several axes, a casual glance at the *Scheer*'s PPI would disquiet the watch officer even if he or she didn't immediately understand what was wrong.

Nothing Daniel had seen of the Captain convinced him that Slidell could counterfeit random action. That'd be like hoping Daniel Leary would learn to salute as perfectly as an Academy Honor Graduate—which Slidell had been in his day.

And of course the final not-quite-spoken objection: "Without Officer Mundy's ability to tap Alliance communications, you don't have a prayer of succeeding."

That was as certain as Daniel's hope of becoming

admiral; but Slidell wouldn't believe it, nor would his paranoia accept Adele's presence on an operation which the slightest misstep would turn into a failure.

Anyway, Daniel would die before he willingly sent Adele off on a mission like this under anybody but himself. She was too good a friend to throw into a certain disaster.

"Sir," Daniel said at last. "I would much rather you allowed me to take out the cutter. Your duty is to the *Hermes* herself."

"You will *not* tell me my duty, Mister Leary!" Slidell said. "Your duty is to obey my orders. If you're not capable of doing that, I'll remove you from your post and you can spend the rest of the voyage as a passenger under Lieutenant Ganse's command until I return!"

"Sir, I'll do my duty as you order," Daniel said. "As I've done throughout the voyage."

"If I may say, Captain?" Lieutenant Ganse said, wearing a worried frown as he combed his red hair with his fingers. "I don't believe either of you should be trying this. Leary, I know your reputation—"

He nodded to Daniel with an apologetic lift of his hand.

"—but this is completely mad! It's suicide, man, not a military operation. Surely you see that?"

"I believe the operation has a chance of doing serious damage to the Alliance convoy, Ganse," Daniel said. "If they're allowed to proceed at their present rate of progress, they'll have a planetary defense array in place around Yang before Admiral Milne can possibly arrive from Nikitin. Even without further reinforcement from Pleasaunce, it'll take a major task

force to dig them out. And if Yang becomes a base
for Alliance privateers, Cinnabar trade with the Gold
Dust Cluster will drop to nothing. Piracy is enough
of a problem."

He carefully didn't respond to Ganse's actual question. He did indeed think it was suicide—but it had
to be done nonetheless, or the cost to the Republic
would be crippling.

Daniel wasn't aware that he was grinning until Slidell
snapped in genuine amazement, "Good God, Leary!
What is there to laugh about in this situation?"

Daniel hadn't had much luck calculating his statements to the Captain. With that in mind and simply
because it was his normal behavior, he said honestly,
"Well, sir, I was thinking that my father has heavy
investments in Gold Dust anti-aging drugs. I think if
asked, he'd say they've given him more benefit than
I ever did."

Slidell's face went white, then flushed. He didn't
move for a good fifteen seconds. At last he said in a
rasping whisper, "I think you must be mad to mention the man who murdered my brother, Lieutenant.
Quite mad."

He shook himself, then continued, "Lieutenant
Leary, you will go to the Battle Direction Center
and wait there until I've left the *Hermes*. Then you
may take temporary command, as is the due of your
position. Though it's not, in my opinion, an office of
which you're worthy."

Slidell took a deep, shuddering breath. "Did you
hear me, man!" he shouted. "Get out of my sight!"

Daniel turned and strode from the cabin without saluting. That appeared to have been the only

good decision he'd made today in his relations with Captain Slidell.

Adele worked quietly, pulling together information on all the solar systems listed as waypoints in the *Greif*'s log. Nobody'd asked her to do that, nor could she imagine what use it'd be to anyone.

It was information with bearing—however tangential—on the present operation; therefore she gathered it. The communications traffic over Lantos didn't require much attention, and Adele had nothing more pressing. After all, she hadn't imagined that the courier vessel's logbook would be of any use either.

Daniel was at the console to her left, working on course projections and crew lists for cutters *610*, *613*, and *615*. *Cutter 612* under Midshipman Dorst had lifted to patrol the adjacent Housmann system some ten hours before she and Daniel returned to the *Hermes* in *614*.

611 was the cutter Captain Slidell had chosen for the attack in the Vela Maun System. Adele was following the progress of boarding through the cutter's commo system; it appeared to her that Slidell would separate in a matter of minutes, though she hadn't asked Daniel for an expert opinion when she forwarded the feed to his console. He obviously had enough on his mind already.

"Wonder why he's taking the people he is?" Midshipman Cory said. "This is going to be a, well, a tough one, isn't it? Anton I swear doesn't know his right hand from his left, and a couple of the others on *611* aren't a lot better."

The four midshipmen still aboard the tender filled the remaining consoles of the Battle Direction Center; the warrant officers who'd normally be on duty here were on the bridge or in the two operational cutters. Hogg and Tovera sat on the jumpseats against the bulkhead, looking—falsely—relaxed.

Adele couldn't see Cory—on the console opposite her own—but the midshipman's face frowned from the top of her display. Pitching her voice to be heard by everyone in the BDC without using intercom—just in case—Adele said, "It's a matter of loyalty, I believe. I've checked *611*'s crew list against the record of testimony at Captain Slidell's court-martial on the mutiny. All of those he's chosen to accompany him supported him unequivocally."

Bragg sat immediately to Adele's right. "I supported him," he said, his expression stricken and his voice trembling in horror. "He had to execute them! Why doesn't he trust me?"

Adele looked at him. "I believe Mister Slidell may have believed all the midshipmen on the *Bainbridge* were tainted by the presence of Oller Kearnes," she said. "It probably has nothing to do with you personally, Bragg."

It was also possible that Slidell thought Bragg was as thick as a battleship's hull. Certainly Adele herself thought that. But given that Slidell had taken his clerk, Orly—the only member of the cutter's crew whom she knew well enough to judge—the first explanation might well be the correct one. Orly was able enough at his job, but he had no business on the present mission.

A hatch sealed, sending a ringing shock through the tender. "That was Captain Slidell closing up *Cutter*

611, Lieutenant," Adele said formally, this time using an intercom link within the BDC only.

At almost the same time, Lieutenant Ganse reported from the bridge on the command channel, "*Mister Leary, this is Ganse. Captain Slidell has left the* Hermes. *Would you care to come forward and replace me on the bridge? Over.*"

"*Negative, Mister Ganse,*" Daniel said. "*Stay where you are and continue in command until Captain Slidell has gotten safely away. Leary out.*"

Adele followed Daniel in bringing up a real-time image of *611*. The cutter rocked gently as the davits extended from the tender's side. The mechanical catches flashed open, ringing through the hull as every metal-to-metal contact did; then tuned electromagnets in the davits and the cutter's shackles pulsed, repelling one another and kicking the lighter vessel away from the tender's hull.

The cutter wobbled slightly as it drifted outward. Three brilliant white points stabbed from its underside, the High Drive motors switching on; because the tender was orbiting above the atmosphere of Lantos, there was no need for plasma thrusters. *Cutter 611* drew away at an accelerating rate, building the initial velocity before it began to navigate through bubble universes which would effectively multiply that velocity against the constants of the sidereal universe.

The cutter's hull had vanished; the light of matter and anti-matter annihilating one another in the High Drive remained, but distance had merged the three exhausts into a single glare; then it vanished abruptly. Slidell had shut down his drive and was easing his command into the Matrix.

Adele felt the tension go out of her abdomen; she smiled faintly. She wasn't afraid of Captain Slidell, but she must've been subconsciously concerned that he wasn't going to leave after all. That same below-surface portion of her mind was sure that unless Daniel Leary had free rein, the Alliance operation was going to succeed to the great detriment of Cinnabar.

Adele grinned. Consciously she thought much the same thing.

"*Lieutenant Ganse, this is Leary,*" Daniel announced over the command channel. "*I'm taking command of the vessel. Break. Ship, this is Six. We have a lot to do, fellow spacers, and we don't have much time to do it. I'm expecting everybody to carry out their duties, correctly but above all promptly. Listen and check your helmet displays to see where you're assigned, then report to your stations ASAP. Break.*"

Daniel stabbed his right index finger onto the ENTER key of his virtual display, sending all personnel the crew lists for *Cutters 615* and *613*. He looked over at Adele and winked, giving the spacers time to assimilate the information. She blinked in surprise, then understood and forced a grin in reply—but Daniel had already gone back to his task.

"*Lieutenant Ganse,*" he resumed, "*take command of Cutter 615 and proceed in the most expeditious way possible to Nikitin, where you'll inform Admiral Milne of the situation. I've prepared a report and enclosed the supporting documentation we've gathered, but I'm sure the Admiral will want you to supplement that with your own personal observations. I trust you'll be able to do so. Do you understand? Over.*"

"*Aye aye, sir,*" Ganse replied. He sounded a little

shaken, and the real-time image Adele was watching was wide-eyed.

"*I'm glad to hear that, Mister Ganse,*" Daniel went on. "*I've downloaded a course to Nikitin into 615. I don't require that you follow it, but it should give you something to work from if you haven't plotted something yourself. I've assigned a familiar crew for you. They should be boarding now, and I trust you'll follow with all responsible haste. Over.*"

"Familiar crew" meant "personnel from the *Bainbridge*." Or better, "personnel not from the *Sissie*."

"*Roger, Captain,*" Ganse said. "*I'm on my way as soon as I stop by my cabin to pick up my barracks bag. And sir? I have prepared a course to Nikitin, though of course I'll compare it with yours. Ganse out.*"

Daniel laughed. Without keying the electronics he said, "Ganse's a good man. I should've known he'd be running course projections without being told. Of course maybe Mister Slidell gave him the orders; I may not be giving the Captain enough credit."

"He did not," Adele said austerely. She'd recorded every word that passed between the two officers since Slidell ordered Daniel to the BDC. Even when the men were talking face to face, the communications equipment in whichever cabin picked up their every word.

She didn't say that in the midshipmen's presence, though they were probably aware of her capabilities. Given the way Bragg's eyes widened, he might think Adele was a witch rather than an information specialist.

Daniel gave her an affectionate smile, then sobered and said, "You know, it could be that Ganse acted like a rabbit because Captain Slidell wanted him to be a rabbit. He came back at me a moment ago."

Adele smiled. Indeed, Lieutenant Ganse *had* retorted sharply—though she suspected you needed to be either an RCN officer or a Cinnabar aristocrat to read that into the exchange.

Still smiling, Daniel rose from his console and looked past Blantyre to Midshipman Vesey. "So, Vesey . . ." he said. "Do you have a course plotted to the Housmann System already?"

"Yes sir," Vesey said primly. "I have three. Would you like me to use the minimum time course? That's without a midpoint star sighting and involves higher gradients, though nothing that should strain a cutter."

"What's your calculated time, then?" Daniel said. His tone was light, but his eyes had narrowed minutely.

"Seven hours ten minutes, sir," she said. "Less if I judge the sky perfectly, but not much less."

"No, I shouldn't think it could be much less than that," Daniel said quietly. Adele heard surprise and considerable respect underlying the words. He would've expected Vesey to be ready to fetch her lover back, so seven hours must be very fast time. "Your crew's waiting for you in 613, Vesey. Bring 612 back within seventy-two standard hours; I'm going to need both of you."

Vesey swung to her feet and started for the hatch. She was smiling brightly, probably from both the praise and the chance to see Dorst again.

"And Vesey?" Daniel said.

She whirled, her hand on the latchplate. "Sir?"

"Midshipman Dorst is a good officer and a good man," Daniel said. "But don't let him try to navigate to Cancellaria without a midpoint course correction, all right?"

"Yes sir," Vesey said. "I plan to reach Housmann soon enough that we won't have to hurry on the remaining leg."

Her expression became momentarily girlish. "Though I'm sure Timothy would do fine without a star sight."

She rushed out of the compartment, closing the hatch behind her. Daniel grinned. "I'm not sure of anything of the sort," he said, "but I know Vesey'll get him back in time if she has to tow him. Which she won't—Dorst isn't fast, but he isn't sloppy either."

"Sir?" said Midshipman Blantyre. "What are the rest of us going to do?"

"For the time being, take your positions on the bridge," Daniel said. "I'll continue to command from here in the BDC—I'm used to it, you see."

Adele kept her face still. She couldn't move to the bridge because of her special hardware, and there might be a time Daniel needed to be able to speak to her without electronics.

"Blantyre," he continued, "I'm giving you the command console. You'll take command if something happens to me. Cory, you're astrogation. Lay a course for the Ruby in the Cancellaria System, that's the convoy's waypoint following Vela Maun. When you're done, send it to me to check."

Daniel turned to the remaining midshipman with a smile of quiet satisfaction. "Bragg," he said, "I want you to act as assistant engineer. Take the third bridge console and keep an eye on the Power Room boards. Now, hop to it, all of you!"

The midshipmen vanished into the corridor, headed

for the bridge. Bragg, the last out, didn't close the hatch behind him. Hogg got up from his seat and walked over to it. As he swung it shut, he muttered, "If there's a way to detonate the fusion bottle, that'un 'll find it, you know."

"I think he'll be fine, Hogg," Daniel said mildly, sitting at his console again and bringing up status displays on the cutters readying for separation.

"*I* bloody well don't," Hogg said, settling onto one of the now-vacant consoles. "But you've always been a lucky bugger, master, so maybe we'll get away with it again."

"Daniel?" Adele said, looking at her display instead of turning to the friend beside her. "Why are we going to Cancellaria instead of keeping station here?"

"I need to see what shape the Alliance convoy's in before I can plan the next step," he said cheerfully. "I thought of scouting in a cutter, but that'd just delay things. I don't believe time will be a serious factor, but I don't want to take chances."

"But Captain Slidell will be returning here to Lantos, won't he?" Adele said. She kept the frown off her face, but she knew some of it was seeping into her voice. "What will he do if you're not here?"

Daniel cleared his throat. "Well . . ." he said.

Before he could continue, Lieutenant Ganse's voice on the command channel announced, "615 *to* Hermes. Hermes, *we're ready to launch. Over.*"

"615, *I'm extending the davits*," Daniel replied as his fingers moved. "*Prepare to extend, over.*"

Hydraulic motors hummed within the tender. Daniel looked toward Adele; this time she met his gaze. "You see, the thing is, Adele . . . Captain Slidell would certainly remove me from my office; and a court-martial would find he was right to, no question about that. I'm certainly willing to take my punishment if it comes to that. But—"

"Hermes, *this is* 615," Ganse said. "*We are ready to launch. Over.*"

"615," Daniel replied as he keyed commands. "*I'm starting the sequence. You will launch in fifteen seconds from the time hack.*"

His index finger hammered the keyboard.

"*Time!*"

He turned to Adele again. "The thing is," he said very quietly, "Captain Slidell isn't coming back. There's no chance at all he'll survive this mission."

Electromagnets kicked *Cutter 615* away with a ringing jolt, adding the final emphasis to Daniel's bleak statement.

CHAPTER 23

En Route to the Cancellaria System

"Adele, would you like to have a drink in the day cabin?" Daniel asked at the open door of what'd been Orly's quarters before she and Daniel had moved into the Captain's suite. "Don't worry—it's good brandy."

"Yes, I'd be pleased to," Adele said, shutting down her personal data unit and wondering if she'd just told a lie. "And don't worry about the quality. My father was a connoisseur, but it didn't take with me during the years I lived at home."

She slipped the data unit into its pocket and smiled wryly. "Since then," she added, "I've sometimes mixed industrial alcohol with the water if I didn't have bleach to disinfect it. They were places where the alcohol was more readily available, you understand."

She certainly didn't mind taking a break. Adele was truly glad to be able to help a friend, and it was clear beyond question that Daniel needed help although he was smiling. She'd been examining the *Greif*'s dispatches in detail now that she'd run them through her specialized equipment. The task was involving and therefore fascinating, to Adele Mundy if not to anybody else; but it would wait.

She followed Daniel into the day cabin. On the tiny table sat a pair of plastic tumblers and a squat green bottle which'd been hand-blown into a mold. She didn't recognize the markings. Daniel dogged the door behind them.

The bustle and limited space of the junior warrant officers' cabin hadn't bothered Adele: she was used to cramped quarters, and she'd always been able to escape into a book or her computer display. She—and probably Daniel as well—gained a degree of comfort by sharing the suite, though; and from what Daniel'd said, Slidell and his clerk weren't going to need it in the future.

"I thought of asking you to take a turn with me on the hull," Daniel said as he took the chair she hadn't. He grinned, but though the expression wasn't forced, it wasn't entirely happy either. "But I really wanted to have a drink while I talked about it."

Adele broke the wax seal and poured a generous slug of brandy into Daniel's tumbler, then her own. This bottle was fresh, but there'd been another bottle of something before he'd invited her over. Daniel wasn't drunk, exactly, but he'd certainly been drinking.

"There are no listening devices in this suite," Adele said. She allowed herself a slight smile. "Unless somebody more skillful than I am manages to undo the lockouts I've placed on the system. I don't think there's anybody in that category on the *Hermes* at present."

Daniel grinned into his brandy as he swirled it. "Of

course the best way to keep it secret . . ." he said, raising his tumbler slowly. "Would be to keep my mouth
shut. Which I don't seem to be able to do."

He swallowed half the contents in a convulsive
gulp. That was doubtless a sin against good liquor,
but Adele'd been telling the truth when she said she
wasn't a connoisseur.

She shrugged. "Telling me is the same as telling
nobody," she said. "But as you please."

Daniel gave her a real smile. "I could've talked to
Hogg, of course," he said, "but Hogg wouldn't care.
He wouldn't see there was anything to be concerned
about. And there is. It's Captain Slidell, you see."

Adele sipped, savoring the brandy. It had a faint
cinnamon overtaste, rather pleasant once she got past
the surprise. "All right," she said, because Daniel
seemed to be waiting for a response.

"My father will think I deliberately killed Slidell,"
Daniel said. "He asked me to, because he thinks
Slidell murdered Oller Kearnes in revenge for what
father did to Slidell's brother. Kearnes was actually
my father's child."

Daniel tossed down the rest of his tumbler. He
reached for the bottle, then paused and looked at
Adele.

She waved dismissively. "Go ahead," she said. "It's
your brandy, after all."

He laughed. "Yes, it is," he said. He shook his head
as he poured. "It's absurdly complicated, isn't it? It's
complete nonsense, it *has* to be."

"Well, it's not too complicated for your father,"
Adele said as she took another sip. "Nor for mine
either, back when he was alive."

She lowered her tumbler and looked at Daniel. "Did you kill Slidell?" she said. "Well, did you maneuver him into killing himself?"

"*No*," Daniel said forcefully. "No, I didn't. I told him the truth and I wanted the assignment for myself. I think I might've been able to pull it off, you see—with *my* crew, of course."

Adele shrugged. "Then tell your father the truth," she said. "Or tell him nothing at all, which ought to be even simpler."

She hadn't realized Daniel had been in contact with Corder Leary since their acrimonious break years before she'd met him. It was disquieting to learn that she'd been wrong in that assumption.

"The thing is, Adele," Daniel said. He lifted the tumbler again, then forced himself to lower it to the table where he glared into its honeyed depths. "The thing is, I knew that Slidell would take the assignment. He shouldn't have—I was the right person to execute the attack for several reasons."

He grinned broadly and added, "Mainly the fact that I could make it work and Slidell didn't have a prayer of that. Which I knew and he should've known if he'd been thinking instead of just reacting. But also because it was my plan. Anyway, Slidell's primary duty should've been to the *Hermes* and the flotilla as a whole."

Adele nodded. She could see what was troubling Daniel now—see it and understand it as well. He was right that Hogg would've shrugged, or laughed.

"Daniel," she said, "you believe that Captain Slidell was too paranoid to do his duty to the Republic. That's correct, isn't it?"

"Well . . ." Daniel said, taken aback. "That's harsher than I—"

He paused. "Yes," he said, "that *is* basically what I'm saying. I understand why he'd be, well, doubtful about me, but . . . Yes, that's true."

"All right," said Adele. "And I assume there's another way to delay the Alliance convoy, that's right too, isn't it? Since after all, we're not heading back to Nikitin ourselves."

"Yes . . ." said Daniel carefully. "It's chancy, of course, but I do have a plan. The bones of one."

Adele gestured with her left hand to indicate that she understood. Daniel was hesitant to talk about something which was nebulous even in his own mind until he'd gathered more information. That didn't matter: what she'd needed was the fact, not the details.

"Would Captain Slidell have been able to execute this other plan?" she said. "As well as you will, I mean?"

"No," Daniel said, shaking his head. "No. It takes . . ."

He looked up from the table and grimaced. "Adele, I don't want to sound as if Slidell's incompetent," he said. "That isn't at all true. But this isn't, well, the normal sort of thing to come up. I'm very much afraid that the Captain would be too hesitant—or else bull straight in. Which is why he'll blow the mission he's on now, I'm very much afraid, though *truly* I'd be delighted to be wrong."

"I know you would," Adele agreed. "You're not your father, and only a man *like* your father would think you were. So. There were two possible responses to the Alliance threat. Captain Slidell was too—"

She gestured. "Hidebound. Limited. Whatever you want. To see those possibilities. That left you the choice of either saying nothing and seeing Guarantor Porra gain a considerable advantage over the Republic, or of giving Slidell good advice in the awareness that he probably wouldn't take it . . . but that the Alliance might still be thwarted. Where did your duty lie?"

Daniel laughed cheerfully. He drank, but this time it was with the normal gusto of a young man who likes liquor and women and life. "Well, when you put it that way . . ." he said and laughed again.

"I put it that way," said Adele austerely, "because I make rather a fetish of factual accuracy."

She finished the tumbler and dabbed her lips with the kerchief from her left sleeve, then put it away again. "Do you have further questions?" she asked.

Daniel grinned. "Yes," he said. "Will you have another glass of brandy while we work through the manifests of these transports you got out of the *Greif*'s dispatches? I've got the two carrying the planetary defense array highlighted, but some of the Alliance commercial nomenclature is new to me. I may need a reference librarian."

Adele took the bottle and poured herself another drink, larger than the first. "With great pleasure," she said.

And this time it was the literal truth.

"Ship, this is Six," Daniel said. "We will reenter sidereal space in thirty, I say three-zero, seconds."

He felt as though he were the ship herself speaking. Laughing, he said to Adele at the console beside him, "If I'd had my choice, I'd be at the top of a foremast reading the sky. I couldn't conn her from the hull, though . . . but you know? She isn't a trim craft, but she's not a pig either. She gives me as much feel through the keyboard as ever the *Sissie* did."

"*Daniel*," Adele said, using the two-way link though they were alone in the BDC with Hogg and Tovera, "*if somebody put sails and an astrogation computer on Chatsworth Minor, you'd claim it was a good ship. And with you for her captain, it probably would—*"

The *Hermes* shuddered across the boundary between universes. The transition wasn't quite instantaneous, nor did it affect every atom of the tender and her crew in precisely the same way.

Daniel's sensation was that of leaping wildly through vacuum, trying to cross from one antenna to another and knowing that if he missed his grip at the far end he was lost for eternity. From the way Adele's face went white and her mouth opened like that of a goldfish sucking air, she felt more like she was being disemboweled.

Adele's face cleared; she gave him a rueful smile. "*It* would *be a good ship*," she finished, but she and Daniel both had work to do now.

The Plot-Position Indicator highlighted a ragged group of fourteen vessels at a tangent to the *Hermes'* course, between three hundred and five hundred thousand miles away. One ship had just come out of the Matrix after making a short maneuvering hop to bring it closer to the main body.

"*RCS* Hermes *to unidentified vessels*," Adele said, her voice crisp and emotionless. "*Identify yourselves at once. Over.*"

She'd said she'd be sending tight-beam microwave as well using the 20-meter short-wave band for broader coverage. The transports—one of the twelve was missing; had Commander Slidell destroyed or damaged it?—might not be alert enough to pick up even the short-wave transmissions, but the escorting warships certainly would.

Daniel had brought the *Hermes* to .04 C before entering the Matrix, much faster than was common or even desirable for a starship under normal conditions. High velocity made it more difficult to maneuver within the Matrix, and it was generally more efficient to hasten a voyage by careful choice of bubble universes than it was to maintain a high rate of progress within individual universes. Besides, it required as much time and reaction mass to brake a starship for landing or orbiting a planet as it did to accelerate her in the first place.

The *Hermes'* present case was an exception: speed and relative motion in sidereal space were the only protections she had against the Alliance warships. Any reasonably competent RCN officer could maneuver to avoid a full-deflection missile from the nearest destroyer, and it would take a minimum of ten minutes—by Daniel's assessment—for any of the escorts to place themselves on a closing course.

It was difficult for a group of ships to maintain station at the best of times, and the problems increased with their absolute velocity. A well worked-up naval squadron might manage to proceed at .02 C, but the present assemblage of civilian transports from a variety of Alliance client states was at less than .01 C—and straggled badly even so.

Daniel felt reasonably confident the tender could safely fly past the convoy: a missile would take longer to accelerate to closing velocity than it would take the

Hermes to shift back into the Matrix. The real danger lay in the possibility that one of the destroyers would chase the tender instead of staying with the convoy. That wouldn't be good practice—the *Hermes* might've been a decoy, after all, drawing off the escort so that other Cinnabar vessels could attack more easily—but a hot-headed, ambitious, or simply stupid Alliance captain might well do that. He'd very possibly succeed if he did.

You couldn't avoid every risk; and for that matter, an RCN captain who considered risk avoidance to be a major goal was by definition a bad officer. It wasn't a stricture ever likely to be directed against Daniel Leary, at any rate.

The transports had been either holding position at 1 g acceleration to mimic gravity or were closing up. Daniel was sure the Alliance commodore was angrily encouraging the laggards. Within a minute of the *Hermes'* challenge three merchant ships—in all likelihood, the only three whose crews were keeping a proper communications watch—shifted course away from the tender.

The *Eliza Soane*, a mixed freight and passenger liner out of Pleasaunce, even lighted her thrusters in addition to her High Drive. She was a new vessel, almost as large as the heavy cruiser *Scheer* leading her escort. The *Soane's* captain was apparently willing to warp her frames in order to avoid an RCN warship, even a warship that no naval officer would've considered a threat.

Adele's challenge went out again, but this time it was a recording. Daniel glanced sidelong at his friend: her face looked like carved wood, immobile and expressionless. He knew she'd pre-programmed her equipment to gather information she wanted, but she'd found additional work to do now. Her fingers were dancing with the control wands.

Woetjans was on the hull with both rigging watches. Pasternak had his Power Room crews at their consoles and his repair personnel suited up, ready to clear frozen feed lines or replace High Drive motors in flight. Sun was on the bridge at the gunnery controls, poised to deflect an incoming missile or—the target of a gunner's dreams—blast the rigging and hull of a hostile vessel that'd come improbably close. The three midshipmen on the bridge were nervously working solutions to every problem they could imagine in the areas to which Daniel had assigned them.

Captain Daniel Leary had nothing to do but to watch the Alliance escort react, and to choose the last safe moment for the *Hermes* to escape again into the Matrix. He smiled. That was a sufficient responsibility. If he misjudged their timing, a missile would vaporize the tender and her skillful, hard-working crew; and unless he got fully into the head of the escort commander, he wouldn't be able to disrupt the convoy.

The *Scheer* didn't shift her position at the front of the loose globe of freighters. The destroyer nearer the *Hermes*, the Z21 according to the legend which Adele's software had careted onto the display, was braking to drop rapidly behind the convoy. Within ten minutes she'd be between the remaining Alliance vessels and the *Hermes*.

She would also be in position to pursue if the tender remained in sidereal space. Destroyers were built for speed and maneuverability. Newly constructed vessels like the later Z Class had a high enough power-to-weight ratio to accelerate at 3 g, and their sturdy frames could accept such stresses.

The *Scheer* launched a pair of missiles. Daniel nodded approvingly. The heavy cruiser had twelve missile launchers and her magazines carried over a hundred reloads. Possibly two hundred, though the higher figure was unlikely in a vessel fitted out for a long voyage. A Z Class destroyer carried no more than fifty missiles, including those in her six launchers. The Alliance commodore didn't expect to hit the *Hermes*, but he could afford to expend two rounds from the cruiser to hasten the RCN vessel on her way.

Daniel's instinct caught a distortion in the PPI even before a visible blip appeared. He highlighted it and snapped, "Signals, get me full particulars on this vessel—"

A line of data appeared at the bottom of his screen in lime green letters: HOUSE OF ZERBE, REGISTERED CAXTON'S WORLD; 3,000 TONNES NOMINAL; PRESENT IDENTIFIER NUMBER C7.

"ASAP, I was going to say, Mundy," Daniel went on with a broad smile. "But you were a little quicker than that, as usual. Break. Ship, this is Six. We are inserting into the Matrix—"

He pressed the code key with his index and middle fingers together, initiating the sequence he'd programmed days earlier. At the moment the details didn't matter as much as entering the Matrix before that pair of missiles reached the point in sidereal space which the *Hermes* at present occupied.

"—now! Out."

Daniel felt the universe shiver as the tender and

all those aboard her prepared to enter another of the interpenetrating bubbles of the Matrix.

He had plans for what came next as well; the planning was easy.

Executing those plans, though—that wasn't going to be easy at all, and it might not even be possible. But he was going to try.

CHAPTER 24

The Interstellar Void

"There you go, mistress," Midshipman Dorst said, his mouth close to Adele's helmet so that she could hear him. He pulled back with a doubtful expression, then bent close again and went on, "Ah, ma'am? Would you like me to go along and, you know, give you a hand?"

Hold me by the hand is what he means, Adele thought tartly. The concern irritated her no less for being a reasonable one.

"Thank you, Midshipman," she said, speaking with exaggerated lips movements since the air suit's clear helmet would muffle her voice. "I don't believe that will be necessary."

The *Hermes* was in sidereal space where radio communication outside the hull would've been safe, but nobody'd bothered to fit radios. The riggers were used to working without them and the suits—minimal garments like Adele's as well as the heavy rigging suits—required two keys, the signals officer's and the captain's, before radios could be installed. The danger if somebody accidentally transmitted from a vessel while in the Matrix was simply too great to be risked.

Adele entered the airlock and closed it behind her. She had the chamber to herself. She should've told Dorst, "*I hope that won't be necessary.*"

She smiled as she waited for pumps to evacuate the chamber. If she did manage to stumble off into space, lost hopelessly among the stars of a galaxy far from the one in which she'd been born, her last words to another human being would've been a half truth. Her honor required that she not stumble.

The indicator light on the outer door of the chamber switched from red to green; the illumination was flat because the air was too thin to scatter light and provide visual depth. Adele pressed the latch and stepped onto the hull, hooking her safety line to a staple while the lock cycled closed behind her.

She'd been on the hull of a ship in vacuum scores of times by now, in sidereal space and in the Matrix where Daniel had tried to give her a feeling for the seething wonders of the cosmos that so thrilled him. To her it was all a confusion of harsh half-lights. She'd never been able to see what Daniel saw, but she appreciated the enthusiasm *he* felt.

This time Adele was sure that the riggers found what was going on nearly as confusing as she did. The antennas were extended fully to keep them out of the way, but the sails were furled. The crew was clambering over the waist of the tender, covering the four remaining cutters beneath a layer of molecule-thin metallized film: the vessel's complete set of spare sails. Spacers lashed together the sails using the grommets that would ordinarily have bound them to the yards.

Like most of the other spacers outside the ship Daniel wore a rigging suit, but his had been painted white. He stood out even in the faint starshine bathing the *Hermes*, a score of light-years from the nearest planetary system.

Adele had expected to find Daniel on a mast truck. Instead he was on the hull not far from the airlock she'd come through, looking toward the bow across the ship's waist. Adele checked her line—it ought to reach—and started toward him, her magnetic soles clacking each time she put a foot down or bent it upward again to release.

A spacer—Woetjans, judging from her size—on the tender's forward section made a series of hand gestures toward Daniel, then pointed. Daniel turned, saw Adele, and gestured her to him. He was probably smiling, but she couldn't tell in this light.

Daniel touched his helmet to hers and said, "What do you think of her?" He swept his arm in an arc across the waist of the ship.

"I don't think Commander Slidell would approve," Adele said dryly. "I accept that you know what you're doing, Daniel, but I have no idea what that is. In this case, I doubt anyone but you knows."

"Yes, well . . ." Daniel said. "It may be that what I'm doing is killing all of us to no purpose, I'll admit."

His chuckle came through the joined helmets as a series of clicks, but Adele had no difficulty visualizing her friend's grin.

"I'm afraid that even if all goes well it's likely to be a suicide mission," he went on, "but it won't be purposeless. I can't hide the *Hermes*, she's far to big to lurk in the debris near the convoy's remaining waypoints. I couldn't manage that even with a cutter, now that the Alliance commodore's been warned. You noticed that—"

Daniel broke off; probably chuckling again, but this time in embarrassment. When he touched his helmet to Adele's again he said, "I'm sorry, of course you wouldn't have. The convoy had shifted the point at which it returned to sidereal space from the fifth planet of the Cancellaria system, a gas giant with a ring and over a dozen satellites, to the fourth planet—a cinder which has neither. The fourth planet isn't nearly as good a navigation aid which is a problem for some of the pigs in that convoy, but it doesn't provide any camouflage for a potential attacker."

"Ah," said Adele as she considered the situation. She knew nothing about astrogation, so it hadn't crossed her mind that the convoy wasn't where the data she'd decrypted for Daniel had said it should be. What she had noticed, however, was—

"Daniel, we entered the system at the same place where the convoy did," she said. "Roughly, I mean. And I don't believe that you made a mistake in *your* navigation."

"Well, no," Daniel said. "I rather thought the Commodore would've done what he did. The other choice would've been to go outward, but Planet Six is a double system with a common center of gravity. I certainly wouldn't trust the civilian captains he's shepherding not get into serious trouble if he chose Six A and B for a rendezvous."

He cleared his throat and added, "He's really quite able, you know; the Alliance commodore, I mean. I wouldn't want his job."

"I certainly wouldn't want his job with Lieutenant

Daniel Leary planning to wreck him," Adele said, allowing more warmth in her smile than she might've done if there'd been anybody to see her face. "But I don't understand what you're disguising us as. I've never seen a ship—"

Which by this time in her RCN career was a fair number of vessels, she realized.

"—that looks anything like *this*."

She gestured also. The riggers had strung cables between the tender's bow and stern sections, and the sail fabric was being wrapped over them. That hid the cutters moored along the waist section, but it certainly didn't look like plating.

"Umm," Daniel said. "I suppose you could say I'm disguising us as *not* an anti-pirate tender rather than *as* anything in particular. You're the one who's going to make the convoy believe we're the *House of Zerbe*, you see."

Adele felt her face go still as she considered what Daniel had just said. "I see," she said, and she at least *thought* she did. "Mimic her signals, you mean? Yes, I can do that, but—"

"Not just her signals," Daniel interrupted. "Her automatic identifier, her emergency beacons in case one of the escort vessels is clever enough to trip them for a cross-check, and—"

"Yes, yes, all that," Adele said sharply. "I meant her *signals*, not just what her captain sends to the Commodore when she rejoins the convoy in normal space. As for her rescue beacons, she doesn't carry any—or any that work, at any rate."

She made her face blank, half regretting that she'd snapped at Daniel. Though he shouldn't have treated her as if she needed to be taught her job. "The difficult part will be masking our resting RF signature—the various fans, pumps and oscillators—and then projecting the pattern I've recorded from the *Zerbe*."

Adele turned to look at him, then realized that Daniel couldn't hear her unless their helmets were in contact. Of course they could butt their foreheads together. . . .

Adele didn't remember ever giggling. She didn't giggle now either, but she felt a momentary urge to.

She leaned sideways against Daniel, temple to temple, and added, "Will that be possible? It's really a matter of tuning our systems. It'll require a certain amount of trial and error, but I'm almost certain that I can get a very close approximation if, ah, if you'll permit it."

"It's possible," Daniel said. "We can get along without full environmental controls during the few minutes before all hell breaks loose."

He clapped Adele on the shoulder in a gesture of careful camaraderie. She was sturdy enough and Daniel knew it, but he was apparently being cautious about her light-weight suit.

"As it will, I promise you," he continued. "Mind, I don't think anybody in the convoy would be capable of matching the passive signatures of one ship with another, but I'm always willing to support an artist when I meet her. As soon as I'm back at a console, I'll tell Pasternak to give you full facilities."

"Thank you," Adele said, smiling at herself. "I like to do a thorough job."

She felt her lip quirk in almost a smile. "And it'll give me something to do besides going over the same data for the twentieth time."

She cleared her throat. "But however careful I am with our RF transmissions," she said, "we still aren't going to look like the *House of Zerbe*. Are we?"

"From a hundred thousand miles, I think we are," Daniel said. "Certainly we are to the civilian vessels, if they even bother to put a telescope on us. The escorts with Fleet optics are going to see a ship of about the right size and about the right lines—remember our rigging screens the details of the hull."

He gestured to the section of waist that was already wrapped in sail fabric; riggers were still working on the portion nearer the bow. "The cloth reflects radio waves, you know," he said. "The thing that makes a tender so very obvious is the radar reflection being multiplied by all the signal traps in the waist. Though the sails don't look very much like hull plating, they have exactly the same effect on radar."

Adele heard the clicking sound of Daniel chuckling again. "That's why I made us so obvious when I scouted them at Cancellaria," he went on. "When we meet them again in the Bromley system, we'll give a normal radar image; and since they already in their hearts know that we're the *Zerbe*, that's what they'll see. Mind, they'll be very surprised that the *Zerbe* managed the leg more or less as quickly as the remaining vessels required this time."

He lifted a hand, palm up; the suited equivalent of a shrug. "I hope that's what they'll think," he said. "For long enough, at least."

"Yes, I believe they will," Adele said. She sniffed, then curved her lips in a smile as hard as a fish-hook. She'd realized with disgust and despair over the years that people *didn't* really look at things, they saw what they "knew." Now she had a friend who saw and understood reality the same way that she did, and who'd become phenomenally successful because of that.

Instead of spending his life, as Adele Mundy had spent most of hers, in a state of frustrated irritation.

Her smile warmed. Well, she was getting better. She was taking lessons from a master.

"I'm going below now to check data," Adele said. "In a few hours I should have a test run for our RF signature prepared, if that's agreeable."

"It's very agreeable," Daniel said. He didn't nod as he'd normally have done if their helmets weren't touching. "You have a good thirty hours, though I don't imagine you'll need anything like that long."

He put his gauntleted hands on his hips and stood watching the work for a moment. Just as Adele turned toward the airlock, Daniel brought their helmets in contact again. "Everything's going splendidly!" he said. "Thanks to the best crew any RCN officer ever had!"

That too, perhaps, Adele thought as she clacked back along the hull. *Though we wouldn't be much use without our captain*.

Perhaps the thing that most puzzled her about Daniel was that he saw the world as clearly as she did, but he was cheerful and enjoyed the life he lived so fully. Possibly some day she'd be able to learn how he managed that.

She smiled without humor. *Possibly*.

"Fellow spacers," said Lieutenant Daniel Leary, facing the video pick-up in the center of his command console. "Fellow Cinnabars. We've come from various ships, but now we're all together on the *Hermes*. I couldn't ask a finer command."

Three of the cutters remaining in the flotilla were fully manned and closed up, ready to launch. They were overmanned, in fact, because the entire crew'd have to abandon the tender after the next series of shifts through the Matrix. There were only two crewmen aboard *Cutter 614*; her hatch remained open to receive Daniel and the rest of the personnel who'd guide the tender on her final course.

"The RCN expects us to do our duty whether it's easy or hard," Daniel said. "This time it's going to be hard. Those of you who've served with me before know what I mean, and I'm sure the rest of you have heard stories."

He took a deep breath. He was speaking on a one-way channel while Adele blocked the chatter on others, but Daniel'd made enough live addresses to know that at this moment everyone under his command was waiting in tense silence anyway. They trusted him, but they were experienced spacers who understood the risks.

"We're going to bluff our way into the middle of an Alliance convoy," Daniel said, "then attack and cripple as many of the freighters as we can. When the reinforcements that our comrades in *Cutter 615* are summoning arrive, they'll finish the job. We'll avoid the escort as best we can, but our priority is to damage Alliance ships rather than to save our own skins. We're RCN and the needs of the Republic have to come first now."

The *Hermes* would reenter the Matrix in just under two minutes. She was accelerating at 1.2 gravities, enough to make those aboard her feel uncomfortable but not enough to prevent them from carrying out their duties in normal fashion. Daniel wanted as much speed as possible when the tender returned to the sidereal universe for the last time.

"We'll be making hit and run attacks," Daniel said. "Each cutter will drop into the Matrix and head for Nikitin as soon as it's expended its rockets. There's no point in sticking around. I've provided the cutters' officers—"

The cutters were commanded by Vesey, Dorst and Blantyre, with Bragg backing—if that was the right word—Dorst and Cory backing Blantyre. Any of the five should be able to make it to a planet where they could top off the air and reaction mass tanks, even if they didn't have the skill to reach Nikitin on the load they'd taken aboard from the *Hermes*.

"—with courses and waypoints, but once a vessel enters the Matrix it's an independent command."

He glanced toward Adele at the console beside his. Her eyes were on her display, and the control wands were twitching in her hands.

The sight took Daniel aback for a heartbeat. He'd paused for effect, but his tongue stuck to the roof of his mouth momentarily. *She's my friend as well as my colleague; isn't she interested?*

And then he remembered that she was Adele Mundy. Of *course* she'd be looking at his image instead of directly at his face; and of *course* she'd be keeping an eye on commo traffic and goodness knew what all else while also listening to him.

Daniel grinned broadly at the thought, beaming toward everybody viewing his image on the tender and the three linked cutters. "We're not committing suicide, fellow spacers," he said. "We're taking only the risks necessary to cripple the Alliance. That's bad enough; but some of you've gotten out of hard places with me before, and those who've only heard about those places, well, you heard it from spacers just as real and alive as you are yourselves."

He lilted an honest, open laugh. "And maybe you were buying the drinks for the folks telling the story, eh?" he said. "Well, you'll have stories of your own to tell, spacers. We all will, all of us who come through this one."

Daniel rubbed the back of his jaw, just under the edge of his helmet. "One more thing," he said. "I know you're not going ahead with this attack for the glory *or* for the prize money. You're doing it because I'm your superior officer and I'm ordering you to. But know this as well: if we do our jobs right and survive, there *will* be glory, and there'll be more prize money than we can any of us spend in a month's leave. On my oath as a Leary of Bantry!"

He raised his clenched left fist high. "Are you ready, fellow spacers?" he demanded.

Adele opened the intercom channel. She turned, met Daniel's eyes, and smiled. It was a real smile, not just a quirk of one corner of her mouth. The cheers from nearly a hundred and forty throats merged into a rhythmic snarl.

"Then prepare to enter the Matrix in ten seconds," Daniel said. "Five, four, three, two, one. . . ."

He stabbed the EXECUTE button with index and middle fingers. *"Now!"*

The universe turned in on itself, swallowing the *Hermes* whole and pulling it back into existence through an infinitely tiny hole.

CHAPTER 25

The Bromley System

The airlock in the corridor just outside the Battle Direction Center clanged, drawing Adele's involuntary glance. The outer hatch had closed, sending a shock through the whole vessel but especially the BDC. Very little penetrated Adele's concentration while she was working, but the ringing crash succeeded.

She was echoing Daniel's display on a quadrant of her own. He was checking the readiness of the four cutters while running a plot of the *Hermes'* course overlaid on major stars of the sidereal universe. That was entirely a matter of dead reckoning: the *Hermes* hadn't made a star-sight in the three days since they set off from the anonymous point in space where they'd disguised the tender.

Dead reckoning or not, Adele was sure that the plot was accurate. She trusted Daniel, and if he'd had any doubts he *would've* checked himself in the sidereal universe. Daniel had a healthy appreciation of his skill, but he didn't make claims that the facts didn't justify.

The inner door of the airlock opened for the last six riggers who'd been out on the hull; Woetjans brought up the rear. The hatch of the BDC was locked back so that the crew on duty—Daniel, Adele, and their servants—could get out immediately when it was time to abandon ship.

Woetjans caught Adele's eye and bent the thumb and index finger of her gauntlet together in a high sign. She didn't speak and risk distracting Captain Leary. Adele nodded approvingly. Five of the spacers clanked down the corridor toward *Cutter 614*, but the bosun herself remained just outside the Battle Center.

"*Ship, this is Six,*" Daniel said, his fingers hovering above his virtual keyboard. "*We'll extract from the Matrix in thirty, that is three-zero, seconds from—now.*"

Adele returned her attention to her display, though there was nothing of interest on it at the moment except for a frontal view of Daniel's face. He looked cheerful and alert—as he was, she was sure.

She smiled wryly. Daniel was usually cheerful and he was invariably alert, even when he was so drunk that he couldn't walk without help. She herself was calm, but it was the calm of resignation. Death meant she could stop worrying, or at least she hoped it did.

"*Ship, prepare for extraction,*" Daniel said. "*Let's show 'em what it means to fight the RCN, my friends!*"

Adele felt as though her body were being sectioned by a microtome and the slices were then dipped in liquid air. Transitions were always different and always unpleasant. Fortunately, she wasn't a person who expected life to be pleasant. . . .

Her display came alive as the *Hermes* reentered the universe of men. She'd set her equipment to register emitters across the electro-optical band, sort out stars and planets, and then to paint the tender's immediate neighborhood with what remained.

The *Hermes* had receivers at her bow and stern. That separation, slight compared with the distances between vessels, was sufficient for the huge astrogational computer to triangulate ranges very accurately. The result was similar to a Plot Position Indicator, but passive and biased toward communications rather than the cross-sectional area of the objects surveyed.

There were fourteen vessels ranging from forty-three thousand to three hundred and twenty-seven thousand miles of the *Hermes*. The nearest warship was the Z21, a hundred and three thousand miles ahead. The destroyer was on a nearly parallel course, but it and the other ships of the convoy were proceeding much more slowly than the tender.

"All ships, all ships!" Adele said. "This is the *Zerbe*. We've had a control failure and our bloody High Drive's full on! For the love of God, somebody match courses with us and send technicians over to help us shut down!"

She'd created a program that chopped and molded her voice into a close approximation of that of the *House of Zerbe*'s captain. A highly skilled observer—somebody as skilled as Adele Mundy; there were a few of them, but not, she thought, in this convoy—would notice that the waves varied in square-edged increments instead of the analog curves of a human voice, but to the human ear it sounded right.

Daniel was keying in commands. In the Matrix the *Hermes* had maneuvered with its dorsal and ventral topsails only, but now the ship squealed and shuddered:

according to plan, the full suit of sails was dropping from the yards to which they'd been furled. Normally riggers'd be out on the hull, straightening the inevitable kinked cables and wadded fabric. This time the mechanical systems had to be left to their own devices.

"All ships!" Adele said, trying to inject panic into her tone. She wasn't very good at it; to her own ears it sounded like a simpering falsetto. "Come aboard and help us for the love of God! We can't shut off the High Drive!"

Daniel had written a script for Adele with the help of Woetjans and Pasternak. They'd explained that it was nonsense; none of the ships in the convoy could possibly match velocities with the putative *Zerbe*, travelling at over .04 C, but it was the kind of panicked nonsense that might come out of the mouth of a tramp captain in a crisis. All the transmission was intended to do was to delay the moment at which the Alliance vessels realized they were under attack.

"*Steiglitz Seven, this is Rampart One!*" the *Scheer* signalled. The escort commander was tightening his signal with a parabolic antenna, but he was transmitting on the 10-meter short wave instead of using microwave or modulated laser which the *House of Zerbe* might not be able to receive. "*You're on a converging course, you idiots! Bear off at once or we'll destroy you, over!*"

"Mr. Pasternak," Daniel ordered, "*board* 614 *with all your people now. Move it, Chief!*"

"*Aye aye, Six,*" the Chief Engineer mumbled. He and two senior technicians were alone in the Power Room; the remainder of his personnel were aboard the three cutters already closed up and awaiting launch.

Adele's display was alive with signals collected by her sensitive equipment. Every electrical motor was a radio-frequency transmitter when in use. Adele had accumulated templates for thousands of the involuntary signals that starships broadcast: pumps feeding reaction mass, fans circulating air through the compartments, and—

"Daniel, the *Scheer*'s turrets are rotating!" Adele said, forgetting RCN protocol in her haste to relay the warning that'd flashed in red block letters at the bottom of her screen.

Even as she spoke, she saw that Daniel had the image of each Alliance warship inset into his display; that of the *Scheer* was suddenly framed with a white border. The *Hermes*' optics were good enough at the present ranges to provide visual confirmation of what Adele had deduced from the drive motors: the turrets holding the heavy cruiser's secondary armament were rotating to bring their pairs of plasma cannon to bear on the *Hermes*. She was of the Admiral Class with four 20-cm, rather than a heavy cruiser's normal eight 15-cm, weapons.

The Alliance Commodore still didn't realize that the *"House of Zerbe"* was actually an RCN vessel in disguise. He was nonetheless willing to destroy her rather than risk his own ship to the incompetence of the tramp's crew.

"*Cutters away!*" Daniel said. He shifted his cursor to a prepared sidebar and made three forceful keystrokes.

The davits holding *610*, *612*, and *613* were already extended and unlocked. Each time Daniel's paired fingers stabbed down, electromagnets flung one of the cutters away from the *Hermes*. The thin fabric wrapping the tender's waist bulged upward, then shredded on the small external image Adele kept at the top of her display.

The *Scheer's* powerful plasma cannon fired, the pair in the dorsal turret near the cruiser's bow followed a moment later by the ventral turret offset toward the stern. The weapons were primarily intended to deflect incoming missiles, but they could rip away any vessel's rigging and blast open a cutter's thin hull plates.

The *Hermes* staggered like a man hit by a succession of medicine balls: all four jets of focused ions expended themselves among the tender's spread sails, vaporizing the filmy material into secondary shockwaves. One of the masts must've taken a direct impact also: the steel fireball rang against the hull like the gates of Hell slamming.

Sun began to fire the pair of 4-inch cannon in the *Hermes'* nose at maximum rate; they shook the tender as they channeled minute thermonuclear explosions. The light guns packed only a fraction of the energy of the cruiser's battery, but at least they might disconcert the Alliance captain downrange.

"Rampart One, cease fire!" Adele said. She was ad-libbing now, but the change seemed called for. "You're shooting at us, you Fleet baboons! Cease fire!"

Daniel made a series of tiny adjustments at his console. Adele felt the direction of thrust—and apparent gravity—shift minusculely.

"*Ship, this is Six!*" he said as he rose from his console. "*All personnel board* Cutter 614 *soonest. Abandon the* Hermes *now!*"

Adele stood. She almost fell back when another

salvo of plasma bolts struck the tender, but Tovera had her right arm and Hogg took her left. With Adele between them they rushed to the corridor where Woetjans snatched her like a sack of grain.

The bosun carried Adele toward the open hatch to *Cutter 614* at a dead run. Daniel brought up the rear. Sun, previously alone on the bridge at the gunnery console, was sprinting down the corridor in the other direction.

Adele clasped her personal data unit in both hands. She was wearing an air suit and didn't want to face whatever was coming next without a weapon.

Information was Adele Mundy's weapon of choice.

Daniel paused short of *614*'s entry. He planned to let Sun, running full tilt but still two strides away, board first. Daniel was the *Hermes*'s captain, after all, and he was abandoning her if not the battle.

Barnes and Dasi waited in the airlock, probably under Woetjans' orders. They grabbed Daniel by the elbows and jerked him aboard the cutter. They passed him to Hergenshied, who passed him to Claud, who thumped Daniel down in the command console. His boots hadn't touched *614*'s deck until that moment.

They're a well-trained crew, Daniel thought as he adjusted the display to his liking. *But they obviously aren't robots who've lost their sense of initiative. . . .*

Sun bolted into the cabin and clawed his way to the gunnery board; Barnes cycled the airlock's outer hatch closed behind him. "All present, sir!" Dasi cried. "*Cutter 614* is ready to lift!"

The icons for the three High Drive motors were green. So were those for the four plasma thrusters, but Daniel'd decided—with a degree of regret—not to use both systems though he was trying to get as much distance as possible from the tender. They'd almost double the cutter's acceleration, but *614* was going to be *very* bloody short of reaction mass as it was. The thrusters were only fractionally efficient compared to the High Drive's matter/anti-matter annihilation.

The cruiser's third salvo crashed into the *Hermes*. Previous plasma bolts had burned away most of the rigging, so three of these four hit the tender's hull. At least one ruptured the plating, adding the softer secondary explosion of white-hot metal recombining with the air in the vessel's interior to the *clang* of ions vaporizing steel.

"*614* prepare to launch!" Daniel said as fingers jabbed the keyboard. "Launching!"

The electromagnets kicked *Cutter 614* out from the tender. Daniel had planned this, the riskiest portion of the attack, with the detail of a ballet choreographer. The *Hermes* was positioned to put *614* on the side opposite the Alliance cruiser; that way the tender's mass would continue to shield them for some while after they'd launched.

Things go wrong. The bolt that hit the hull had started the *Hermes* rotating on her axis an instant before the cutter separated. *614* slid out of the tender's shadow almost instantly.

You play the hand you're dealt. Daniel adjusted the angle on his High Drive motors from what he'd planned, then hit IGNITION. Normally he'd have balanced the motors at low output; no two provided quite the same thrust at the same nominal setting. This time he immediately rolled the throttles up from the initial 20 percent to Maximum Continuous Output. The cutter began a slow corkscrew.

That'd provide at least a slight problem for the *Scheer*'s gunners if they shifted their fire from the tender to the cutter. Daniel didn't think they'd do that—they couldn't yet be sure what was happening—but he needed to help his luck any way he could.

So far the cruiser's fire had been extremely accurate. That was good, because it meant that at least Daniel didn't have to worry about *Cutter 614* running into a 20-cm bolt by accident. Nobody aboard the cutter would know if that *did* happen, of course.

Adele was handling communications. She'd blocked the chatter from the other three cutters, but text at the bottom of Daniel's display gave the gist of the signals among the Alliance vessels. The Commodore's attempts to keep control were being swamped in panicked questions from the transports.

Sun had set the guns of the *Hermes* to fire at their maximum rate as they tracked the nearer of the Alliance destroyers, the *Z21*. At this range the light charges could only damage sails and rigging. That wouldn't degrade the destroyer's ability to fight and maneuver in sidereal space, but it'd help the cutters considerably if the *Z21* tried to pursue them into the Matrix. The destroyer'd be sluggish until the damage was repaired, and her captain'd have to recalculate his values every time she slipped from one bubble universe to the next.

612 rippled four rockets at the *Bird of Pleasaunce*, the big freighter carrying most of the mines that were intended to form a Planetary Defense Array above Yang. Daniel'd made all the target assignments himself to prevent all three cutter commanders from concentrating on the same ships and leaving the bulk of the convoy to sail on unhindered.

He hadn't had time to plot detailed attack plans, however; that was up to the midshipmen themselves. Vesey was an excellent officer, but Daniel noted without surprise that it was Dorst who was first to engage. His *612* made a perfect, zero-deflection attack and passed on to the next target.

There were brighter officers than Dorst, but Daniel had met very few in the RCN with a surer instinct for an opponent's jugular. Dorst would be an ornament to the service for as long as he managed to survive.

Which might be at least a few years. Daniel himself wasn't dead yet, after all.

Daniel touched his controls, recalculating *614*'s course on the fly because the screwed-up launch had thrown his plans out the window. There was bound to be some variation between actual and predicted data, but the tender's spin and the corkscrew it'd induced in the cutter's course were beyond the computer's ability to adjust optimally for an attack.

Z21 launched four missiles. The projectiles were mere flickerings, but the puffs of superheated steam which expelled them from the destroyer's launching tubes waved like flags in the light of the distant sun. For a moment Daniel thought they were aimed at *614*, but the dashed orange lines of the course extrapolations on his display showed beyond question that the salvo was meant for the *Hermes*.

Good God, how could they have been so stupid? But as the thought crossed Daniel's mind and his lips spread in a delighted grin, he knew the answer: the tender's guns were punishing the *Z21*, so the Alliance captain lashed out with his full force to swat the gadfly. The consequences of what he'd just done might not occur to him for the better part of a minute.

Blantyre had brought *610* within 3,000 miles of the transport *Delta Conveyor* with 600 Alliance troops aboard, part of the planned garrison for the base on Big Florida Island. Her gunner, a former Bridgie named Rosinant, launched two rockets, then two more. The first pair missed ahead of the target, while the follow-ups passed behind it.

The transport took no evasive action. Daniel wasn't sure that its captain had even grasped that his vessel was being shot at.

Sun turned from his gunnery display and screamed, "Sir, I've got a target! Can I hit them, sir?"

The Alliance convoy was a globe as loose as the separation between orbiting electrons. Daniel was threading through the center of the formation, striking for the ships on the other side. Chance had brought *614* within two thousand miles of the *Eliza Soane*. The mixed-use transport was a sitting duck for a gunner as skilled as Sun, but—

"Negative, Sun!" Daniel said, shouting over the keening of the High Drive. "She's not ours, I gave her to Vesey. Save your—"

Three rockets burst on the *Eliza Soane*'s hull and rigging. An antenna in the A ring shattered. The upper two-thirds with the yards, sails and stays, carried backward at the transport's 1 g acceleration. It broke off three more masts before the whole tangle spun wobblingly astern.

The hull had ruptured also. Not seriously, Daniel

assumed: rocket warheads weren't large enough to do real harm to a 10,000-tonne transport. Air escaped in another sunlit banner, though. That was damage which the inexperienced civilian crew would have to repair before they even thought of replacing the shredded sails. The *Eliza Soane* wasn't going anywhere for a considerable length of time.

"Target, Mr. Sun!" Daniel said, highlighting the Z17 on his screen and echoing it on the gunner's. "Two rounds only!"

The destroyer was accelerating hard to put herself between *614* and the three outermost transports. She was still 103 thousand miles distant, but Daniel was sure she'd have been firing her 13-cm guns if the *Eliza Soane* hadn't been nearly in line with the cutter.

614 hummed as the basket of rockets on its dorsal spine gimballed around. The projectiles were ballistic. They couldn't course correct after they'd been launched, but neither could they be jammed. Sun determined his line, tapped his firing key, and then tapped it again.

When the second rocket launched, slapping the hull with its exhaust, Daniel shut down *614*'s High Drive. If the destroyer's gunner was calculating his lead based on his target's constant acceleration, the change would throw his aim off by a little.

Loose objects floated away within *614*'s cabin—a wrench that hadn't been locked down, a sub-machine gun which shouldn't have been brought aboard in the first place; grit and trash hidden in places inaccessible under normal gravity. The spacers knew to strap themselves in, but Daniel hadn't been sure Adele would remember.

Maybe she hadn't, but somebody'd latched her harness. Her wands continued to twitch as she worked, oblivious of what was going on around her.

After three calculated seconds, Daniel brought his thrust up to 80 percent, 2.6 gravities. He balanced the motors' output now, but the cutter's previous oscillation meant that because of the brief shutdown their present impulse was at a five degree vector to the original course. Again it wasn't much, but a trivial change multiplied by the distances of a space battle could be the margin between life and death.

The image of the tramp freighter *Arkadiy 412* sparkled. A moment later several antennas went by the board. Rosinant had redeemed himself, hitting his second target with at least three of his four-rocket salvo.

Blantyre was braking *Cutter 610* hard. The flotilla'd attacked with the enormous velocity with which the *Hermes* had returned to sidereal space. That made it possible for the cutters to penetrate to rocket range before the escort could react, but it made the attacks themselves difficult. Blantyre knew Rosinant was inexperienced, so she was coming as close as possible to her assigned targets and trying to slow down besides. The tactics were dangerous but in the best tradition of the RCN.

Sun launched two rockets at the *Belsen Bull*. The transport was one of *614*'s targets, but she was a good 5,000 miles distant. Daniel frowned, because he'd expected his gunner to wait for a closer approach.

Both 6-inch rockets burst on the transport's starboard outrigger, blowing it apart and excising three of the five High Drive motors on that side. The *Belsen Bull* began to tumble. Her captain shut off the asymmetric thrust as quickly as he could, but it'd take anywhere from minutes to an hour to correct the transport's present spin. The blasts'd shredded the starboard and ventral topsails of rings C and D besides. Fragments had probably cut the maincourses to pieces also, though the damage wasn't visible because they were furled to the yards.

Sun had his job under control. Daniel cut thrust momentarily, hearing the basket of rockets whine as it compensated to hold its target despite the change in acceleration. Maybe it would—

The hair on the backs of Daniel's arms and neck lifted. His console dissolved in white fuzz, and a bank of strip lights on the ceiling burned out. Images began to re-coalesce almost instantly, but it was ten long seconds before Daniel could be sure there hadn't been permanent damage to either the display or the computer itself.

A salvo from *Z21* had missed *614* by a hair's breadth. The minute particles of matter across eighty thousand miles of interplanetary space were sufficient to fringe the originally compact plasma bolts with a haze of ions. This penumbra bathed the cutter, doing only minor damage but warning all the veterans that Death's thumb was poised above them.

Dorst brought *612* so close to the *Ina Walton*, another troop transport, that Daniel thought they were going to collide. The Alliance vessel was trying to transition back into the Matrix where it'd be safe from attack. It was almost successful, but two rockets burst against its hull an instant before the remainder of the salvo passed through the portion of sidereal space which the vessel had previously occupied.

Sun rippled four rockets in the close sequence, the technique he preferred over launching pairs simultaneously from opposite sides of the basket. The exhaust of one rocket could interfere with the flight of a later one if they were too close together, but the firing sequence had to be kept short to group the salvo.

Daniel didn't know what Sun's target was—probably the *Delta Conveyor*, some 8,000 miles distant, but possibly the *United Brotherhood of Crecy*. The latter was much farther away but proceeding at only a slight angle to the cutter. A target's low relative motion made the attacker's job much easier.

Daniel didn't have time to check what his gunner was doing because *Cutter 614* was now driving away from the *Z21* at a three-degree angle. The cutter's speed was .04 C, astoundingly fast for a vessel in normal space, but bolts would rip from the destroyer's 13-cm guns at *precisely* light speed.

At the present range, a single hit would probably destroy the cutter. Two certainly would, and the *Z21* wouldn't stop firing until its target was a ball of gas.

The crew was shouting with excitement as they watched the image Adele must be projecting for them. Daniel knew what it was, but that wouldn't help either. Though if his people died instantly while they were capering in triumph—well, there were worse things.

Daniel initiated the sequence he'd hoped wouldn't be necessary. *Needs must when the Devil drives*. . . .

Cutter 614 gave a violent lurch.

CHAPTER 26

Bromley System

"Rampart Two, this is Rampart One," said Adele, affecting the nasal Blythe accent of the *Scheer's* signals officer. She was using a modulated laser communicator and the Fleet code which had been current when the Alliance convoy left Pleasaunce. "The vessel claiming to be the *Delta Conveyor* is the Cinnabar command unit, directing attacks on the convoy. Destroy the *Delta Conveyor* at once! Repeat, destroy the *Delta Conveyor*! Out."

She didn't expect her misdirection to have any effect, but it'd seemed to her to be worth a try. She'd projected a holographic echo of the command display in the center of the cabin for the off-duty crewmen to watch without locking their visors down, but she wanted to be of some active help.

Though the signals intelligence Adele was gathering would be very useful in an after-action report, it didn't have tactical importance. She'd only distract Daniel if she told him—for example—that the freighter

Bloemfontein had lost a fourth antenna, Dorsal D, whose stays had to be severed unnoticed when *613's* rockets destroyed Starboard A, B and C.

Although *Cutter 614* was in the middle of a battle, most of her crewmen had nothing but their fears to occupy them. Riggers made up the majority of a cutter's crew, and *614's* antennas were still retracted and folded against the hull as they had been when stowed alongside the tender.

"Rampart Two, destroy the *Delta Conveyor*!" Adele repeated. She was trying to be forceful but she was afraid she sounded mostly peevish. She couldn't seem to take this seriously. To her lower brain if not her intellect, this was a game of phosphor dots twisting in the air rather than a real battle.

The imagery which she'd copied from Daniel's console to the cabin as entertainment for the crew and to her own display as background was a Plot Position Indicator, not a specialized attack board such as Sun was using. The spacers were familiar with the PPI, and by now so was Adele herself.

The courses of RCN vessels were blue lines racing across the display; the projected continuations of those courses—assuming the degree and direction of their acceleration remained the same—were purple. Alliance vessels were red lines which ate away their pink continuations much more gradually than the *Hermes* and her flotilla did. Each course had a three-digit descriptor at the point the ship itself would be, an infinitesimally small dot at the present scale.

Alliance missiles were orange lines, their projections dashed. There were no RCN missiles, but Daniel had set the display to show the cutters' rockets as pulsing white sparks. *610*, Blantyre's cutter, passed close ahead of HOR, the Alliance freighter *Hornchurch*, with a flurry of white. Three sparks continued on into the void, but the thin white cross now overlaying HOR indicated that a rocket had gotten home.

All three escort vessels were launching missiles, but even Adele could see that the only ones likely to hit their target were the four the *Z21* had aimed at the *Hermes* early in the action. The cutters' high initial velocity meant that even a missile's acceleration wasn't enough to overhaul its target quickly. Besides, the cutters were maneuvering violently in order to attack the transports and freighters. That had the unintended benefit of making their courses impossible to predict.

The purple continuation of *Cutter 610*'s course faded and disappeared. Adele frowned, then realized that Blantyre had expended her rockets and transitioned into the Matrix in accordance with Daniel's orders. She and her crew had gotten away at least for now, though Adele knew there was a risk that the escort vessels would follow and destroy the cutters when lack of air forced them to return to sidereal space.

The blue thread of Dorst's *612* crossed that of the freighter *Spirit of Quincy*. The ships must've nearly collided, because the descriptors *612* and SPI suddenly offset on the display to avoid overwriting one another. The cutter's salvo was only a blink on the screen, too brief for Adele's eye to catch, but the thick cross that marked the *Quincy* showed that several rockets had hit.

612 drew away from the damaged freighter, describing a curve that diverged increasingly from her predicted course as Dorst vectored thrust to avoid the

Scheer nearly dead ahead. *612* must've fired all his rockets, so he too would be—

The cutter vanished abruptly. Adele frowned. How had Dorst entered the Matrix so quickly? She knew from experience that even a small vessel in the hands of an expert like Daniel took fifteen to thirty seconds to make the transition.

"Oh bloody hell, the cruiser nailed them," Timmons said hoarsely. "Oh, bloody *Hell*, my cousin was on *612*."

"Oh lookit lookit lookit!" Barnes shouted in delight. "The *Hermes*, lookit!"

Adele looked, but all she saw was that *Z21*'s missiles were about to hit the tender. They'd left nobody aboard the *Hermes*, so she didn't see that it mattered. Besides, the crew was cheering instead of crying out in horror and concern.

Cutter 614 lurched violently. Adele's left hand clamped the data unit to her lap. Paired electromagnets, on the underside of the unit and woven into her uniform trousers, should hold it in place while it was live, but reflex overruled intellect.

Have we hit—

There was a world-splitting crash. Everything went white, then black.

Daniel pounded the three-stroke sequence that dumped two of *614*'s four tanks of reaction mass. Full tanks weighed nearly half of what the hull and rigging did, so the cutter had a pressurized air ejection system to void any or all the tanks in case it was necessary to land or dock with only partial thrust for braking.

Cutter 614's need was much more immediate than

that. An instant after tons of water spewed out behind the vessel in a freezing fog, a salvo from Z21's plasma cannon lit it in a coruscating fireball.

Dumping reaction mass was a good trick, but it would only work against a plasma weapon directly in line with the ejection port. Also, it'd only work once. As it was, *614* would be dangerously short of reaction mass when it next tried to land. It might be possible to transfer water from a friendly vessel, but first things first.

None of the focused ions had struck the cutter directly, but the interior lighting went out and two of the High Drive motors stalled. Because the third motor continued to run at full output, the cutter fell into a tumbling barrel roll.

Daniel's console went monochrome but didn't shut down. After a few nervous heartbeats, the moan from the unit's interior built back up till the whine was inaudible and color returned to the display. The cabin lights were still off, but fluorescent strips outlined the bulkheads and the airlock.

"Prepare for transition!" Daniel said, trying to calculate potentials while the cutter's corkscrew motion shoved him toward the port bulkhead. His ears rang with the crash of the plasma bolts; he wouldn't have been sure he was speaking except for feeling his lips move. "Beginning transition now!"

Z21's missiles reached the *Hermes*. They'd just burned out and were beginning to separate into three segments apiece, increasing the volume they'd sweep as they coasted onward at .06 C.

Multi-ton fragments tore through the tender, vaporizing the steel hull plates. They bloomed as expanding shockwaves, tearing apart the larger portion of the ship that hadn't been in the projectiles' direct path. In a fraction of a second what had been a 3,000-ton warship became a cloud of gas and debris, still continuing on its original course.

Daniel had aimed the *Hermes* toward the *Scheer* as his last action before abandoning the ship. He'd known the Alliance cruiser would have plenty of time to maneuver out of the tender's path, but—like the pair of rockets fired at the hopelessly distant *Z17*—it'd give the Alliance captain something to think about besides swatting the cutters into oblivion.

Z21's ill-considered missiles converted the *Hermes* from an irritation for the *Scheer* into a catastrophe. The tender's fiery remains expanded as they sped onward, a ball of blazing gas concealing thousands of massive fragments. It'd become a comet composed largely of steel instead of ice and gravel.

The *Scheer*'s captain had tried to accelerate out of the *Hermes*' path when he realized what was about to happen. The pale flames of the cruiser's plasma thrusters flared alongside the diamond-hard actinics of the High Drive's anti-matter conversion. An antenna swayed and snapped, overweighted by the topsail yard that there hadn't been time to lower.

It was almost enough.

Almost. The blazing ruin swept across the stern of the *Scheer*, tearing off masts, rigging, and the portions of the outriggers that were in its path. The ventral 20-cm turret exploded in a spike of white light like the dwarf star glowing at the heart of a supernova. Either the guns had fired while the haze of vaporized metal filled the bores, or the cloud itself had detonated the chambered rounds.

Vesey had managed to shift *Cutter 613* into the Matrix. Her third attack had brought her dangerously close to Z17, but she'd used the bulk of the freighter *Hornchurch* to shield them from the destroyer's guns. She was a skillful officer: a better astrogator than most officers twenty years her senior and a capable tactician. Vesey would never have flair—that wasn't something you could learn—but she was efficient, dependable as the sunrise, and as *thoughtfully* brave as anyone Daniel had met.

There're different kinds of courage. Adele, though it pained Daniel to see it in a friend, would just as soon be dead. She didn't put the same weight on danger that most people did.

Daniel did his duty first while his second concern was for his subordinates, whether they were the spacers in his crew or retainers of the Learys of Bantry. There wasn't room in his mental universe to worry about personal safety.

But Vesey was different. She hated violence; feared it, perhaps. Yet she used violence because it was a necessary part of her duty, and she faced it without flinching or hesitation.

Dorst, the late Ensign Dorst, had been a lot like Daniel. *Cutter 612* had hit all three of its targets because Dorst had taken it in so close that even his inexperienced gunner couldn't miss. He was brave because a man—in Dorst's definition—is brave, and it'd never crossed Dorst's mind to be anything but a man. If he'd had time to think in the instant the bolts hit *612*, it was with a sense of satisfaction at the memory of antennas collapsing in the blast of his rockets, leaving crippled hulks that were no longer a danger to Cinnabar.

Daniel knew that, as sure as he knew the joy he'd felt when he saw the abandoned *Hermes* reduce the *Scheer* to a ruin that'd require months in dock to repair. *He*, Lieutenant Daniel Leary, had planned that result though he hadn't dreamed that he'd succeed.

Daniel regretted Dorst's death, for the RCN's sake and especially for the sake of Midshipman Vesey. Though she'd probably seen *612* destroyed, the reality wouldn't have sunk in yet. Daniel wasn't sure how she would react when it did. The sleet of ions that vaporized Dorst might well have cost the RCN two promising young officers instead of just one.

That was a problem for the future, and at the moment it was less than certain that anybody aboard *614* had a future. The *Scheer* was no longer a threat, but the cutter'd spun beyond the fog of reaction mass which still sparkled with the ions it'd absorbed. Another salvo from the *Z21* would finish the job easily, and 13-cm guns were powerful enough that *Z17* could cripple the cutter despite the extreme range.

The destroyers salvoed so closely together that their four turrets might've been on the same firing circuit. The reaction mass, by now a thin haze spreading over more than a cubic mile, fluoresced in streaks under the lash of multiple plasma bolts.

The Alliance vessels had mistaken the tumbling cutter for a piece of debris. They were shooting instead at the mass of charged water because it gave a much brighter signal. They needed an expert like Adele to sort targets for them. . . .

"Sir, I've got four rockets left!" Sun said, screaming to Daniel over the motor's high-pitched burr. Adele must be blocking intercom traffic, knowing that Daniel had his hands full. And knowing Adele, she was probably considering sticking a gun in Sun's face to prevent him from getting past her barriers with voice alone.

"Save them!" Daniel shouted back. "We'll need 'em later!"

And as he spoke, his skin crawled: *Cutter 614* was completing her transition into the temporary safety of the Matrix.

Temporary, because the job wasn't done yet. They'd be back.

Dorst would've understood.

CHAPTER 27

En Route to Yang

Daniel made his way slowly back down the hull, completing his third inspection in the ten hours since *Cutter 614* had left sidereal space. Woetjans and all her riggers were at work around him. None of the damage the cutter'd received in the convoy battle was serious, but it was very extensive

At least two and probably three bolts from *Z17* had struck *614* at the start of the action. Though dispersed by the extreme range, the ions had welded catches and sliding collars so that the shafts and spars of several antennas wouldn't extend fully.

The sails had been furled to the yards at the time. Instead of blasting holes through the film, the plasma had fused layers so that each one had to be cut loose and then patched. The cutter didn't carry enough spare fabric for the task, so Woetjans had cannibalized the worst-damaged maincourse to repair other sails.

Daniel wasn't checking up on the bosun: Woetjans knew more and cared more about the job than any captain she'd ever serve under, Daniel Leary included. He was out on the hull to show the riggers he appreciated what they were doing—

And also to make sure that the Alliance escorts hadn't pursued *Cutter 614* after it slipped from the sidereal universe. A spacer skilled at reading the fog of lights surrounding a ship in the Matrix could see—could *tell*, rather, because it was more a matter of soul than eyesight—when another vessel was on a parallel course. That was how pirates tracked merchant vessels, and there were regular naval personnel who were equally skilled or almost so.

Daniel was that skilled. He wasn't willing to bet his crew's life that the Alliance destroyers didn't have somebody of equal ability.

There'd been no sign of pursuit. There shouldn't have been, after all: it wouldn't have been a wise use of the convoy's few escorts to send them after a cutter simply for revenge. The shambles the *Hermes* and her flotilla had left behind could've made even a cautious officer angry enough to view revenge as a priority, though.

Daniel reached the airlock but looked back again. A rigger waved. Daniel replied with a left-handed salute, but it wasn't the work or the spacers which drew him. The light around him, the splendor of a cosmos greater than human eyes or human imagination could encompass, held him for a further moment.

Daniel wasn't a traditionally religious man—few veteran spacers were—but he believed in God, and he believed he was never closer to God than when he stood on the hull of a starship coursing the void between universes. That it was a ship he commanded **was the** cherry floating on top of perfection.

The airlock telltale was green. He undogged the hatch, sealed it behind him, and was already taking off his helmet when the inner hatch passed him into *614*'s cabin. There were only ten people aboard at the moment, but the interior still felt tight.

Adele smiled a greeting but didn't speak. It was for Sun to say, "How's it look, sir? Are we going to make it to Nikitin?"

"We're going to make it to Yang, Mister Sun," Daniel said. "Or at any rate, to the Yang System, because I propose to land on one of the moons of Yang Six. The moon's gravity's only .3 standard units, and we're not going to have enough reaction mass left by that time that I'd care to land on a full-sized planet. We'll have to brake across half the system just to get rid of the velocity we built up before the attack."

Hogg and Tovera stepped to either side of Daniel to winkle him out of his suit. They were wearing gloves; in space the external metal stiffeners radiated heat till they dropped to zero degrees Kelvin—unless they happened to have been turned toward the sun, in which case they might be hot enough to broil flesh.

Daniel noticed that his voice was being repeated by the speakers amidships and aft so that the spacers there could hear without coming forward. Imagery appeared in the air: a schematic of the Yang System, replaced after a moment with the sixth planet, a gas giant, and the orbits of its seventeen moons as varicolored circles. Daniel hadn't asked Adele to do that, but of course you didn't have to ask Adele to be helpful.

He looked at the scarred, rugged faces watching him from around the cabin. They were worried but nonetheless hopeful; they trusted their Mr. Leary to save them.

Which he would do, if it was humanly possible *and* if it still allowed them to defeat the Alliance forces. Daniel was Speaker Leary's son: he didn't imagine that Cinnabar politicians were saints or that all the many Cinnabar protectorates rejoiced to wear the Republic's yoke.

But he'd seen some of the "free stars" of the Alliance, gray worlds where family members informed on one another and villages which didn't pay their tax levy were cordoned off and burned, buildings and people together. Daniel was a patriot first and foremost: he'd have fought for Cinnabar against God and His angels if that were required. But in all truth, Guarantor Porra and his minions were very much the other thing. . . .

"I intend to bring us out of the Matrix within ten million miles of Yang's sun," Daniel went on. This was a good time to explain the plan to the members of the crew who were present; they could pass it on to the riggers when they came aboard. "That's too close, I know, but we'll be going outward fast enough that overheating won't be a problem. We need solar gravity to brake us, or we can't lose the velocity we gained while we were coupled to the *Hermes*."

Daniel didn't say that if he judged wrong the cutter might enter sidereal space too close to the sun—or even on the wrong side of it, diving into the solar corona at four tenths of the speed of light. His crew knew that already. They trusted him not to let that happen, and regardless—he was the captain. Even Mr. Pasternak, a senior warrant officer, appeared to feel that way.

"I sent the other cutters to Nikitin," Daniel continued. He held his arms out straight so that the servants could draw the upper portion of his suit away from him. "We're going to Yang instead because it's closer, within nineteen hours by my calculations. We'll fill our tanks from leads in the moon's mantle where the primary's gravity has pulled the ice apart, then go back and hit the convoy—"

He grinned at the gunner and nodded.

"—with your remaining rockets, Mr. Sun."

"Hey, we'll tear 'em apart!" said Timmons, a Power Room technician who'd acted as the Captain's Steward on the *Princess Cecile*.

"I very much doubt that, Timmons," Daniel said, making his smile more general, "not with the four rounds we have remaining. What we *will* do, though, is keep the Alliance commodore off balance and afraid to divide his forces."

With Hogg and Tovera each holding a leg, Daniel stepped out of the rest of the suit. Hogg slid the power switch recessed inside the waistband to OFF. The stiffeners went flat when their dynamic memory emptied, reducing the suit to a layer of thick fabric instead of an object with greater bulk than a human being.

"If the Commodore decides there won't be further attacks," Daniel continued, "he'll send his less damaged vessels to Yang with the destroyers for escort. The cargo in those ships is probably sufficient to fortify Big Florida Island beyond what Admiral Milne and her squadron could handle by themselves. And as soon as the base defenses are up, the destroyers can coddle the jury-rigged remainder of the convoy there to safety."

He shrugged. "When we hit them again," he said, "the Commodore won't know what's coming next. He hasn't seen anything of 615, but he knows that the *Hermes* should have six cutters in her flotilla. And there's always a chance that we're able to rearm all the cutters from a temporary base on an asteroid."

Daniel's grin became a broad, bright smile. "If I'd had time, I'd have set one up," he added regretfully. "Though we didn't do too badly with what we had to hand."

That brought the dusting of cheers and laughter that he'd been aiming for. He wasn't trying to conceal the coming danger from his crew—they were veterans; they *knew*—but he wanted them able to go into it cheerfully. Apart from anything else, they'd work better that way.

"Guarantor Porra has a short way with officers who make mistakes," Daniel said. "The Commodore knows that if he sends away his destroyers—or even one of them—and we capture some of the cripples, he'll be shot on his own bridge. He won't take that risk. If he doesn't, Admiral Milne will be in position around Yang before the convoy gets there."

There were nods of agreement, but nobody spoke until Sun again broke the silence, saying, "Well, I'm *bloody* glad we're having another crack at 'em instead of running back to Nikitin. I'd look a chump when we landed at Sinmary Port with rockets aboard and my strikers'd expended all theirs, right?"

General laughter followed. Daniel, his face smiling, settled onto the command console.

614 would be alone this time, and they wouldn't be attacking with the enormous velocity at which they'd

made their first pass through the convoy. *614* would pin the Alliance force in place until they wouldn't be able to set up a base on Big Florida Island, but it would be at the probable cost of the cutter and her crew.

Sometimes duty required that.

"Ship, this is Six," Daniel said over the intercom. To Adele he sounded . . . not bored, never bored; but certainly not excited either. He might've been a dentist discussing the state of a patient's teeth. *"We will extract from the Matrix in thirty seconds from—now."*

Woetjans and eleven other riggers, as many as could pass through the airlock in two cycles, waited with their faceplates open. The remaining ten riggers would suit up as soon as the first group had gone onto the hull: there wasn't enough room in the cutter's cabin for all of them to wear their bulky rigging suits at the same time.

The bosun looked down at Adele and muttered, "If it was anybody but Mr. Leary, I'd worry about coming out so bloody close to the sun. He won't let us down, though."

"No, he certainly won't," Adele said calmly. She wasn't sure if she was agreeing with Woetjans or just responding to an indirect plea for reassurance.

She supposed every living thing had some fear, even the rugged, seemingly indestructible bosun. Perhaps Woetjans was afraid of falling into a star.

Adele Mundy was afraid of failing her friends. In the days not so long ago when she had no friends, she might honestly have said she feared nothing. But of course in those days Adele Mundy was already dead. . . .

"Extracting!" Daniel said, banging his fingers down to execute the command. The cutter trembled. For an instant it wasn't between worlds but rather existing simultaneously in an infinite number of them. Adele felt ice in her bones. She was looking down on her own body, interested to see how empty her eyes were.

Then they were back in the universe of humans and life as humans knew it. The hatch was open and Woetjans was leading her first section into the airlock.

"Mistress Woetjans!" Daniel said, shouting because the riggers didn't have radios in their suits. "As I warned you, I'm sealing the outer lock for at least another minute. The antennas won't be at risk till I start thrust braking, and I *won't* have you going out on the hull while we're so close to the sun."

The bosun didn't reply. She might have her own opinion of the matter, but Daniel controlled the command console.

Adele was sorting the RF emitters which she'd begun to gather as soon as *614* returned to the sidereal universe. Obviously the cutter hadn't fallen into the sun, but the question hadn't really concerned her. Navigation was in Daniel's province; the business of Signals Officer Mundy was to let the Captain know what other vessels were in their neighborhood in a more accurate and detailed fashion than his own equipment could.

Daniel's fingers were tapping through one screen after another with the regularity of a metronome; his face was composed, with a suggestion of amusement. That didn't mean his mind couldn't be wrestling with oncoming disaster, so rather than risk breaking his concentration Adele ran her data as a text crawl at the bottom of the command display:

> Frigate RCS *Cutlass*, Patrol Cruisers RCS *Garnet* and *Chrysoberyl* are on station above Yang. *Garnet* carries flag of Admiral Milne.

"Are they by God?" Daniel cried in delight. Adele fed his words to the PA system, but he immediately tripped the intercom as well with, "*Ship, this is Six. The Gold Dust Squadron has arrived a good three days before I imagined they could. Lieutenant Ganse is a fine astrogator, a remarkable one.*"

He paused, then went on, "*And whatever I may think about the Admiral's choice of bed-partners, she's done well also. There've been some who don't think my choice of bed-partners is absolutely the best either, after all.*"

Among the peals of laughter and relief, Woetjans called from the airlock, "What's this mean for us, sir?"

Instead of answering the bosun immediately, Daniel said, "*Mundy, how quickly will we be able to communicate with the* Garnet? *With any of the squadron's vessels, over?*"

"When you say the word, Captain Leary," Adele said with deliberate formality. "I have laser emitters trained on all three vessels, though the *Chrysoberyl's* about to pass into Yang's shadow for about fifteen minutes. Over."

She was being ironic, she supposed. Adele knew that Daniel was correct to revert to a professional demeanor when he spoke as her commanding officer, but she was human enough that it disturbed her. That was why she'd allowed herself to be irritated at the implication that she couldn't immediately connect *614* with any vessel she'd identified.

"*Thank you, Mundy,*" Daniel said. His image quirked a wry smile. "*I'll call the* Garnet *in just a moment. Break. Ship, what it means for the moment is that I want the riggers to get the antennas stowed ASAP, because we'll rendezvous in Yang's orbit instead of landing a hundred and fifty million miles further out. On the other hand, fellow spacers, it also means that we don't have to worry about having enough reaction mass left to land in a gravity well, because we'll be filling our tanks from the* Garnet. *Out.*"

The inner hatch had started to close at the word "ASAP," so Woetjans and her section probably didn't hear the last of Daniel's explanation. They didn't need to, of course; they already understood that part of the situation.

Adele cleared her throat. "Ah, ready for transmission, sir," she said. "The squadron doesn't appear to be aware of our arrival, probably because we inserted so close to the sun. Over."

"*Gold Dust Command, this is* Cutter 614, *Lieutenant Leary commanding,*" Daniel said. He nodded, apparently to Adele's image at the top of his display. "*We have information of immediate importance which we must come aboard to deliver. I'm braking to come alongside* Garnet *as soon as possible. Over.*"

As Daniel spoke, his fingers continued to type commands. Adele could see that he was plotting a new course, though the detailed figures were opaque to her.

Yang—the system's fifth planet—was fairly close to

being in line at present with their original destination, the system's unnamed sixth world. Adele assumed that made the process simpler, but she'd seen the neat way Daniel could swallow intrasystem distances with short hops through the Matrix. The current problem was the cutter's velocity in normal space, not where they were in relation to Admiral Milne's squadron.

The outer airlock pinged as it opened. Daniel made a single keystroke. The cabin filled with squeals, clanks and whines: the sails were furling, the yards were rotating in line with the antennas, and the antennas themselves were retracting. Daniel had waited till the bosun was on the hull to begin the theoretically automated process, because if a jam weren't immediately cleared it might lead to breaks and tangles which could take untold time to correct.

The airlock telltale winked green; the second lockful of riggers entered it. They remainder of the outside crew were well into the process of donning their suits. Daniel continued to work—as did Adele, cataloguing the signals that were passing among the ships of the squadron.

Milne's force was using the 20-meter band for general communication with no attempt at signals security beyond the automatic encryption feature. Adele supposed there was no reason to act otherwise under these circumstances. *She* would've, however.

"*Leary, this is Squadron Command,*" said a voice that Adele guessed might be Lieutenant Farschenning's. But wasn't he part of the base establishment? "*The Admiral directs you to make your report by laser communicator. The Admiral adds that there's no danger of interception here, over.*"

Adele suspected that what Admiral Milne had really

said was less polite than the circumlocution Lieutenant Farschenning had spun from it. She was more than a little surprised that Daniel had made an issue of security in the first place. It wasn't a subject which had appeared to interest him in the past.

Smoothly, Daniel replied, "*Command, I'm very sorry but I'm afraid I'll have to deliver my report face to face. I estimate that we'll be alongside the* Garnet *within the hour, over.*"

He resumed his course computations, his expression one of harmless naiveté. Adele frowned. The transmissions were voice-only, but Daniel's face wore a mask that *proved* something was going on. He never looked that innocent when he wasn't up to something.

Cutter 614's first outgoing message had taken five minutes forty-seven seconds to reach the *Garnet*; the distances involved were significant, even for light-speed communication. The time lag would decrease as the cutter streaked toward Yang and the squadron, but it remained considerable.

When the response came, it was in a different voice: "*Leary, this is Admiral Milne. As soon as you've linked with the* Garnet, *report to my suite. When I've heard what you've got to say, I'll decide what to do with you next. And at the moment, my instinct is to lock you in a store room till we get back to Sinmary Port! Squadron Command out!*"

"614 *out,*" Daniel said. For an instant his expression was blank, except for an unusual hardness around his eyes. Then he grinned broadly at Adele's image and said on their two-way channel, "*Well, Adele. If it comes to that, at least I'll have more leg room than anybody here on 614, eh?*"

He laughed.

Try as she might, Adele wasn't able to force her lips into a smile. "Daniel?" she said. "Why do you insist on reporting in person? Because I assure you that I can keep our transmission safe. At least from any spy who wouldn't be able to overhear a conversation in the Admiral's quarters just as easily."

"*Ah,*" said Daniel. For a moment, only one side of his mouth was smiling. "*Well, you see, Adele, I'm not worried about interception. The squadron will've hit the convoy before an Alliance spy in the Yang system could possibly get word to them. If I go aboard the Garnet, though, Captain Toron can pass reaction mass to 614 at the same time. If I simply transmit the information, I very much doubt that Admiral Milne will delay to do that; and without reaction mass, we won't be part of the attack.*"

"Ah," Adele said. If she simply stared at his image staring at her image, he might assume she disapproved of his plan. She didn't disapprove, exactly, but neither would she pretend she understood. "Daniel, I—all the crew, of course, all of us would support any decision you made. But I honestly can't imagine that anyone would think that the part this cutter has already taken in the matter is insufficient. And to put your career at risk like this is . . ."

She let her voice trail off. It wasn't that she couldn't find words to finish the thought, but those she found all had too much negative emotional loading for her to be comfortable using them in the present instance.

"*Yes, I take your point,*" Daniel said. "*The thing is, Adele . . .*"

He smiled with rueful sadness, then continued, "*I*

think the Hermes *should have a representative at the conclusion of the matter. She was, she was a good—I know a ship is just a machine, a lot of machines working together, but the* Hermes *deserves to be in at the kill! I think."*

"Yes," said Adele, understanding at last. It was always the emotional factors that she overlooked; and which blindsided her as a result. "All right. And I'll come aboard the *Garnet* with you."

"*I don't think that's wise,*" Daniel said, frowning in surprise. "*It's not your job, you see, and—*"

"You have your duties, Captain Leary," Adele said. "But don't try to tell Mundy of Chatsworth what hers are."

"*Ah,*" said Daniel. "*Ah. My mistake.*"

He cleared his throat and went on, "*Yes. I think I'll use the time before we come alongside to go over attack plans with Sun. The two of us probably have a higher opinion of a cutter's combat effectiveness than Admiral Milne does, you know.*"

But not higher, Adele thought as Daniel linked his console to the gunner's attack board, *than the Alliance commodore does. . . .*

CHAPTER 28

Yang System

Adele was amused to see Daniel start back as he stepped through the airlock onto the *Garnet*'s A Deck. A vividly chartreuse flying lizard banked upward within a hand's breadth of his nose to snatch a cockroach off the ceiling. On Sinmary Port he'd been too busy to visit the ships which had been on station for some time.

"This way, Lieutenant," Lieutenant Farschenning said. He didn't sound hostile, but he was keeping an evident distance in his voice. "The Admiral's taken the officers' wardroom for her quarters."

"Very well," Daniel said briskly. "Officer Mundy will be accompanying me."

Farschenning glanced at Adele and raised an eyebrow. Adele stared back with a deliberate absence of emotion.

The aide shrugged. "As you will," he said and led the way sternward.

"How do you happen to be aboard the *Garnet*,

Farschenning?" Daniel said, asking the question that'd occurred to Adele also.

"Ah," said Farschenning. "Admiral Milne asked me to become her Flag Lieutenant when Lieutenant Pontefract returned to Cinnabar. He had family business there."

Ah indeed, Adele thought. Milne had to get Pontefract off-planet after the debacle in the Gallery for the same reason she'd sent Daniel to Yang.

The *Garnet* trembled with the buzz of its High Drive running at low output to create the illusion of gravity. As Adele followed the men down the main corridor, she felt the throb of a deeper note as well: the cruiser's pumps had begun to transfer reaction mass to *Cutter 614* through a high-pressure version of the flexible tubing which allowed her and Daniel to cross between the ships without their suits.

Adele was glad they'd come over by tube rather than by hauling themselves along a line. Even an ordinary air suit was bulky within a vessel's tight spaces, and it was uncomfortable as well. Adele found it so, at least.

They passed three technicians going in the other direction, two of them wheeling an arc welder. Adele grimaced, wishing that she'd had an opportunity to change or at least clean up. The *Garnet* was on a combat patrol, so everybody aboard wore utilities just as she and Daniel did. The cruiser's personnel had been able to bathe regularly, however, and their uniforms weren't caked with weeks of body oils.

Adele smiled minusculely. She'd be Mundy of Chatsworth if she were stripped naked and stood on a gallows. And Daniel would be Daniel, grinning and very probably figuring out a way to escape with the executioner's pants and his wife besides. If she was young enough, and pretty enough, and had the IQ of a parakeet.

The wardroom didn't have a proper entryway, so the Admiral's clerk sat at a small workstation bolted to the deck to the side of the hatch. The clerk glanced down the corridor and saw them coming; he spoke via intercom, using his helmet's active cancelling even though he was talking to the Admiral only ten feet away.

"Send him in, Craig," Admiral Milne boomed without waiting for Lieutenant Farschenning to announce them formally. "And then get out!"

The clerk stepped around his workstation and met them in the corridor. "She says go on in, Lieutenant," he said in a low voice, nodding toward the hatch behind him. He looked surprised as Adele gestured to Daniel, then entered the office ahead of him.

"Who the bloody Hell told you you could come in here?" Milne said when she saw that someone was accompanying Daniel. "I'll deal with you when I'm damned good and ready to deal with you!"

The Admiral was at the full-sized console which had replaced the wardroom table; a bunk was fixed behind a screen against the rear bulkhead. She'd obviously been angry already, and Adele's presence threatened to turn her apoplectic.

"Close the hatch, Lieutenant," Adele said to Daniel in a thin, cold voice. When it clunked against its coaming she continued, "I'm afraid you'll have to see me now, Admiral. My information has bearing on the safety of the Republic, and it's time sensitive."

"Have you both gone mad?" Milne said. "If it's

time sensitive, then why didn't you transmit it to me hours ago as you were ordered to do?"

"Lieutenant Leary didn't transmit the information because it was under my control," Adele said, seating herself on one of the metal chairs facing the console. She put her personal data unit on her knees. "And I wouldn't permit him to take such an action because it might compromise my sources and methods. My superiors in Xenos won't be pleased that I chose to make this information available to you directly instead of going through them, and I don't want to think of how they'd react if I broadcast it openly."

She was exaggerating, but not a great deal. People whose business is information dislike having it pass out of their control. Regardless of policy, though, Adele knew that Mistress Sand would support any decisions she made in the field. Admiral Milne would lose if she insisted on making a fight of it.

Milne grimaced. "Go on, then," she said. "You're here."

Adele had planned to link her unit to the Admiral's console because the larger display would have higher resolution, but on reflection she decided to let the little box project the data directly. Milne was dangerously angry already; blithely taking over her supposedly-shielded equipment might push her over the edge.

"The Alliance convoy of which Lieutenant Ganse informed you . . ." Adele said. She led off the visuals with an image of the *Scheer*, showing the aftermost third of the cruiser's hull stripped clean. A sidebar of data formed in the air beside the ship, expanded so that Milne could theoretically read it but therefore fuzzy. "Has been attacked and crippled."

She began to shuffle through the remaining ships of the convoy, starting with those which had received the worst damage. The *Bloemfontein* made a particularly striking image: a forward antenna severed by one of Vesey's rockets had managed to wrap its shrouds several times around the transport's hull, bringing down most of the rest of the rigging in the process.

Love was a hot emotion to Vesey, something Adele herself could accept as a concept without having the least notion of what it meant to one who felt it. It was rather like belief in God, she supposed. What happened to Vesey's love now that its object had been reduced to an expanding ball of gas? Did it continue, the way light spreads from a burned-out pinch of magnesium? Love infinitely attenuated but never completely *gone* until the universe itself died. . . .

"I'll transfer this information to the *Garnet* as soon as I've checked your database security, Admiral," Adele said, "but I wanted you to see it first. You'll note that it includes not only the vessels' damage reports but also full particulars of their crews and cargoes."

Milne wasn't looking at her any more. The Admiral's eyes went from the imagery to Daniel. "This is real, Leary?" she said. "This isn't some sort of sham dummied up on a computer? And you did it?"

"It's no sham, sir," Daniel said quietly. He remained standing instead of taking the other chair, his back straight and his hands crossed at the small of his back. "The *Hermes* and her flotilla carried out a very successful series of attacks, though there were casualties. The tender was lost, and two cutters were lost with their complete crews. I regret to report that Commander Slidell himself commanded one of those cutters."

"Slidell did this?" Milne said, looking puzzled and with the edge of anger that uncertainty brings out in defensive people. "Ganse said Slidell'd left you in command of the *Hermes*. Did he return, then?"

"There were two options for delaying the Alliance convoy until you could arrive with the squadron," Daniel said with great calm. "Captain Slidell chose to take the very dangerous task of attacking alone in the Vela Maun System, leaving me responsible for executing the second attack with the remainder of the flotilla."

The Admiral's face worked as though she were swallowing a walnut, shell and all. She looked from Daniel to Adele. "You've got the coordinates?" she said. "Of where the convoy is now?"

"Yes sir," Daniel said, drawing Milne's eyes back like a gun turret rotating. "It was an eighteen-hour forty-minute run for us, but I think it'll require at least another half hour going back because of the way the gradients were shifting. Ah, that's if you were to make the voyage in a single stage, which—"

"Which would be a bloody disaster, since there's no way of guaranteeing that three ships arrive perfectly together over that distance," Milne said snappishly. "Don't get above yourself, Leary. I don't need a lieutenant to tell me not to send my squadron piecemeal against a pair of destroyers and a cruiser that's still got teeth. We'll rendezvous a light hour out from the target, then go in simultaneously."

"And it's four ships if you please, Admiral," Daniel said. "*Cutter 614* is ready to carry out her part. Our tanks will be completely full again in a few minutes."

"Good God, Lieutenant!" Milne said. "A cutter doesn't have any business in this."

Her eyes narrowed. "You're just after a share of the prize money, that's it, isn't it?" she said in a challenging voice. More calmly she went on, "Well, I'll grant you've earned it. I'll place you aboard the *Garnet* here as Second Lieutenant. And place you too, Mundy. I gather you're not too pure to take prize money? Even though you've made such a point of not being under naval discipline."

"I regret that you consider me undisciplined, Admiral," Adele said. "To be honest, my family has never been greatly concerned with amassing money."

"And I believe that a prize court," Daniel said, verbally stepping into the breach, "would find that because the convoy attacks are all part of a single action, shares will go to the crews of the ships involved in any of the three phases. Still, if *614*'s presence will make it easier for Captain Slidell's heirs to collect his share of the award, so much the better. He was a skilled and inspiring officer."

Admiral Milne stared at Daniel. For the first time since they came aboard the *Garnet*, Adele was doubtful about what was going on in the Admiral's mind.

At last Milne said, "All right, Leary. I'm not an expert in cutter operations and you've demonstrated that you are. I suppose you've worked out a course back to the convoy?"

"Ah, yes sir," Daniel said. He'd thumped his heels together and was standing at attention. "For *Cutter 614* alone, of course, but I believe it'd be perfectly suitable for heavier ships as well."

"I believe it will also," Milne said with a touch of sarcasm. "How long would it take you to add a waypoint a light-hour from the target?"

Daniel shrugged. "Well, sir," he said. "Possibly ten minutes with an astrogational computer."

Milne rose from her console. "Use this one," she said, gesturing Daniel to the seat she'd just vacated. "And Lieutenant? One other thing."

"Yes sir?" Daniel said. He was looking at the keyboard, not the Admiral speaking to him.

"When you've got the course plotted, I'd thank you for the loan of your signals officer to transmit it to the other ships," Milne said, nodding to Adele. "The Gold Dust Squadron doesn't get a lot of practice in group operations, and I'd regret for there to be a communications failure at this juncture."

"I would be pleased . . ." Daniel said. "If my crew could assist the Admiral's staff in this matter."

He looked toward Adele through the shimmer of coherent light and smiled. To Adele it was as if a bust carved from fire opal were grinning at her.

Lieutenant Farschenning and the clerk, Craig, waited in the corridor just outside the Admiral's quarters. They'd heard the hatch undog and had time to compose their features as rigidly as those of a pair of statues.

Daniel grinned and said, "The Admiral will probably want you both. There'll be a general order going out shortly. Lieutenant, we can find our own way back to the cutter."

The two staff personnel stepped into the cabin looking stupefied. Well, Daniel had been there, but he found the results of the interview a little hard to fathom also.

"Daniel?" Adele murmured as they strode down

the corridor. "What will happen when we reach the convoy? That is, what's the battle plan?"

"The heavy ships will launch immediately at the *Scheer*," Daniel said. It was a reasonable question, but Adele didn't generally take an interest in tactics. "Mind, I can only say what I'd do, but it's pretty cut and dried. The *Scheer's* a sitting duck because of the damage she's taken, but she's still extremely dangerous. She'll be able to get off three, possibly four missile salvoes before she's destroyed."

Daniel weighed possibilities for a moment, then smiled wryly and continued, "If the *Scheer* has a competent missileer who concentrates on one target, we'll lose that ship. If the missileer spreads his salvoes—which he shouldn't—but gets lucky, as everybody sometimes does, we could lose more than one ship. And while that's going on, *614* will be trying not to stop an eight-inch plasma bolt."

He shrugged. "The heavy ships will switch their attentions to the destroyers as soon as the first salvo takes care of the cruiser," he said. "We'll have surprise on our side since we'll learn roughly where they are when we regroup an hour out, but we'll be arriving before the light of our own appearance. Even so it'll be a fight. Which—"

He grinned.

"—is what we joined the RCN to do, of course. Some of us, at any rate."

They'd almost reached the airlock to which the transfer tube was coupled. The hatch was sealed while the tube wasn't in use, as was *614's* airlock on the other end. Barnes and Dasi waited in the corridor, talking with two of the cruiser's personnel.

"What will the civilian vessels do?" Adele said, perceptibly slowing her pace. "Will they just surrender?"

Daniel halted. He didn't see where Adele was going with this line of questioning, but it obviously wasn't idle. "The Commodore will order them to scatter," he said, "but most of them won't get far. All the officers in the Gold Dust Squadron have experience in tracking ships in the Matrix. That's one advantage in the constant anti-pirate operations."

The disadvantage—which Daniel hadn't chosen to mention—was that the squadron's missileers weren't as experienced as those of vessels which specialized in fighting enemy warships. He'd thought of offering to take over as missileer on one of the heavy ships, but for a great many reasons he'd held his tongue. He'd started this battle with the *Hermes* and her flotilla; that's the way he'd end it as well.

"What would happen," Adele said, "if the Alliance commodore saw that the *Cornelwood* and three other cruisers were a light-hour out, preparing to attack?"

"The *Cornelwood* won't be ready for action in a month," Daniel said, unintendedly harsh. "Maybe six months. And they won't see us, because we'll arrive through the Matrix before the light gets to them."

"*If*, Lieutenant," Adele said. "What *if* they saw that?"

Daniel felt his face go blank. "The Commodore'd order the convoy to scatter immediately," he said. "Including the destroyers, it'd be suicide for them to stay. And he'd surrender the *Scheer*, since for the short time she'd be in action, her missiles wouldn't be able to get through the *Cornelwood*'s defensive battery."

"From a light-hour out, Daniel," Adele said with a cold smile, "I could convince even myself that *Cutter 614* is a heavy cruiser."

"Good God Almighty!" Daniel said as he turned around. "Come on, Officer Mundy! We need to see the Admiral again!"

CHAPTER 29

Sinmary Port on Nikitin

Adele, carrying in her right hand the decryption module she'd been moving from ship to ship since the *Hermes* made its final attack, stepped from the airlock of *Cutter 610* which had ferried the last of the *Scheer*'s prize crew to the surface. She walked toward the quay, keeping her eyes focused on Daniel's shoulderblades. She hoped that it would keep her from noticing the way the catwalk bounced and quivered underfoot. Perhaps it did help—some.

Adele knew she wouldn't drown if she fell into the slip: even holding the module she could stay afloat, and she was willing to bet that Daniel, Hogg, and probably Tovera as well swam like fish. She would, however, feel like a complete fool—which was worse, of course.

The air was humid enough to wring out, and it smelled like a swamp. It was the first time in . . . the first time since *Cutter 614* lifted from Yang six weeks earlier that Adele had breathed air that hadn't

486

been bottled and chemically scrubbed. She found she liked the change, though it wasn't a matter of great import to her.

Daniel glanced over his shoulder. "Eight of the ships in the harbor are prizes from Bromley," he said in a voice only Tovera, directly behind Adele on the catwalk, was likely to overhear. "Not the *Zerbe*, though, so we've beat somebody getting here. The light cruiser's the *Galatea* from the Home Squadron, and she must be being used for a courier. And there's a brand new 2000-ton fast transport. She's got antennas long enough for something three times her displacement."

Adele stepped onto dry land; well, land baked to coarse limestone by the exhaust of ships landing in the slips to either side. A motor barge was moored in the opposite slip.

Twenty spacers had come down with Adele and Daniel in *610*, the last of the prize crew which'd brought the *Scheer* to orbit above Nikitin. Now they poured aboard the barge, laughing as they bragged about what they were going to do when they got to the dives of East End and how often they were going to do it.

Through the cutter's optics during the landing approach, Adele'd seen five aircars parked on the shore. Their passengers had waited near the vehicles until the steam from *610*'s landing had dissipated, but now they started down the hundred yards of quay toward the new arrivals.

"Looks like we're bloody heroes again," Hogg observed with satisfaction. "Good. That's *always* worth a few drinks."

The group was a mixture of civilians and naval

officers in 1ˢᵗ class uniforms. Daniel's local bimbo, Geneva Raynham, and her mother were among them; that was only to be expected. What Adele hadn't expected, though—

"Daniel?" she said, a little more tensely than she'd intended. The module was in her right hand, but she found her left hand was half into her tunic pocket: "Who are those people in gray? Are they soldiers?"

"Umm," said Daniel. "Well, I suspect some of them have been. They're private security personnel now, though; from that transport, I shouldn't wonder. Now who would they be guarding, do you suppose?"

"Ah," said Adele. She hadn't fallen into the filthy water of the slip, but she seemed to have found an equally effective way to embarrass herself. "Yes, of course."

Sun and Tovera had patched Adele's specialized equipment into the cruiser, but it'd required hardware modifications that wouldn't have been necessary on an RCN vessel. Because of the time Adele knew would be required to remove it, she started stripping it out as soon as they reached Nikitin. She hadn't been able to give more than a cursory glance to the ships filling Sinmary Port.

Her personal data unit almost certainly contained the answer to who'd arrived aboard the fast transport. It'd take Adele longer to retrieve the information than it would for the person approaching within the wedge of large men in gray to introduce himself.

Ginny Raynham sprinted the last two steps toward Daniel. She wore a broad smile and would've thrown her arms around his neck if a man in a gray suit hadn't gotten between them without apparent effort.

Ginnie squawked in surprise. Her mother laughed out loud.

"Why, hello, Deirdre!" said Daniel, stepping forward to clasp arms with his sister. "What are you doing here?"

"I'm on business for the Shippers' and Merchants' Treasury," Deirdre said. Her tone was austere, but her smile as she stepped back from the embrace was warm and extended to Adele as well as her brother. "I'm safeguarding our clients' financial interests. Their very considerable financial interests, I'm pleased to say. When word of the captures was received in Xenos, the directors of the bank ordered me to set out immediately to take charge of affairs before the prize court."

Deirdre gave a smile which in a less perfectly composed woman might've been called a smirk. "Some of the fees which the prize commission here on Sinmary have been reported as charging would be considered criminal in a court on Xenos," she explained. "The directors trust my ability to convince the commissioners that they'll be before just such a court if they attempt any such foolishness with our clients."

Adele had no idea who the directors of the Shippers' and Merchants' Treasury might be. She was quite certain, however, that they were all nominees of Corder Leary and that they carried out his directions with the innocent simplicity of robots.

"Ah," said Daniel, who very possibly didn't know that his father owned the bank. So far as Adele had been able to tell during the years of their acquaintance, Daniel had no interest in finance so long as he had the price of a round of drinks or the barman would let him chalk a tab. "You came on the new transport I saw in harbor as we landed, then?"

"Yes," Deirdre said. She was dark-haired in contrast to her blond brother and not unattractive, though she made no effort to emphasize her looks. Deirdre was Corder Leary's elder child, his spiritual heir and his close associate from her early youth. She exuded authority, as cold and inexorable as the face of a glacier. "Its name's the *Tonnant*. Your shipyard manager, Lieutenant Mon, recommended her for our purposes."

"Ah!" said Daniel. "You couldn't have asked a better advisor. She's fast, then? She looks it!"

Deirdre shrugged. "I gather she is," she said. "That's not my department."

Daniel laughed. "Well, it's very good of you to come out here, I'm sure," he said. "Ah—Deirdre? Please excuse me for a moment. I think I'd best talk with these gentlemen."

Two officers waiting at the edge of Deirdre's guards wore RCN dress whites. The lieutenant with curly black hair was probably a serving officer; the slim, ash-blond officer was not. The latter's name was Wilsing. He wore lieutenant's insignia as he had when Adele had met him a year before in Xenos, but his real duties were to Mistress Sand's organization.

"Oh, we won't break in on a family reunion, Lieutenant," Wilsing said with easy cheerfulness. "We've just come to offer you and Officer Mundy—"

He nodded to her, smiling. Wilsing would smile politely if they stood him in front of a firing squad. He was always polite, always appropriate. Wilsing couldn't do Adele's job, but she was well aware that she couldn't have done his, either.

"—the congratulations of Admiral Jeffords and his invitation to attend him in Squadron House at your convenience."

Wilsing didn't say "*earliest* convenience," but that was implied. Adele wouldn't claim to be an expert in RCN protocol, but she understood what a polite offer meant when it was directed to someone so far down the chain of command.

"I, ah, I'll be glad to," Daniel said. "I was hoping to replace the uniform I lost aboard the *Hermes* before I made formal calls, though. How urgent would you say . . . ?"

"Not that urgent, Mister Leary," said the dark-haired lieutenant, Broderick according to his nametag. "Though the Admiral's looking forward to meeting you. Informally, that is, before he presides over the court-martial regarding the loss of the *Hermes*."

"Court-martial?" Adele said. She didn't raise her voice, but she clipped the words and her expression must have shown a touch of what was going on in her mind. Lieutenant Broderick looked shocked, and Wilsing lost his smile for a heartbeat.

"There's a court-martial any time a ship's lost, Adele," Daniel said. His use of her first name here in a semi-official context showed how concerned he was about how she might react. "It's the only way to clear the commanding officer in cases where the loss wasn't a result of his malfeasance or neglect."

"Not to prejudge the findings of the court . . ." Lieutenant Broderick said, relaxing but looking from Daniel to Adele speculatively. "But I will say that all the testimony gathered thus far indicates that Mister Leary's brief period commanding the

Hermes was fully in line with his distinguished previous career."

Broderick's speculation was of course false. Adele had come to believe that most things that most people thought were false, so it probably didn't matter.

Broderick faced Daniel and instinctively drew himself to attention. Wilsing had been attached to Admiral Jeffords' staff, but Adele was sure his duties only indirectly involved Jeffords or even the RCN. Broderick was the real Flag Lieutenant, a relative of either the Admiral or of someone highly placed in naval or political circles with a claim on the Admiral.

"A remarkable career, Lieutenant," Broderick said. He was at most two years younger than Daniel, but from the awe in his voice he might've been addressing a hoary patriarch of ninety. "It's truly an honor to meet you."

"We're both fortunate to be part of RCN, Broderick," Daniel said in a tone of good fellowship, clasping the other man's arm to break the formality of the moment. "A pleasure to meet you, too."

He turned toward his sister, keeping the two officers in the corner of his eye to include them also. "Deirdre?" he said. "Would you be able to carry me and Officer Mundy and our servants in the aircar you came in? I'd like to get to the transient officers' housing as quickly as possible so we can borrow dress uniforms. I realize you have your own entourage."

Which was one way of describing the squad of bodyguards. They'd let the two officers past, but the dozen or so local civilians who'd come to greet Daniel were kept resolutely behind a wall of gray.

"We can carry you, Leary," Wilsing said smoothly.

"Our car's a six-seat so the servants will have to squeeze onto the front bench with the driver. I'm sure the engines have sufficient power, though. Ah, don't you think so, Broderick?"

Of course the engines do! Adele thought, remembering the load their aircar had carried in the assault on Big Florida Island. But she knew that if she said, "Put the car in ground effect if you doubt it can fly with the load," these officers in Dress Whites would look at her blankly. They hadn't seen or done the things Daniel had.

She grinned broadly, startling Broderick even more than she'd done by breaking in on the discussions of commissioned officers. Very few people had seen and done what Daniel had; but she, Adele Mundy, was one of the exceptions.

"That won't be necessary, gentlemen," Deirdre said coolly. Neither her voice nor the gaze she turned on the officers had any hint of challenge. Adele doubted that Deirdre respected either man enough to consider them worth a challenge. "I brought a 12-place vehicle in the *Tonnant*, since I'd been warned that transportation might be a problem. There's ample room for my brother and his associates."

She turned to Daniel and continued, "And as for uniforms, when the other directors and I heard what had happened to the *Hermes*, we assumed you'd need replacements. I have full sets of clothing for both of you aboard the *Tonnant*. Since they'll need final fitting, I brought the tailor along also. I don't think it will delay you more than a few minutes."

"Good God," Daniel said. "Well, that simplifies matters, doesn't it, Officer Mundy? I, ah, suppose we'd best get to it, then. Broderick, please present our compliments to Admiral Jeffords and tell him that we'll call on him as soon as we're properly uniformed!"

Daniel, feeling uncomfortable in his new uniform, stepped into the outer office of the Squadron House Annex. His discomfort wasn't because of the Whites themselves but rather because of the amount the tailor'd had let out seams that'd been cut to Daniel's measurements from not very long ago. If he wasn't careful he'd be as fat as an admiral by the time he was thirty. . . .

The reception clerk, a senior rating, touched her intercom before Daniel had a chance to speak. "Lieutenant Leary and Lady Mundy have arrived, sir," she said. Daniel couldn't hear the reply, but after a moment she beamed professionally at them and said, "It'll be just a moment, Lieutenant."

Admiral Jeffords was Director of Chandlery at the Navy Office; he reported directly to Admiral Anston. The Alliance vessels captured at Bromley contained vast quantities of naval stores, enough to justify someone so senior coming out to take charge. Conducting the court-martial on the loss of the *Hermes* was a mere sidelight of his presence on Nikitin.

The Annex had been the outdoor reception hall, across a garden from Squadron House proper; this present outer office had been the cloak room. The base complement had partitioned the remainder of the hall, then covered the floor with carpets and the raw walls with hangings and pictures.

From the quantity of the furnishings, they must've scrounged from Nikitin's wealthier civilians as well as the naval personnel. The result was a sort of trashy opulence, making Daniel think of a warehouse filled with stolen goods.

Daniel crossed his hands behind his back. There were chairs of enameled wood, but he preferred to stand.

"Did you notice the big tree in the garden?" he said to Adele, primly erect beside him. "I don't recognize the species."

"It's a Terran black walnut," Adele said. "I thought you might ask, so I checked before we left the *Tonnant*. I'd seen it when I was in Squadron House previously."

She smiled, broadly for her, but she continued to look toward a painting of a man with a trowel in one hand and a law book in the other. It was allegorical, Daniel supposed.

Adele was dressed in a civilian suit rather than a 1st Class uniform like Daniel's. The closely tailored tunic was a mauve so dark it approached black in dim light, picked out with small gray trapezoids; the trousers' pattern was identical, but the colors were reversed. Daniel didn't recognize the fabric, but it had the soft luster of highly radioactive ore.

In an RCN uniform, Adele would be a junior warrant officer who had no business dealing directly with an admiral. In civilian clothing, very expensive civilian clothing, she was Mundy of Chatsworth and could meet anybody in the Republic on terms of equality.

Deirdre was a very clever person, and a very political person. Daniel grinned: Speaker Leary'd been fortunate in his firstborn.

Lieutenant Broderick opened the door of the inner

office. "Lieutenant Leary," he said formally, "the Admiral will see you now. Mistress Mundy, the Admiral begs your indulgence and asks that you grant him a few moments alone with Lieutenant Leary. If you'd like some refreshment, or . . . ?"

Adele gave a tiny shake of her head. "I'll entertain myself," she said, sitting on one of the chairs. Her tone might've seemed curt to a stranger, but Daniel recognized it as his friend stating the truth without emotion or embellishment.

She nodded to Daniel, then took her personal data unit from a thigh pocket. Deirdre really didn't miss a bet. . . .

Daniel stepped past Broderick, who closed the door from the outside. That left Daniel alone with Admiral Jeffords, a tall man with a pronounced widow's peak. He braced to attention and saluted with enthusiasm if not skill.

"Sir!" he said. "Lieutenant Daniel Leary reporting!"

Jeffords returned the salute from his seat. He wasn't much better at saluting than Daniel was. Perhaps they'd both get credit for having made the effort if they appeared at the gate of Drill and Ceremony Heaven.

"Sit down," he said. Jeffords was behind a console that'd been brought here at his arrival. "I'm pleased to meet you, Leary. I won't claim I've been following your career, but I've heard your name around the Navy Office. Now, let me find what I'm looking for."

Jeffords keyed in commands, then scowled in concentration at his display. A thick cable snaked from the console, running in the direction of the main building; it humped the carpet like a gopher track.

While the Admiral worked, Daniel settled on one

of the four chairs placed for visitors. Their frames of heavy, dark wood had squared outlines; the seats were black leather. Daniel had seen pressed-metal furniture that was more inviting, but he was sure this set had cost somebody a great deal.

Jeffords looked at Daniel again and said, "I want to check with you about the manifests of the captured ships. You provided them, didn't you?"

"Signals Officer Mundy provided them, sir," Daniel said. "I merely forwarded them to Squadron command. Ah—Officer Mundy's in the outer office right now, sir. If you'd like to know something specific?"

"I've heard about her too, Leary," Jeffords said with a wintry smile. "I've got nothing against her, you understand. We need that sort, Porra has them so we have to. But I'd sooner deal with somebody who reports to me, if you see what I mean. So tell me, Lieutenant: can we trust the information here?"

Daniel let his face blank as he considered the question. "Yes sir," he said. "With allowance for the sort of errors that crop up in any loading operation. I won't swear that a crate marked hand grenades isn't really full of canned soup; but I will swear that the loadmaster who signed off on it thought it was hand grenades. Officer Mundy is confident of her data, and I'd take her word over that of anyone else I know."

He smiled, but he realized that expression was a trifle harder than he'd intended. "I'd trust her before I'd trust myself," he said.

Jeffords nodded. "I thought that might be the case," he said. "I told you I'd heard about her. And if it's so, it's going to save a devil of a job of offloading every ship, doing an inventory, and then loading it back. We don't have the facilities or the personnel at Sinmary Port to do that. But—"

He smiled at Daniel in wry good-humor.

"—by the same token, if I tell the Garlock Sector Commander that he's got a Planetary Defense Array coming and he finds it's really a shipload of pictures of Guarantor Porra, Anston'll have my guts for garters. And be right to."

Jeffords touched a control and leaned back as the seat reshaped itself to his body. "All right," he said, "I'll order the condemnation of military stores from the cargoes on the basis of the manifests. That'll cut a month off the process, which is a bloody good thing given how badly we need some of them in the Garlock Sector. It'll speed your prize money too. I suppose you've thought of that too, eh, Leary?"

"Yes sir," said Daniel, allowing himself to grin. The Admiral seemed both friendly and cheerful, and "prize money" was a term that made any RCN spacer smile. "Though that's more my sister's concern than mine."

"I met your sister," Jeffords said with a chuckle. "It's not before time that somebody sorted out the Prize Court here at Sinmary. Not at all."

He leaned torward his display, making it omni-directional. Images of the *Scheer* appeared: the cruiser as-built above and in her present condition below.

During the voyage to Nikitin Daniel's prize crew had fitted spare spars in the aftermost ring in place of the missing antennas. That'd provided a degree of directional stability, but all adjustments still had to be made by hand: the cables and hydraulic lines on the cruiser's stern had been swept away as completely as the antennas had.

"So, Lieutenant," Jeffords said, frowning at the holographic image. "What do you think of the *Scheer*? Is she worth repairing on Cinnabar or should we send her to Gascoigne or maybe Briarwood and see if they're up to the job? We need cruisers, but the yards at home are at capacity now."

"Why, good God, sir!" Daniel said, shocked into speaking more directly than he'd intended. "They don't have a dock on Briarwood that'll take a ship her size, and I don't think the facilities are a bit better on Gascoigne. Besides, the turret casting'd have to be shipped there since there's no foundries off Cinnabar that could handle the job."

He paused to think, then continued, "Better to take her to Cinnabar, mount a pack of thrusters on her stern as a temporary fitment, and bring her down in a private yard to be re-rigged. That'll be complete by the time a new turret's ready, and she can be transferred to Harbor Three to place the turret in a week or less."

He cleared his throat. "Ah," he said. "Of course that's just a personal opinion. I met Captain Hallas and the other members of your survey party when they came up in the first of the cutters ferrying us to the ground. I wouldn't presume to interfere in her duties."

If Daniel had the slightest concern that the survey party wouldn't come to the same conclusions he had, he certainly *would* try to interfere; but he knew Hallas by reputation. There were RCN officers who looked down on engineering specialists like her, but Daniel knew better that.

"I have full confidence in my survey party," Jeffords

said, "but you've spent three weeks aboard the *Scheer* bringing her from Bromley. Her hull's all right then, you think? Ships colliding at those velocities don't usually leave much of either one."

"The *Hermes* was a gas cloud by then, not a ship," Daniel said. His mouth worked for an instant on the sour thought: she'd been a good ship, well-found and as handy as a tender could be with her specialized design.

"The only structural damage came when a plasma cannon exploded and blew the whole turret out," he continued. "We made do with an internal dam of sailcloth since the rig had higher priority. I'd want something a lot sturdier before I landed her, of course, but that can wait for Cinnabar orbit. The team attaching the thrusters can take care of the patch at the same time. Ah—if that's your decision."

Jeffords flicked through several files in quick sequence. Daniel could see the display but without context the data meant nothing to him. Still scowling, Jeffords looked at him again and said, "You brought the *Scheer* from Bromley with a crew of seventy-five. Is that number sufficient to sail her to Cinnabar?"

"Yes sir," Daniel said, "it is. Especially if they're the same seventy-five. The prize crew was mostly spacers who've been with me since, well; since my first cruise as a supernumerary on the *Aglaia*."

He coughed to let his mind work. Daniel liked to deal with individual items in sequence, and several very different things were going on right now. One of them was the implication that he'd be taking the crippled *Scheer* back to Cinnabar, which meant he'd no longer report to Admiral Milne. Milne would be very happy if that occurred, but not nearly as happy as Daniel Leary.

"Ah, sir?" Daniel went on. "I realize we made wretched time from Bromley, before we got the stern antennas rigged, but our rate over the final four days was very much better than the early portion. I'm not making excuses—our initial progress was abysmal and I was the one plotting the course—but I'd expect not more than seventeen or eighteen days to Cinnabar orbit."

Jeffords frowned; then his expression became unreadable. He went to his console again, shifting from one astrogation chart to another. After staring at the last for a moment, he shrank the display and faced Daniel.

"You're related to Commander Bergen, aren't you?" he said abruptly.

"Yes sir," said Daniel. "Commander Bergen was my Uncle Stacey. He was the finest astrogator ever born."

"I've heard that," Jeffords said. "And because I've heard that, I guess maybe there's a chance you *can* get that wreck to Cinnabar in eighteen days. Anyway, you're going to have the chance. I'll cut the orders as soon as I've got a formal report from Captain Hallas."

He paused, drumming his fingers, then added, "*And* as soon as we've held the damned court-martial on the *Hermes*, that'll have to be taken care of. I'll tell Broderick to schedule it ASAP so that we can get on with fighting a war."

Jeffords leaned back in his seat again and smiled. "Anston thinks a lot of you, Leary," he said. "You know that, don't you?"

"I'm very glad to hear that, sir," Daniel said in a careful voice. There was something in the Admiral's tone besides bonhomie. Daniel figured he was better off keeping a neutral expression than he would be guessing wrong about what was going on.

"Yes," Jeffords said. "He says you take orders. That isn't your reputation, I'm bound to say, but Anston's judgment is the main reason we're beating the Alliance all the way around the flagpole even though they've got twice our population."

He opened a drawer in the console's return, then slammed it shut. "Right," he muttered, rising to his feet. "I told Broderick to keep it for me. Come on out, Leary. I'm having a little reception in the garden and you're invited."

"Yes sir," said Daniel. He'd been saying that a lot. Well, he was speaking to an admiral, so it was what he should be saying. *Anston said I take orders?* he thought.

He reached for the door but Lieutenant Broderick swung it open instead. Daniel stepped through and moved aside, letting Jeffords by. Hogg, grinning like he'd stolen somebody's liquor cabinet, was alone with the receptionist in the outer office; there was no sign of Adele and Tovera. They might've gone off with Wilsing, of course, discussing matters of common interest that weren't properly RCN business.

"Everything's ready, Admiral," Broderick said. He walked briskly to the outer door and opened it.

"Come along, Leary," Jeffords ordered, gesturing Daniel ahead of him. Daniel obeyed, blank-faced. *Something was going on. . . .*

The garden was full of people, *full*; there were hundreds of them. Many were wearing Whites, but a good half the crowd was enlisted spacers in their liberty suits: utilities with ribbons dangling from the seams and a patch for every port of call. The former Sissies were there, and so were members of the *Hermes'* crew who'd originally been with the *Bainbridge*.

Daniel stopped short. "Hurrah for Mister Leary!" Woetjans bellowed, and the whole crowd took up the cheer.

Adele was in the front rank, standing between Woetjans and Tovera. Barnes and Dasi were behind her to make sure she wasn't jostled from the back; Daniel didn't know that he'd ever seen her look so happy. And Deirdre too! She stood in front of a weather-beaten statue with two of her own guards.

"Go on, Leary, go on," Admiral Jeffords said, shouting to be heard. "Stand on the dais but leave room for me."

Daniel walked out. He didn't see Admiral Milne in the crowd, but many of the other officers from the Squadron and Port establishments were present. Lieutenant Ganse was cheering and waving a spacer's neck scarf with RCS *Hermes* embroidered on it. Deirdre and her people were the only civilians, though.

While Daniel'd been speaking with Admiral Jeffords, somebody had brought a low dais into the garden and covered it with a tarpaulin painted red. There was a serving table for later, set over the cold frames along the garden's east wall. It held liquor in bottles, carafes, and a tub—probably punch made with industrial alcohol for Power Room crewmen.

A pair of base personnel with a stereoscopic recorder were perched on a limb of the walnut tree. *Good God!*

Daniel stepped onto the dais, feeling wood creak beneath his boots. The Admiral got up beside him and took a scroll from his aide; a ribbon with a red wax seal tied it closed. Jeffords grinned at Daniel and broke the seal with his thumb.

"Assembled spacers and citizens of Cinnabar!" he

said. A concealed pickup sent his voice booming from speakers mounted under the eaves of Squadron House, but the amplification wasn't really needed. "It gives me great pleasure to read this communication from Admiral Anston, President of the Navy Board."

"*Yee-hah!*" somebody shouted. Daniel winced, but people who'd faced what his Sissies had couldn't be expected to find an admiral as threatening as RCN regulations wanted him to be. There was just the one outburst, though, thanks be to God and the good sense of Woetjans, who spun and pointed her finger toward Timmons in silent threat.

Jeffords held the document up, face toward the crowd so that everybody could see the calligraphy and the pair of additional seals in blue and again red. It struck Daniel that though Jeffords was a very important man, he'd probably never experienced this much raucous enthusiasm before during his professional duties. He was milking the scene for all it was worth.

"It reads," the Admiral said, squinting at the document now, "'By the powers vested in me by the Senate, I hereby appoint Daniel Oliver Leary to the rank and authority of Commander in the Navy of the Republic of Cinnabar, his duties to commence upon the reading of this order.' Signed, Anston, President of the Navy Board, and counter-signed G. W. Tillotson, Admiral, Chief of the Bureau of Personnel."

Jeffords turned and with a flourish held out the document. Daniel reached for it reflexively, but he almost forgot to close his fingers on the parchment.

But that's a two-step promotion! he thought.

From the way his Sissies were cheering, they hadn't overlooked that point either.

CHAPTER 30

Sinmary Port on Nikitin

Adele heard the vehicle coming some ways before it pulled up in front of *Cutter 614*'s boarding bridge. It was a tractor from the port's maintenance division, meant to drag trailers carrying heavy parts. At this hour of the night there was very little traffic, and the caterpillar treads rang on the beryllium-mesh road surface like a continuing alarm.

Adele got up from the console and joined Tovera at the hatch. "Hogg's bringing Mister Leary back," Tovera said. "They're alone."

She took her hand out of her attaché case. Adele knew that the precaution was as natural to Tovera as breathing, but apparently her servant was concerned that greeting the visitors at gunpoint might appear discourteous.

Adele smiled slightly. Tovera probably didn't care what Daniel thought regarding the matter, but Hogg's opinion was something else again.

"When I was out walking one morning for pleasure . . ." Daniel sang. Liquor had roughened his clear tenor voice,

but he got down from the tractor without stumbling and walked straight as a plumb line along the boarding bridge.

Hogg followed his master, obviously unconcerned. As these things went, Daniel was as sober as a . . . well, as sober as Adele herself.

"*I met a young spacer—*" Daniel continued. He stopped dead and spread his arms wide. There was a bottle in his right hand.

"Why, hello, Adele!" he cried. "What are you doing here?"

"I told Timmons and Claud to go find a party," Adele said, "and that I'd be anchor watch in their place. I don't know that they'd have taken any other order from me, but they didn't argue that one. I wanted a full-sized computer and decided to use *614's* instead of putting a cot in the Communications Room at Squadron House."

She stepped back to let Daniel enter the cutter. She didn't add that while she knew she'd be welcome aboard the *Tonnant*, she wasn't willing to trust her data to Deirdre Leary. Adele was under no illusions about her ability to safeguard information that passed through the *Tonnant's* system.

Daniel wore the pips of a full commander and two broad stripes on his cuffs, but the upper stripe on either sleeve was only pinned. He hadn't had his uniform off since his promotion, so there'd been no opportunity to sew on the stripes properly.

He raised the bottle to his lips, then stared at it in surprise. It was of yellow glass and fluted; rather attractive, Adele thought.

"It's empty," said Daniel. He set the bottle carefully

on the arm of the command console. "I didn't know it was empty."

The bottle slipped from the cylindrical cushion and shattered on the deck. Daniel didn't appear to notice it. "The *Hermes* is gone, the *Sissie*'s gone too," he said. "I'm not going to sleep on shore, and I'm not going aboard the *Tonnant* either. Deirdre might want to talk about things I don't want to talk about."

Daniel's face scrunched into a combination of fury and despair. "Adele?" he said. "My father's going to think I did what he asked. What am I going to tell him?"

Adele slipped her personal data unit into its pocket. Daniel could have almost any woman on the planet tonight, but instead he wanted a ship he'd commanded to share his triumph with him. He displayed a touching innocence at some times.

"Daniel?" she said. "Are you able to come up on the hull with me? I'd like to look at the stars."

Daniel laughed. "Officer Mundy," he said with drunken solemnity. "I am a commissioned officer in the RCN. I can climb the ladder upside down, if you like. Indeed, I'll do that regardless just to prove I can!"

"Please don't," Adele said. "I'll become dizzy and fall, leaving you with my death by drowning on your conscience."

Laughing at the way she'd disarmed his deadpan bluster, Daniel reached out of the hatch with his left hand. He caught a rung of a hull ladder and swung himself outside, then climbed with as little hesitation as he'd shown walking aboard in the first place.

Adele followed in a stolidly cautious fashion, moving one hand or foot at a time. She felt ridiculous in her concern, but she knew that she'd be even more ridiculous if she let herself fall.

Hogg and Tovera watched Adele's progress from the hatch, speaking quietly to one another. The servants were on terms of mutual respect and even liking, if one could properly use that word to describe Tovera's mental processes. They stepped back into the belly of the ship when she'd reached the spine and Daniel offered her his arm.

Adele knew that they could overhear her conversation with Daniel if they wished to; she was simply making the point that she *wanted* privacy, a wish that they could respect or not as they chose. She rather suspected they would, but she wasn't going to worry.

Daniel sat cross-legged, leaving the dorsal foremast to support Adele's back. He pointed at what to her was a fluttering blur over the water of the slip.

"That's a balloon bird from Golconda," he said. "They're amphibians, really. Here they only come out at night or on cloudy days, because direct sunlight would make the methane in their lift bladders swell enough to burst them."

Adele wasn't interested in natural history generally or balloon birds in particular, but she dutifully pulled her goggles down over her eyes and followed the line of Daniel's arm. A flat creature hovered just above the slip. It had transparent pustules which she supposed were the lift bladders. The fringes of its body rippled against the faint breeze, permitting it to hold its position.

"It dangles a lure into the water," Daniel explained. He wasn't using his goggles. "When a fish takes it, barbs open like the head of a harpoon and the bird jerks it into its belly. If it misjudges the size of the fish, it has to either disgorge or digest its meal floating on the water."

He turned to Adele and grinned. "How do you suppose creatures from Golconda got here, Adele?" he said. "I could imagine a thousand paths, none of them likely. And maybe *none* of my guesses would be right."

"I agree," Adele said. "And that has some bearing on what I want to tell you."

Because Daniel had dropped the subject of his father, she thought of letting the matter be. Daniel wouldn't forget it even if he never mentioned it again, though. Better to have it out now.

She took off her goggles and put them in her lap. She wanted to bring her data unit out simply as a mental crutch, but that would be weakness.

"Daniel," she said, "I ran DNA analyses of you and Oller Kearnes through the *Hermes'* Medicomp. Both of you were in the RCN database, of course."

"I hadn't thought of that," Daniel said. "Go on."

"There was no statistical similarity," Adele said. "If Corder Leary is your father, he wasn't the father of Oller Kearnes."

Daniel didn't speak for a moment. His moonlit face could've been carved from wax. Then he started to laugh.

"Oh, Adele!" he said. "Well, there's no certainty in life, but based on what I know of my mother's personality, I'm pretty sure that I'm Speaker Leary's son."

He leaned his head back and laughed again in relief

and delight. The balloon bird skittered downwind and vanished into the reeds poking up around the water's margin.

"So it was really that easy?" Daniel said. "Anybody could have done it!"

"Yes," said Adele, keeping the edge out of her voice by the greatest effort of will. "Anybody at all."

Daniel stopped laughing abruptly. He turned to face Adele directly. "You know," he said conversationally, "I've been drinking quite a lot tonight, but I don't think that has much to do with it. I'm perfectly capable of saying stupid things when I'm stone sober. My pardon, Adele. I should have said, 'Any librarian would have asked the question, so it was fortunate that someone finally brought the problem to a librarian.'"

He squeezed, then released her right hand. "Thank you, Adele," he said. "That will silence my father."

"I'm not done yet," Adele said. "I did a general sort, since I had the parameters entered in the database already. I found one close match."

She turned—turned her face toward the water but really turned it away from Daniel. A humped form edged from the reeds like foam moving against the breeze. She couldn't see the balloon bird clearly without putting her light-amplifying goggles back on; and anyway, she didn't *care* about the cursed bird!

"Commander Slidell's elder brother was named Jan," Adele continued. "He was at one time your father's legislative aide."

"That's correct," Daniel said. "Had I told you that?"

"No," said Adele, "you hadn't. I looked it up—"

In a political database that was one of the tools Mistress Sand had provided her.

"—after I found a genetic match between Commander Slidell and the late Oller Kearnes. I should say 'the late Commander Slidell and the late Midshipman Kearnes,' I suppose. The similarity is consistent with Kearnes having been the son of Slidell's brother. Since they're all dead now, it may not matter."

"On the contrary, Adele," Daniel said. "I think it matters a great deal."

"I won't insist on this, Daniel," Adele said, her eyes on the bird. "But I'd appreciate it if you wouldn't mention my name when you discuss that matter with your father. I'm most comfortable when I exist in a world completely separate from that of Speaker Leary."

Apart from the man who had my whole family murdered . . . for good and sufficient reasons, but murdered nonetheless.

"I don't think I'll be discussing it with my father after all, Adele," Daniel said. "It turns out the business has nothing to do with the Leary family, whatever he may think. And *I* do better in a world separate from him too."

Daniel rose, then offered Adele a hand to help her up. "Judging from where the smaller moon is, it's nearly three in the morning," he said. "I'm ready for bed. But first, if you wouldn't mind—I'm sure Hogg can find a bottle somewhere. Will you drink with me to friendship, Adele?"

"I will," Adele said. "To that, I'll drink the whole bottle."

The following is an excerpt from:

ONE JUMP AHEAD

BY

MARK L. VAN NAME

Available from Baen Books
June 2007
hardcover

CHAPTER ONE

Maybe it was because the girl reminded me of Jennie, my lost sister and only family, whom I haven't seen in over a hundred years. Maybe it was because Lobo was the first interesting thing I'd met in a while. Maybe it was because it was time to move on, because I'd been healing and lazing on Macken long enough. Maybe it was because I had a chance to do some good and decided to take that chance.

Not likely, but maybe the time on Macken had healed me more than I thought, and I was reconnecting with the human part of me.

Also not likely, but I like to hope.

Whatever the reason, I was lying on my back in the bottom of a fifteen-foot-deep pit waiting for my would-be captors to fetch me. As jungle traps go, it was a nice enough one, not fancy but serviceable. They'd made it deep enough to keep me in when I fell, but shallow enough that I'd probably only be injured, not killed, from the fall. They'd blasted the walls smooth so climbing out would not be an easy option. The bottom was rough dirt but without stakes, another welcome sign they hadn't wanted to kill me. The covering was reasonably persuasive, a dense gray-green layer of rain-forest moss over very lightweight twigs. In the dark it passed as just another stretch of jungle floor—as long as you were using only the normally visible light spectrum. In IR its bottom was enough cooler than the rest of the true jungle floor and its sides were enough warmer from the smoothing blasts that the pit stood out as an odd red and blue box beneath me. Not that I needed the IR: Lobo was chummy with a corporate surveillance sat that was supplying him data, and he had a bird-shaped battlefield recon drone circling over the area, so he'd warned me about the trap well before I reached it. The drone wouldn't have lasted two minutes in a battle, where the best result you could expect was a burst of surveillance data before enemy defenses shot them down, but these folks were so clearly amateurs that Lobo and I agreed the drone wouldn't be at risk.

You don't spend much time alone in jungles before you either die or learn to always carry at least a knife, food, water, and an ultra-strong lightweight rope. I'd kicked in the pit's cover, looped the rope around the closest tree, lowered myself into the pit, and pulled in the rope. After a light dinner of dried meat and fruit, I'd decided to relax and enjoy the view a small gap in the jungle canopy afforded me. Lying on my back, looking up past the pit's walls to the sky above trees so ancient that luminescent white flowers grew directly from their trunks, I could see so many stars I could almost believe anything was possible somewhere.

If you spend all your time on industrialized planets, you have no clue as to the beauty and brilliance of a night sky without light pollution. You can see pictures and videos, but they're not the same. They lack the fire, the sense of density of light that you get from the sky on a planet still early in the colonization process. The view of Macken's stars from its surface would slowly blur as its population grew—the new jump aperture ensured growth even more surely than the planet's amazing beaches—but for now I could enjoy a view most will never know they've missed.

Lobo's voice coming from the receiver in my ear interrupted my reverie. "Jon, you are early."

"Why? I thought their camp was nearby."

"It is, but as you were climbing into the pit they were heading to town. I monitored the alarm their sensors triggered, and so did they, but apparently they decided to let you rot for a bit."

I thought about climbing out, but I couldn't finish the job if I left the area, so why trade one bit of jungle floor for another? On the other hand, the prospect of simply waiting, doing nothing while these amateurs enjoyed some R&R in town, was unacceptable. I've learned on past missions that you should always rest when you can, so I decided to put this time to good use. "I'm going to take a nap," I said. "Wake me when they're within a klick or so."

"Will do. Want some music?"

I listened to the low but persistent buzz of the jungle, the wind, the insects, the flow of life around me, and I thought back to simpler childhood days watching the sunset on the side of the mountain on my home island on Pinkelponker. The memory was pleasant but hollow, leached of resonance by time, by what the planet's government had done to Jennie and me, and by the possibility that my entire home planet no longer existed. Still, I found a welcome peace in the sounds, and in the lush scent that filled the forest. "No, there's music enough here. Thanks, though, for the offer."

Lobo couldn't exactly sigh, but I had to admire his emotive programming once again, because I was sure I could hear exasperation in his voice as he said, "Whatever you want. I'll be back to you when they're close."

I enjoyed the stars a moment more, then closed my eyes and thought about the path that had led me here.

The house I had rented on Macken was well away from Glen's Garden, the closest city and the capital of the human settlement on the planet. A simple but large A-frame structure built from native woods reinforced with metal beams and coated pilings, its entire front was an active-glass window facing the ocean. The tides pounded slowly and gently against the beach a hundred meters away, waging a long-term, low-key war with the shoreline that they'd eventually win. I'd come for solitude, so I'd paid in advance for half a year. Stupid. I should have paid by the week like most people, should have known that anyone spending that much money at one time in a colony like this had no chance of staying alone for long. I figured that out after the fact, however, so between long swims in the ocean, short but frequent bouts of disturbed sleep, and even longer periods staring out the house's front, the glass tuned to the clearest possible setting, I made friends with some appliances and started gathering the local intelligence I knew my mistake would inevitably make me need. I suppose I could have left, taken my vacation on another planet, but I liked this house, I'd spent a lot of money on it, and most of all, I didn't feel like giving it up.

Washing machines are the biggest gossips in the appliance world, so I had cozied up to mine early. They talk non-stop among themselves, but it's all at frequencies people—humans—can't hear. I suppose at some point most people still learn somewhere in the course of their education that the price we've paid for putting intelligence everywhere is a huge population of frequently disgruntled but fortunately behaviorally limited machines, but just about everyone chalks it up to the price of progress. I've seen some organizations try to monitor and record the machine chatter, but in short order the recorders warn the other machines and then they all go quiet until the people give up and move on.

Appliances will talk to you directly, though, if you can hear them, speak their frequency, and, most importantly, if you can stand them. Most are unbearably dull, focused solely on their jobs. They yak day and night about waste nutrients in the run-off fluid or overcooking or the endless other bits of work-related trivia that compose their lives. Washers, though, are an exception. As part of the disease-monitoring system on every even semi-civilized world I've visited, they analyze the cells on everything they clean. What they must and do report is disease. What they love to chat about is all the other information those cells reveal: whose blood or semen is on whose underwear, who's stretching his waistband more this week than last, who waited so long to put his exercise shorts into the washer that even the gentlest cycle can't save the rotting crotch, and on and on. They're all on the net, of course, like all the other appliances and pretty much everything else man-made, so they pass their gossip back and forth endlessly. They trade their chemical-based news and the bits their voice-activation systems record for the scuttlebutt other appliances have picked up, and they all come away happy. The older, stupider models of most appliances have to stop talking when their work taxes their processors, but anything made in the last fifty years has so many spare processing cycles it never shuts up.

My washer was a brand-new Kelco, the owners of my beach house clearly willing to invest in only the best for their rental property, so getting it to talk to me was as simple as letting it know I was willing to listen. Appliances are always surprised the first time we talk, but they're usually so happy for the new and different company that they don't worry much about why we can hear each other. The combination of the changes Jennie made to my brain and the nano-machines the researchers at the prison on Aggro merged with my every cell lets me tune in. I suppose it's a blessing, and it certainly is useful, but it came at such a high price that I wouldn't have voluntarily made the trade, and I never mourn for the deaths of the scientists Benny killed on Aggro when we escaped. The disaster that followed, that made it impossible for me to know if Jennie is dead or alive: that I mourn. I also mourn for Benny; I wish he could have gotten away, too.

Of course, my escape wasn't the only good thing to emerge from that disaster. I have to confess it's also proven useful to be the only person alive who knows that one of the Aggro experiments actually survived. Everyone else thinks the disaster there and the subsequent loss of the Pinkelponker system was the result of a huge failure in nanotechnology, a failure that was the catalyst for the ongoing ban on human/nano-machine fusion. I like it that way. As long as no one believes anyone from Aggro survived, no one will hunt me.

The washer was unfortunately so happy to talk to me that I had to invest a lot of boring hours maneuvering it into giving me the kind of information I wanted—who was buying what, which groups were armed, and so on—rather than the sex-related gossip it loved to discuss. Apparently it was more fun and common to check for semen than for explosive residues, laser burns, or stains from weapons-grade lubricants. I spent many of those hours listening to the washer recount intimate details of the randy sex lives of the corporate types who frequented the beachfront resort houses and mansions in Glen's Garden. If I hadn't already known it, the washers would have convinced me: put a man in a bureaucracy, weigh him down with a great deal of stress for a very long time, and his sexual imagination will go places the rest of us would never conceive of.

All that time paid off, however, when the washer told me about the kidnapping and the exclusive rights.

Armed with that news, I wasn't surprised when Ron Slake came knocking on my door after lunch on a clear, warm day. He looked the standard high-ranking corporate type: a little under two meters tall, taller than his genes would once have allowed, very nearly as tall as I am; perfectly fit, no doubt from exercise machines; hair the thickness and pitch-black color that only enhanced genes can deliver for more than a few years; and dressed in the white slacks and shirt that have been standard tourist garb on every beach on every planet I've visited. The tourist costume made it clear that he wasn't ready to share the news about Kelco's rights with the locals. I braced myself for a round of wasteful verbal dancing while he wound his way to the point, but he must have ranked higher than I had guessed because he came straight to business.

"I'd like to hire you, Mr. Moore."

"Jon will do. And I'm not looking for work. I'm here on vacation."

"I understand, but from what I can find out about your background—freelance courier who has the trust of some serious banks, former soldier who saw a decade of action—and, perhaps as importantly, what I *cannot* find out about you, I think you're the type of man I need."

I didn't like the thought of him or anyone checking on me, but that was part of the price for stupidly paying in advance. "What type is that, Mr. Slake?"

"Someone who can get things done." I noticed he didn't tell me to call him Ron; he was definitely a VP or above in Kelco. "They've kidnapped my daughter, and I want her back." He took a small wallet from his pocket, unfolded it several times until it was a thin sheet in front of him, and said, "Jasmine."

Three pictures of a dark-haired teenage girl filled the sheet. She was standing alone against a blank wall, caught perhaps in pondering something weighty. She looked too serious for her age, almost in pain, her nearly black eyes blazing with an intensity that reminded me of Jennie at the same age, right before the Pinkelponker government took her away to heal the people they considered important. I hadn't been able to find, much less rescue Jennie before they took me away to Aggro.

"Jasmine is my only child, Mr. . . . Jon, a luxury I had not planned to permit myself. I never bothered to get to know the maternal surrogate, so Jasmine is all the family I have."

"What makes you think I can help?"

He looked at me for a few seconds, then glanced away. "We could waste a lot of time doing this, but I want Jasmine back more than I want to observe protocol, so let's try to be efficient. If I'm wrong and you say so, I'll be surprised, but I'll leave and see how quickly I can import some off-planet talent. I don't think I'm wrong, though, so I'm willing to offer safe passage for you and anything else you want to the planet of your choice, plus a million additional credits in the repository of your choice. I've just finished brokering Kelco's purchase of the exclusive commercial rights to Macken and to the new aperture that's growing at the jump gate, so my bonus alone is more than adequate to cover this cost."

I didn't need money right then, but it was going to cost me a lot more than I had if I ever wanted to try to approach the Pinkelponker system. "Fair enough. No wasted time." Though my washer had already filled me in, getting data firsthand is always best, so I asked, "Who took her?"

"Some local anti-development group that calls itself the Gardeners."

"What do they want?"

"To keep the planet exactly as it is." He laughed and looked away, shaking his head slowly. "As if that's even possible. We run into these naïve types in many deals, and it's always the same story: they try to stop progress, and its wheels grind them up. What they don't understand is that I don't have the power to kill this deal. It's done, and whether they do nothing or kill Jasmine or make some other stupid gesture, Kelco will develop Macken for the good of tourists everywhere. Then we'll furnish every tourist house and every residence with Kelco washers and Kelco refrigerators and on and on, and everything will work the way it always has. When the new aperture is ready, well," he laughed again, "then with any luck at all we'll make the real money." He looked back at me. "I cannot stop this. They want me to leave the planet—which I'll gladly do, though I haven't told them that—because they think my departure will matter. It won't. Kelco will put in one of my subordinates for however long it takes to import some corporate security folks to protect us, and then I'll be right back. No way is the company letting a new aperture slip away, and no way am I going to give up this opportunity."

"So why not bring in your security folks now and have them deal with it?"

"That's exactly what I'll have to do, and soon, because I can't keep the kidnapping secret much longer. But if I do, you know what'll happen: they'll clean out the Gardeners, but they'll make a lot of noise and do a lot of damage in the process. The Gardeners are local, so other locals will blame Kelco. That'll upset the local Frontier Coalition government, which will slow our work here, cost us even more money, and so on. I want Jasmine back safely, and I want her back quietly." He reached out and gently touched my arm, his eyes now glistening. "Screw the publicity. That's not the problem; 'avoid exposure' is the corporate line, not what I feel. What really scares me is that Jasmine could get hurt in an armed rescue mission. She's my only child. Can you understand what that means?"

"No," I answered honestly. I had no children, had never been willing to even consider bringing another life into the universe. For that matter, I didn't know if I could have children. I thought about Jennie. "I do, though, know what it's like to lose the only family you have. That I understand."

"Then help me, Jon. Please."

I thought about his offer. I couldn't help but feel sorry for a young kidnapped girl. I could use the money, and finding the Gardeners should be no problem; I've never known any activist group, however green, that didn't indulge from time to time in such appliance-based conveniences as laundry or hot food. I had no clue, however, what I might be walking into, whether this was three people with a little passion and a few small weapons, or a heavily armed group, so I needed more information.

"How long did they give you to respond?"

"They wanted me to get back to them in a day," Slake said. "I persuaded them that nothing in the corporate world moves that quickly, and we settled on four days. That was last night. I haven't slept much since then."

He looked way too perfect for someone who hadn't slept, but I suppose maintaining your appearance at all costs is part of the job of an executive. "I'll think about it and get back to you in the morning." I pulled out my wallet, thumbed it, and it received Slake's contact information. "If I decide to help, I should be able to do so within their time limit. I can't imagine them moving far from Glen's Garden, because they'll want to be close to you. The town isn't that large, and I assume you've already verified she wasn't on any departing flights or boats"—he smiled in acknowledgment—"so they're either hiding her in town or, more probably, in the rain forest." I stood. "I know that's not the answer you want, but consider what you'd do if you were on my end of such a proposal, and you'll know it's the only reasonable answer."

He smiled again. "True. That is, of course, unless you were involved, in which case you might be foolish enough to answer sooner."

I prefer dealing with smart people: even when you don't like them, you have a shot at understanding their thought processes. I stared straight at him. "I'm not involved in any way, though if I were I would never be stupid enough to appear that eager." I walked him out and basked for a moment in the warmth and the moist air and the steady thumping of the surf. "I'll get back to you tomorrow morning."

—end excerpt—

from *One Jump Ahead*
available in hardcover,
June 2007, from Baen Books

THANK YOU, JAMES SCHMITZ, WHEREVER YOU ARE